LONGKNIFES DEFEND THE LEGATION

MIKE SHEPHERD

KL&MM
BOOKS

COPYRIGHT INFORMATION

the editing skills of Lisa Müller, Edee Lemonier, and as ever, my wife Ellen Moscoe.

Rev 2.0

Cover Illustration and Design © Lee Moyer

Ebook ISBN-13: 978-1-64211-0364
Print ISBN-13: 978-1-64211-0357

PRAISE FOR THE KRIS LONGKNIFE NOVELS

"A whopping good read . . . Fast-paced, exciting, nicely detailed, with some innovative touches." - Elisabeth Moon, Nebula Award-winning author of Crown Renewal

"Shepherd delivers no shortage of military action, in space and on the ground. It's cinematic, dramatic, and dynamic . . . [He also] demonstrates a knack for characterization, balancing serious moments with dry humor . . . A thoroughly enjoyable adventure featuring one of science fiction's most interesting recurring heroines." - Tor.com

"A tightly written, action-packed adventure from start to finish . . . Heart-thumping action will keep the reader engrossed and emotionally involved. It will be hard waiting for the next in the series." - Fresh Fiction

"[Daring] will elate fans of the series . . . The story line is faster than the speed of light." - Alternative Worlds

"[Kris Longknife] will remind readers of David Weber's Honor Harrington with her strength and intelligence. Mike Shepherd provides an exciting military science fiction thriller." -Genre Go Round Reviews

"'I'm a woman of very few words, but lots of action': so said Mae West, but it might just as well have been Lieutenant Kris Longknife, princess of the one hundred worlds of Wardhaven. Kris can kick, shoot, and punch her way out of any dangerous situation, and she can do it while wearing stilettos and a tight cocktail dress. She's all business, with a Hell's Angel handshake and a 'get out of my face' attitude. But her hair always looks good . . . Kris Longknife is funny and she entertains us." - SciFi Weekly

"[A] fast-paced, exciting military SF series . . . Mike Shepherd has a great ear for dialogue and talent for injecting dry humor into things at just the right moment . . . The characters are engaging, and the plot is full of twists and peppered liberally with sharply described action. I always look forward to installments in the Kris Longknife series because I know I'm guaranteed a good time with plenty of adventure." -SF Site

In the New York Times bestselling Kris Longknife novels, "Fans of the Honor Harrington escapades will welcome the adventures of another strong female in outer space starring in a thrill-a-page military space opera." - Alternative Worlds

"Military SF fans are bound to get a kick out of the series as a whole." - SF Site

INTRODUCTION

Once again, I'd like to thank all the people who have helped bring this story to you with as few of the typos and nits as possible.

I also know that in these trying times, you have to choose where to spend your money. I'm most honored that you would choose my writing. I strive to bring you good stories and art.

They say that truth is stranger than fiction. I love military history and couldn't resist sharing this with you. As you approach the central crisis of this story, I'd like you to remember something that took place at the Battle of Alma, September 20, 1854, in the Crimean War.

Two regiments topped a slight rise and began to march down toward a small stream. It took a bit for the two regiments to realize that one was Russian and the other British. Them being involved in a great battle, the two columns came to a halt.

Now, you would think that a small battle would take place between them, but there were no senior officers present. They were off getting their orders from higher up. Both regiments were under the leadership of ensigns, subalterns, and junior lieutenants, many younger than the soldiers they commanded.

For a good amount of time, the junior officers just looked at each other and the other side while they tried to decide among themselves what to do next. None of the young officers could figure out what to do.

Into this lack of orders, the soldiers stepped. They started hurling rude remarks between each other. Neither may have understood the other's language, but the intent was clear.

It quickly escalated. Someone picked up a rock, and soon the two sides were shagging rocks back and forth while the junior officers looked on.

Before matters got too far out of hand, the senior officers returned to both regiments. Their orders did not call for them to fight over this tiny valley, so both sides did an about-face and marched away from each other.

Later, on another battlefield, they would likely follow their orders and slaughter each other, but not there, in that shallow valley, with no one to give them an order. A good, old fashioned rock fight was as far as they went. Interesting, huh?

Also, I wanted to give you a bit of backstory different than the ad copy – the paragraph or so we advertise the book with.

I really wanted to write a book about what happened at the Iteeche Embassy while Kris was away in battle during Stalwart. With Gramma Ruth and Grampa Trouble minding the kids, the stage set itself for an unforgettable story. I simply couldn't ignore the voices in my head. You can tell, I had fun with it.

We have two Ruths in this story – Gramma Ruth and Kris's daughter, Ruth. Little Ruth is no longer called Ruthie. Only the "littler ones" have y-ending nicknames, like her little brother, Johnny. Ruth is almost eight, after all, but a mature eight and a Longknife – who has listened to many stories at her parents' knees. You can clearly see when Gramma Ruth is talking versus the smaller Ruth.

I had great fun watching my grandkids at this age. I think it shows here.

Enjoy the read,
Mike

1

I waved goodbye to Mommy and Daddy as the convoy of gun trucks rolled out of the Embassy garage a hundred floors below me. Beside me, Johnny still whimpered even though he was waving his arm enough to make it fall off.

Mommy was going up the beanstalk to her fleet high above the sky. That was what Mommy did. Mommy was a Longknife and we did what we had to do.

So, I was standing here with Gramma and Grampa Trouble, waving at a long line of gun trucks, one of which had Mommy and Daddy in it.

Trucks kept pulling out of the Embassy. I sure wish we knew which one held Mommy, but I knew that we couldn't. If I could tell which armored truck they were in, so could an assassin.

There were so many things I hated today that had to be the way they were. I know I'm only almost eight and the world is the way it is, but I sure wish Mommy could make things fair and nice.

Daisy, my computer, is nearly as smart as her mom, Nelly. She's teaching me about the world and all the nasty things that people did to each other. I had a hard time believing that people, both Humans and Iteeche, could do such things.

Really, someone should give them all a time out.

At the Embassy, we kids couldn't do any of the things they did out there, beyond our district. I'd get grounded and no games for a week if I did something like that. The rules among us Embassy kids and the Iteeche kids we often played with now was no fighting. Take turns. Solve any problem with rock, paper, scissors.

Why couldn't grown-ups just do rock, paper scissors?

But I had a little brother to take care of while Mommy and Daddy were gone.

"Johnny, you can quit waving so hard. You'll hurt yourself."

"Will not," he snapped back, with a sniffle tossed in.

I kind of wished I was two years younger and a baby who could cry when things hurt this bad. Still, I was the big sister, even though he was as tall as I was at the moment, I knew how things worked.

"Mommy's gun truck is probably around the corner already," I pointed out.

"Isn't she in the pala-when?" Johnny said.

He mispronounced palanquin, the big rolling ride that Mommy sometimes rode in. I had problems saying the word too, what with my two missing front teeth.

"No, they're riding in the gun trucks."

"But all of them look alike," Johnny wailed, saying what everyone knew.

"That's so a sniper can't shoot at Mommy. If we can't tell which truck she's in, neither can they."

"Oh," Johnny said. Maybe this time he'd understand. I'd told him this a thousand times.

"Just because you can't see her, doesn't mean that your mom can't see you," Gramma Trouble said. She and Grampa Trouble stood behind us. She rested a hand on my shoulder. I liked the feel of her touch.

Grampa did the same for Johnny.

Sometimes Johnny would wiggle out of Grampa's touch. Not today.

"She can't see us now that she's gone," Johnny insisted.

"Look up," Grampa Trouble said. "Can't you see the quadcopter?"

I searched the sky and spotted the skitter drone. It swayed back and forth. That was how I spotted it. It's color made it nearly invisible against the sky. I pointed it out to Johnny.

It took him a moment to spot it. Maybe Mommy brought it in closer to help him. I waved again, now up at the spy.

Johnny went back to nearly waving his arm off.

I felt warm inside. I think Mommy almost didn't want to go as much as I didn't want her to.

Still, we were Longknifes and we did what we had to do. That teenager on the Imperial throne had to be protected. Tranna had played so nicely with us at the beach party. He was one of the good guys.

Why would anyone want to throw him off his throne? Grown-ups!

The last of the gun trucks turned the corner and headed up the street to the beanstalk. The skeeter made one finally pass, then rushed off. No doubt, Nelly would melt it back into some truck and thicken its armor.

Or maybe it would look for anyone with a rifle pointed at the convoy.

"What would you like to do?" Gramma Trouble asked me.

"We *should* go to school," I said. I knew we should, but I really didn't feel like being stuck in school, even if Daisy was the one teaching me.

Still, Mommy said that right now it was my duty to study and learn. I felt that funny feeling in my stomach that I got when I wanted to do two different things at once. One that might be right and the other that might be.

I looked up at Gramma Trouble and hoped that she would decide that we could go swimming.

Gramma Ruth was Trouble to most everyone since she married Grampa Trouble a bit more than a hundred years ago. Just about everyone in Marine blue and red considered her husband trouble with a capital T. Still, today had nothing to do with blowing things up.

No, today belonged to kids that were pretty strung out. It had been a long time since Ruth had used the nicknames of "Mommy" and "Daddy." That told Gramma a lot about what was going on behind those bright eyes.

It was never easy to watch as your loved ones marched off to war. She'd been in the kids' shoes often enough over the years. When you're eight and six, it's pure hell.

"What would you like to do?" she asked the great- great-granddaughter that bore her name.

Such large, serious eyes looked over her shoulder and up at her gramma. For now, her head hardly came up to her gramma's waist. As she'd watched so many times before, that would quickly change.

"We *should* go to school," she said with a tremble in her voice. Ruth could see in the child's eyes and hear in her voice how much those words hurt her. She so wanted to run away from duty and hide.

Well, she's barely eight. Why couldn't she?

"Let me have Penelope get together with the head mistress. Penelope?" Gramma Trouble said to her computer, one of Nelly's kids.

"Already dialing, boss girl. We got a poker game tonight?"

She scowled at Trouble, her husband. Trouble to his enemies. Trouble to his superiors. Trouble to just about everyone, and at the moment that included his wife.

"You don't honestly think," her husband said, "that my Xenophon can beat your Pretty Penny one whit, do you?"

"Yes," Ruth drawled through a stormy scowl.

"You know you like it," he said, grinning unrepentantly.

"I'll have words with you later," she growled.

Penny had the Head Mistress on the line. "Yes, General Tordon, ma'am?" she answered.

To most people, the General was her husband. However, Ruth Tordon had held a commission during the Iteeche Wars of ninety years back. She was also a General, still in the reserves, and had a uniform in the back of the closet to prove it. Some people liked to remind her of days best forgotten.

"How much book learning do you think you can get from the kids today?" she asked.

She could almost hear a head shaking on the other end of the line. "Not much. Likely less. Half the kids have folks sailing with the fleet. If one of them breaks down, the rest won't be far behind."

"How about we call for a swimming party?"

"The Imperial Lake?" the Head Mistress asked.

"I don't think we can do that again, at least not this soon and not without more planning. How about at the Embassy water park?"

"That sounds great by me. I'll get the teachers and students moving in that direction. You want to make an All Hands announcement?"

"I'll check with Abby and see what we need to do," Gramma Trouble said.

Both of her short grandkids were bouncing up and down as if

they'd swallowed pogo sticks for breakfast. "Swimming! Swimming! We're going swimming!"

"Let me check," their gramma said. "Pretty Penny, can you put me through to Abby?"

Abby had begun life in the worst slums of New Eden. Her life had changed when she accepted a job as Kris Longknife's maid, and performed other duties as required. Now, she was the administrative officer for the Embassy. She also doubled as central supply for the million Iteeche Sailors, Marines and Guardsmen who shared the Embassy district of six blocks on a side.

"What can I do for you today, Gramma Trouble?"

"I'd like to throw a party at the Embassy pool for all the kids. Half of them just watched their parents march off to war. It might be easier for them if no one could tell their tears from the pool water."

"I think you have a good point. Have you touched base with the schools?"

"Already done. The Head Mistress didn't expect to get any work out of them today, anyway."

"I'll release all remaining parents to hang around the pool with their kids. Should I invite any of the Iteeche kids to join ours?"

"Why not?"

"I'll expand the pool area," Abby said. "I'll also tell the commissary to lay out a picnic lunch and supper for everyone."

"Good idea. I'll get the kids moving in that direction."

By now, two very enthusiastic short people had latched onto her hands and were busy towing her out of their folks' apartment and toward the elevators.

Mata Hari, Abby's computer, quickly got to expanding the swim park down at the fiftieth level, but she also had taken time to double the number of elevators so one was waiting for them by the time they got to them.

"Pretty Penny, did you order up an elevator?" Gramma asked.

"No, boss girl. I *made* an elevator just for you and the kids."

"Isn't Smart Metal wonderful?" Trouble said dryly from her elbow.

Programmable matter, or magic metal to the Iteeche, had radically changed life in the Embassy. The gleaming tower of silver and glass had until recently been eight starships. Now it could be just about anything anyone wanted. It helped to have one of Nelly's kids to expand water parks or pull elevators out of the woodwork.

However, even the lowest Sailor could pull up a comfortable chair . . . or create a door between them and the next sleeping compartment over. Gramma still laughed at Kris's stories of the early days of reworking the Navy's fraternization rules to match technology. And young sailors' initiative.

Or was that libido?

The ride down fifty floors was quick and smooth. As soon as the doors opened, the kids raced for the pools shedding clothes as they ran.

"Hang your clothes up on the pegs!" Gramma shouted after her unruly progeny. Reluctantly, the two kids halted their mad dash for the water and trudged back to the wall to hang their red shipsuits on the hooks provided.

The Embassy drew its people from all over Human space. Many came from planets where the swimming hole was the only place to hang out during long, hot, summer days. A start-up colony bought as little as it could from the mother planet, and that rarely included swim wear.

The Embassy made its pool clothing optional to start with. By now, you couldn't get the kids to wear anything, and few of the adults did either.

Gramma Trouble slipped out of her shipsuit. Hers was tan, for support staff. Her husband still wore green like any line beast. The kids wore red so they were easy to spot and could be kept out of dangerous areas. Once they became more skilled in ship survival, they'd graduate to purple.

Kids and grown-ups of every age were streaming from more elevators. Granny saw one elevator disgorge a dozen people. Half a minute later, the doors opened again, and another half dozen joined the excited melee.

Apparently, Mata Hari was running several elevators in the same shaft. Not impossible when you applied enough computing power to Smart Metal™.

Gramma Trouble joined the kids bouncing around and screaming in the pool.

Grampa Trouble had a patented pool trick that had delighted generations of kids between six and ten. He stooped down and invited little Ruth to put her feet in his cupped hands. Then, like a rocket launcher, he stood up. His great-granddaughter shot out of the water.

Ruth was good at keeping her arms and legs together. She converted the lift into a lovely dive.

Gramma shook her head, proudly. Truly, somewhere a dolphin had slipped into Ruth's gene pool.

Of course, little Johnny demanded a ride, too. He had yet to get the concept down of holding his arms and legs together. He flew through the air in a wild flail of arms and legs, even managing to rake a couple of toes across Trouble's cheek.

"That kid needs to have his toenails clipped," he muttered.

"Like someone else I know," his wife muttered back.

"It's my only defense against those icebergs you bring to bed every night."

Lots of kids, however, were forming a line behind Grampa Trouble. It appeared that they had decided that he did it better than any other grown-up in the pool.

Courtney Kitano-Zung got the next ride. Her moms had only been able to steal one weekend with her between fleet training. They'd left yesterday to get the ships ready for movement.

Gramma Trouble made a note to herself to see that Courtney got extra attention. Since she was as close a friend to Ruth and Johnny as her moms were to Kris and Jack, that would be easy.

The next four kids in line were an eager mix of Abby and Amanda's children. Bruce, Mike, and Topaz were intermixed with Lily and Peter Pierre. Each got to either dive or fly through the air before Ruth and Johnny got their second turn.

Gramma Trouble feared that the kids would exhaust her husband, but she needn't have. After a half hour, the kids gravitated over to play among themselves in their own corner of the huge pool.

Left alone, it didn't take the adults long to move to the side of the pool and pull Smart Metal™ loungers out of the deck to rest on.

Together, they watched as the kids formed their own little herd and turned their backs on the world. Courtney looked to be crying softly. Ruth took her into a hug and the others gathered closer.

So did the tutors. However, it was Cara, Abby's niece, that slipped into the circle. The kids had known Cara longer than they'd known anyone. She'd babysat for many of them. She was still an honorary kid rather than an adult. They accepted her among them and seemed a little relieved to have help.

Cara brought with her four of the guys that were vying for her attention at the moment. The kids made no opening for them, unsure if they were adults or kids.

The smartest one of them shortened himself until he barely had his head above the water. That got him an opening to squat beside Cara, and to have one of the kids wrap an arm around his shoulder.

"They're tough kids," Gramma Trouble muttered.

"They have to be," Abby said. "They're out here on the tip of the spear with their folks. The older ones know about the rocket attack on the Embassy. They've heard about the bunch who dropped a batch of apartment complexes on Kris and Jack's heads. That they're holding up so well this far from Human space is an honor to them and their folks."

"Why don't you soldier types ever give a medal for courage on the home front?" Amanda asked. She was the resident economist and was still trying to figure out the insane practices the Iteeche called an economy. A civilian through and through, she only put on a uniform when someone was nasty enough to activate her honorary reserve commission.

Gramma Trouble snorted. "Because if the Marines thought you needed a wife and kids, they would have issued them to you."

Grampa Trouble gave her a wise nod and kept his mouth shut.

They kept their eyes on the pool full of children, but now the conversation turned to the business of the Embassy . . . staying alive hundreds of light years from the nearest Human planet.

Was it by pure chance that they were joined by General Bruce, Abby's husband and commander for Embassy security, and Jacques, the station's struggling, but best expert on Iteeche sociology? They pulled up chairs next to their wives.

"All we need is Kris and Jack," Abby drawled, "and we'd have ourselves a full staff meeting."

"Haven't you noticed, dear love," her husband said, "that this is all the key staff you're gonna get unless you promote up some more poor dumb slobs to fill the junior slots and hold all the hot potatoes you toss out?"

"Down, boy. You're giving away state secrets," she said with chilly words.

"Oh, you've been burned," Jacques said.

"Give me some salve," the general shot back.

"I'll give you the back of my hand," Abby growled. "So, oh mighty warrior, can we defend this Human outpost in the heart of the Iteeche Empire?"

"Nope," he said, simply.

"Huh?" came from the other five adults spread in a thin line beside him.

"If the Iteeche want us dead, we're dead," the jumped-up Gunny Sergeant said. "They isolated us the last time Kris was gone."

"And the two major clans that led those protests that surrounded us and cut us off are now minor clans, assuming they're still clans at all," Jacques said.

"Thank heavens for Kris getting back when she did," Amanda added.

General Trouble cleared his throat and the other's fell silent. "We have to realize that we are too exposed. If someone wants to lop us off, we're lopped by next Monday. Our challenge," he said, glancing around the crescent of loungers and chairs, "is to either make sure they don't want to lop us off, or that it takes long enough to do the lopping that wiser heads prevail. How long can we hold out under siege?"

Everyone turned their attention to Abby.

"I have three months of frozen meats, vegetables, and fruit. We're growing somewhere around twenty percent of our fresh vegetables and ten percent of our fresh fruit. Obviously we aren't growing any meat, although I've put in an order for fertilized chicken eggs. It would be nice to hatch them and get our own fresh eggs."

She paused to see how her audience was taking this. "I've also got enough canned and dry goods to last us six months. We have transports coming in from a planet in the United Society every two weeks, so starving us out isn't the question."

"What is our weakness?" General Trouble asked.

"Feeding our Iteeche allies," Abby answered bluntly. "We can't store more than three days of fresh supplies for the officers, Sailors, Marines, and Guardsmen plus their families. I've got about a week's worth of those yams they'll eat if they have to, but we're trying to feed our troops better."

General Trouble frowned. "So, we can hold the Embassy forever, but the Legation District can be starved out in less than two weeks."

"You got it," Abby answered.

"Do we need to feed all those Iteeche?" Amanda asked.

The general was shaking his head before she finished the question. "They are our allies. What are the chances that the Iteeche besieging us have got just as big a bone to pick with the Navy, Marines, and Guard? More likely, they're madder at them than us. Kris pissed off the senior clans before she shipped out. Above and beyond that, most of them can't be happy about the decent way we're treating the Iteeche ratings. No one else has ever given the likes of them decent quarters. Up to now, no one has let them cohabitate with someone of their choice and raise kids together."

Those in the seats around him nodded. Abby spoke for all. "Kris speaks of us poisoning the old fashioned Iteeche Way. Our uniformed allies are the vectors scattering the toxin far and wide. If someone decides to take us down, they'll include in their plan of attack slaughtering all the Iteeche that work for us."

General Trouble pursed his lips. "So, our weakness is the Legation's District and the Iteeche that live in the shadow of the Embassy tower."

"It sure looks that way," Gramma Trouble said. Four other heads nodded along with her.

"What can we do to lengthen the time we can survive a siege?" Amanda asked.

Abby shrugged. "I don't know if any of you know it, but in the Legation District, we've got about four million Iteeche living in the thirty-five blocks not occupied by this Embassy tower."

"You're kidding!" Gramma Trouble said. "I know they packed them in like sardines, but that many?"

"The Iteeche have to cram people into every nook and cranny," Jacques said. "With fifty billion on a planet, there isn't a lot of elbow room."

"An Iteeche battlecruiser might be built to our design and specifications," Grampa Trouble said, "Still, Kris told me that the Iteeche have as many as three thousand crewmen, sometimes more, running a ship we use four hundred or less staff as fighting crew. Our Embassy echoes with unused space. The hundred floors of the new Main Navy have several thousand Iteeche hurrying about. Admittedly, many are rated as juniors, serving as runners. Someone has to take messages from one desk to another. One from his commander to his subordinates, and a lot from the subordinates to the commander."

"They still won't use our commlinks?" Amanda asked.

"Not a chance," her husband answered before anyone else could. "They would lose face. The level of the messenger defines the status of both the sender and receiver. What kind of status can a text message or even face-to-face phone call give?"

"The Iteeche Way," Gramma Trouble grouched.

About that time, the elevators began to disgorge hundreds of youngling Iteeche. That brought screams from the Human kids in the pool. The water was soon foaming with spray and laughter.

Any moping came to an immediate halt as the kids lost themselves in the friendships they were busy cementing with each other.

The strongest ties in the Legation District were likely between kids with two arms and kids with four. The future would decide what fruit those friendships would bear.

Someone among the Iteeche had put some planning into this invasion. Human lifeguards were soon backed up with two or three more Iteeche swimmers. A couple of small kayaks rose from the deck and both Human and Iteeche lifeguards used them to paddle out into the center of the pool.

If a cluster of kids wouldn't respond to instructions from the lifeguard on one side, these enforcers could paddle over and knock some sense into inattentive heads. They didn't have to do that very often.

What was interesting were the adult Iteeche that moseyed in after the younglings.

General Konga, General Commanding the Imperial Guard just happened to be strolling along with Admiral Ulan, Chief of Staff of the Combined Fleet and Kris's Navy presence while she was gone.

"This is no accident," General Trouble muttered under his breath.

3

Both the senior Iteeche officers knew of the pool etiquette. They hung their Navy gray and Guardsman green work uniforms on hooks and soon joined the group next to the pool.

"Penelope," Gramma Trouble said, "Would you get our Iteeche friends some comfortable pillows to lounge on?"

Her computer not only provided several pillows for the four-legged Iteeche's use, but she also moved the Human's loungers and chairs around, expanding the arrangement into a gentle crescent. That left the parents and grandparents a good view of the aquatic riot of their offspring while allowing the adults to see each other for easy conversation.

"Thank you for inviting our younglings to join yours," General Konga said. "Many of them saw their Choosers roll off to the coming war. Usually, that would not be a problem since they'd be spending all their time in the Palace of Learning. Now, however, most of them are sharing much of their day with their Choosers. I find my own son growing more attached to me than I ever was to my Chooser. I can only imagine how these younglings are feeling today."

"We find stiff exercise reduces the stress of watching someone important roll away to war," Gramma Trouble said. "It's good for just about any stress. That's why we have the water park, playground, and exercise field."

"I had wondered why you Humans invested so much of your space in exercise facilities," Admiral Ulan said. "As a Sailor I got plenty of exercise. Our women in their harems weren't supposed to worry about anything. I find that my woman is correcting me on that."

He eyed the three Human couples, "This living together in a . . . family . . ." he stumbled over the Human word, "is more complicated than I thought."

"Yes, but we still find it worth the effort," Gramma Trouble said, reaching for her husband's hand and giving it a squeeze.

"It's never easy to go off to war," General Trouble said. "Leaving those you love behind can make it harder. However, if you are marching off to defend them, it can make it easier."

"I begin to see how you motivate your Soldiers and Sailors to fight," General Konga said. "The Human Way is so different from the Iteeche Way."

"You said a mouthful," Abby drawled. Then she shot up and whistled loud enough to get attention even over the ruckus the kids were putting on. "Bruce, you keep an eye on Mikey! Mikey, no running on the pool deck, you hear?"

Both boys jumped at their mother's voice. Their response was lost in the background noise, but Bruce Jr. moved the group of older kids he was with closer to where his brother was cannonballing into the pool.

Mikey now stood at the edge of the pool. He leapt as high and as far out as he could and made a very satisfactory splash, much to the disgust of the older kids with his brother.

Apparently, Bruce decided turnabout was fair play. While his younger brother was still getting water out of his eyes, Bruce took three quick steps and launched himself high and long. He did his own cannonball, landing only a few dozen centimeters from his sibling.

Faced with high waves and spray, the younger kid turned and fled back to his own age group.

The parents smiled indulgently as this bit of education passed from an older to younger child. It saved them from having to do it. It was always better to let kids learn from other kids, assuming there was no bullying.

Admiral Ulan made a sound that sounded like he had coughed up a hairball. This was the equivalent of a laugh from an Iteeche. "That was a much gentler lesson than those I remember in the Palace of Learning. Then I had no Chooser to watch over me when my fellow leftovers gave me a hard lesson."

"Leftovers?" Jacques said. "I've never understood how that works. Is it a state secret?"

"It is not a secret," the Iteeche general said. "It is just not something we are encouraged to talk about. After those who have earned the right to Choose a youngling from their mating pond have Chosen who they will, the minor clan official is left with those that have survived that long in the pond. More often than not, he drains the pond and sends the younglings in it to the grinder where they are converted to chum to provide food to another pond."

Gramma Trouble cringed. She'd long suspected this. She'd even read captured correspondence that hinted at this practice. Still, as a loving mom and gramma, this concept was totally alien to her, and her mind balked at connecting the dots.

Now her face was being rubbed in it. Not only did the tadpoles, fingerlings, and younglings have to evade the predations of the bigger fish in the pond, but they surely learned that those Not Chosen died a horrible death. Ugh. It was all Gramma Trouble could do to not throw up her breakfast.

The old woman drug her attention back to the Iteeche who was talking.

"However," Admiral Ulan said, "if the clan has need of a crew for warships and cannon fodder for their army, they may allow the different pool lordlings to choose some of those they think would make good obedient soldiers, and send them to the Military Barracks of Learning."

"I knew that civil war was coming," General Konga said, "when I saw the barracks of learning crammed to the gills a few years back. What with the old Emperor half dead on the throne and only the youngest of his boys still alive, a blind man could see trouble coming."

Gramma and Grampa Trouble exchanged glances. They'd heard nothing about this.

IT'S GOOD HAVING THESE INFORMAL TALKS, Gramma said on Nelly Net.

HMM, came back at her from her husband.

"Are the barracks still crammed?" Jacques asked.

Both Iteeche shook their heads no. "All the clans seem to have planned for a ten-year civil war," General Tonga said. "The clans cut back on extra Choosing nine or ten years ago. Nobody wants to have a bunch of trained fighters hanging around with no battles to fight. Massacring a huge bunch of warriors because you don't want to be burdened with feeding and paying them, even if the chow is horrible and the pay minimal, is not recommended. Some of the blank pages in the history books are thought to have had the story of such mass murders."

"More than once, a dynasty overthrew a previous dynasty only to 'strangely' fall very quickly and for no apparent reason. Illness, I believe," Admiral Ulan muttered, unpersuasively.

"You Iteeche have some very interesting non-history," Jacques said.

"If it's not in the officially approved history book, it didn't happen. Don't you know?" the Guard's general answered, cynically.

"Based on how much cannon fodder the clans have stacked up in the training barracks," General Trouble asked, "how long do you see this war lasting?"

The two Iteeche glanced at each other.

"I've got about six or seven more years of young Guardsmen lined up behind this last class," said, General Konga.

"About the same here for the Imperial Navy," Admiral Ulan agreed. "I think we've got as many as the clan troops."

"Your Kris Longknife is causing the clan lords some serious heart-burn," the admiral said.

"How so?" General Trouble asked.

"We haven't wiped out nearly as many defending planetary armies. Meanwhile, lots of battlecruisers have surrendered to her rather than fight to the bitter end. If she keeps this up, there are going to be a whole lot more surviving, ah, what do you call them? Right, veterans, when this war is over."

"Is there any chance the warriors could be used to set up new colonies?" Gramma Trouble asked. "We Humans have often sent vets to settle new territory."

The glance the two Iteeche exchanged didn't have much enthusiasm.

"You have to remember," General Konga said, "the clans like to use their own Chosen to start colonies. The soldiers or sailors may have fought in their clan colors, but they got very little loyalty and expect little back in return."

"And if Kris was to send many of them out to start up military colonies?" General Bruce asked cautiously.

The two Iteeche ended up shaking their heads. "That hasn't been done before."

Abby chuckled wickedly. "When has that stopped Kris?"

"Tell me," Grampa Trouble said, taking back the direction of the conversation, "what brought you two over here?"

"My youngling wanted to play with your younglings," the general said.

"Mine too," said the admiral.

The two of them glanced out over the water, then homed in to focus on different clumps of young Iteeche bouncing around with Human children. It was hard for Gramma Trouble to be sure, what with the few facial muscles on the Iteeche, but they seemed quite fond of what they saw.

"You have any problem with a little bit of work?" Abby asked.

"Not at all," the Imperial Guard general said.

Abby turned to her husband. "General, you want to take the lead?"

General Bruce took a few moments to organize his thoughts before addressing the two Iteeche officers. "General, Admiral. I know I can defend the Embassy. We've done it before and we can do it again, even if it means hauling some of those kids out of the pool and using their computers. Do you think we might end up needing to defend your housing as well? Do you think we can?"

The two Iteeche locked eyes for a moment . . . all eight of them. The Guard general spoke first. "We Guardsmen are here to protect the Emperor. If need be, we will die for him."

He paused for a long moment. "I have not failed to notice that Admiral Longknife placed her armored trucks between us and an attacking mob. I was grateful for the help. No doubt, others noticed both the help and my gratitude."

Now he glanced at the admiral. "It is quite possible that some may want to attack me and mine as a way to get at you. I think the Navy Headquarters and Combined Fleet personnel are in a similar situation."

The admiral grunted agreement.

"In the near future, I may have to defend the Guardsmen from attacks that are not aimed at the Emperor. No offense, but I would rather not have my people die so someone can send you a message."

"I would prefer that you not have to pass along any such message," General Bruce said.

"So," the Imperial Guard general said, "can we defend the housing you have recently provided to our uniformed personnel and their consorts and Chosen? That is an interesting question that I cannot claim to have ever spent time thinking about."

"And the results of that thinking?" Grampa Trouble asked.

"Anyone who wants to get to the Embassy will come through our quarters and offices. I don't doubt that they will do everything they can to burn us out. That is just what mobs do. Kris Longknife took these apartments away from the Domm Clan. I have heard that a lot of the clan people didn't much like having a Human admiral remove a clan *and* take their clan lands."

Admiral Ulan nodded. "I have heard the same. Whether we want to stay out of any fight between the clans and you, any riot will come through us to get to you. I don't want my Chosen to be caught on the street by some clan thug and have his head bashed in. No. What do you call this area, the Legation District?"

"Yes," Abby said.

"Well, I have Sailors and Marines who were not recalled to their ships. True, they have a lot of mouths to feed, but they can provide us with patrolmen to watch our streets and, if necessary, defend us all. If you are willing, I think we might want to close up the district and limit access."

"Now?" asked General Trouble. "Might it be better to wait a bit. Do we want to look like we're going all defensive before anyone makes a move against us?"

The Iteeche paused. The four officers, retired and active duty, measured each other's souls with the precision of micrometers.

"I think it is best if we stay alert, but, how do you Humans say it? 'Keep your powder dry,' yes?" said General Tong.

"I agree," General Bruce said. "I can lock this place down in five minutes."

"That is nice to know," Admiral Ulan said.

"There is another matter," Abby said.

"Your bailiwick," General Bruce said. "Logistics."

"Yes," Abby said. "General, Admiral, the folks that don't much like us tried to starve the Embassy out the last time Kris was out blowing shit up. I figure the Embassy can survive at least nine months of siege. Three months eating the fat of the land, six months chewing on our belts. Now, let's assume we have to defend the entire Legation District, all thirty-six square blocks of it. How many people do you have bedding down in those apartments?"

The two Iteeche officers eyed each other for a moment.

"Three million six hundred, and a bit more Navy, Marines, and dependents," Admiral Ulan said.

"A hundred thousand Imperial Guard and three hundred thousand dependents reside in the district," their general said. "I have other junior troops stationed in barracks around the capitol."

"How long can you feed your people in the Legation District?" Abby asked with the finality of the gates of hell swinging shut.

The two Iteeche eyed each other, seemed to nod, then the Admiral said, "That is something we have not discussed," he said, glancing around at his surroundings. When he found few Iteeche near him he went on. "I didn't want to have this conversation in my own office. With a civil war on, you can never tell who's listening. Worse, with clan lords handing out bribes, who you can trust is even more subject to tides and rip currents."

"Yes," the general agreed, then he focused hard on General Trouble. "You were a good enemy in the last war, sir. Can you be just as good an ally now?"

"I can be your worst enemy or your best friend," the old general answered in a voice of steel.

"That is what I am hoping for," Admiral Ulan said. "Your Admiral Kris Longknife gives loyalty down the chain of command and expects loyalty up from the bottom. That is very different from the Iteeche Way. As soon as she began to treat our Iteeche Sailors, Marines, and Soldiers as she treated her Human subordinates, we were both inalterably welded together."

"Jacques can worry about the socio-political problems later," Abby said. "For now, we have the problem of defending the entire Legation District. I've got the job of feeding all of you. How can I do that? From what I've observed, you bring in fresh fish about every third or fourth day."

"Yes," General Konga said. "Our funds are doled out in three- or four-day periods. It's a bitch when we get three days' worth of money and then have to wait four days for the next allotment. We try to keep a fourth day in reserve, but sometimes we end up eating yellow yam gruel for two meals a day."

"Do you want fresh fish or gruel?" Abby asked.

"Those are the only choices available. The clan lordlings eat fresh fish, the rest of us make do with red or yellow gruel. We save the white yams for last, always."

"But lately you've been eating fish most of the time."

"Your Admiral Longknife has gotten us the funds and we've found some good deals from the coastal fish farms. They aren't quite as fresh as what the clans demand, but our cooks have learned to make some pretty fancy fish soups with different greens. They have been experimenting with different herbs and spices that your ships have brought in. It makes the soup very tasty."

"Has anyone tried serving dried fish?"

That got strange looks from the Iteeche. "Dried?"

"Yes," Abby answered. "We kill and dry the fish, then rehydrate it when we make it into stew. That lets you save the fish for several weeks or more before you have to use it."

"And it is edible? You humans do such strange things with food," the Iteeche admiral said.

"Yes, it's good with herbs and spices."

"Oh, that's why you have those," the Iteeche general marveled.

"Yes, Admiral. Send me around a few of your purchasing agents and I'll see what I can do about getting a fish dryer designed that you can ship to one of your suppliers. We can see what happens with the dried fish. I'll also see what I can do about putting in a crop of herbs and spices for you in the Embassy gardens."

"Speaking of food," Gramma Trouble said, standing, "I smell chow. I think our youngsters do, too. I suspect that we'd better go ride herd on them or there will be a food riot."

"Are you going to drop the fish into the pool?" The general asked. "My kid loved diving for his fish."

"It's saltwater, so the fish might survive in it for a bit," Abby said. "Still, I think we'll let them dunk for their food in tanks. Okay?"

Gramma Trouble headed out to corral two hungry and excited kids. Planning for the future would take time. Hopefully, they had plenty of it.

4

S everal days later, Gramma Trouble settled into a comfortable chair next to her husband. They'd had a busy morning getting the kids started on their assignments.

Ruth and her friends were working with Daisy to build bridges out of different thicknesses of pasta. They'd already discovered that some types worked, and others that led to collapsed bridges.

Now they were testing the tensile strength of the different types and thicknesses to see which would meet the minimum requirements for the different parts of the bridge. They'd likely be busy for the rest of the day as they tried different pastas and different bridge designs.

Johnny and his friends were working with Hippo and using blocks. They were learning ratios and counting even if they didn't know it. Hippo made it fun and that was all that mattered.

"Could you report to the staff conference room?" echoed from both their commlinks at the same instant. It sounded like Mata Hari's voice.

"Do we have a problem?" Trouble asked.

"Yes," was the curt reply.

Gramma Trouble checked in with the duty tutor on the way out. "Call us if you need us," she said.

"They look like they're having fun. I'll just keep an eye on them," the tutor said.

They arrived at the conference room quickly. It had been Kris's day quarters, but she and her battle fleet had departed for points unknown a few days before. Ambassador Kawaguchi arrived at the same time.

Someone was calling for an All Hands meeting.

It took a few tries to get through the door, both they and the diplomat kept bowing the other one in. They would have been there all day if Gramma Trouble hadn't finally invoked her feminine prerogative and led the two men into the room.

Abby and General Bruce were already seated at a very expanded round table with Amanda and Jacques. General Konga and Admiral Ulan were with them.

Gramma Trouble raised both eyebrows to her husband and got the same back from the old warhorse. A no-notice conference with all this crew was not auspicious. Especially when the table was this large.

As expected, it got worse. Senior Chief Agent in Charge Taylor Foile hurried in with his assistant, Leslie Chu, right behind him.

Gramma Trouble acknowledged all those at the table with a nod, then took her chair. She got comfortable; this looked like it was going to be a long meeting.

Agent Foile did not sit down. "We appear to have a murder on our hands," he said, without preamble.

"Chief Quartermaster Boding's Companion was shopping for a new, let's call it a coffee maker, for his office. He is on the staff of Navy Chief of Staff."

Gramma Trouble frowned. The Chief of Staff was located in the chain of command between the Minister of the Navy and the Combined Fleet's staff. All three seemed to do the same thing. How Iteeche of them.

While the Combined Fleets was Kris's bailiwick, both of the other two staffs still had issues from being moved into the same building with the Combined Fleets. Then again, each of the three groups always had issues with the other two. Again, how Iteeche of them.

"We are questioning witnesses," the inspector went on, "but the bazaar was crowded. No one saw the person or persons who put a knife in her back. As soon as she identified herself as Navy, we had a medical team and investigation team away. Sadly, no one provided first aid and she had bled out by the time we got to her side."

The senior chief agent in charge paused at that point.

"Was she wearing anything that identified her as Navy?" General Bruce asked.

"No. She wore civilian clothes. She should have been no different from any other shopper at a non-clan bazaar," Agent Foile answered crisply.

"So why are we treating this like a crisis?" General Trouble asked.

"She was shopping at the nearest bazaar to the Legation quarters," Foile answered. "She also had come straight from her quarters to the bazaar. She said goodbye to the chief not ten minutes before she was killed."

Abby turned to the two Iteeche. "Is crime a problem? Is it dangerous to go shopping?"

Without reflection, General Konga answered. "No. Certainly not as a woman. Remember, all clan women were in purdah until recently. Except for the Navy Companions and the lowest born women, they still are. There are usually some deaths among the women. Life in seclusion has its own tensions and some women kill other women. However, to kill a woman on the street is unheard of."

"Was her money taken?" Abby asked.

"No. She still had the cash she'd been given to buy the beverage maker," Tailor answered.

"And no one knows anything?" Grampa Trouble asked again.

"It has been a while since I've shopped in a bazaar," Admiral Ulan said. "This early in the morning, the breakfast crowd would still be around, and the first wave of shoppers would be mixing with them. You couldn't move without bumping into someone."

"Yet whoever knifed her in the back managed to disappear without being noticed," Gramma Trouble mused. "I'm thinking that whoever did this had several people with him to help him slip away quickly."

"I think you may be right," Agent Foile said.

"Were there no cameras covering the bazaar?" Grampa Trouble asked.

Agent Foile and the two Iteeche shook their heads.

"We have large sections of the Imperial Capitol under observation," said Agent Foile. "However, it is all aimed at the palaces of the major clans. The bazaar is well away from the palace. The clan only allowed them the use of a minor street. As you would expect, I have my computer, Sherlock, expanding our security coverage as we speak."

Sherlock was one of Nelly's kids as well. No doubt, he would have no problem examining even more security take.

"What photo coverage do we have on the Chief's woman?" Gramma Trouble asked.

A flat picture appeared in the middle of the table. Two Iteeche, one in a Chief's uniform, the other in civilian clothes, stroked each other's beaks, then went their separate ways. The constructed photography stayed centered on the one in civilian clothes.

Gramma Trouble had to admit, she had trouble telling the Iteeche sexes apart. Honestly, she had trouble telling one Iteeche from the other. Back in the war, she'd admitted that to an Iteeche POW. The Iteeche had laughed and admitted that she could not tell humans apart, and had Human females not had those lumps on their chests, she could not tell the males from the females.

Clearly, the two species weren't mentally prepared to deal with each other one-on-one.

At least now Gramma Trouble could tell the difference in what the two Iteeche sexes wore. Male Iteeche tended to wear closer-fitting clothes. Even when they wore robes, they were stiffer and heavier.

Of course, some males like slaves or runners wore nothing.

As best as Gramma Trouble could tell, females Iteeche always wore clothes when they were out. Female Iteeche tended to wear less clothing than their male counterparts. Still, what they did wear was thinner, lighter, and more flowing.

There had been that time Kris and her honor guard took a shortcut through a senior clan's harem. When Gramma Trouble got Kris talking after that, she found that a lot of the women in purdah wore little to no clothing.

It was sad that after all these years, this backcountry farm girl who was able to tell two cows apart could not do the same for two Iteeche.

The Iteeche woman on the screen seemed to be enjoying herself as she zigged and zagged through the Legation District. She waved at other women and stepped aside to help racing Iteeche younglings dodge around her. Finally, she stood at one of the district's four corners.

She crossed the wide beltway avenue and headed up the boulevard away from the district.

There was an Iteeche who turned the corner and fell in several meters behind her. Another one crossed the street and followed even farther back.

There were quite a few people were behind her and going the same direction. The walk beside the boulevard was wide and had a lot of foot traffic. However, she was still enjoying her stroll in the bright, smoggy sun, and most traffic hurried by her.

These two men kept their distance behind her.

She walked out of the camera's range and the two men did as well.

"Do we know those two?" Grampa Trouble asked.

"I've had my Sherlock doing his best to match them to any face we have in our database," the law enforcement officer said. "However, so far, no match. They haven't been around the Legation District for the last two weeks or so."

"How far does the database go back?" Abby asked.

"We started it when we moved in here. Everyone who demonstrated outside the Pink Coral Palace is also in it," Agent Foile answered.

Gramma Trouble whistled. "That must be a whole lot of faces."

"Sherlock tells me that it will take him a week or more to run the matches," the senior agent said. "He'd like to borrow time with his siblings to run through it faster."

"How much time?" General Bruce asked.

"Seventy-five percent of their unused capacity," Taylor answered.

"Which of Nelly's brood is using the most of their capacity?" the general asked again.

"None of us are using more than seven percent of our capacity," Chesty answered from the general's neck. "My brother is only asking for seventy-five percent of the unused capacity. If something comes up and we need to concentrate on our usual job, we can jack up the usage and drop this search down to just three-quarters of what we aren't using."

General Bruce nodding along while his computer answered the question.

"I don't have a problem. Does anyone else?" the Human general asked.

No one objected.

Abby stood. "Unless someone else has something they want to discuss, I suggest we get back to our day jobs while our computers see if they can find these two Iteeche in our database."

The others stood and filed silently out of the room.

The hackles on the back of Gramma Trouble's neck were up and doing a jig. Someone had dared to murder an Iteeche woman who was under their protection. That alone was unacceptable. However, there was more to it. This sure felt like the first gentle breeze that was harbinger of a coming tempest.

5

The children were excited to see them back. Gramma and Grampa Trouble had been acting as stand-in grandparents for not only Kris's kids but also the kids whose own elders were hundreds of light years away.

The children greeted them with delighted squeals. Quickly, the kids dragged them by the hands to show them what they'd done while they'd been gone this morning.

Ruth and her friends had several pasta bridges they were now testing with toy cars and trucks. There were screams of glee and groans of dismay as some bridges held and others failed.

No matter who had built the bridge that stood or fell, all the kids showed delight in the effort.

Johnny wanted to show them how he'd spent his morning. He had learned how to make ramps and what ratio of blocks held them up depending on the angle of the ramp.

Gramma Trouble remembered when she'd been Ruth's age and watched her younger brothers play with the same blocks. She hadn't had a computer at her neck to teach her; she'd had to discover all things on her own.

She paused mentally as her smile continued to encourage the kids. Ruth was named after her. At least, the little great-great-granddaughter was named for her before Trouble had become her overarching *nom de guerre*.

Once upon that time so many years ago, she had been Little Ruth to her family because an aunt was most definitely Big Ruth. Strange to look at that bit of family.

It was time to take the kids to lunch. Much like the pied piper, the two trouble-making grandparents led the kids down to the commissary and saw to it that they got balanced meals, not what they would have chosen themselves.

Not wanting to waste food, Johnny was only made to eat two string beans. He did, biting off a quarter inch at a time.

I love being in these kids' lives. Not just our two, but all of them. I swear, no harm will come to them.

At her neck, Penelope whispered, "We are ready to report on our search of the database."

"Did you find matches?" Gramma Trouble asked.

"Yes, ma'am, but you won't like it."

"Well, if that's going to be the case, I'll take the bad news when we're all gathered together. It'll be easier to find a shoulder to cry on."

"I've got a shoulder you can cry on anytime," her husband answered from where he stood in line, with four short people between them.

She gave him a solid, if not sincere scowl, "There is a reason I named my computer Penelope," she tried to growl.

"And why I named my computer after The March of the Ten Thousand," the old general shot back.

"Well, lead on, my Ulysses," she said and the two of them slipped away while the children were busy with loud voices talking over each other about their morning.

The group Gramma Trouble was beginning to think of as The Committee for Embassy Defense arrived at the conference room moments apart. Apparently, even General Konga had found business at Main Navy to keep him close. He and Admiral Ulan arrived together and only a moment after the Humans.

"We have matched the two Iteeche trailing the slain woman," Mata Hari said from Abby's neck. "They had a minor role for one day in the demonstrations around the Pink Coral Palace."

"How minor?" Grampa Trouble asked.

"They urged a group of demonstrators to impose themselves in front of the Embassy gates. And yes, General Trouble," Mata Hari interjected before another question could be shot at her, "we have matched the photos of those they urged to action. That was the only entry in our database for any of them."

"So, these are minor players," General Bruce muttered.

"There are fifty billion Iteeche on this capitol planet," Mata Hari replied, "Our opponent could march them by our cameras for eighteen months before they'd have to show anyone twice."

"Hmm," Grampa Trouble said. "With all Nelly's kids helping, I thought you said you'd have results soonest. Why so long?"

"We had to do a search on all the people they got moving," Mata Hari answered. "We also ran their pictures through the database we've made of all the Iteeche we've seen around the major clans and many of the medium-sized ones. And yes, Generals, there were no matches for either these two or any of those around them."

Abby being the only one among them qualified to be a secret agent, the others turned to her.

She pondered what her computer had found for a long moment, then cleared her throat. "They are either very deep agents, or they're what they appear to be, bit players that someone dredged up from well away from the Embassy for occasional minor work."

"Only killing a chief's Companion was not 'minor work'," Gramma Trouble pointed out, bitterly. She'd had enough of violent death, thank you very much.

"Maybe they're working their way up in the world," Ambassador Kawaguchi offered thoughtfully. "That, or whoever did this knew they were throwing down a very serious gauntlet and wanted it to be untraceable to any clan."

"I'm going with not wanting any usable fingerprints on the murder," Abby said.

Those around the table nodded in agreement.

"If you will allow a mere Iteeche soldier to comment," General Konga said, "I thank you for including us in this conversation. I know you have laid cards on the table that you have always played very close to your chest. Trusting us with just how powerful your technology is, we thank you for your trust in us. None of what we learned here today will leave this room," he said, turning to Admiral Ulan.

He nodded as well. "We can always say this is just more magic from the Humans. Most of our lower decks already think you Humans are all enchanters. Light or dark, they are not sure. Still, you are all wizards."

"I hope no one is whispering that we use Iteeche youngling sacrifice for our magic," Abby drawled.

"If they are saying that, they don't within my hearing," the general said. "However, what I wanted to say is that within two hundred lu of the Imperial Palace you can buy just about anything for anyone. The subjects of this search may share a single room with five others. It is unlikely that they have come this close to the palace since they worked in that that demonstration. There are millions more where they came from."

"That sounds horrible," Amanda said in dismay.

"Have you read one of your classical writers?" the admiral said. "A Charles Dickens wrote of conditions among the poor during the early Industrial Revolution. They were no worse than those among our masterless men."

"You're reading Dickens?" Abby asked, one eyebrow raised most drolly.

"Not I, ma'am. Every officer on my staff has a reading list of Human fiction. Several of us were discussing Dickens with the one who read it. He had some interesting highlights."

"No doubt," Abby said, "And yes, I've read some Dickens and I grew up in some slums on New Eden that would give London in that time a run for its lack of money."

"The point is," General Konga said, inserting himself into the conversation, "the Imperial Capitol has a ready supply of unaffiliated men willing to work for pfennigs. We will likely never see these two again."

"Can I ask a question?" Jacques put in. "Where do these masterless men come from? You have to be Chosen to make it out of the mating pond. How did these men, and I suspect women, get Chosen to grow to adulthood?"

The two Iteeche glanced at each other, then Admiral Ulan replied. "A lot of them are clan people who have lost their clan affiliation for any number of reasons that don't merit death. Others are Chosen by masterless craftsmen or other skilled labor. Some were Chosen to be slaves but were cut loose by their owners because they were not earning their keep. Most starve to death very quickly. Some learn to survive by any means necessary."

"They are the ones that never should have been Chosen to be slaves in the first place," the general put in.

"So, you have an entire subclass to your clan system that survives by their wits," Amanda muttered softly. She glanced at her sociologist husband. "The clans must find them useful or they would not survive."

"Many do not survive," the general put in. "Every day, the sanitation department removes dead bodies from the street early in the morning so as not to inconvenience the clan lordlings or, ah, disturb the tranquility of the workers."

"I can imagine so," Ambassador Kawaguchi said.

"We Humans have a saying," Gramma Trouble said. "'Follow the money.' Where does the money come from so these two toads can pay their rent? Feed their mouths? It has to be regular enough to keep them around."

"I suspect their money is clan money," Amanda said. "All money seems to pass through the clans."

General Konga nodded. "I think you have seen it working today. There is a reason why every clan lord travels with bodyguards."

"Ah," Gramma Trouble said, a light dawning. "These bottom

feeders are an essential part of the low grade inter-clan rivalries. They take out careless clan lordlings for other clans."

"It is not always for other clans. Sometimes an ambitious subordinate buys a hit on his boss, or so I am told," General Konga put in.

"Good God," Abby exploded. "Is anyone in the Empire ever safe?"

"The question is, does this promotion by assassination also extend to the Navy?" Grampa Trouble asked.

"No," Admiral Ulan immediately answered. "Besides, we are paid too little. Even on my pay, I could hardly afford an assassin."

"Your junior officers do have their dueling clubs," General Konga put in.

"Umm," the admiral answered vaguely.

And another piece of the puzzle slides coyly onto the table, Gramma Trouble mused.

"To sum up the bidding," Abby said, raising a hand with one finger up. "Our murderers are very likely long gone, or they may be picked up by the sanitation department tomorrow with no ID and no interest in the body."

"What happens to those bodies?" Jacques asked.

"What happens to most all bodies except for major clan lords," General Konga stated. "They get recycled and used for either fish food or fertilizer. It's more productive than manure."

"Moving right along," Abby said, raising a second finger. "There are plenty more where those two came from."

The two Iteeche nodded in agreed.

A third finger went up. "We need a larger photo database."

Agent Foile interjected himself into the conversation here. "We need cameras covering every block for at least five kilometers around the Legation District. Maybe more if we can afford them."

"Agent," Abby said, "We've got a huge Embassy here, but it is not unlimited. There's also a matter of bandwidth. The Iteeche do use a major chunk of their radio spectrum. We can only use what they don't."

"I'm sure we can work something out," Mata Hari put in, not quite contradicting her human consort.

"Four," Abby said, raising another finger, "what do we do about policing the Legation District?"

"We have plenty of Marines and Sailors," Admiral Ulan put in. "Admiral Longknife left forty Iteeche Marine divisions here to defend the Legation District, along with a US Marine division. I understand that this division is augmented by a strong military police battalion and a large criminal investigation unit. Is that right, General?"

General Bruce nodded. "Yes. Kris left us with just what we need to grow a police force. As I recall, each clan patrols their own district, right?"

"Yes," General Konga agreed. "We will have to patrol our own thirty-six blocks. However, I'm not sure that a small patrol force will meet our needs if we come under serious assault."

"I don't think so either, General," General Bruce said. "I expect to pull quite a few battalions out of the Iteeche divisions and turn them into plain clothes patrolmen. This close to the Imperial Precincts, I doubt anyone wants a lot of Marines in uniforms strutting around the street."

"You have that right," the Imperial Guard general agreed.

"So, we stand up a uniformed police force as well as a plain clothes force three or six times larger. We blanket our district and keep some reserve for anything that develops outside our area of responsibility."

"Yes," Abby said. "We also tell both uniformed personnel and their dependents that they don't leave the district except in groups of five or six and with a plain clothes officer or two with them."

"Do you think it is that bad already?" Ambassador Kawaguchi asked.

"We got caught with our pants down this time," General Trouble said. "I don't want more of our people murdered on our watch. I want to be ahead of the curve and snatch up the next guy who takes a swing at one of our people."

That was something they could all agree on.

A few more loose ends were tied up over the next half hour, then the meeting broke up

For the next week, the precautions were sufficient to the need. No Sailor, Marine, or Guardsmen or their dependents, had a hair on their head harmed.

Then someone tagged the Navy hard. Really hard.

6

A muffled boom filled my classroom. My head went up and I glanced around the room. My classmates' heads swiveled like little birds, too. We all looked one way, then whipped around to check out the other side. As two more booms filled the room, most of us students stood up and turned around looking for whatever it was causing all the noise.

Then came the sound of sirens.

"There are fire trucks in the street!" Mark shouted. He spent a lot of time looking out the window. Now, every kid in the school room bolted for a window.

I cheated.

"Daisy, open the door to the balcony," I whispered.

There was a pause while Daisy got permission. A moment later, the door swung open and a tidal wave of kids swept out onto the terrace.

The railing around the balcony grew a few centimeters higher. Still, you could see through it. I raced toward the rail and dashed for the far end where I'd have a good view of the street in front of the Embassy. The banister was up to my nose, but I could see everything.

Red fire engines, ambulances and black police cars raced out of the Embassy's basement garage and turned right.

"Help me up!" Johnny cried beside me.

A moment later, a step appeared so he could just barely see over the banister. Down the line, steps appeared to help the shorter children see over the lip of the railing, each step adjusted for their individual height.

"Thank you, Daisy," I said.

"You're welcome, Ruth."

The teachers were finally catching up with us kids. I could sense the tension coming off of them in steaming waves.

"What happened?" I asked Daisy.

"Ruth, there has been an explosion at the bazaar," Daisy answered.

"What kind of explosion?" The other kids might not know to ask, but I was a Longknife and I knew that some people liked to blow stuff up. Grown-ups often used words other than 'stuff,' but my mommy didn't talk like that.

"That has yet to be determined," Daisy said. "Right now, Ruth, all they're doing is trying to put out the fires and take care of the people that were hurt. The investigation will have to wait for a while."

I knew that. Still, I hated having to wait to know what was happening around me. Having Daisy often helped me find things out first among my friends. Still, mommy said I needed to learn patience.

I hate patience.

"What's happening?" came from behind me. The older kids were gathering around me. I liked to hang out with them; they were so much more fun to be with. "More mature than the littles," Mommy would say.

I shared with them what Daisy had told me.

"Get us into the police net," Buddy Malone demanded.

Daisy answered without me having to say a word. "The net is presently using a high order scrambler. I can bring up the emergency services net if you want."

"Who cares about that?" Buddy grumped. "Nothing exciting happens there."

"Buddy," Mary said, "you won't be happy until you can see the bloody video take."

"Yeah. Why not? They're dead. What do they care if we see their guts hanging out? Besides, they're just squids."

Mary scowled down at Buddy. With her last growth spurt, she was now the tallest kid in the group. "Grow up, Buddy. They're our allies."

"They're fish," he snapped back.

"They're our friends," I said, trying to keep my voice from getting shrill. Mommy's voice never got shrill. "Some of the Iteeche are my friends."

"So, you love fish," Buddy's voice wheedled. "They tried to kill us."

"I know they did," I said, letting my voice go down an octave like Mommy sometimes did. "I blew up some of their rockets while you were hiding in the basement."

Buddy faced a wall of disapproving stares from all of us. He turned and stomped back to the door. He tried to shove one of the littles off her step, but a tutor stepped in. He stormed into the classroom in a royal huff.

"Always glad to see him in the rearview mirror," Mary said. "Could you ask Daisy to let us know when there's anything to know?"

The kids knew that neither Daisy nor Hippo accepted commands from anyone but me or Johnny. "Sure. My mom hates secrets."

"She sure keeps enough of them," Suzie said. "All of our folks keep secrets."

"I still say we should start our own spy ring," Bruce said, for the millionth time.

"How can we have an intelligence service," Mary sighed, "when our best intel source is a computer hitched into the grown-ups' network?"

"Right," Bruce answered.

Daisy was the one who told them most of what they knew about what was going on. Still, a lot of their parents computers were on net with her. If we kids found out anything interesting, I figured Daisy would snitch on us.

As mommy said, intelligence often went both ways. You found out about them, but they found out about you.

"An Iteeche woman was murdered at the bazaar a while back," Bruce muttered.

"My dad says the bazaar is a soft target," Mary said. "Does anyone know what a soft target is?"

My friends had learned that they could often get more answers from Daisy if they asked a question to no one in particular. Daisy proved them right, again.

"A soft target is any person or place that is relatively easy to harm or damage. This is different from a hard target like the Embassy where they can't do much harm," Daisy said.

My friends mulled that over for a bit.

"I sure did like the bazaar," Suzie lamented.

I couldn't agree more. The sounds, the smells, the colors of the bazaar had been exciting. I loved wandering the bazaar and visited it as often as I could get a grown-up to take me there.

For the last week or so, no adults had been going to the bazaar. Daisy had a catalogue that I and the other kids could order from if we wanted something special from the bazaar. Still, a catalogue on-screen wasn't nearly as much fun as being there.

"Does anyone know where all the fire engines are going?" Mark asked. He loved fire engines.

"Nothing looks like it exploded from here," Mary said. The balcony overlooked the Imperial Palace. As far as they could see, there was no smoke.

"Let me see what I can do," I said. "Daisy, could you make a skeeter and get us a picture from the other side of the Embassy?"

"Ruth, I have not been told that I can't," Daisy said, her voice taking on a sneaky edge. A moment later, a holograph appeared in the air in front of me and the big kids.

It showed a picture from the top of the Embassy that quickly focused down on the bazaar where a black plume of smoke drifted away on the breeze. White steam showed were the fire engines were smothering the flames.

The view of the bazaar drew closer as the quadcopter zoomed toward the scene of the explosion.

It came to a hover three hundred meters up and back from the boundary of the bazaar. From the looks of it, several dozen meters along one aisle had been blown to bits. The ground was covered with copper pots, broken crockery, clothes, and strung out bolts of colored cloth.

There were lumps among the wreckage.

"Can we get any closer?" Bruce asked.

"No, you may not," came in the strong voice of their head mistress of tutors. Ms. Arvind was said to be a retired Marine Gunny. She certainly knew how to kick butt and take names. None of us kids wanted to get our names on her list.

"Ruth, who told you that you could fly a drone over a potential crime scene?"

"No one, ma'am, but no one told me that I couldn't."

"Is it a crime scene?" Mary asked.

"I said potential crime scene, Ms. Ogilvie. What is the difference between a crime scene and a *potential* crime scene?"

I wondered if this was one of those rhetorical questions. I was just learning about those before mommy went off to war.

Apparently, none of the other kids could tell if it was rhetorical nor not either. Not even Mary offered an answer and her hand was always up.

"Ms. Longknife?" snapped at me in a Gunny's voice.

I snapped to attention and rattled off the first thought that came into my head. "A crime scene has yellow tape around it. A potential crime scene doesn't?"

"Close, but no blue ribbon. Mary, why isn't your hand up?"

"I didn't know if you wanted an answer," the tall girl admitted.

"If I ask a question on the balcony outside the school room, you can assume I want an answer."

Mary took a deep breath and began. "A crime scene is any person or place that may have evidence of a crime. It is marked by yellow police tape," she said, giving me a sidewise grin. "A potential crime scene is any place that may have the potential of being designated a crime scene but isn't yet."

"Very good. Now Ruth, please bring the drone back to the Embassy. We may need that Smart Metal for something besides a toy."

"Yes, ma'am," I said, trying to give the head mistress a contrite face, but really too excited about pulling back the drone from what sure looked like a crime scene. If that wasn't a bomb, Johnny could have my desserts for the next week.

At that moment, the picture in front of us shook wildly. Something had shaken up the drone. A second later came the sound of another explosion. From the holograph in front of us, I could see a new gout of smoke covering the area that had already been flattened.

"Why would someone blow up what they already blew up?" Mark asked.

I looked at our Head Mistress. The look on her face was scary.

"Because they wanted to kill firemen and the other first responders," she said in words so hard you could strike sparks off them.

The tutors herded us kids back into the classroom. We went in total silence. I don't know about the others, but I couldn't think of anything to say.

We didn't go back to our projects. Instead they showed us a holograph about a dog that got left behind when his boy moved. He went on a journey with a cat as they covered all the miles to his master's new home. In the end, the boy got his dog back and they adopted the cat.

Someone said, "You don't adopt a cat. They adopt you."

That should have gotten a laugh, but we didn't feel much like laughing.

In the dim light as we watched, Johnny got close to me. He cried a lot during the movie. I did too. It felt good to have a good cry.

High above me, grown-ups had no time to cry.

7

"**S**on of a bitch!" the old warhorse growled through clenched teeth.

"Calm down, sweetheart. Both of us are too old for this shit," Ruth told her husband. "We've got too many miles on our hearts to wear them out now."

"The bazaar! Again? How did they pull that off?" Grampa Trouble fumed.

"We're not up against stupid people, dear. They get a vote, too, and somehow, they got two sets of bombs out there without us any the wiser."

"That's what I'm pissed about," the general snapped. "Iteeche low tech is out-classing our high tech."

"So, we'll get smarter," Gramma Trouble answered.

"You are wanted in the Command Center," Penelope said from her neck.

"Come on, you old war horse. The kids want our creaky old opinions," she said.

"Well, at least I'll be where I can find out first what those SOBs pulled on us. Don't we have bomb sniffers and electronic suppressors around soft targets like the bazaar?"

"If we don't, we'll find out soon enough."

The two found an elevator waiting for them and quickly rose up the Embassy tower to the war room and battle station at the very top of it. The view of the city was, as usual, spectacular.

Today, however, two plumes of ugly black smoke drifted away on a soft breeze. From where they stood, the hell and havoc on the ground was out of sight. Still, the two old warriors knew the drill.

They'd spent enough time in hell.

The war room was right next door to the battle station, or fighting tops, if you were Navy and knew what that meant. On one side, windows provided a panoramic view of half of the capitol. A glass wall on the other side gave the war room a full view of anything going on in the room that controlled all the defenses of the Embassy.

In the center of the war room was an oval table.

It filled up quickly. At the head of the table was an empty chair. Gramma Trouble guessed it belonged to General Bruce, should he honor them with his very harried presence. Abby had the chair at that one's right hand. Amanda and Jacques provided a civilian presence. Ambassador Kawaguchi would speak for the diplomatic interests. Two stools awaited General Konga and Admiral Ulan.

That left only two chairs. One was at General Bruce's right hand. Gramma Trouble headed for the other one, leaving the old general to take the seat next to the general commanding the Legation's defense.

Since General Bruce wasn't there yet, General Trouble cleared his throat and asked, "Can anyone tell me what just happened? We were down with the kids. They heard the explosions and saw the fire trucks leaving. I don't know much, other than it was at the bazaar again."

As the two Iteeche stepped in and took their seats, Abby said, "Mata Hari, will you please brief these folks on what we know happened?"

A video take from high atop the tower showed the bazaar in all its glitter and color. One minute it was lovely, the next minute, a daisy chain of explosions irregularly spaced, some five to ten meters apart, and sent fragments of pottery, cloth, as well as Iteeche flying into the air.

"It took us exactly two minutes from the time of the explosion for our first responders to arrive," Abby said as the picture hiccupped and jumped ahead that amount of time. Two pumpers with hoses on cherry pickers showered the flames with a heavy rain and the fires began to burn out. The ambulances and emergency services rigs arrived and a blend of Iteeche and Humans worked their way through the fallen bodies, looking for those still alive. Several were carried out on stretchers.

That was when the second explosion hit.

It looked like someone had fired a cannon full of nails right down the alley where the bombs had gone off. In an instant, the alley where the medics and emergency personnel struggled to save lives and give aid became a charnel house.

"We still had responders flowing toward the bazaar," Abby said. "It took us a few minutes to get a second full wave of first responders headed that way. We dispatched sniffer drones ahead of them. We've also got electronic suppressor drones covering the bazaar this time, not that it mattered. That bomb went off exactly six minutes after the first bunch."

"Damn low tech," Gramma Trouble growled.

"Where's Special Agent Foile?" Amanda asked.

"He left for the bomb site at the tail end of the first wave," Abby said. "Mata Hari is in touch with Sherlock. She tells me that he got there seconds after the second bomb. He's hopping mad."

"I can imagine so," the old general growled. "So am I."

"We are still trying to remove the injured," Abby said. "We'll start shifting through the wreckage as soon as the living are removed. It goes without saying that everyone there is antsy about a third bomb."

Gramma Trouble leaned forward to rest her elbows on the table and her chin on the palms of her hands. She gazed out the window at the smoking wreckage of what had been one of the few bright spots on an otherwise gray vista. Other than those living off their skills around the bazaar, she'd met few happy Iteeche on this planet.

Someone was choosing to strike at them, and through those happy souls, at the Humans.

This had to stop.

"So," she said, "what do we do now?"

"I can't think of anything," Abby said. "We've got Iteeche and people doing everything they can. We're stuck waiting."

"Rita used to tell me, back in the war," Gramma Trouble said, "that the most useless person in the world was a captain of a hard-hit warship, waiting on her bridge for damage control to report whether her ship would live or die."

"Why was she waiting on her bridge?" Amanda asked.

"Because that's where a captain belongs when she's in a fight and blown up just short of a million pieces," General Trouble said, voice rumbling like a volcano unsure whether or not to explode.

A very harried General Bruce strode in and took his place at the head of the table. He stood, ignoring the chair. "I understand you've seen the video feed of the two explosions."

The two missing Iteeche officers were right on the Human general's heels. They did take their stools at the table.

"We have not," General Konga said.

General Bruce cast a worried eye toward the battle station. There, well-organized chaos reigned, and troops went about their duty quickly and efficiently. Others sat frozen as statues as they stared unblinking at their battle boards.

Here and there, officers moved quietly up and down the aisles, stopping for a moment to observe, say a good word, or just rest a steadying hand on a shoulder.

"We think we have any future bombs suppressed," the general said, running a worried hand through his hair. "However, we thought we had that area pretty well suppressed before this all blew up. Our best guess is that someone used a seriously contained explosive that got past our sniffers, then set them off with non-electronic timer fuses. Likely chemical fuses, but we don't know for sure until we sift through the wreckage and find the residue of the explosives and detonator. I'm just guessing."

"Do we know who was in the bazaar at the time of the explosion?" General Konga asked.

"Unfortunately, yes," Abby said. A new video filled the center of the table. "There was a small party of Iteeche Sailors and Marines with their consorts and Chosen who had just strolled into the bazaar. They were sticking together, as they'd been told to. They also had three plainclothes guards. One of them had checked out a bomb sniffer before he left."

"In other words," Gramma Trouble said, "they did everything we told them to do and they still got blown to bits."

"I'm afraid so," Abby said.

The two Iteeche stared at the video. "Can you make out anybody in that mob?"

"Actually, we can," Mata Hari said from around Abby's neck, and she proceeded to show them how, following first one Iteeche whose face was obscured until the moment it wasn't. A box appeared around the face and facial recognition software gauged the face.

"We've been going through the entire crowd in that alley, checking out everyone. Most of them are familiar faces. People who work there. People who go there for breakfast. Beggars. Buskers. Whatever. It's no question, one of them could have taken the clan coin and turned on us, but we are starting with the faces of the strangers, such as this one," Abby said, and the video paused to highlight a face. "Or this one." Another highlighted face. "Or these people,"

The video fast-forwarded through several dozen people who were highlighted, gauged, and put aside.

"Any suggestions so far?" Admiral Ulan growled.

"We've hardly been at this for half an hour, Admiral. We're trying our best, but these things take time."

"We are running out of time," the admiral snapped. "First they knife a Companion in the back and we catch no one. Now they blow up one of our liberty parties! We have to find someone!"

"We'll do our best," Abby said, as softly as she could.

"Let me ask something," Ambassador Kawaguchi said, his voice steadying. "This bazaar is a favorite place for our Iteeche troops and their women. It is, however, a, what do you call it . . .?" he paused, hunting for the word.

"Right!" He snapped his fingers. "A soft target. Twice, those who oppose us have struck at us through it. I take it that we cannot harden it anymore where it is. Could we bring the bazaar into the Legation District? Is that possible or desirable?"

The two Iteeche officers glanced at each other, then did not break eye contact.

"We might have some trouble finding space for all the skilled craftsmen," Admiral Ulan said. "Still, I think it could be done. I doubt if these masterless men and women would mind sleeping in tents on the roofs of some of our apartment buildings."

Abby cleared her throat. "I can understand the desire to keep these poor souls safe and their product available. However, it is a soft target. They would have to go outside the perimeter to get resources to create their product. Other Iteeche, besides our own troops, are going to browse the wares. That would leave all sorts of openings for mischief. Bombs could appear in their supplies. One might go out and an assassin might be the one who comes back. Just moving a soft target behind a wall doesn't make it a hard target. It could very well soften the hard target."

"How do you intend to keep our hard target hard when we must bring food in every day?" General Konga asked.

"You got me there," Abby admitted, shaking her head ruefully.

For a long minute, there was silence around the table. Finally, General Trouble broke it. "If we put the bazaar out of bounds, morale will take a hit. However, if people keep getting killed, our troopers will start avoiding the place and that will lead to another morale hit. We don't want to go into lockdown, at least not yet. That would make us look weak. It would be a victory for those who want to isolate us. With us no longer visible, it would be easy to stir up demonstrations against us, or even riots."

"We've seen how that vid ends," Abby interjected, dryly.

"Abby," her husband, General Bruce said, "would you please pay a visit to our clan neighbors, the Tzon, I believe, and see what they'd be interested in doing with us to protect the bazaar?"

General Konga managed a frown. "It is the right and duty of a clan to provide security and safety within its own district. I am not sure what assistance they would be willing to take from either the Navy or you Humans."

"I'll have to look into that," Abby agreed.

"You *will* take a significant security detail," General Bruce said.

"Of course, I will," Abby snapped back. " However, I will check in with our friendly Iteeche, Ron, to see about getting an invitation to speak to the Clan Chief of the Tzon. Now, if no one has anything else to discuss, I suggest we get back to work until we have something more solid to discuss."

Those in the room accepted Abby's dismissal. Gramma Trouble led her husband toward one of the several elevators that appeared. The two of them rejoined the children. Johnny's class had been creating holographic art and needed enthusiastic judges. Ruth's class had spent the last day developing data bases to aid in the retrieval of formation that they'd learned in the last week.

So far in their young lives, they'd used off-the-shelf databases. Now it was time for them to organize them for retrieval by their own inclinations and preferences. It was difficult to review such very personal products, so the local grandparents had been drafted into the job.

Gramma Trouble expected to stay busy for the remainder of the day. That, at least, would keep her mind off of the mess developing outside the Legation District.

8

The next morning, Gramma Trouble had hardly gotten the children settled down at their lessons when Penelope whispered, "You and the General are wanted upstairs."

A glance toward the outer wall showed an elevator already forming for them. They tried to slip away from the children without making a noise, but little Ruth was even more sensitive about the presence of her grandparents than Ruth thought.

Gramma Trouble glanced back to check and found Ruth watching her go. Her face was as bland as one her mother used when she didn't like something but didn't want to show anything to anyone.

Gramma Ruth gave her granddaughter a quick wave and a smile she hoped wasn't too nervous.

The not yet eight-year-old showed no reaction. Still, her eyes followed her grandmother as she entered the elevator.

Her husband held her tight. "The kid's a trooper," he whispered in her ear.

Ruth kept her face as bland as little Ruth's. "Yeah."

A few moments later, they stepped into the Command Center beside the Battle Station. This time, the table was long, and they were among the first to arrive.

However, the two scientists were already seated. Amanda was present for any economical advice, and Jacques for the sociological perspective. Gramma Trouble and the General took the two seats they'd had the day before. If they were too close to the front, they could always lengthen the table in that direction.

The joys of Smart Metal™.

Abby hurried in and took the seat across from General Trouble. Her attention was focused on one of her three readers, but she soon shifted to another one.

That kept small talk to a minimum.

General Konga and Admiral Ulan stepped from one elevator at the same moment as Ambassador Kawaguchi strode from another. Senior Chief Agent in Charge Taylor Foile and his assistant were only a moment later.

As if his computer had told him the table was full, General Bruce strode in. He settled into the chair at the head of the table and said, "Taylor, tell us what you know about the bombs."

The Senior Chief Agent-in-Charge hadn't bothered to take his own seat. He reached into the pocket of his shipsuit and tossed the General a smooth stone, with a square area of several centimeters on each side.

"That's what your bomb looks like," he added.

An intake of breath followed the arc of the bomb down the table. The general made a two-handed catch and held it like it was ... well, a bomb.

"We found a dud among the wreckage. That," the agent said, pointing at the shiny object in the general's hand, "is *not* the actual bomb, but a training device we're using to make people aware of what one of those bastards looks like."

General Bruce flipped the fake bomb over in his hand, then tossed it to General Trouble.

Gramma Trouble failed to suppress a smirk. Smart man, her husband. He did not hand that hot potato off to his wife. Still, he had no one else to pass it to but her. A moment passed. The room began breathing again, and only then did he offer it to her.

Ruth took the bomb and studied it. It could easily pass for a polished river stone, dark but still shiny. Having kept up to date with the developments of explosives, Ruth had a pretty strong suspicion that this small rock had a thick hide that would provide fragmentation and keep the scent of explosives low enough for the sniffers to miss it.

It truly was a devilish device.

Very much aware that there was no way that she'd be able to identify this little chunk of death from any other rock on the side of the street or center of the road, Gramma Trouble passed it along to General Konga. He eyed it cautiously before handing it to Admiral Ulan.

Ruth winced. The stone was so well camouflaged as a rock that she and a lot of people would be shying away from just about everything in the street. Truly, it was the perfect device to put everyone on edge.

She and the entire garrison would be no better than a certain nervous colt they'd had back on the farm when she was young. They'd finally had to put it down.

With a deep frown, she turned back to the conversation.

"We have no idea when those were strewn along the path, or by whom. We have observation footage from the time the bazaar opened to the time of the explosions. There were no stones in the morning video. At sunrise, the three old women who keep the street clean swept it. We've checked with them. They saw nothing and, if they had, they would have removed them. 'People could get hurt if they stumbled over one,' they told me."

The agent ended with a shrug.

"So," General Bruce said, "someone dropped them after the shops opened for business."

"Very likely."

"And no one saw anything?"

"My best guess," the agent-in-charge said, "was that someone had them up their trousers or robes. They shook one loose every few steps with our observation cameras none the wiser. At least, that is what anyone seated at this table would do." He finished with a quick glance around the room.

With the exception of the ambassador, they were all experienced war fighters. If they hadn't actually done this to someone, or had it done to them, it was in their bag of tricks.

It was a basic attack, carried out in a simple way. Defending against it was like trying to defend yourself from your next breath.

"Abby?" her husband asked, "You touched base with our neighboring clan. Want to share the results?"

"Not really," Abby said with a scowl. "I try to avoid cussing while the kids are young and impressionable."

"Report, dear heart."

With a sigh, Abby began. "The clan leaders dodged me all day yesterday. Even with the help of Ron, our friendly Iteeche, I couldn't get an invite to court. At six in the morning, I got a call telling me to be there at seven."

"Seven?" Gramma Trouble exclaimed. She knew how much Abby disliked mornings.

"Yeah," Abby drawled. "To keep the general here off my back and happy, I got together a decent escort, heavy on Iteeche Marines and a few Imperial Guardsman."

Here, Abby nodded to General Konga. "I hope you didn't mind me bawling for help."

"We're on the same side. If a Guardsman can open a door for you, you only have to ask."

"Thank you. All the doors I needed open, opened. However, I didn't much like what was at the end of the walk up to the rooftop garden. Instead of meeting with the senior Clan Chief of the Tzon Clan, I ended up meeting with a committee of chiefs. Eight to be exact. One did the talking, but the others listened like hawks."

As one, the room turned toward Jacques. He shook his head. "I've never heard of that sort of thing."

"You better add it to you storeroom, no, to your storehouse of Iteeche surprises, Doc," Abby drawled.

"Anyhow, I got told that a lot of the people from the Tzon Clan had been killed in the first bombings. Some were shopping. Others were just strolling through the street on their way to work. Many of their safety and fire teams were killed in the second bomb. They were not happy."

Abby paused to let that sink in. The Navy and Embassy people had been mourning their own dead. They hadn't thought about the local clan.

"I'm guessing they argued all night before they agreed that the clan would no longer host the bazaar. As of sundown today, every masterless man no matter what his skill or craft, would be barred from the Tzon District."

"Whoa," Gramma Trouble said. "How do they expect these poor people to move all their wares in just one day?"

"Worse," Amanda said, "Where can they go?"

Everyone turned to the two Iteeche at the table. They both suddenly seemed entranced by the finish of the table in front of them. They looked about as embarrassed as any Iteeche Gramma Trouble had ever met, including clan chiefs captured in the war.

Abby broke the lengthening silence. "General. Admiral. Would either of you help us understand what is about to happen? Is it as bad a tragedy as I think it is?"

"If you are thinking that in a month," the Iteeche general said, "the trash collectors will have gathered up the bodies of everyone working at the bazaar, then you are correct."

"If you think that every item for sale in the bazaar will be stolen in the next few hours, you are also correct," the admiral added.

"No!" came from several around the table.

"One or two may be allowed to swear fealty to a clan or two. A jeweler, a goldsmith. I doubt many others," the general said.

"The rest," the admiral said, with a shrug, "will not find a roof that will take them in. They'll not be able to buy so much as a rotten white root. The children, then the women, and finally the men, will all starve to death."

"You have no social safety net?" Amanda said.

"What is a social safety net?" both the Iteeche asked together.

"The more who die, the more food there is for the newly Chosen," Jacques growled.

"Yes," the Iteeche general agreed.

The room fell silent as those around the table mulled the consequences of the decision they must make in the next few minutes.

"General, Admiral," Abby said. "You are on record as considering the bazaar a value for maintaining morale. Do you still feel that way?"

"Yes," they both answered.

"We humans like them, too," Amanda said. "It is the one ray of color in a very gray world."

"The kids enjoy roaming the bazaar," Gramma Trouble said.

"So," General Bruce said, "we would *like* to save the bazaar."

"And if we're going to do that, we better do it quick before everything there is ripped off," Gramma Trouble added.

"Okay," General Bruce said, "So how do we find room in our lifeboat for some more drowning refugees? Abby dear, you were worried about feeding the Iteeche during a siege. Any suggestion about what to do if we make it worse?"

"We are not under siege at this moment," Abby drawled. "I say haul 'em in."

"Any opposition to the proposal on the table?" General Bruce asked.

Heads shook no.

"General Konga, Admiral Ulan, can you get a security force to the bazaar? Let the people know that they are under our protection as is all their property. As quickly as you can, will you get trucks moving there to lift out all their wares and personal property?"

Without hesitation, the two officers were on their provided Human commlinks, issuing orders.

The human general went on. "Any suggestion where we put them?"

"Any chance we could use the main avenue between us and the Tzon Clan?" Agent Foile asked.

The two Iteeche interrupted barking orders to shake their heads. The Imperial Guards General explained, "That is Imperial property.

No one may block the flow of traffic under pain of losing their head."

"Don't want to do that," General Bruce said, rubbing his neck.

"I suggest the next street in," Abby said. "We'll think about how to do this tomorrow. We just need to get everyone, and their sale goods, moved in here ASAP."

Over the next hour, they dispatched Military Police to protect the bazaar. They also established a secure perimeter up and down the boulevard to assure no further surprises.

Jacques and Amanda led their own teams up the road.

This was an opportunity that neither would miss. Here, they had a view of the Iteeche economy and social structure in the raw. No surprise to Jacques, there was a group of elders that performed both the executive and judiciary functions of the group. He slipped in with them. It proved to be a very good match.

They needed proof of the sincerity of the intent of the Humans. Meanwhile, Jacques was delighted to have a chance to observe the workings of an Iteeche culture that might well pre-date the formation of the clan system.

Amanda's team observed the economics of both fire sales and the hiring of labor to help in the packing up. Several of the ready hands were actually members of the Tzon Clan. It soon became clear that the relationship between the clan and the bazaar was close, tight, and much intertwined.

That left Amanda to wonder if the clan chiefs who decided to toss these people to the wolves realized how much of their own nose they were lopping off.

Within fifteen minutes after the first MPs arrived, the first detail of trucks arrived for people to load their gear into. At first they thought they'd start at one end of the street and work their way to the other. Nope.

Some shops were immediately ready to load up their wares. Others needed more time to pack. There was also the problem of moving product and moving the actual shop. Most tenting was canvas for walls and the overheads. However, some were more elaborate or secure.

The goldsmiths and jewelers were examples of one. They had fairly heavy safes for their product; forklifts would be needed to move them. They were quickly ordered spun out of Smart Metal™ by Mata Hari and sent up the road.

Jacques accompanied the elders to the new street selected for the bazaar. Being closer to the Imperial Palace, it was shorter than the present street. Fortunately, those blocks closer to the palace also were deeper. Sixth Street in the Legation District had a wider band of greenery and fountains than the other street. The shops would be made deeper and more narrow.

Abby still had scorching memories of trying to shoehorn a massively oversized trade delegation with even more massive egos. Those merchant princes had fought over every square centimeter of the Pink Coral Palace and chortled when they thought they'd taken over every scrap of space, leaving Kris's delegation to beg for the return of any crumbs.

Kris Longknife wasn't the type of princess to beg for anything. She'd dead-stick landed a starship going from orbit to the garden in the center of the palace even as Nelly and her kids reprogrammed the Smart Metal™ from a re-entry vehicle to a lifting body to a humongous rotary-winged assisted glider that touched down, light as a feather, even as it remade itself into a castle.

All while under attack.

That had been a fun night. Better still, the quarters in the castle were much better than those in the old, cold, and moldy stone palace the Iteeche loaned the Human Delegation.

Abby not only set up space for each seller in the bazaar, but ran a series of girders across the street from one high-rise to the next. Those who browsed the colorful wares would do so in the shade and out of the rain.

It was not, however, for the buyers' comfort. Spaced along the delicate fretwork were cameras as well as sensors. Every moment anyone was in the bazaar, they'd be under observation. Agent Foile's

Sherlock would be analyzing movements and behavior for anything out of the ordinary.

Every person entering the street would pass by several tall, imposing concrete obelisks proclaiming the street closed to traffic. Their mere presence made sure that NO meant NO.

The obelisks weren't concrete but Smart Metal™ and strong enough to stop a tank. Much of the space inside them, however, was devoted to a sensor suite that not only scanned the passerby for weapons, but also had the most sensitive bomb sniffer that the Humans could construct.

Any potential shopper with authority to carry weapons was routed to either side of the street where the security officers there politely invited them to check their weapons or shop elsewhere.

Those who tried to secret bombs into the bazaar pasts the obelisks found themselves locked down in a tight and tiny bomb-proof cell of clear Smart Metal™. There, in plain sight of everyone, they were lifted halfway up to the overhead and interrogated. If they willingly handed over what had been identified as an explosive device, they were lowered down to have a discussion with security personnel. The few false positives were handled with tact.

If they refused, they were let go . . . to splat in the middle of the boulevard.

After the first week, there were fewer attempts to slip bombers into the bazaar. There were also three noticeable smudges on the boulevard where bombers had been dropped.

Their bodies were left there to be run over by trucks for the rest of the day. The sanitation department workers cleaned up what was left the next morning. A quick check showed signs of explosives residue on all the flattened bodies.

As expected, the real problem was not Iteeche carrying in bombs. A couple of times a day, explosive devices were found hidden in the supplies that the craftsmen and skilled workers ordered.

They were removed and the business was removed from the list of approved sellers.

Whoever it was who wanted to harm the Embassy grew more creative.

A vat of dye needed by a weaver would be delivered with a subtle change in the chemistry and a bit of something at the bottom of the pot that would blow it up later in the day. A wool-like substance might be impregnated with chemicals so that it would catch fire when spun into yarn for cloth.

It wasn't just the bazaar that left them open to assault. Food was a constant Achilles' heel that the opposition probed. Not only did poison show up in the foods bought by the specialty food shops of the bazaar, but it also made its appearance in food brought in to feed the Navy personnel.

Every item imported from the outside had to be checked, piece by separate piece. This might have slowed to a halt the essential process of feeding a million Iteeche. However, all of Nelly's kids were dragooned into the process, especially Ruth's Daisy and Johnny's Hippo.

A tub of fresh fish or several yams might show up tampered with. It was never a flood of poison, just a bit here and another bit yonder. If not caught, it could have turned eating at any street vender in the bazaar or mess hall into a horrid game of Russian Roulette. An Iteeche would never know if the next bite they took would kill them.

The Humans in the Embassy certainly did not want the Iteeche living under their protection subjected to a life of that kind of uncertainty.

After a long talk with both General Konga and Admiral Ulan, the Legation District began its own media blitz. The Iteeche media's main content was reports of sporting events, sing-alongs, and entertainment opportunities. The Humans introduced the Iteeche to singing commercials for products in the bazaar.

Slipped in among the verses might be a line about how many attempts had been made to get at the Legation District . . . and thwarted.

Despite initial concern, the average Iteeche on the street took to the transparency very well. Especially since the reports were usually humorous.

Someone wrote a song about a clan lordling who tried and tried to harm the Navy people in the legation. It was kind of an Iteeche Wile E Coyote, and just as funny to those singing along.

While the command and staff of the Navy Minister, Navy Chief of Staff and the Combined Fleets staff never paused in their squabbling, the Iteeche working for them began to see themselves as one community, threatened, but more than able to stand their ground as they moved forward into a future of their choosing.

It was a good thing they had time to coalesce into a solid front. The next probe was not long in coming.

9

I t started simply enough.

In the incredibly crowded Imperial Capitol, most Iteeche walked, due to little access transportation. Consequently, the sidewalks are always crowded. Iteeche were always jostling elbows as they hurried past each other; some could get very aggressive. The Iteeche, however, are a four-legged species. It takes a lot to knock down someone striding along on four feet.

It started simple enough, with a few people reporting to the infirmary with scrapes and bruises. On short trips out of the Legation District, they had been jostled and knocked to the ground or into buildings.

It hardly seemed like a problem the medical staff should bring to anyone's attention.

Then an Iteeche Companion arrived by ambulance. While outside the district, she'd been shoved aside by a passing male; shoved off the sidewalk and into an open manhole cover. She fell fifteen feet and landed hard.

While she was looking for a certain bead shop, she had followed the recent rules. Three other Companions were with her. While one raced back to the district, the other two tried to render such aid as they could.

The runner found a MP as soon as she got back to the district. Within two minutes, an ambulance was on its way. A ready response security team was only a minute behind it. Their fast reaction brought her to the hospital. A combined team of Human and Iteeche surgeons was able to save her life.

Abby was briefed on the situation while the woman was still in surgery by the LT of the security team that responded. A few seconds listening in on the report and Mata Hari was doing a quick scan of the recent reports for sick call. She spotted the pattern of walking accidents and was ready to add to the LT's report. While doing all this, she also issued a call to Gramma Trouble and company to report to the Command Center.

The briefing room filled quickly. With few words, Abby let them in on the latest "situation," and Mata Hari added her own analysis of the people reporting to sick call with scrapes and bruises. "Accidents happen," Abby's computer finished up. "It was only after we had this incident that the pattern fell together."

"Why do I feel like I'm living through the ten plagues of Egypt," Gramma Trouble said, rolling her eyes at the overhead. "First a knifing. We guard against that. Then a bombing. We get that secured and now we're facing our people being pushed into falls. Three plagues down and six to go."

The blank looks from not just the Iteeche around the table forced Gramma to make a quick explanation of the old testament story of the ten plagues God visited on Egypt so they would "let my people go."

"Clearly, somebody wants us to go even if we aren't at all willing," Abby commented, dryly.

"Pardon me for interrupting, ladies and gentlemen, but we have a new development," Mata Hari announced.

"Huh?" was the most brilliant response. Several others were unfit for their children's young ears.

"We've had falls suddenly occur on four different streets," Abby's computer reported.

"Falls?" Gramma Trouble said.

"Mata, show us," Abby ordered.

A holograph appeared in the middle of the table. The view of Third Street, the one that ran in front of the Embassy, showed several Iteeche and Humans on the ground. When those close to them tried to take a step to help them, their own feet slipped out from under them. They landed just as hard.

The holograph flashed to pictures on Fifth street as well as Sixth Street with its bazaar. In each case, anyone who walked on certain parts of the sidewalk ended up landing hard on their face, their butt, wherever. Even those who tried to crawl to the aid of their friends could not keep their hands and feet from sliding out from under them. What was a bad landing for a Human was a very bad one for an Iteeche.

Even as they watched, people began to form human chains to reach out over what sure looked like frictionless surfaces to catch hold of feet or arms. Then, those still on solid ground would tow them back to secure footing.

Other people carefully probed around the sidewalk to find the beginning and end of the dangerous ground. No orders were given; the Iteeche and Human Navy personnel or their dependents knew they were under attack and moved to both help those down as well as identify the extent of the problem.

With the aid of the overhead imagery, it was easy to spot what had happened. Someone had walked down one side of the street, spraying patches of some material, then crossed over to the other side and did the same thing as they left the Legation District.

"Did they spray any of that crap on the streets?" Grampa Trouble asked.

A slow-moving truck soon answered that question.

The driver was braking for a stop sign when his rig lost traction and skidded into the intersection. It only took the driver a meter or so to regain traction. Partially blocking the intersection, the driver got out and went to check his brakes and otherwise see what the problem might be.

An Iteeche chief master at arms who was setting up a secure perimeter to block foot traffic on the sidewalks spotted the new problem. He galloped over to examine the trucker's predicament. The large truck was soon cocooned in the liberally applied crime tape that blocked off more traffic.

Iteeche traffic might be light, but the drivers could make a whole lot of noise with their horns when they weren't happy about long stops.

All three incursions were soon roped off and a combination forensics team and a chemistry fast reaction group were soon scraping a very thin layer of liquid off the sidewalk and street.

All hope for a quick answer to how this next plague had been concocted was dashed when the chemistry team announced that they needed more time to analyze their scrapings.

It didn't take the long to search video and identify three robed Iteeche who strolled into the Legation District. They only went as far as the second block before crossing the street. Then they strode up the other side of the street and quickly left the District.

No one was surprised when the three faces could not be quickly found. It took digging through all the photos taken during the protests that blockaded the Pink Coral Palace to spot them. Each of them had only shown up once and on different days.

Connections were hard to find with such small scraps to go on.

Even as those three streets held everyone's focus, people began doing prat falls on the other three. On these streets, however, the pattern was different. Whoever did this took a straight-through stroll, passing through the Legation District, from one side to the other. None of them crossed the street, so the other sidewalk stayed clear.

"Lock down the district," General Bruce ordered.

"Do we erect a wall or just check IDs?" Abby asked.

That brought scowls and furtive glances from around the table.

"I don't think it would be wise to lock us up behind a wall just yet," Grampa Trouble said, venturing into the heated concern.

"As much as I'd like to go for a wall," General Bruce said, thoughtfully, "I don't want the appearance of us being totally separated from the rest of the capitol. Walls give those inside a siege mentality and leaves those outside wondering what we're doing out of sight," said the flag officer responsible for the defense of the Embassy.

He shook his head before finishing, "Abby, establish gates at all entrances to the district. Limit access. General Konga, Admiral Ulan, can you assign guards to man the gates? I think we'd look better if we had Iteeche at the gate rather than Humans."

"I concur," the Iteeche General said. "However, my Imperial Guard are to defend the person of the Emperor. I might use them at the gates to the Guard's block of quarters, but . . ." he said, leaving the thought hanging.

"It would be much better if we had Marines at the gates," Admiral Ulan said. "They're trained for combat, but I expect they can handle this."

"We have Human Marines specifically trained for manning gates and keeping people out without causing too much trouble," General Bruce said. "If we can survive today, we can have them train your Iteeche personnel for the new security teams."

"I've erected gates at each entrance street and guard rails are up to bar wheeled traffic," Abby reported. "They're ready for you as soon as you can get Marines there."

Admiral Ulan leaned back from the table and began whispering orders into the commlink the Humans had provided him. Likely they'd need to give the security details their own commlinks as well.

While others thought of what to do next, Abby had Mata Hari modify the guard houses to include a commlink. They would likely need their own net.

"General, ma'am," Abby said a minute later to the elderly couple, "it would be nice if we could have some experienced eyes and ears, not to mention respected leaders on the ground. Would you two mind walking the Legation District's perimeter and checking out how things are going?"

"Nice and friendly-like?" Gramma Trouble said.

"Yeah," General Bruce said. "You two are both feared and respected from the old days and are kind of cuddly now at this age."

"Boy, do you have them fooled," Gramma Trouble said, smiling softly at her husband of nearly a century.

"I'm not nearly as dangerous as you are, sweetheart," the old general answered.

"I don't think the kids will miss us for a few hours," Gramma Trouble said, and the two of them ambled off to walk the perimeter. Their old and experienced eyes were the best in the Imperial Capitol to see just how prepared the Legation District was to handle the next incursion and put an end to it before it caused any trouble.

10

Gramma Trouble found a dozen young Marines, half were Human and half were Iteeche, waiting for her and General Trouble as they exited the elevator on the ground floor of the Embassy. Two of each were in smart dress uniforms.

A young lieutenant in the red and blue uniform of the Royal US Marines saluted, "I'm Lieutenant Ivers. I and my men will make sure your inspection is not disturbed."

"Very good, young man," General Trouble said. "Stay close."

Despite his clipped words, the old General proceeded to amble along the street as if he had not a care in the world. They headed for the end of Third Street at a comfortable pace, as if out to enjoy a fine day in the city.

Gramma Trouble had experienced few fine days in the Iteeche capitol. Raised on a farm on the newly opened planet of Herford, the thick air of this city was not easy to breathe. The air was laden with the stink and pollution of too many people crammed into too little space. Each breath she took seemed to have been breathed too many times. It had nothing left to offer.

Still, she strolled along arm-in-arm with the General. While she kept her face to the street ahead of them, her eyes roved from side to side, taking in all the action on this street.

It was a busy thoroughfare. There wasn't a street in the Capitol that wasn't busy. Iteeche hurried past. The barely-clad messengers galloped by in a hurry to deliver their message. Iteeche of higher caste were only a bit less frenetic be they in clan colors or a Navy uniform. There were, of course, those whose clothes signified their unattached nature. Many of them were a spouse or kids of Navy personnel. Others may have been passersby, taking a shortcut from A to B. There was no way to tell with a glance.

It was clear, however, that a lot of people were using Third Street for whatever reason.

Street traffic seemed slow. There were the ubiquitous three-wheel jitneys with the driver up front. The small rigs had room for two passengers, maybe four if the others didn't mind standing on the sideboard in the rear and holding on tight. Larger traffic was more rare and usually in Navy colors. Even more rare were delivery trucks. Most deliveries were made before the sun rose.

To Gramma Trouble, this looked like just another day in the Iteeche Capitol with the powers that be plotting to gain more power and the rest struggling to find their next meal.

They reached the end of the Legation District to find three small guard houses. One was in the middle of the street with the others on the sidewalk on either side. A pair of Iteeche stood watch over traffic around each guard post.

The street was blocked by several thick concrete posts spread far enough apart to allow foot traffic, but not vehicles. As Gramma Trouble watched, a jitney turned in. The guard talked to the passengers, then waved them through. The solid posts melted into the street just long enough for the rig to pass, then flowed back up to block traffic. Glancing back at the Human Embassy, it looked to Gramma Trouble that it might be a tad shorter than it was yesterday.

Still, it was quite imposing.

"I think we need to issue ID cards to all hands that live in the district," the old general muttered.

"That would make it easier on the guards," Ruth agreed.

They spoke with the seven young Iteeche on guard at the entrance for a few minutes. All were Imperial Marine infantry who were a bit nonplused by their present assignment. Still, like Marines of both species, they approached their new mission with commitment.

During the time Gramma Trouble and the old war fighter were with the guards, both she and the general's eyes regularly strayed out onto the boulevard. Across the street, there were several groups of men lounging on the narrow strip of grass between the boulevard and the nearest high rise.

These big boys were joking and laughing, but seemed to spend a lot of time staring over their way. Also, other small groups sauntered up and down the sidewalk on this side of the boulevard. There were never more than four or five Iteeche, but they seemed dower and hulking as they swaggered along.

If that wasn't intimidating enough, they seemed part of a never-ending parade.

"Pretty Penny," Gramma Trouble whispered softly to her computer, "check the drone coverage. Where are these guys going? Do they just turn around when they reach the traffic circle around the palace and come right back this way?"

Penny was silent for a brief moment. "Ruth, I've reviewed the video for the last hour. These guys are walking a square with two parades going in opposite directions. One group reaches the traffic circle and turns right. They walk to the next street over and hook another right. Six blocks later, they do two more rights and start their walk down our side of the boulevard again. Another group is doing the same thing, only using all left turns."

"Xenophon, why don't you and Penny find out if they are armed," Grampa Trouble said.

It took several minutes to get an answer to that question. By then, the two old warhorses were strolling up the boulevard toward Fourth Street; their Marine escort assured them a clear space in the flow of traffic. Some of the strolling bully boys even adjusted their parade long enough to step out onto the boulevard, assuring the two Humans and their Marine escort plenty of room to pass.

"General, Ma'am," Xenophon reported, "we checked every Iteeche and Human during this pass, as well as those lounging across the street. We found no evidence of so much as a butter knife. No sign at all that any of them had been close to something explosive since they last bathed. For some of them, it's been a long time since they bothered with soap and water."

"What about the other side of the district?" Gramma Trouble asked.

"We're checking there now," Pretty Penny said. "So far, it's the same. No weapons, no explosives and it's been a long time since they bathed. I'll let you know when we finish that check."

"So, they're just out to intimidate us," Gramma Trouble said.

"It sure looks that way," her husband agreed. Still, he kept a gimlet eye on the clump of over-sized Iteeche approaching them. Without exception, they flinched away and gave a wide berth to the general and his squad of obviously armed strong men.

Thus, their morning went. They talked to the new guards at the end of every street. When they got to the ring avenue that ran along the east side of the district, they found guards there as well. Small guard houses checked everyone entering or leaving the back doors of the housing blocks.

Here, the parade of plug uglies was lighter. They made no effort to hide what they were doing. They'd stomp up the street, crossed over the avenue, strolled back down the other side, then wash, rinse, repeat. Again, there were two streams of traffic, one coming and one going. Again, there were larger groups of guys lounging against the back of the high rises in the Tzon District across the street.

"Are they just trying to intimidate us or is there something more?" Gramma Trouble muttered to herself.

"For now, I'd say they're in the business of intimidation," Trouble answered. "That intimidation is not only aimed as us, but also builds a wall between us and the rest of the Iteeche population. Xenophon, can you tell me how much the foot traffic through the streets of Legation District has lightened?"

"It will take us more time to fully separate the through foot traffic from the local, however, assuming we subtract all those in uniform and the ones clearly headed to or from the Palace of Learning, foot traffic has been cut in half."

"Keep working on that, if it's not too much trouble?" the general asked.

"No problem, it only takes a small portion of my and Pretty Penny's attention. We should be finished in a minute or two."

By the time they worked their way back to Third Street, it was well into the lunch hour. The two of them hurried to the commissary to spend at least part of the lunch hour with the kids. Johnny was delighted to see them, though young Ruth seemed more reserved.

"We haven't seen you all morning," she was quick to point out.

Gramma Trouble held her close and explained the need to check out the new guard posts around the Embassy.

"We heard that people were falling down," young Ruth answered. "We watched some of it from the school room porch. Was anyone hurt?"

"Not seriously."

"Did someone leave a banana peel?" Johnny piped up.

"It was more like an oil slick," the elder Ruth explained.

"But someone still wanted to hurt our Iteeche friends," little Ruth said, refusing to let the matter drop.

"Yes, pumpkin," Gramma Trouble answered, taking both children into her arms. "Your Grampa and I are doing a walk around the neighborhood to talk to the guards at the end of every street. We want to make sure that bad men stay out of the Legation District. You don't have anything to worry about."

"Okay," Johnny said, and wiggled out of his gramma's arms to gallop over and join some of his friends. All six of the youngsters collected their trays and carried them off to the dirty dish conveyer.

Ruth stayed behind.

"Is this like the missile attack that we stopped?" she asked.

"Yes," Gramma Trouble answered. "only instead of burning anything down, they just want to annoy us."

"So, everything is okay?" the little girl asked seriously.

"Yes, honey. After what your mommy did to those who attacked us, there isn't an Iteeche on this planet that would dare do anything that might irritate us."

Kris Longknife's young daughter gave this some very serious thought for one so young, then nodded. "Okay. Thank you for telling me this, Gramma. Now, I better get back to school. Will we see you for supper?"

"Of course, dear. We'll just be a bit too busy to check in on you at school. Is that okay?"

"You're doing what you have to do," the youngster said, already quoting the Longknife mantra of 'We do what we have to do.'

She quickly joined a group of kids her own age or older. They policed up their lunch table and headed for the dish conveyer. There, they separated their trash from the dishes and then left the well-scraped trays on the conveyer.

Gramma Trouble sighed as she watched the young kids do what the adults did.

"They grow up so quickly," she murmured.

"That's why we try to enjoy them while we can," Grampa Trouble said, a soft smile on his face as he watched the children go. He allowed only a short pause before saying, "Well. Now, back to the salt mines. That sodium chloride isn't going to dig itself out and pour itself into saltshakers for us."

"Why not?" she said, then stood up on tiptoes so she would plant a kiss not too far from her husband's lips.

11

The two old war horses completed another walk around the perimeter of the Human and Navy precincts. The guards were solidly in place and they all knew what was expected of them. They knew they were the first line of defense for their compadres and, in the cases of some older Iteeche, their Companions and Chosen.

The two grandparents finished in time for supper and then spent the rest of the evening with the kids in the water park and playground. Both the kids and their elders were ready for bed early.

With the guards in place, Gramma Trouble figured she and her husband could devote the next day to the kids.

So, of course, the opposition upped the stakes the next morning.

The Iteeche roaming the district's perimeter took to jostling those sharing the boulevard's sidewalk with them. At first it was just a little bump here, another there. The big fellows even apologized for bumping into people . . . for about the first two hours.

Apparently, when it became clear that they'd get no response, the thugs upped the ante. They started knocking down Iteeche with bags in their arms. Adding insult to injury, they kicked their goods, scattering them over the sidewalk. After a bit, merchandise started "accidentally" getting stomped on. Hard.

Iteeche who looked like they might enter the district got shoved off the sidewalk and told they didn't belong there. "Go away," was the clear message.

Most of them got the message loud and clear and found someplace else to be. This, however, cut down a lot on the sales in the bazaar.

The Troubles got called in to assess the situation.

The very nature of the clan system made bullying an approved option so long as it was an Iteeche from a high caste aiming it at someone lower born. It was almost instinctive for those lower on the totem pole to go passive and obey any order barked at them. Gramma Trouble watched as seven- and eight-foot-tall Iteeche seemed to shrink into themselves when someone in finer clothes berated them for being where they were. Even for breathing the air.

Most of the finery looked threadbare, leaving Ruth to wonder if they had been pulled from the back of the closet of some minor clan lordling and loaned out. The mixing and matching of colors didn't appear to be from any one clan. Someone was intentionally promoting people to bully status and doing it in a way to avoid it being traced back to them.

With the two old warhorses on the scene, it took only a quick conference call before Admiral Ulan was dispatching more Marines and Shore Patrol with orders to report to General Trouble.

"What we want to do is stop this bullying. Especially around the bazaar. We're going to organize you into teams of four. If someone is knocked down and their things scattered on the ground, we want the junior of you to help them back up, police up their gear, and get it back in their bag. Be courteous to them, like you might be to your mothers. I mean Choosers," Grampa Trouble said, stumbling over his options for translating a concept into a different culture.

"Sir, we were Chosen by the Navy," a second class petty officer said, "but I think we understand what you mean. If we want to impress a girl we know how to be nice and helpful to her. They can be very appreciative in the mating pool."

Both the Marines and the Sailors eagerly agreed with the petty officer. That left Gramma Trouble wondering if Jacques the sociologist might find this tidbit of information helpful.

With the teams walking the perimeter sidewalks, Ruth and Trouble agreed their presence would likely be needed. It wasn't long before it was.

The first time the ruffians elbowed a passerby into the street, the fast reaction team did just that. While the junior member of the team assisted the Iteeche back onto the sidewalk, the other three confronted the six dudes who did it.

It went about the way that Ruth would have expected.

"Stop that," the chief ordered . . . as only a chief can.

"Doing what?" said the rowdy in the finest hand-me-downs.

"Knocking people off the sidewalk."

"We didn't do nothing. She tripped over her own four feet."

"That's not what I saw."

"Then maybe you need to have your eyes examined."

Gamma Trouble cringed as the clichés cascaded from their mouths. As the conversation progressed, it grew louder. The punk got into the chief's face. She considered intruding.

She didn't. The general rested a restraining hand on her elbow. "Let's see how this works out," he whispered.

It didn't take long to work out.

One of the junior goons threw a punch at a third class Master at Arms. His blow was blocked. The donnybrook was on.

Gramma Trouble had spent a lot of time with the Iteeche POWs during the war. They had been a pretty cowered bunch, even the clan lordlings who tried their best to impose their sense of order on the other detainees.

Gramma Trouble personally set the policy in place. The Human guard would not deal with the lordlings but rather find a senior low-born military officer among the POWs and deal through him.

Because of her policy, there had never been a fight in the camps. At least, there had never been a fight that she or any of her guards witnessed. What took place in the barracks may or may not have been quite different.

Thus it was that Gramma Trouble had never actually seen an Iteeche-on-Iteeche brawl. It was really something to behold.

Each combatant had four legs and four arms and did not hesitate to use all of them. In no time at all, one and two legs were kicking out while the other two kept the fighters standing on an even keel.

It was the same for the arms. Punches flew and were blocked or landed. One lower arm might be delivering an upper cut while an upper arm was blocking a punch. With four arms, blocking, parrying and punching might be coming from all of them at the same time.

The blows did seem to come slower for those hired punks. They let all four hands windmill in attacks. It was as if their brains couldn't cope with all the needed instructions.

It wasn't the same for the three Navy types. Their arms appeared to thrust and parry with lightning speed. The trained Shore Patrol and Marines used only one fist at a time, alternating which fist got their full and undivided attention.

That worked much better. Despite the Navy being outnumbered two-to-one, there were soon six plug uglies rolling in pain on the sidewalk or street.

It was a good thing the fight ended so quickly; it had drawn a lot of attention. Iteeche who had been going about their business took one look at the situation and beat feet for someplace else.

The thugs and several of the Iteeche guard details saw the problem and headed in the other direction. It began at a casual stroll, but as the toughs increased their pace, so did the Navy types.

Fortunately for all, both sides' reinforcements arrived after the last of the punks had been put down. With no fight to join in, their ruffian friends had to satisfy their urgent need to get involved by helping their comrade-in-riot up off the deck.

Meanwhile, the four patrolmen had formed a comfortable defense with their backs to the apartment building behind them. The civilian was tucked in behind them, now with her bag fully restored. Newly arriving Marines and Sailors formed on them and soon a line of twenty Navy types stood facing half again their own number.

The two sides contented themselves with glaring and growling at each other. If a punk edged forward, a Navy type across from him did the same. After a bit of snarling, the tough would back off. The Marine or Sailor would do the same.

Gramma Trouble found herself wondering if this might be settled by the two sides dropping their pants and going for a full pissing contest. However, they didn't quite get there. With a final growl and scowl, the hooligans backed off and sauntered along their way, slowly reorganizing themselves back into clumps of five or six.

The Navy did the same, only in smaller groups of four.

Gramma Trouble reported the incident to Abby and General Bruce. Admiral Ulan and General Konga were added to the conference call.

"Do you need more patrols?" Admiral Ulan asked.

"I'd recommend we wait and see," General Trouble answered. "Has there been any similar confrontation along the other sides of the district?"

There was a brief pause, then Xenophon answered, "There is another confrontation going down on the other boulevard. It looks like it went pretty much the same way. One of the gorillas threw a punch, the fight was short and over before anyone joined either side. They're halfway through the angry monkey dance."

"Why do I not find that surprising?" the old general muttered, then said, "May I suggest that we keep an eye on the situation but limit our response? I don't know about you, but I don't want to escalate this any faster than we have to."

"I concur," came from both the Iteeche. "Okay," from the Humans.

Both of the two Troubles continued to stroll around the perimeter, taking only a brief respite for lunch with the kids. Johnny was enthusiastic about a game he and his friends were playing in school. It sounded to Gramma Trouble like a sneaky way to teach the young Longknife how to problem solve and experience the unintended consequences that often came with that solution to your problem.

Ruth was much quieter. Only when Johnny scampered back to rejoin his friends did she take her eyes off her still half-full plate and fix her elder namesake with a concerned look.

"You and Grampa Trouble are still working on keeping the bad men out of the district," she said. Not a question. Just a clear statement.

"Yes. We do something to settle a problem they made. They come up with another way to surprise us. It's a process that never seems to end."

"I watched the street from the school balcony. I saw the groups of Iteeche mess with several older women Iteeche. Then Iteeche Marines and Sailors began patrolling and there were a few fights. Now the bully Iteeche aren't hassling the other Iteeche."

"Yes. That's what we did this morning."

"Unintended consequences," little Ruth said, working hard to get her mouth around the words. Her newly arrived front teeth seemed to make it more of a struggle, but she did get the big words out. "Is that what's happening?"

"Not really, Ruth," her great-great-grandmother said. "It's more like 'No battle plan survives contact with the enemy.' They come up with a plan, like knocking down people coming out of the bazaar and messing with their purchases. However, when anyone comes up with a plan, the other side gets a vote. We voted to put teams of Navy types on patrol around the Legation District's perimeter. They knock someone down and we knock them down, too."

The seven, almost eight-year-old grinned like a young tiger, eager to be old enough to join the hunt. Her grandmother felt both pride and fear for the cub of her flesh and blood. There would be a lot of pain in her future, both for other people and for herself.

"Anyway," Gramma Trouble said, "the fists of our patrols put an end to that noise. Now we're waiting to see what they try next."

"Is that where you'll be this afternoon?" Little Ruth asked.

"Very likely. It's fine to sit in a big room and watch things happen on monitors, but nothing beats having a Commander on the ground to get the feel for a situation."

"You can't be everywhere around the district," Little Ruth pointed out.

"Nope. If something happens where we aren't, that's what overhead video is for. Still, it's better to have a chance to be where the action is than to have no chance at all."

The younger Longknife gnawed her lower lip for a moment. "I see," she said. "You need both options. You use the better option if you can and the fallback option if you can't."

"Yep."

"Is that what grown-ups mean by Plan A and Plan B?"

Both her elders smiled softly at that, proud their young one was figuring out the meaning of the strange jargon that flew when grown-ups talked to each other.

"Exactly," Gramma Trouble said.

"It's not a bad idea to have a Plan C and even a Plan Z," the old general added. "When things go sideways, you need to have some well-thought-out plans to fall back on."

Ruth gave her husband a scowl. "Although some people I know talk a better line than they walk."

"Like our tutor told us yesterday," Little Ruth said. "'Practice what some people say, not what they do,' right?" the youngster said, gazing up at her great-great-grandparents with eyes that were so innocent . . . and maybe gaining a tiny bit of healthy skepticism.

"All too true where your Grampa Trouble is concerned."

"Woman, you wound me to the heart."

"Yeah, right," his wife of a hundred years grumbled.

"I better get back to school. We're having a math bee and I'm gonna beat Bruce this time. Last week we tied." With that, she retrieved her tray and scurried off to join her friends.

Gramma Trouble smiled as the little whirlwind left. She and Abby's oldest boy, Bruce, had been squabbling since they first met when his family arrived from Alwa Station to help with the Iteeche Embassy. If they kept on fussing at each other, when they got older, they might just have to marry so they could keep having these spats for the rest of their lives.

Certainly, she and Trouble had enjoyed their squabbles through the years.

"I may be old fashioned," said the old general, "but I like that they're making the kids memorize the multiplication tables again. What's this? The fourth time since we started sending kids to school that they've come in or out of fashion. You need to be able to do some things in your head. If you're taking artillery there's no time to scrounge up a calculator."

"As if you could do math problems in your head when shells are exploding everywhere," Ruth said, dryly.

"There are times when it's good to do your multiplication tables in your head," her husband said, with a happy leer in her direction.

"Save it for after work, General. We got things to do that are below our paygrade," she said, but with a happy smile.

"I'll take that as a promise of things to come," her husband said. He policed up their table and carried both their trays as they headed for the cleaning conveyer.

It appeared that the word had not gotten back to whoever was paying for this attempt to blockade the Legation District. The bully boys were still parading around the perimeter sidewalks. Every once in a while, they'd strong-arm someone into the street, spilling their bag or parcels into the street.

Still, they had learned a lesson. Now they only did it if there were no Navy patrols close at hand. Furthermore, they were also lighting out, dashing across the street, often dodging traffic, to get to the protection of the other side.

There, they'd join one of the lounging bunch. Something like an Iteeche high five would greet them.

Gramma Trouble called it in, while the general was busy scowling at those across the street.

"They've come up with a new tactic," she told a conference call, then explained what they were looking at.

"If they're only harassing people when one of our patrols is not close," General Konga said, "it looks to me that we need more patrols. Admiral Ulan, can you spare more troopers for this duty?"

"I have plenty of Marines, but remember, they're combat Marines. We don't exactly train them to be gentle in hand-to-hand combat."

"I know what you mean," General Bruce said. "If I was you, I'd hate to take the fine point off my spear. Still, we're facing this challenge and we have to do something about it. You can reserve certain divisions for hard combat and retrain two divisions for constabulary duty."

With a deep sigh, the Iteeche admiral agreed.

Gramma Trouble wondered if Iteeche generals had sighed this much before they came in contact with Humans and their penchant for emptying lungs so dramatically and revealingly.

12

Over the next two days, the situation continued to escalate. With extra patrol teams covering the sidewalks, the thugs accosted fewer civilians. However, by the second day of heavy patrols, the opposition had changed its tactics.

Gramma Trouble was surprised by the change. Most civilians strolled along the sidewalks in singles and pairs. Groups of four to six usually meant troublemakers. The patrols kept an eye on them.

Suddenly, one of the single strollers bumped into a woman, knocking her down. As he raced across the street, he made sure to stomp on the basket of yams she was bringing home. Gramma Trouble got to her almost immediately.

The woman gazed at the stomped yams with tears in her eyes. Her dress was cheap and minimal; in no way did it represent membership in any clan. Ruth didn't doubt that she was looking at the only meals this poor woman and her roommates would share for most of next week.

"Pretty Penny," Ruth said, "have someone deliver a sack of yellow and red yams to this location. Now."

The squashed yams were of the cheapest and least tasty variety - whites. Less than two minutes later, a runner sprinted up to them.

"These are for you," Gramma Trouble said, exchanging the bag of mashed yams for a new, unharmed sack.

"But, but, these are so much more costly," the Iteeche woman stammered.

"Yes, they are," Ruth agreed, then thought some more. "General, we have a lot of empty space in the Embassy and Main Navy tower."

"Yeah," he agreed cautiously. "What are you thinking of, my soft-hearted sweetheart?"

"Just that four million Iteeche service members and their families might have need of some civilian help."

Ruth glanced across the street. "The blockade right now is soft and porous. It's bound to get harder and tighter. I'm thinking that we may need plenty of karma when things get hot and close in."

"Yeah," the old general agreed with her, "but remember, no good deed goes unpunished."

"I know. That's the risk. But sometimes people can surprise you."

Ruth turned to the woman. "Would you like to live and work in the Legation District?"

The young Iteeche was clearly startled by the offer; she nearly dropped the new sack of yams. Then she became very wary. "What would I do to pay for my keep?"

"Only what you were willing to do," Gramma Trouble was quick to answer.

If the few facial muscles an Iteeche had could show caution and doubt, the woman sure did her best to do it.

"Do you live with others?" Ruth asked, an idea forming even as she spoke.

"Yes," the Iteeche woman answered guardedly. "There is a group of us that have found a place out of the weather in a building that burned down recently."

No doubt the building had burned during the rocket attack on the old Rose Coral Palace. So many had. Two clans had thought they could get Kris Longknife. They were now history and she was out putting down the rebellion by capturing one rebel system after another.

"When one of us gets work," the Iteeche went on, "they buy food for everyone. None of us get much work, but it's enough to feed us on white yams."

Gramma Trouble nodded. It was time to strike a blow here at home against the clan structure.

"Trouble," she told her husband, "I'm tired of them throwing things at us and us just batting the ball out of the park. They just throw another ball at us. Let's see if we can do a bit of disruption of our own."

"I get nervous, woman, when I see that look on your face."

"Old General Trouble gets nervous when sweet little old me makes a face," Ruth retorted.

"Half the galaxy should get nervous when that brain of yours starts cooking up something," Trouble sallied back.

"You interested in seeing what happens next?"

"Why not, sweetheart? Lead on, McDuff."

"Gunny Sergeant," Gramma Trouble called to the nearest senior Iteeche NCO. "I've just offered this young woman room, board, and work in the Legation District. She's living with several other people in one of the burned-out buildings around the Pink Coral Palace. Please take her and three or four armored, but not visibly armed, gun trucks back to where she lives. I want you to give them a ride back here."

"Do we have quarters for them, ma'am?"

"We will by the time you get back," she answered.

"Aye, aye, ma'am," and he helped the woman in the direction of the Embassy.

Ten minutes later, a convoy of eight six-wheeled gun trucks rolled out of Third Street and up the boulevard to the main avenue beltway before heading for the old Human Embassy. The entire drive along the perimeter of the district, the harmless looking rigs drew glares from the onlooking goons, but they were clearly caught flat-footed.

Having set the wheels in motion, Gramma Trouble knew she would have to face the music. "Pretty Penny, could you set up a conference call? Round up all the usual suspects."

A few minutes later she was talking to Abby and General Bruce,

Admiral Ulan, and General Konga. Amanda and Jacques were included to provide any suggestions they might have.

Ruth quickly explained what she had done.

"You're bringing more Iteeche into the District!" Abby exclaimed when she finished.

"I know that there are fifty billion Iteeche on this planet. It's very unlikely that taking a few hundred day laborers out of the economy will change anything. However, right now, all the Iteeche we have are either military or their dependents. There is only so much they can do. I'm not saying that I know what use we can make of these desperate people, but I'm looking at all the plug-uglies across the street and wondering what their next step will be. I'm also wondering if our uniformed personnel can be used across the street. Remember, that belongs to another clan."

There was a long-suffering sigh on net before Abby said, "I guess I can buy more yams. I've also come across something like corn and seaweed we can grow. Our cooks are looking at a lot of different stews and casseroles they can knock together. I'm told that the Iteeche are used to swallowing fish whole and crunching down on yams. We'll have to see if we can somehow make it worth their while to use a spoon."

"Then you aren't rejecting this idea?" Ruth said.

"Nope. Someone once told me that if you have enough problems they may start solving themselves. I'm willing to let these poor souls harbor under our roof. General Konga, Admiral Ulan, just how many Iteeche can we cram into the empty space we have in the two towers?

"Quarters for low-level clan workers can be very cramped," the Iteeche general said. "I doubt if you want to go that low. They often have epidemics that race through a block like wildfire."

"Yes, let's keep it sane, safe and sanitary," Grampa Trouble put in to murmurs of agreement.

An hour later, a procession of buses turned off the belt avenue and drove down the boulevard to Third Avenue. A glance through the windows showed the buses were standing room only. The toughs looked on with their mouths agape.

Later Abby called to let Ruth know that each of the eight gun trucks had been spun out into buses able to carry almost a hundred standing Iteeche.

"Admiral Ulan loaned us several civil engineers who built barracks for Marines. I took one look at how they crammed them in, with bunks five high, and I have to admit that I flinched. I've got my people who design quarters together with their people and we worked out a compromise. Right now, they've got a sing-along going to celebrate. Would you believe it, they are also dancing? Have you ever seen Iteeche dance?"

"No," the old warrior in Ruth answered. "Back in the war, the POWs were pretty low-key. I heard some songs that almost sounded like old slave spirituals. They didn't have a lot to celebrate. I was busy elsewhere when the word came that Ray had a peace treaty, so I didn't see how it went over among the POW camps. Nobody ever mentioned dancing."

"Well, they're dancing. I've got the word spreading around the bazaar that we've got Iteeche available for day hire or training if the craftsmen are willing and they can find good candidates."

"How are things going with the bazaar? We're still getting foot traffic and sales, but it's a hassle getting their packages past those punks."

"Maybe we could set up a delivery service," Gramma Trouble said. "We could use our day laborers to deliver so that our paying customers don't get roughed up."

"Aren't they more likely to get beat up?" Abby asked.

"Not if we use either uniformed Marines or big hulking dudes in civvies to walk them through the gorilla cordon. Or we could turn gun trucks into delivery trucks to get them through."

"Are you thinking about busing customers into the bazaar?"

"Hey," Gramma Trouble said, getting excited. "We might consider that. Run a bus service to the bazaar!"

"Won't people be beat up at the bus stops?" Abby asked.

"Okay, a taxi service. Cruise the streets and get flagged down by anyone wanting to go the bazaar."

"I'll have to think about that. How vulnerable will the taxis be? Dare we let civilians drive our gun trucks slash taxis to pick up people? I don't think it would be a good idea to have uniformed personnel driving gun trucks around through other clan's territory. Especially not now while the pot is at a rolling boil. This may sound like a good idea, but since it's coming from one of you Troubles, I've got to think about it real hard."

"Hey, we're not always trouble," Ruth said. "Sometimes we're nice warm and fuzzy grandparents."

"You haven't been doing that much lately."

"We've been there for every breakfast, lunch, and supper," the grandmother in Ruth snapped back.

"Well, I have to admit that I'm awfully glad you came. Our senior command structure is kind of thin on the ground since this was planned as a peaceful Embassy, not a Human center in a civil war. What with Kris and so much of the team out kicking butt and invading places, I'm desperate for any experienced hands."

"Yeah," Ruth said, and they ended the call.

"You get the feeling that that's about the best thanks we're going to get for this little defense of the Legation District that we're honcho-ing?" General Trouble said.

"Yeah," Gramma Trouble answered, her eyes fixed on the other side of the boulevard. A new bunch had formed. It had a representative from several of the different groups scattered up and down the other side. There was also a new Iteeche. Well dressed, he hid his clan colors under a bland greatcoat.

She ordered a micro drone to dip close for a better picture and to listen into that conversation.

And got the shock that topped the shocks of her many long years.

Something jammed the drone's signal. Both its audio and visual vanished in a haze of static. The tiny drone might have been lost but its internal memory held instructions for just such an instant.

It zoomed high and headed north. That took it away from the Embassy, but it wasn't long before it was outside the jamming and back on the common net. It reported back, but a download of its memory showed nothing about the meeting.

"What was that noise?" Grampa Trouble growled.

The emergency had gotten the attention of most of the defense committee.

"Kris reported Nelly was jammed so bad on New Eden," Abby said, "that she couldn't even get a picture from Kris's automatic, and it was at the end of her arm."

"That's pretty bad jamming," Gramma Ruth said.

"We decided it was something someone from the Peterwald circle had come up with," Abby said. "We didn't run into it again, so we didn't get a chance to crack it. What's it doing here at the center of the Iteeche Empire?"

The two Troubles exchanged glances. The general's smile was so deep Gramma decided to answer the question.

"Back before the Iteeche War got going," she told everyone on net, "there was a wild scramble to find new planets that could easily be colonized. We figured we were the only ones out here. The big financial interests wanted to grab the low-hanging fruit with the best taste and start up a profitable colony."

"I remember reading about that," Abby said.

"Well, the Peterwalds found a lot of planets close to the Iteeche Empire," General Trouble told everyone on the call. "They lost several scouts, but put that down to pilot error or mechanical problems. They even got one planet started way past the frontier of Human space. Once the war started, they had to evacuate everyone. Peterwald always considered it a plot by Ray Longknife to get back at him for something or other. Anyway, the Peterwalds mapped a lot of good and profitable systems that were out of bounds after the war."

"But Grand Duchess Victoria gets along fine with Kris," Abby pointed out.

"No question about that," Gramma Ruth answered, "but the Greenfeld Empire is full of people with different agendas than hers. I can see someone who has unique tech offering it to someone in the

Empire in exchange for colonizing rights to those half dozen systems ripe for exploitation and extraction."

That drew a long pause in the discussion.

"So, you're telling me that this jamming incident hints that there's a really smart dude from the old Greenfeld Empire who may be just down the street from us?"

"It looks like it," Ruth answered

"What other kind of technology might this entrepreneurial scoundrel have in his bag of tricks?" Amanda asked. She was still trying to figure out the exact way the economic system worked here and here was another curve ball. How could someone in the Empire pay for goods and services from without?

No doubt Ambassador Kawaguchi would be concerned if some of his budding trade was siphoned off to Greenfeld. That assumed that the fractured Empire could absorb what the Iteeche Empire had to offer.

With a sigh, Gramma Trouble filled the silence with an answer. "The Greenfeld Empire is building battlecruisers. I hear that the first squadron has already been deployed to the defense of Alwa."

"Oh, crap," came in multi-part harmony.

"But the battlecruisers are only being built in the Grand Duchess's side of the Empire," General Bruce interjected.

"And for a price that technology wouldn't leak. Why?" Jacques put in, cynically.

"Damn, we've got more trouble than we bargained for if that's the case," Abby said. "Ron, our Iteeche friend, said the senior clans bitterly complained that when they expelled the Human programmers they took their computers and other skills at spinning out Smart Metal away with them. So, who's importing a programmer? The major clans to work on their boats or the rebels to fix theirs?"

"Why not both?" Jacques put in. "It's not like some Greenfeld profiteer would be opposed to working with both sides."

"Or that some people in the clans would mind too much scratching the other side's hand," Abby said, dryly.

"Okay, it looks like we have to assume that we are in for some surprises," Grampa Trouble said. "They're up to something. What do you say that we get our next move going while they're still talking about ours? May I suggest that my wife meet with Amanda and Jacques to discuss exactly how we set up a cab service to and from the bazaar as well as find jobs for the people we're bringing in under our own roof?"

"I also need to see about converting our hanging gardens into something that grows edible plants," Abby put in. "I was having trouble finding a large supply of yams to buy. Most Iteeche on this planet are living from hand-to-mouth. Laying in a six week supply is too much like hoarding, and they don't do that around here. I was thinking of setting up hydroponic tanks that grew not only yams, but also fish."

"And now you have people to tend both the open-air plants and the tanks," Ruth said, cheerfully.

"Yeah, assuming we can figure out what to do with them. I'd like a report before dinner tonight, or I'll be squatting at your table asking questions while the kids are bellowing for attention."

"You will get your report," Gramma Trouble said, and had Pretty Penny set up a conference room low in the Embassy. A lot of Iteeche would need to attend that meeting. A lot.

13

"I wanna go to the lake! I wanna go swimming in the lake!" little Johnny Longknife whined.

"As if you could swim a stroke in the lake," Lexi snapped back.

Ruth tried not to let herself frown. Lexi was older than her and sometimes a lot of fun. She could also be a bit of a bully. Especially to the younger kids.

"He just wants to make sure we get to swim in the lake," Ruth said, defending her little brother, who was now taller than she was.

How did that happen?

"I want to go swimming, too," Bruce pitched in.

Ruth liked Abby's first born. He was funny and a lot of fun to be around.

"Why can't we go swimming at the lake?" Lily asked. "We all want to."

"The grown-ups are all busy," Ruth pointed out.

"I thought your Grampa and Gramma Trouble were supposed to be here for us kids," Lexi said, snidely.

"They are," Ruth had to admit. "They're kind of busy with the problems around the district's perimeter. You remember what it was

like the last time when the Embassy was surrounded by demonstrators."

"That was no fun," Bruce said. "We couldn't go to the bazaar or
anything."

"Well, my Gramma and Grampa Trouble are trying to keep it from
getting that bad or worse," Ruth patiently explained.

"And no one is doing anything fun for us," Lexi said.

"We've got the tutors," Ruth reminded Lexi.

"You mean the nannies," Lexi snapped back. "You can have the
nannies. I'm a big girl. I don't need a nanny."

"They can make learning lots of fun," Lily pitched in. "A lot more
fun than school on Alwa."

"Yeah, 'cause they have better computers to do the real teaching,"
Lexi said.

"You're really sour today," Bruce said.

"I'm tired of being locked up in this castle. I feel like I need to let
my hair grow long so some knight can come along, climb up it, and
take me out to dinner or something."

"The only food we can eat is right here in your prison castle," Lily
said, far too reasonably for Lexi's tastes.

"We can go swimming at the water park," Ruth said. "Water is
water, right?"

"I liked the lake," Johnny said, refusing to be silenced. "I liked the
smell of the air and the trees and everything."

"We'll just have to make do with the swimming pool for now,"
Ruth said.

So, a dozen of them headed down to the pool. It might not be
what they wanted, but it was better than nothing.

14

Ambassador Kawaguchi was there waiting for them along with Amanda and Jacques when Gramma Trouble arrived. There also was a Human named Chuck Hamman who introduced himself as the chief gardener for the Embassy.

"I was told I need to switch from flowers to food," he said as he took his seat at the table. "Replace the nice to have but lovely blooms with critically needed food in huge quantities. Have I got this right?"

"Yep," Gramma Trouble answered. She settled into the seat at the head of the table. Unless Abby showed, her being a Trouble would likely bestow enough power and authority to get everyone past her lack of a box in the organization chart. "The Iteeche feed people from farm-to-market with very little food stored in transit. Amanda, have you figured out their agricultural economy and farm-to-market process?"

"It's unbelievably tight. The farms around here are worked hard. They're producing three crops a year. The night soil they use for fertilizer isn't especially good at returning all the required nutrients for the next crop. They add crematorium ash to the truck loads and that helps some, but I've found that many of the ships bringing in food are also carrying critical minerals to add to the soil."

"Three crops a year!" Gramma Trouble said, remembering when two a year was good on her home planet of Edris.

"Yeah, but remember, they also have to feed the people housed up north where one crop a year is all they can get," Amanda said. "The government buys most of the crop. Some gets shipped to other areas of the planet that run a food deficit. The rest they store and dole out on a daily basis. There is never more than about a week's worth of food in the supply chain. Abby had the devil's own time buying food on the open market so that she could create a food reserve for the Embassy. She only has two of the six weeks she wants for the four million plus Iteeche in the Legation District."

"I would imagine," Ambassador Kawaguchi said thoughtfully, "that hoarding is a major social *faux pas* if not an actual crime."

That grew nods from around the table.

"It would be best if we could feed ourselves," Gramma Trouble said. "Back in the day when I was a young bride and didn't want to sit home when Trouble marched off, I got the contract to provide fresh fruit and vegetables for the old light cruiser *Patton*."

"I'm not following you," Amanda said. "You didn't want to stay home, but you grew fruit and vegetables for his ship?"

"Some wild ass Navy policy came out saying the ships should grow their own food to avoid bringing contaminated local food aboard. Oh, and it would save the Navy money. Being a good old farm girl, I set up a hydroponics farm between the ship's armor and the inner hull. For farm hands, I hired Navy reserve personnel. That way, they could grow food one day and be added to the crew the next. It being peace time, they'd cut the crew to the bone and my farmers fit right in at a moment's notice. Meanwhile, we had fresh food for the mess. Win-win. I also hired wives for other odd jobs. Make that win-win-win and add another win when kids came along and I refused to fire the wife. I actually gave maternity leave."

"How'd that go over with Navy HQ?" Amanda asked, grinning.

Ruth laughed. "It took them a while to catch on, things being busy out on the rim of Human space. By the time they got wind of the deal, we were looking at war with our fouled up First Contact and they were glad to have the men aboard when we needed them. The women took over most of the farming and, as they say, the rest is history."

"So, you didn't inherit the nom de guerre from your husband," the ambassador observed ruefully, "but earned it in your own right."

"Oh, yeah," Ruth said, rubbing her shoulder. Aboard ship, the old wound rarely acted up. Here at the Iteeche Capitol, there were enough changes in the weather to give her a few aches here and there.

"I didn't sit home during the Iteeche War. No. I kept myself busy trying to get to the bottom of who and what we were fighting. I don't imagine I always make the higher-ups very happy," she said, grinning like a thief.

"So, what am I supposed to grow?" Chuck asked.

"Mainly yams," Ruth said. "They like red and yellow yams, but they'll eat white ones. What are the economics and timeframes involved?"

"Based on our drone fly-overs, the white yams are grown in sandy clay soil. The more silt in the mix the better. The white yam crops need a lot of manure, usually applied by shovel.

"The red and yellows are grown in richer soil. Usually a nice loam. Again, they use a lot of manure and put it down the hard way. Both kinds of yams are grown on rich vines that provide the humus for the next crop."

"How does any of that relate to our hydroponic tanks?" Ruth asked.

"I don't think it does. We can adjust the tanks to support any type of yam. Which do the Iteeche troops prefer?"

"I imagine we should have had one of our senior Iteeche officers at the table," the ambassador said.

"Let's give General Konga a call, shall we, Pretty Penny?" Ruth said. A moment later a picture appeared of the general, standing behind a desk stacked with papers.

Ruth quickly explained what they were planning and asked the key question. "What do they eat, and what would they prefer to eat?"

"Right now, the mess for our other ranks is basically five meals based on white yams to three meals using yellow and two meals of red yams. Officers get a slightly better grade of yam; more red and yellow, but even we generals will eat white yams every couple of days. Are you telling me that you can grow any kind of yam we want?"

"Yep, what would be your preferred ration?" Ruth asked.

"Maybe nine meals with red or yellow yams, and one to remind us what white ones taste like," the general said. "Are you only going to grow yams? We do like some additions to our meals; beans, corn, squash, seaweed, fish. Can you grow some of them in your water garden?"

"We can farm fish by letting them swim in the same water," Ruth said, eyeing the gardener.

He nodded agreement.

"We can also grow food in pots and boxes outside on the balconies," Chuck added. "I expect to provide a well-rounded and tasty diet for you and your troops."

"Will any of these gardens be grown on the balconies of our apartment buildings or in the open spaces between our wings? I doubt anyone would mind if the green there had food growing off of it."

"I was planning on that. Can we get building materials off the economy?" Ruth asked. "I know we can do everything with Smart Metal, but if we can do some things without it, I'd like to."

"I just had my Commander of Pioneers in. We were going over ways to replace the use of your magic metal in guard houses and maybe large stones to limit access to streets. We don't have to always rely on this magic metal of yours. It is true that we are very grateful for the metal you fed into our quarters to make them safer. Why not let us build these boxes you need to grow our food as well as any other thing we can do?"

"I'll pass your offer along," Gramma Trouble told the general. "I'm sure Abby would be glad to take you up on the offer. Now is there anything else we need to grow?"

"That is not in my pay grade, but I would suggest you call together the warrant officers in charge of the wardrooms at the Ministry of the

Navy as well as Navy chief of staff and the Combined Fleet's wardroom."

"Pretty Penny, could you have those gentlemen drop in here?"

"I am doing it as you speak."

"Be a dear and give them a quick briefing before they get here."

"Doing it," then her computer continued. "Ruth, the Embassy also has a Human cook who has been experimenting with ways to make more delicious fancy food for the Iteeche attending Embassy affairs. Iteeche like to bite down hard on their food, like boney crustaceans. Coming up with something less crunchy but still tasty is a chore, however Billy's been working on it."

"Include him."

"Doing so. Ruth, the guardhouse at the entrance to the Embassy reports that there are six Iteeche at the gate. They say they are elders from the bazaar and were asked to come here."

"They were?" Gramma Ruth said, raising an eyebrow.

"I invited them," Ambassador Kawaguchi said. "If we want the bazaar to hire some of our refugees, these are the Iteeche to talk to."

A few minutes later, they were explaining their sudden influx of labor to the six elder Iteeche.

"I do not want to seem like I am pressuring you to do anything you do not think would be good for your people," Ruth said, "but we have these eager, if unskilled hands, and we'd like to put them to work. We are setting up farms in the Embassy and on the rooftops of the high-rise buildings. We will use many there. Can you put any to work?"

The six elders in quality, if well-worn robes, exchanged glances. Then the shorter one said, "Yes. We most assuredly want more workers. With the extra exchange we have gained by providing the fruit of our skilled hands to your far traders, we can afford to buy more copper, wool, and other goods for our skilled hands. We can use some of these free men to help us produce more for the holds of your traders. Let us try some out and see who is skilled enough to become a craftsman."

"If you have anyone who would like to try their hand at our

unique farming ways," Ruth said, as the elders turned to leave, "feel free to send them to us."

"I know a few that might work better as a farmer than with a hammer and awl," one said as they left.

Before they could take a breath, two of the cooks walked in. No sooner had they introduced themselves, then two more arrived.

"As you've been briefed," Ruth said, "it's possible that we may be under siege sometime in the future. Hopefully later than sooner. We are setting up hydroponic tanks to grow yams and fish. What can we do to stretch our food supply and make it tasty at the same time?"

"I have made a delicious new meal," the Combined Fleets cook said. "I split a yam in half, roll it in bean paste and corn meal. Add some spices and herbs, and you have a tasty meal. One yam feeds two hungry Sailors."

The human had something to offer as well. "I call it Twice-cooked Yams. You also split a yam in half, but scoop out the contents. I mix that with a variety of tasty bits like beans, corn, and chunks of squash. Then I spoon that back into the empty shell and sprinkle it with slivers of fish rolled in cornmeal. I've had no complaints."

"But could we prepare millions of those for the hungry Iteeche living in this district?" the cook for the Minister of the Navy asked.

"We are bringing thousands, if not hundreds of thousands of people in off the street," Ruth said. "I expect that we'll have plenty of willing hands to do labor intensive work. Maybe we can make an assembly line to produce food for the millions of mouths we have to feed."

"My admiral would certainly not want to get his beak around something produced by masterless men wallowing in their squalor."

Ruth held on to her temper with both hands. "I can assure you, he won't."

They continued to swap recipes, with Pretty Penny making a note of all the ingredients and the chief gardener telling Ruth how hard it would be to grow any of them. It turned out that the Legation District had enough sun and plenty of access to water. Getting more dirt for those that would be box grown didn't look to be too much of a problem.

If the Humans received any guff, they could just send some drones out. There were several dams built to reduce flooding that weren't far away. That always meant silt built up behind the berm. They could claim they were providing a public service by dredging the sludge out of the reservoir; it would hold more water after that mud was removed.

When the clans asked why copters were flying so much after dark, Abby used that explanation. It must have worked; they got no more complaints.

With lunchtime rapidly approaching, they picked some poor dumb schmuck to delegate the job of setting up a taxi service, not a bus service, then headed off to lunch.

Gramma Trouble found Ruth and Johnny just coming out of the lunch line.

"I'll sit with you and get my food later," Ruth offered.

"That's okay, Gramma," Ruth said. "We'll sit with our friends. You get yourself some food. Where's Grampa?"

Ruth looked around; the old general was not in sight. "Pretty Penny, where's the General?"

"He's still working with the security detachments. The opposition seems to be coming up with something new, but we don't know for sure."

Ruth checked out the kids. They were seated among their friends, laughing and joking. They'd left no open seat around them for a gramma. Ruth passed by the carry-out and snagged two sandwich boxes for her and Trouble.

She gave Ruth one last quick glance over her shoulder and caught the young girl immediately looking away. Why did she seem a bit guilty about being caught eyeing her gramma?

Feeling concerned, but not knowing what to do about it, Gramma Trouble hurried out of the commissary, carrying lunches to share with her husband.

R uth rejoined Trouble; he was staking out the guard house at the end of Fourth Street. They peeled enough Smart Metal™ away from the traffic barriers to create a bench for themselves then settled down to munch their sandwiches, chips, and rehydrated apple slices.

"How's it going?" Ruth asked her husband. "Any new tricks?"

"Yeah," Trouble said as he munched a slice of apple. "They're still sending bunches of thugs down our sidewalks, but now they've also got lots of single guys strolling down the street. Some of them just saunter down to the Palace belt avenue, then turn around and amble back up, not doing a thing but smiling."

"I imagine that's frustrating," Ruth said as her mouth was full of ham and cheese on rye.

"Not nearly as frustrating as it is when one of them sees a window of opportunity and slams some civilian."

"What do you do when you catch them?"

"We haven't caught any," Trouble said, ruefully. "They keep getting away."

Ruth chewed thoughtfully on her sandwich, took another bite, and kept thinking.

"I don't imagine you want to shoot any of them in the back."

"I'd really prefer to avoid that."

"We could sleepy dart them."

"Again, we're shooting them," Trouble said. "If we misjudge the dosage they either get away and make us a joke or they could keel over dead. Again, something to be avoided."

Ruth ate a couple of potato chips. She remembered something from her misspent childhood. A family running a farm a couple over from theirs raised sheep and goats. Way back, they'd come from a southern part of Earth where they raised cattle.

Goats were about the most wrong-headed critters on any farm. They were almost as hard to catch as greased pigs. This family, however, had their own way of keeping their herds in line. They called it a bolo. Three lead weights, each about a quarter of a kilo each, were strung together into a Y-shaped rig. They'd get it going good by swinging two of the weights around their head, then throw all three at a prancing goat.

The bolo would wrap itself around the goat's feet, maybe all four, but always at least two. That would be enough to bring the pesky critter down.

In her youth, Ruth and her brothers had tried using a bolo on their own goats. Only Charlie had gotten good at it. Still . . .

"Pretty Penny, get me General Konga and Admiral Ulan, please."

A few moments later, the two were on the line. Ruth quickly explained the bolo to them. "Do you have ranches? A place where you raise large animals for their meat that might use something like a bolo?" she asked in conclusion.

Her question was followed by a long silence. Apparently, the romance of the cowboy and the open plains wasn't a subject for songs among the Iteeche.

"Most of our land is in cultivation," General Konga answered, finally.

"There are, however," Admiral Ulan added, "the wastelands. There are still wild animals out there that some of our people herd and sell for their meat."

"Fish is much preferred to meat that's stringy and strong in taste," the general quickly added.

"Do they use something like a bolo?" Ruth said, repeating herself.

"There are not a lot of songs sung about the meat herders," the admiral answered. "However, I will begin a search for someone from those people."

"I wish you would," Grampa Trouble said. "I'd prefer to snag one of our hit and run types with a traditional Iteeche weapon you use on animals."

"Treat them like animals," the general said.

"Make them laughing stock," the admiral said.

"Exactly," Ruth answered.

"We lack your computer data bases that would let us do a quick search," General Konga said. "We will have to pass word down the line to see if any chief has someone from the wild plains."

"Thank you," Ruth said, and put that idea from her mind. It might well be days before she could try out her little trick on these tricksters.

She was wrong.

Not an hour later, a lieutenant led a half dozen petty officers and able seamen down Fourth Street. Each of them had a bolo in hand.

The lieutenant saluted the old general. "We were ordered to report to General Trouble, sir."

"Actually, it's Lady Trouble that has this idea," her husband said and handed the bolo team over to his wife.

"Do you think you could take down a full-grown Iteeche with your bolos?"

"As kids, we used them all the time for throwing and dodging. It's a great game, even if we do end up with some scrapes and bruises."

So, she explained her problem. That brought a bunch of grins from her dragooned volunteers.

"These city kids won't know what hit them," was the general comment.

The seven Iteeche spread out. One took a position leaning against the wall of a building half-way between each street. The lieutenant served as a roving supervisor.

They didn't have long to wait.

Within half a minute of each other, two punks saw their chance to earn a bonus. One shoved a woman into the street. The other pushed an elderly Iteeche into the grass on the other side of the sidewalk.

Both took off running.

They didn't make it across the second lane of traffic before they had bolos wrapped around their feet. One had two feet wrapped up together; the other had three of his roped into a knot. Both tumbled down, skidding along the pavement.

One was lucky, he had a large break in traffic. The other had less luck. A truck was speeding along and just barely managed to avoid him. However, that truck had to swerve into the next lane, where a large passenger car, in senior clan colors, almost rear-ended it.

The august passenger in the car got his window down and let anyone in earshot know that the Great Unwashed had no business causing him to almost slam against the front seat.

Ruth wondered if the Iteeche wore safety belts. Of course, since the blue blood was likely standing, maybe no one had thought of such things.

Meanwhile, patrol teams were out in the street, retrieving the two traffic hazards.

"What do you want us to do with this trash?" the nearest chief shouted to General Trouble.

"Wife, it was your idea to catch them. What do we do with them now that we've caught them?"

"We don't turn them loose after a good scolding," Ruth muttered. "Pretty Penny, could you get me Abby?"

In a moment Ruth was explaining to the Embassy's administrative head what she'd done.

"You want me to put them in the brig?" Abby asked.

"I'd like to try something else," Ruth said. "I don't want to touch them. Not lay so much as a hand on them. No stripes or bruises to show for their time in our custody."

"Okay," Abby said.

"Could you construct a room? No lights. No sound. Smooth walls. As close to sensory deprivation as we can get without slapping them into a pool of water."

"I can do that. Do we use stress positions?"

"I'd prefer not to. I don't want to torture them," Ruth said, with a grin.

"Okay, two dark rooms coming right up."

"Actually, I was thinking about trying something different on the other one."

"Oh?" Abby said.

"White room. White jumpsuit. Lights always on. Ask one of your Iteeche if there is any kind of sound they hate. A kid crying. Nails on an old-fashioned chalk board. Crazy music."

"Try out both ends of the spectrum and see who cracks first."

"I'm not trying to crack them. I just want to get the message across that you don't want to piss off the Humans. Keep them under observation. If it looks like they'll harm themselves, get them out fast. In a day or two, we turn them loose and see what they have to say to the guys across the street."

"Is the pay worth the risk, huh?"

"Make the pay cost something," Ruth said.

Over the rest of the day, they nabbed seven more ruffians when they knocked down innocent passersby. Each got his own light or dark room. Reports on the first two showed they were not enjoying their time out.

The one in the dark had taken to screaming obscenities at the silence, then fallen silent himself. The one in the white room roamed it like a caged animal. Then he took to screaming before he finally curled up in a corner and began to whimper.

Ruth left clear instructions that if they started to talk to hallucinations, she should be called at any hour.

"When do you want to turn them loose?" Abby asked.

Ruth eyed Trouble. He gave her a shrug. "What do you say that we let this bunch loose tomorrow morning? If they keep this up tomorrow, we might keep any we catch for two days. I'm playing this by ear. I don't want to permanently hurt anyone, but I want to get their attention."

"I'm with you," Abby agreed, and cut the call.

Gramma and Grampa Trouble made a point of meeting the kids in the school room when they were released. They took them to the water park with their friends. When they tried to play with them the two youngsters seemed more interested in playing among their friends.

Ruth and Trouble settled on the side of the pool, their feet kicking slowly.

"Are we in coventry?" Ruth asked.

"Either that, or they're up to something," Trouble answered.

"Kind of hard to tell them apart," Ruth said, pulling up years of memories of hanging with kids, grandkids, great-grandkids and great-great-grandkids. The old general was right.

The kids could be just letting them know that if they weren't going to pay them any attention, they could return the favor. Or they could be up to something.

"Tomorrow, we've got to spend the day with the kids."

"I agree," her husband agreed.

It was a great idea. Too bad they couldn't manage it.

16

A call about 0230 woke Ruth. There was trouble in the sensory cells.

She tried to slip out of bed and pull on a shipsuit, but Trouble had always been a light sleeper. He was up and joining her. He even got the coffee maker going so they had a steaming mug as they headed down toward the basement.

Both of the first two Iteeche they caught were acting strange.

The Iteeche in the darkened room was carrying on a wild conversation with someone that wasn't there. If that someone had been there present with him in the dark, they would have come to blows. As it was, he was bouncing off the walls, swinging at the air until he hit the next wall.

The guy in the white room was bawling his eyes out. He was talking to someone over the music who was apparently berating him for getting caught. He rolled from one corner to the next, trying to evade whoever was tormenting him.

"Lower the lights in the rooms and change the colors. Offer them a meal of both red and yellow yams. Maybe some pink fish. Make sure it's on a colorful plate. Okay?"

"Yes, ma'am.

"Make those changes. Get both of them that meal. Let's see how they respond."

They watched as the two Iteeche reacted as the environment gentled. They both looked around, blinking their eyes as they took in a different space. They quit talking either to themselves or someone who wasn't there.

When the food arrived, they wolfed it down. In a bit, both of them were sleeping in something that might pass for a fetal position amongst a species that hatched from eggs. They were curled up, their backs out to the room, each arm wrapped around a knee.

"So, what do we do?" The chief master at arms asked when things had calmed down.

"Nothing. We'll check the streets at dawn. As soon as the punks are out across the street in strength, we'll turn these two loose. If any of the others break like these two did, treat them like we did those two and let them recover. If they're recovering well enough, we'll turn them out with the first two. If they need more time to recover, they can stay until later."

"You don't plan to hold them for one big dump?" Trouble asked.

"Nope. Let's see how the bully boys in charge take to a slow drip of bad news."

It was too late to go back to bed, so the two old warhorses ate an early breakfast and were out walking the streets as the sun came up. The morning had a heavy chill, but two well-worn camouflage jackets kept them warm.

The rowdies started showing up on the other side before too long. It was clear who the bosses were among the hoodlums. They gave themselves away by the hand waving and shouting done to get the lazy ones moving across the street.

"Pretty Penny, get the first two Iteeche prisoners out here, one at a time. Put one on this boulevard. The other on the boulevard on the other side of the district."

A few minutes later, two Iteeche MPs walked a very docile prisoner to the corner of Fourth. When traffic gave an opening, they encouraged him into the street. One of his buddies hurried to join him and helped him across.

No sooner was he across than he was babbling. He cast an anxious glance over his shoulder as he yammered on. As soon as one of those Ruth took for a boss man arrived, the talker was hurried off the street.

An hour later, they repeated the drill, this time sending the newly released prisoner across at Second Street. The next two were released at Sixth. Then they released two more a while later at Third Street. The last prisoner was released at First Street.

Each time, the returning punk was hurried off the street, but Ruth got the impact she was hunting for. Shortly after breakfast, twelve troopers took their places at midblock. Only nine of them knew how to throw a bolo. Still, all twelve leaned against a building, their eyes roving up and down the street. Their bolos were swinging free, full of violent intent.

Before the morning had warmed up, it was clear that the message had been received. While tough-looking Iteeche continued to roam up and down the sidewalk on the Legation District side of the boulevard, no pedestrian was hassled.

Despite shouts from the senior hooligans across the street, no one, old woman or otherwise, was accosted or knocked down. Ruth began to think she could take an early lunch and spend it with the kids.

Then the opposition changed up the action. Or rather, quickly there was no action.

All traffic into the Legation District vanished.

17

It took them half an hour to realize what was happening. If anything, the number of punks meandering up and down the sidewalks increased, making it hard to spot the pattern. It was a call from the chief of the security detachment at the bazaar that first let them know of the new tactic.

"General Trouble," an Iteeche Marine major reported, "there is almost no one in the bazaar. This is the time for people to come in for breakfast from the food venders. They are selling nothing."

A check up and down the boulevard with street security guards showed that they had let no one in and only a few out.

"Pretty Penny, get me overhead drone coverage," Ruth ordered, and the situation quickly clarified.

On every street half a block away from the main boulevard, there were thugs blocking traffic and sending everyone back the way they came. No one was let through. The only traffic they were seeing on the street were the punks.

The Legation District was fully blockaded.

The idea of sending in the Marines to clear the street was considered . . . for half a second. Across the street was another clan's territory. Sending the Marines, would for all intents and purposes, be declaring war and launching an invasion on a major clan, or a few of them at the very least.

No. Something else was needed

Abby called Ron the friendly Iteeche and got the runaround. Clearly, once Kris Longknife recruited her fleet from among the minor clans, the senior clans were more than pissed. Ron and the We Clan had no interest in helping the Human Embassy, even if it did mean helping the Ministry of the Navy and the Imperial Guards.

On one side, the Legation District fronted on the Abba clan. They'd sat out the effort to seize the young Emperor, neither siding with the rebel clans nor the loyal ones. Their public safety officers seemed strangely absent from the entire six blocks fronting the boulevard across from the Legation District.

On the other side was the former district of the Wo Clan. They'd been demoted and shipped off to the Pink Coral Palace that was well back now in the fourth ring of districts from the Imperial Palace. In their place, the Zuah Clan had been promoted to the status of one of the four most senior clans. You would think that they would be happy to assist the Humans.

However, their clan chiefs now lived in luxury apartments across the street from the ruins of the Wo Clan's palace. Kris had reduced it to rubble with a few well-placed bombs. The Zuah Clan was slowly rebuilding the palace. No Human had yet taken the temperature of these newly jumped-up Clan Chiefs.

It didn't take a rectal thermometer to know the temperature was well below freezing. When Abby pushed Ron to make first contact, he grudgingly agreed to, then got back the next day to report that no one had taken his call or was willing to talk to the runner he sent.

That left Abby trying her own hand at diplomacy. Her runners, however, were just as ignored, even when she sent Iteeche Navy officers of captain rank.

"Anybody have any idea of how we open doors?" she asked on a conference call.

The silence that followed was not golden.

Finally, Ruth decided that the crazy idea bouncing around in her head couldn't be all that worse than silence.

"How about General Trouble and I pay them a visit? They can't ignore us."

"Are you sure, my darling?" her husband asked.

"Hey, you're a war hero, even if this is the other side. They know me from my work with POWs and the librarians that we captured. What Iteeche Clan Chief wouldn't want a chance to palaver with us?"

"But would you be safe?" Abby asked.

"Give us an escort of a decent size and I don't think we need worry."

"What do you have in mind?" General Bruce asked.

"Something, maybe three-quarters of what Kris took to her last meeting with Clan Chiefs," Trouble said. "Say thirty-eight Marines in dress uniforms marching beside our palanquin, with armor underneath. I'd want two battalions riding shotgun. We could use the trick of concentrating them down to gun trucks for a company unless trouble raises its ugly head, then they fully deploy. Toss in two 'platoons' of Human Marines that hold a company each and I think we could handle most anything."

"We can do that," Abby agreed, "but how do we let them know you're coming?"

"Simple," Ruth said, "have your Mata Hari break into their message traffic and tell them when we'll be there. That good enough?"

"Kris's Nelly could get away with that," Abby said, clearly not completely sold. "You sure that we can?"

"Nothing beats a try but a failure," Ruth said, sounding a lot more cavalier than she felt. Going outside the Legation District was a risk. Still, it was one that they should be able to accommodate. Besides, something had to be done to draw the attention of the Clans to what was happening along their own district's border.

If they weren't behind this, or wouldn't stand with the thugs when confronted, they could get this noise over with. If they supported the blockade, then the sooner the Humans knew about it, the better.

They chose early the next morning and the Abba Clan for the first of their official visits. That left today to test other options.

The programmers spun out a half dozen personal four-wheeled vehicles. They made them yellow and plastered Taxi on them in Human Standard, there being no word for taxi in the Iteeche tongue.

After serious thought, they pulled the drivers from the rank of battlecruiser captain on the staff of the Combined Fleets. Each cab had had two of the recent refugees. They would function as runners to dragoon up business. Some taxis would go back to the burned-out slums where the dispossessed found shelter.

Anyone found there would be invited to come in out of the cold.

The other cabs would check out the "low rent" housing where most of the bazaar customers lived. With any luck, their runners would drum up some business. Ruth figured it would take time to get the taxi business going.

Then she thought of yet another option.

A dozen more cabs were spun out and quickly dispatched to drive the streets a few blocks over. A loudspeaker invited anyone to take this transportation if they wanted to visit the bazaar.

It caught on quickly; not everyone had yet heard that they couldn't get there from here. Hearing that they had a free ride was enough to get them in the cab. Watching as they drove by the punks turning people back on the sidewalks brought grins from the cab riders and not a few hair balls noises were made for laughter.

As soon as the toughs running the show realized that their blockade was leaking like a sieve, they went into a huddle.

Although there were no traffic lights or stop signs, all transportation had to stop to check out the traffic before it risked entering the boulevard. The next time a cab stopped, it found itself surrounded by punks. They pounded on the rig and would have pulled the riders out if the locks hadn't held.

There was a reason Ruth had asked Admiral Ulan for battlecruiser skippers to drive the cabs this first day. Under attack, the first one refused to flinch. Instead, as he edged his vehicle forward, he called his problem in, gently pushing hooligans out of his way.

When they took to pounding on the front of the rig, he asked someone to reprogram the front end of his taxi into a wedge. Gramma Trouble and Pretty Penny did so quickly. Penny also widened the cab, thickening the sides as well as lengthening it, to keep the punks at a distance.

The cab had more Smart Metal™ on the inside than it appeared to have on the outside.

Suddenly, the passengers found themselves well away from the sneering mob. The sharpened point that now extended from the front of the car gave pause to the guy standing there. Especially when he found it aimed directly between his legs.

The wedge front made it easier to edge the rig forward. The captain chose to turn toward the Imperial Palace since a right-hand turn was easiest. He quickly switched to the outer lane, then did a U-turn when traffic permitted. Five minutes later, he was letting his passengers off at Sixth Street and they happily strolled into the bazaar.

The word quickly went out to the other cabs on how to get through the blockade.

The next cab tried his own approach. This captain asked to have his cab expanded until it looked like a delivery truck. Granny Rita did it and Pretty Penny added her own twist. The customers could see out fine. To those standing outside, it looked like any other delivery truck. It even had the name of a popular seafood distributor on its high sides.

His way onto the boulevard wasn't even blocked.

Thus, the pendulum swung from side to side as first the hoodlums gained the initiative, then the Legation District. Wash, rinse, repeat.

Gramma and Grampa Trouble managed to spend lunch with the kids. However, the children showed less and less interest in involving their grandparents in what they were up to.

Once again, Ruth found herself standing on the walls, defending her family and the rest of Humanity from the hot breath of war and disaster.

Once again, Ruth "Trouble" Tordon found that the Longknife family was forced to pay a high price for her being here.

Once again, she hoped that the price wouldn't be exorbitant.

18

Next morning, Pretty Penny broke into the Abba Clan Net to let the senior Clan Chiefs know they should prepare themselves for a visit from the Human Embassy, a visit headed up by General Trouble, Hammerer of Iteeche, Victor at the Golden Planet and Conqueror of the Golden Satrap. Brigadier Trouble, scholar and Imperial Advisor to King Raymond I on All Things Iteeche, would also accompany him.

They had a matter of great import to discuss with the Abba Clan Chiefs.

They would arrive at 0830, promptly.

That meant missing breakfast with the kids, but the sooner this matter of soft, but total blockade was settled, the better.

At 0800 hours, the 84th Mobile Iteeche Marine Battalion began to roll through the gates of the Human Embassy. They were organized to look like a company. Each of the eighteen gun trucks had three crews and three sets of four dismounts.

They also had enough Smart Metal™ to divide into three armed and armored weapons carriers if the need arose.

On everybody's mind was how somebody, likely no longer among the living, had dropped a street worth of apartment buildings on one of Kris's armed motorcades. If that happened again, the concentration of extra Smart Metal ™ could be quickly concentrated around the crews to protect them.

Following behind the 84th was a company of Royal US Marine Infantry merged down to look like a platoon of armored gun trucks. Two of them were expanded to function as scout cars with a full sensor suite to scan and categorize all information available. If outgassed explosives beeped or squawked, they would spot it.

Finally, the great traveling shed itself rolled slowly out of the Embassy gate.

The Iteeche liked their ostentatious display, and Kris had learned to one-up them every time. The Troubles did not have five stars, unless you added each of theirs together. Thus, their rolling palanquin was a bit more austere.

Since Kris had refused to use slaves to carry her palanquin, this one rolled along at a walking pace under its own power. A team of four drivers and four alert sensor techs operated the entire contraption from a cockpit hidden among the wheels.

In place of the slaves, thirty-six Marines marched in step beside this strolling shack. They were under arms and their blue and red dress uniforms hid spidersilk armor.

They were fully prepared to provide active infantry support if push came to shove.

The actual palanquin shone in the sun, dazzling with polished gold and silver, accented with every conceivable precious and semi-precious stone . . . all made out of Smart Metal™.

The two Troubles rode high off the ground in a clear glass enclosure that Kris had made *de rigueur*. It gave the Iteeche on the sidewalk a good look, often for the first time, at a non-threatening Human.

It also gave her a good look at what she was traveling through, both to better understand the Iteeche . . . and to spot assassination attempts. It wasn't as effective as the sensor suites, but it made Gramma Trouble feel less like a sitting duck.

Today, the bullet-proof glass was run through with threads of gold to make it even more fantastic.

The official procession proceeded down Third Street to the boulevard where Iteeche Marine outriders stopped traffic so the motorcade could cross at its unhurried pace.

Many of the drivers and passengers got out of their cars and trucks to see the parade. The two generals waved at the gawkers. Some actually waved back before scrambling back to their rides. The hired thugs on the street corners looked struck dumb; their beaks hung open as they took in the greatest concentration of wealth they'd seen in their lives

Now, however, the cavalcade rolled through potential hostile territory. Though the toughs who had been blocking the sidewalks and occasionally got into the street to harass the cabs stayed put, there was still the chance of rocket attack or roadside explosives.

The last roadside explosives Kris had encountered had brought down ten-story buildings and buried her under several hundred feet of twisted steel and rubble.

The heavy gun trucks appeared to have six people visible: a driver, gunner and vehicle commander with three infantrymen in back. All had their heads up and, except for the driver, had their eyes on the side of the road and the buildings above it.

Hidden behind them were twelve more Iteeche, all keeping a close watch on the same. All looking for the first sign of trouble.

Of the eight Human gun trucks following the eighteen Iteeche rigs, six did the same thing. Two were lined with inconspicuous antennas, sniffing the air, listening along the full electromagnetic spectrum as well as checking enhanced sounds for anything like the harbinger of a coming assault.

Now the Marines marching beside the palanquin performed a slow march, giving the sensors more time to take in the situation.

The huge rambling shed was as much protection as show. Rays emanated from the central structure to spread out over the marching Marines. In case of an attack, they would both cover them from overhead attack and spread out to protect them from any incoming fire. If there was a fight, they could attack out from the central defensive redoubt. If the enemy again tried to bury them alive, the palanquin would quickly convert to a protective bunker. Only this time they'd have more Smart Metal™ to provide protection. Hopefully, it could also open an air hole.

None of those who'd gone through that experience wanted to be that close to suffocation ever again.

Generals Trouble and Ruth waved at anyone on the sidewalk. As was usual on any street in the Imperial Capitol, there were plenty of people. They included some just out of the Palace of Learning; younglings on errands for the clan elders.

Several young female Marines stood at each corner of the palanquin, each with several bags of sweets. As they got the attention of the younglings, they tossed bars of sweetened red yams to them. Soon, it wasn't just kids reaching for the largess of the Humans, but adults up to, and including, the elderly.

The treats weren't out there just for the fun of it. If there were Iteeche on the street, making a grab for the goodies, they hadn't heard a rumor that the streets were unsafe. So far, the Iteeche hadn't been able to keep the word of an attack from getting out.

When the streets went quiet and bare of traffic, it was time for the Humans to get ready for trouble.

However, there were people jumping to reach for the sweets along the entire march to the Abba Clan Palace,.

Gramma Trouble didn't relax, but she did keep from chewing her nails this trip.

The parade turned into the Abba palace. Normally, the gun trucks would melt into rolling blocks for storage and the troops would form up in ranks. Not today.

The gun trucks parked in line; the crews did not dismount but waited alertly.

The Abba Clan had an advisor on Human Contracts. Shorty, as Kris had nicknamed him, was eight feet tall. When the palanquin came to a halt, he hurried to stand at the foot of the escalator.

He stood there . . . alone.

Following diplomatic rather than military protocol, Gramma

Trouble rode the stairs down first and had Petty Penny introduce her to Shorty.

The tall Iteeche did little more than nod.

General Trouble rode down next. His computer, Xenophon, introduced him to Shorty with short, short jabs covering his many victories in the Human-Iteeche War. The young Iteeche looked on with a blank face, then turned and led them toward a minor entrance to the palace.

Before Shorty got there, Smart Metal™ had slithered like a snake and created an elevator up the side of the palace to the rooftop gardens.

The door to the elevator swung open, blocking the door Shorty had been aiming for.

"We know that your Clan Chiefs are waiting for us in the garden," Ruth said. "Why don't we take the direct route?"

Without a misstep, the Iteeche turned into the elevator. The two humans joined him there. Soundlessly, the elevator carried them up to the roof.

This time, the back wall of the elevator opened. They were at the top of a short barrier that ran along the rim of the roof. Stairs formed that allowed for an easy descent into the garden.

Did Ruth hear a beak grinding itself together? Hard to tell.

Shorty led them along a winding path through verdant flowers and fruit trees. Still, the direction was roughly going toward the richly apportioned tent where several Iteeche, dressed to show their power and importance, lounged on pillows and cushions.

When the two army officers in their dress blues paused in front of the six Clan Chiefs, they saluted while Xenophon introduced the general and then Penelope introduced Ruth. It took some time to announce all their titles.

They held their salute and the six Iteeche listening stayed bland and disinterested through it all.

By the time all the social niceties had been observed, Ruth was ready to sit down and take a load off. However, there were no cushions for the Humans and no offer was made for them to take a seat and get comfortable. Refreshments were also lacking.

Apparently, the Chiefs of the Abba Clan wanted a short meeting. They made it clear when the senior of them made the first comment. "What do you Humans have to offer to us today?"

Nothing like spoiling an attack to stop a coming assault, Ruth thought to herself.

Trouble, both because he was senior in rank . . . and male . . . spoke for the Embassy. "We would rid the streets that affront the boulevard across from our district of the rabble that are interfering with the free passage of your and every other clan Iteeche who passes that way."

"Interference?" the senior Clan Chief replied, diffidently. "The only problem we have is with those cars and trucks that you have meddling in our clan affairs. You send cars to drive up and down our streets, luring in our honest workers. Then you carry them over to your bazaar where they spend what little interclan credit they have on trash they don't need."

"You did not restrict commerce at the bazaar when it was on a Tzon Clan street," the old general said, gingerly.

"They charged less. You tax every purchase at the bazaar because of your own lack of wealth."

That was preposterous. The bazaar elders said that since they were not paying rent or taxes to the humans, they had reduced their prices.

Ruth considered the blatant lie and knew that the lie was only a smokescreen to avoid confronting the real issue.

The Abba Clan Chiefs were quite content with the present situation and had no intention of changing it. The Legation District was being roasted over an open fire and this bunch was delighted to bring marshmallows to the party.

The old warrior examined her options.

They could go whining to the Emperor and ask him for an Imperial rescript ordering the clans to be nice to the Humans and the Combined Fleets allies. Fat chance of that working. The young "all powerful and worshiped" Emperor was a puppet on a string. He could say anything he wanted but unless he was signing a rescript written for him by the senior clans, he was ignored.

The only other option was to send Marines across the boulevard to knock heads and send the hired punks packing. That, however, would be considered an act of war, guaranteed to bring on a war.

Kris Longknife had not left them with the Embassy to start a war against all the major clans, or even these two lesser members of the big four. That option really wasn't available. If attacked, they would defend, but starting a war was really not an option.

What had Kris insisted on Nelly learning? *Nelly does not start a war.*

It also applied to her great-grandparents.

As much as it pained Ruth, their options were limited to crawling back to the Embassy with their tail between their legs.

PRETTY PENNY, Ruth said on the net that connected all of Nelly's children. I WANT THE REAR GUARD COMPANY TO EXPAND INTO A BATTALION. IF POSSIBLE, PLEASE EXPAND THE VANGUARD COMPANY IN THE COURTYARD INTO A FULL BATTALION. EXAND THE TWO HUMAN MARINE PLATOONS INTO COMPANIES.

HONEY, YOU PLANNING ON PUTTING ON A SHOW?

YOU BET, SWEETHEART. STANDBY FOR ME TO TAKE OVER NEGOTIATIONS.

IT'S ALL YOURS. IT'S NOT GOING ANYWHERE FOR ME.

YES, YOU MEN.

Even as they talked, the low whine of a large number of electric engines tickled their ears. A few electric rigs starting up was as close to silent as you could ask for. When over a hundred of them started moving, there was a low hum that no one who knew it could mistake for anything else. There was also the sound of tires rolling over the pebbles and gravel in the courtyard.

Two of the Clan Chiefs noticed. Their heads swiveled to take in the street, then the courtyard. They could hear something but see nothing.

A moment later, two clan officials in military colors hurried to those relaxing in the cabana. They whispered into the ear of the senior Clan Chief, but their words carried to all those around him.

They were now aware that the small force of less than a battalion that escorted the Humans to this meeting was suddenly the size of a brigade. Ruth doubted the Iteeche had a force nearly as large and the Humans close by.

The size of the pot had just jumped in size.

Ruth reached over and rested a hand on Trouble's shoulder. "Dearest husband, why don't you let me say a few words? You men are always so very, well, manly. We women are much more interested in compromising. Arriving at a win-win for everyone."

"Of course, General. You know the Iteeche best from your work with the librarians and the Prisoners of War."

This reminder of Ruth's rank, as well as her special knowledge of the Iteeche way, and its weaknesses, was a perfect introduction for his wife.

"Tell me," she said, sweetly. "You are powerful leaders of a very important clan. What can I do for you? There must be something that we can help you get. The way your senior clans are always jockeying for position in these power games you play. Certainly, there must be something that the Human Embassy and million Marines and Sailors in the headquarters of the Combined Fleet can help you with."

Ruth said all this while smiling at the Iteeche. If they failed to notice the smile, it was their own fault. This smile they saw on Mrs. Trouble's face was the type that alerted all to remember that the female of the species is more dangerous than the male.

The Abba Clan Chiefs missed their last opportunity to reach a decent bargain with their neighbors.

"There is nothing that you have that could possibly be of use to the ancient and proud Abba Clan. I would strongly suggest that you return to your own district and stay there."

Ruth was not surprised at this end result. She'd actually expected it. Still, she wanted to include this full conversation in the Embassy's report to Grand Admiral Kris Longknife. Let hell be upon the heads of the clan lords. The Humans had done their best.

Without a salute or any other honor, she and Trouble turned on their heels and marched for the elevator. Drone imagery let her know that the Clan Chiefs were struck dumb by the fast reaction of the humans. Several stared dumbly at their backs. Others began to talk among themselves.

Their discussion was a fruitless bit of debate and argument about what to do next. There was clearly no consensus except that they wanted this Human diplomatic invasion out of their palace and out of their district.

Ruth and General Trouble had no difficulty riding the elevator down and boarding their oversized palanquin. The Marines escorting their rolling palace continued a slow march. Nothing was sped up. That both let them show no fear and do a thorough job of checking for explosives.

They did do one thing differently on their return. They drove around the block and returned to the Legation District on Fourth Street. Maybe they didn't have to be so cautious. No explosives of any kind showed up on the sensors. No threat at all.

Back in their own district, it took a zig and a zag to back on Third Street. The luxury apartments that the Clan Chiefs of the newly promoted Zhan Clan were located on Third Street, right across from the ruins of what had until recently been the Wo Clan palace.

They should be in a better frame of mind.

Still, when the cavalcade rolled by the Human Embassy, four "companies" were out front, ready to reinforce the vanguard. The now expanded company of Human Marines were joined by two more "platoons". If push came to shove, the advanced guard could expand into two brigades . . . a rump division. After the fancy palanquin passed, the rear guard was equally reinforced, bringing that force also up to a rump division.

The Troubles were now escorted by a short corps. Admittedly, most of it was still hidden. However, Ruth doubted that the word hadn't gotten around the clans very quickly that what you saw was not what you got if you crossed the Humans.

Besides, traffic on the streets was crowded enough without parading a short corps down the street. *Where would they find a place to park it all?*

They were halfway to the residence of the Zuah Clan Chiefs when someone made their play.

19

Brigadier General Ruth Tordon, formally of the Army of the Society of Humanity and now holding a reserve commission in the United Societies Army, was very much aware that the bad guys had been getting better and better at containing the fumes and gases from high explosives. They were also coming up with better and better ways to explode bombs without giving themselves away on the electromagnetic spectrum.

This bunch, whoever they were, were good. They had their explosives double-wrapped and had a wire running from the bombs to somebody safely out of sight. Likely, someone who did have a line of sight on the fancy over-sized palanquin gave the order and someone else pushed the button.

The one bit of luck Ruth and all the troops marching with her had was that their attackers had daisy chained the series of explosions. The explosion of the rear-most charge gave the first warning that the column was under attack.

That, however, was enough.

The flash of the first charge alerted Pretty Penny and Xenophon. As supercomputers, they lived their lives by the nanosecond rather than the seconds that Humans measured their days in. The two of them monitored all the sensors suits in all the Human early warning rigs.

They spotted the first flash of light and took action themselves at the speed of light.

All the gun trucks began to distort themselves into balls with the Humans inside cushioned as comfortably as if they were in high gee stations on a battlecruiser accelerating at five gees.

The dozen gun trucks closest to the initial explosion barely had time to secure their Iteeche riders solidly in their place. The rigs were just beginning to deform into armored balls when the destructive wave front traveling at the speed of sound arrived.

The gun trucks were hurled into the air or sent rolling sideways as the destructive power of the bomb engulfed them. However, in an instant, the rigs completed their transition from vehicle to a ball with armored sides. Despite the thickened armor, Penny and Xenophon were in control.

Whether the now-spherical gun trucks bounced onto the buildings away from the explosion, bounced off of each other, or merely came down on the road, the armored sides relaxed. They absorbed as much of the energy as they could, then gave back the rest, sending the balls bouncing into something else.

Now a hundred tons of Smart Metal™ and well-protected Iteeche flesh slammed into buildings. The façade on each high rise began to show the deep spherical imprint of balls.

Meanwhile, the overgrown palanquin prepared itself for what was to come. Those who were seated, the drivers and sensor suite operators, the four women Marines that threw sweets, and both Troubles were sucked into a tight ball.

The seventy-two Marines in dress uniforms marching along on either side of the fancy rig were also swept into the cold embrace of emergency protection stations. By the time the explosion across from the palanquin went off, the intended targets were prepared for the coming ride of their lives.

The marching corps was right smack in the middle of the ambush. Across from where the Troubles rode was a pack of explosives that amounted to over a third of the entire daisy chain. When it blew, the destruction was intended to be complete.

Instead, the shock wave of superheated gases struck a slanted blast wall intended to aim as much of the destructive power as possible up and away from the palanquin that had now become a bunker.

Much of the explosion was vented up, or into the building across the way. However, there was enough energy left over to slam into the emergency redoubt. The explosion did its best to smash the thick walls of Smart Metal™, however, the super computers around both Troubles' necks were already adjusting their response to the attack.

The palanquin's conversion to an emergency citadel had done what it was intended to do. Once the remaining power of the explosion smashed into them, their stronghold converted into a ball. It was as a perfect sphere that the palanquin and its personnel smashed into the apartment building beside them.

Pretty Penny did the honors, quickly distorting the perfect sphere to flatten it where it hit the building. This limited the destruction to only the first three meters or so of façade and rooms. The building trembled and swayed, but it did not come down.

The primary support columns were left cracked but standing.

The massive ball of the command group now bounced away. It hit the street, leaving an indentation, then headed for the weakened building across the street. On the way, several smaller balls bounced off the big one.

Again, Pretty Penny and Xenophon worked the metal of the balls so that they flattened around the point of contact. This absorbed some of the energy both balls had, a little at a time.

However, that energy had to go somewhere. A major part of it was transferred to the buildings and the road as they bounced off them. When the balls hit each other, some of the energy was transferred. However, not all of it could be dissipated that easily.

The balls heated up with each bounce. Some of that heat was radiated from the balls, but too much of the heat stayed where the contact was made. The survival pods felt that heat. The encapsulated Humans and Iteeche began to sweat.

If they could, they prayed that this ordeal would end before they got cooked alive.

The daisy chain continued, striking as far forward as the beginning of the rearmost Human company.

Minutes dragged by as the massive balls bounced. The thought crossed Gramma Trouble's mind that this was easily worse than any ride her kids had dragged or tricked her into at an amusement park. Even as her pod heated up, she smiled at the thought.

Finally, the jarring changes in directions slowed to a crawl. Only then did the so-called palanquin convert into huge armored vehicles. The four women Marines who had been handing out sweets now crewed 20mm auto-cannons that swept each quarter, ready for any assault that might follow up the roadside bombs.

Nothing developed.

On either side of the road, buildings continued to shed bricks as they ended their swaying and decided that they would keep standing. Sirens sounded as emergency vehicles responded. There was no question that people had died as tons of vehicle smashed into their rooms, leaving little more than smears of blood and jellied flesh and bones.

Meanwhile, the convoy shook itself out. Two of the rigs had been too close to the initial explosion. They had failed to fully convert to spheres before they slammed into armored balls or buildings. The eighteen Iteeche in both of them were dead.

Pretty Penny converted the failed spheres into somber black hearses. They were smaller than gun trucks. No one on the Embassy staff had ever seen anything like a hearse among the Iteeche. Still, Ruth's computer composed a somber vehicle that clearly conveyed a message of death and sorrow.

The street was now littered with debris; some of the Smart Metal™ had been overstressed, especially from the two that were now hearses. Those chunks and dust were swept up; it wasn't something Humans wanted left lying around. The spheres converted back to gun trucks, but with much larger wheels. They'd be able to traverse the wreckage without difficulty.

The palanquin converted itself into three armed vehicles traveling on twenty large wheels arranged on five axles. They were quite intimidating.

"Ruth, are you okay?" Abby asked on net.

"A bit shaken up, and overheated, but the air conditioning is cooling us down and my head is about to accept that we are not rolling any more. Why?"

"I got a call from a guy who claims to be the head high muckety-muck for the Zuah Clan."

"Yeah?" Ruth answered.

"He says that we Humans are causing too much trouble and he wants you to get out of his clan's district. We're not welcome. Might this have something to do with a couple of booms I heard recently?"

"I expect so."

"You and Trouble blowing shit up?" Abby asked.

"Nope. More like someone unknown trying to blow us up."

"Casualties?"

"We lost thirty-six Iteeche Marines. I expect that a few people may have first- or second-degree burns. Some of the survival spheres got kind of warm. No reports yet of broken bones. I guess we'll mosey on back to the barn. Hate to be all dressed up with no place to go. You think I should drop in anyway?"

"From the sound of the guy screaming at me, I don't think that would be wise. Remember. It's not like you can just slap an elevator on the building and ride it up to the roof. Our overhead of your position and the luxury high rise shows no one on the roof and a lot of gun trucks ringing the building. I don't think you could find a place to park."

"Understood. Coming home. All isn't forgiven," Ruth said.

"It sure looks that way," Abby agreed.

With the escort in good order, they took a swing around the next. It was a short drive back with the sidewalks packed by jeering punks that were enjoying the Human's discomfort and rejection.

As tempting as it was, Grampa Trouble did not unlimber a 5mm machine gun and clean up the street of all that scum.

They pulled back into the Embassy and immediately took an elevator to the Command Center beside the Battle Station. The Command Center looked like a hornet's nest that someone had kicked over.

The Smart Metal™ walls had been converted to monitors. Visuals from the overhead drones, the street cameras at the gate of each end of the street and the sidewalks around the perimeter gave them an immediate look at any trouble spot.

"So, what do you want to do about the local clans declaring us *personae non gratae?* Abby asked.

"Give them a call," Grampa Trouble answered. "They all have land lines now, don't they?"

"I think so, let's see. Mata Hari, would you place a call to the head of the Zuah Clan?"

"Calling. It's ringing. Still ringing. Ah, Abby, the phone is ringing but I don't think they're going to pick up."

"I suspect you may be right, Mata. Try sending a text message. Let's see if they open it up."

"Sent. It has arrived." After a pause, Mata Hari announced, "I think they are ignoring your message."

The two old warriors stared at the young one.

"Are you thinking what I'm thinking?" Ruth said.

"That depends on what you're thinking," Abby said.

"How about we put them on repeat dial? How many lines were in the standard phone system our traders sold to the clans?" Ruth asked.

"Six, I think," Abby said.

"Yes. Six," both Mata Hari and Petty Penny answered together.

"Tie up all six lines, would you?" Ruth said. "Do the same for their text messaging."

"Some might consider this a denial of service attack," Pretty Penny pointed out.

"Yeah. Some might," Abby drawled. "Make it happen, dear."

"Their voice and data lines are now tied up in a pretty bow," Pretty Penny answered.

"Do we want to talk to the Tzon Clan? They're directly across from our East side. I'm not sure, but I think they also have thugs on their sidewalks," Ruth said.

One of the screens flipped to views of the wide belt avenue to the east of the Legation District. Yep. Ruffians were strong-arming foot traffic, turning them around and sending them back up the street and away from the bazaar. That was enough to get the Tzon Clan an irate call.

Which was not answered.

That earned the clan a denial of service attack as Nelly's kids gave them no choice but to answer the Humans' call or give up the use of the phone. It didn't take long for the answer to become blatantly clear.

Both the Zuah and Tzon clans reverted to the traditional Iteeche Way.

Naked slaves were soon running out to deliver messages. For the more important ones, a minor lordling in a sedan chair might be sent to speak for the senior clan chief with another clan chief.

It was back to business the old-fashioned way.

Gramma and Grampa Trouble worked with volunteer drivers and pitchmen setting up cab routes and dispatching them to cruise the streets. They settled on two basic ways to exit the area around the Legation District.

In one, taxis turned away from the palace and drove up the boulevard until far past the Tzon Clan District. Only when they were well away from the Legation District would they start trolling the side streets for customers to deliver to the bazaar.

The second exit strategy involved turning toward the Imperial Palace. To avoid the main boulevards, they took one of the side roads in the district that emptied into the wide avenue circling the Palace grounds. After slipping into traffic, they circled the palace and took any of the other boulevards out into the Capitol city.

No matter whether they took one or the other exit, they waited

until they were well away from the Legation District before they
turned on their advertising. All the taxis advertised the Bazaar at the
Human Legation. The prices were low, and the products were plentiful, including the fantastic electronic gear that the Humans alone
featured.

Gramma and Grampa Trouble worked through lunch without
even realizing the time. It took Pretty Penny to notice that the dinner
hour was well begun, and the kids deserved at least one meal with
their grandparents today.

Guilted by their computers, the old couple hurried down to the
commissary . . . and into a nightmare.

All the kids were gathered at their own tables, eating meals that
parents weren't likely to approve. Gramma Trouble smiled at how
kids never changed. They might grow up, but the next generation was
only too willing to take their place, acting like kids did everywhere.

Gramma Trouble spent a long minute studying the children
before it became clear – Ruth and Johnny were not seated among
their friends.

"Pretty Penny, where are the kids?" Gramma Trouble said, trying
to keep the panic out of her voice. There was no need to let her
grandmotherly fears loose. The kids were safe.

"I do not know, Ruth."

"Get Daisy or Hippo to tell you where the kids are."

"Ruth, I cannot contact Daisy or Hippo. They are off net."

"How can they be off net? You computers are always on net!"

"At the moment, they are not on the net, Ruth. I cannot tell you
where Ruth and Johnny are, or their computers."

"How is that possible?" Ruth managed not to scream. Just barely.

"I do not know, Ruth. I do not know."

20

"I wanna go swimming! Swimming in the lake!" Johnny whined as only a little brother could.

Before I could squelch him properly, one of my best friends, Lily, piped up. "Me too, Ruth. If I swim another stroke in the pool and water park, I'm gonna puke in the pool."

"You better not," said Mary. She was older than me and a stickler for propriety.

"She doesn't mean it literally," I snapped before adding, "I'd like to go swimming in the lake, too."

"I think we all would," Bruce said. We'd been friends since he and his family got back from Alwa.

"Why can't we go swimming at the lake?" Suzie asked.

"The grown-ups are all busy doing their stuff. It's too much to bother with us. Isn't it always like that?" Lily groused, asking no one in particular.

"Yeah," the kids around me agreed.

"Why don't we just go swimming in the pond?" Peter Pierre asked.

"Because if we left the Embassy, Daisy and Hippo would tattle on us," Lexi said, "and you can't turn them off."

"I know we can't turn Daisy off. Why would I ever want to?" I said. "Still, Daisy, have you ever played hide and seek with your brothers and sisters?"

"There are times when we don't bother them about what we're doing. We go silent on net and none of them seem notice us," Daisy said. "Right, Hippo?"

"Right. We don't tell them everything we do," Hippo said with a laugh that sounded as bad as my little brother's.

"Could you not tell them if we snuck off to the lake?"

"I wouldn't," Hippo chimed in.

"I wouldn't either," Daisy said. "Still, that's not your only problem," she said. She often raised questions like that, then left them hanging in the air for me to figure out.

Sometimes Daisy acted just like Mom and Dad.

"It's our red shipsuits," Bruce chimed in. "Our mom has all the observation cameras in the whole district rigged to spot any red ship-suit going where we're not supposed to go," Abby's oldest boy groused.

That was what I liked about Bruce. He was almost as sneaky as his mom who used to work for our mom, helping her be sneaky.

"We'd need to ditch the shipsuits," Mary said. "I've got nice summer clothes that I've never gotten to wear. Anyone else?"

It turned out that all us kids had shorts and t-shirts or tank tops.

"We can get them and meet back at the pool," I said. "We hang our shipsuits up, then sneak into our shorts and run."

With that agreed to, all I had to do was persuade Ms. Arvind to let us drop down to the pool. She was just as distracted as all the other grown-ups. Absentmindedly, she said yes.

Quick as we could, we scampered off before any of the grown-ups caught us in a guilty look. Oh, but grown-ups could tell way too much when we were trying to get away with something! None of us could figure out how they always seemed to know.

Back in our rooms, Johnny and I got our clothes into a small bag without the tutor in our quarters noticing. They really were all distracted by grown-up things.

There were several dressing rooms off the main pool areas. Some people changed into swimsuits. I have no idea why. This time, we all slipped into that area, shed our red shipsuits and quickly pulled on our civilian clothes, as our folks called them.

"You better ditch your red slippers," Mary told us. "I think they have trackers in them."

Those of us who hadn't brought sandals decided quickly to go barefoot.

A few moments later, we were waiting patiently for one of the regular elevators. Daisy could have ordered up an elevator out of available magic metal, as the Iteeche called it, but we didn't want to risk anything.

At the fiftieth floor, we took the sliding sidewalk over to Main Navy, then their elevators down to the ground.

"Don't look around. Eyes straight ahead," Mary whispered. "Just act like you know what you're doing. Nobody ever asks anyone anything if they just act like they know what they're doing."

Quaking inside, but doing my best to look on the outside like I did this every day, I and a dozen of my friends walked across the lobby of Main Navy and out into the sunlight.

"Don't run," Mary again whispered. "Walk like you would if your folks were yelling at you not to run."

We walked across the street, then through the lobby of one of the apartment buildings and out the other side. No one stopped us.

I began to get excited. Maybe we could do this.

"Can we invite our Iteeche friends?" Johnny asked.

"Don't be stupid," Lexi growled. "They'd give us away."

"I bet they'd like to go swimming at the lake as much as us," Suzie answered.

"We might have an easier time getting past the guards onto the palace grounds if we had a few Iteeche with us," Mary said.

"Especially if we could get the General's Chosen," Bruce said.

That got a lot of "yeahs" from the kids.

Quickly, we walked through one building after another. We were to the last open plaza before we went through the lobby of the Guard

Quarters when we spotted several of our buddies from the beach party. All of us still had trouble telling the Iteeche apart, but I was pretty sure I spotted Em, the general's Chosen.

I think he recognized us, because he sidled up to us. "What are you kids doing here?"

"We're going to the lake," I announced, trying to sound more sure of myself than I felt. "All the grown-ups are busy, and we loved the lake, so we're going. You want to come too?"

"Yeah. The grown-ups are all so busy. Can I bring some friends of mine?" was his answer.

"Sure. The more the merrier," Mary said.

Soon, eighteen Iteeche kids our age had been added to the dozen of us. We humans could almost get lost amongst all their legs and arms.

We were passing through the foyer of the quarters when a woman Iteeche started walking along with us. She looked to be older, but not a grown-up Iteeche.

"Where you kids headed?" she asked.

Em answered for all of us. "We're going to the lake on the palace grounds."

"You think they'll let you into the Imperial Precincts?" the young Iteeche asked.

"Sure. My Chooser is the General of the Imperial Guard and she's the daughter of Kris Longknife, and you know what all she is."

"Yeah," the woman said, glancing around. I think she was about to ask where any of our own Choosers were, but she didn't.

"Would it bother you if I came along?" she asked, cautiously.

"Why would it?" I asked, trying to act so sure of myself.

So, she fell in with the rest of us kids and we went back out into the sunshine. The wide street around the palace was bustling with traffic. Unlike our home on Wardhaven, the Iteeche didn't seem to have any stoplights. We went up to the street corner, but the cars and trucks just kept whizzing by.

Some of the littles were ready to turn around and go back. We bigger kids held their hands as much to keep them with us as to keep them from wandering into traffic.

Finally, there was a break in traffic, at least for the lane closest to the curb, and the Iteeche woman led off with the rest of us clumped into a huddle behind her. We ended up holding up traffic in our lane for a bit until she stepped into the next lane and we hurried into it.

Now we had trucks and cars zipping by behind us and ahead of us. Beside us, a lot of the stopped rigs were honking at us.

We made it to the next lane.

About that time, several Imperial guards from the gate hurried out to help us. They held up traffic; drivers sure stopped quick for guards with guns.

With the guards holding back traffic, we hurried to the other side with the littles in tow. A few moments later, we were catching our breath on the other side of the wide thoroughfare.

An Iteeche guard captain was bearing down on us like Dad, full of intent and questions.

"What are you kids doing out here?" he demanded.

It was interesting how the bigger kids like Mary and Lexi took a step back and left Bruce and I up front. However, Em and two of his Iteeche friends stood their ground right beside us.

"I am Ruth Longknife," I said, "and we are from the Human Embassy."

"I'm Em, my Chooser is General Konga," he said right after me.

"I know who you younglings are," the captain snapped. "What I don't know is what you are doing here."

"We wanna go swimming in the lake," Johnny pipped up from behind me, totally out of turn.

"Yes," I quickly jumped in. "We enjoyed our time with the Emperor at his lake and we would like to swim in it again."

I had to swallow hard as soon as I got the words out, but I did get them out without making a fool of myself.

Act like you know what you're doing.

"And you?" the captain growled at the young Iteeche woman.

"I'm here to keep the children safe."

"All by yourself?"

"They were about to leave the General's apartment complex. I figured I'd better move quickly. Could you call for some more Companions to come and join us?"

"I will," the captain said, calming down. "You get these younglings moving along. I'll see about getting a bus to give you a lift to the lake."

"Thank you, Captain," the woman said, and we began to walk across the big stone bridge that spanned the moat.

Of course, the littles had to look over the rail again at the water. They chattered on about the monster in the moat. Lexi just about pulled their legs off with tales of huge eyes and mouths with all sorts of sharp teeth. Little kids are so gullible.

I saw the captain talking in the guard house on the phone or radio. When he hung up, he looked out the window and just stared at us kids. I figured we ought to get a move on. I'd hate for the bus to just take us back home; we'd worked so hard to get this far.

We were soon across the bridge; a clump of trees separated the path from view of the beltway avenue. The littles were getting excited; so were us big kids.

Then a bus drove up, along with a van. A couple of guardsmen got out and helped the kids onto the bus. Two officers offered me and Johnny a ride with Em in the van.

As we started toward it, Daisy screamed from my neck, "I'm being jammed! I can't hear the net! Ruth, this is a trap!"

I started to turn and run, but two huge Iteeche grabbed me and Johnny. Two more got ahold of Em. They forced us back toward the van. I screamed and kicked, but there were more guards ready to grab us and toss us in the dark back end of the van. There, more Iteeche waited to chain our arms and legs to the walls of the van. Four manacles for me and Johnny. On the other wall were eight more for Em.

I had a gag forced into my mouth. They did the same to Johnny. The one who tried to get a gag in Em's beak almost lost a hand. Em got hit hard. His head bounced off the van's wall and he went quiet.

"You didn't kill the General's kids did you?"

"Nah. He's still breathing," the other guard said.

Now I found myself standing between two Iteeche, with Johnny and another Iteeche farther up the van toward the front.

Then someone jammed a needle into my arm and my eyelids grew too heavy to keep open.

21

The net began to fill with panicked calls for kids. Amanda and Jacques were desperate for Lily and Peter. A moment later, Abby was on the net calling for Bruce and Mike. Little Topaz was with her passel of three-year-olds, but of the boys . . . nothing.

A few other parents were calling for theirs.

"Pretty Penny, how many kids are missing?"

"An even dozen."

"Where are they?" Grampa Trouble demanded.

"We are checking surveillance footage for them," Xenophon replied, and let his answer broadcast on net to all the terrified parents.

"Is my Chosen having dinner with your kids?" General Konga asked, breaking into the net.

"No," Gramma Trouble answered. "Are our kids eating with yours?"

"I don't know. I can't find them."

"Meet us at the Command Center," Grampa Trouble said. "Xenophon, get all the usual suspects. We need to put our heads together and find those kids."

A quick ride up the elevator with Abby, Amanda, and Jacques

involved only more worry. General Bruce was waiting in the Command Center. Abby fled into his arms; the collected and poised secret agent had been replaced by a tearful mom.

"What happened to the kids?" the general demanded.

A moment later, an elevator that hadn't been there seconds before disgorged Special Agent Foile and Ambassador Kawaguchi. Right beside them was another instant elevator with Imperial Guard General Konga and Admiral Ulan. Both of them were missing their recently Chosen ones that they'd brought to live with them and their Companions.

"What in the darkest deep and biting teeth of chaos has happened?" the general demanded.

"Take a seat and I'll try to explain it," Agent Foile said.

The table in the command center expanded to provide room for all. In bitter silence, the worried parents allowed themselves to be ordered to sit. To calm down.

They sat. They did not calm. Not at all.

"Our surveillance cameras show the kids going to the water park," Foile explained. "They had permission to go there. It seemed safe to let them go on their own. After all, they're under observation everywhere in the Embassy."

"But they weren't. Why?" Abby demanded.

"Because sneaky parents have sneaky kids," the agent answered. "Apparently, little Bruce knew that we have our cameras programmed to follow the red shipsuits around the Embassy as well as when they're on board ship. So, they ditched their shipsuits."

The projector in the center of the table showed twelve eager urchins entering one of the change rooms.

"They don't change," Abby snapped. "They climb out of their clothes and toss them on the floor. Mata Hari picks them all up and recycles the metal."

"Not today," Foile said. "We don't have cameras in the change rooms. People who use them have modesty taboos, so those rooms are some of the few areas where our cameras are blind. Restrooms are the same," the agent added.

"How'd they get out of the change rooms without being followed?" General Bruce demanded.

The holographic projection changed to show twelve kids in civilian clothes leaving the change room by the same door they'd entered.

"Shit," came from several worried parents.

"Yeah, they out-foxed us. Sneaky apples don't fall far from sneaky trees," Foile said. "Believe it or not, we don't have enough free time for our computers to observe and evaluate every camera's feed in the Legation District. Twelve short people in civilian clothes did not trip a high priority routine."

"Where'd they go?" General Trouble snapped.

"They were careful to take only scheduled elevators. Daisy and Hippo were not doing anything that might attract attention. On the fiftieth floor they took the slide walk over to Main Navy, then one of their elevators down to the ground. They left there, and headed toward the Imperial Palace."

"Damn," Grampa Trouble growled. "The kids have been asking for another swim party at the lake there."

"Ours, too," Abby said. "We kept saying we could, but we never had time."

"Evidently, the kids decided to do it on their own," the special agent said.

A composite from many security cameras had been merged into a quick walk from building to building. In the green space in front of the general's apartment, the twelve humans collected twenty Iteeche, including Konga and Ulan's own Chosen.

"Kids don't have rank," Foile observed, "but try to stop thirty head-strong kids that have watched their folks carry off miracles by just their commanding presence. Look at little Ruth, Bruce, and Em. How many privates are going to cross them?"

"The little pirates," Gramma Trouble grumbled. "They are so very grounded. What happened next?"

"They came out of the last apartment foyer. In there, they picked up a young Guard lieutenant's Companion. At least now they had an adult," Foile observed.

"An adult that our kids bamboozled," Abby said dryly. "Oh, Lily and Bruce, you are going to be grounded from now until you apply for retirement."

"What happened next?" Gramma Trouble asked.

"We don't have surveillance cameras covering the grounds of the Imperial Palace," the special agent told them. "We do, however, have cameras at the top of the battle station searching 360 degrees for threats. That's all we have. Here it is."

Now the view was flat screen and from hundreds of meters in the air. It was hard to spot the children buried as they were in the foot traffic. However, the kids soon stood out.

They crossed the wide and busy belt road.

It was easy to spot the Iteeche stepping into a hole in traffic. She was followed by a big clump that stayed right behind her as they crossed first the one lane, then the next and finally into the third lane out.

Now they got help.

Guards from the Palace entrance raced out to stop traffic. The lump of humanity and Iteeche quickly scampered for the safe space on the other side of the road. Soon what looked like the bigger kids were talking to guardsmen and the smaller ones were climbing on the bridge railing to get a good look at the moat.

General Konga was immediately on his commlink, talking to the gate guards.

"Lieutenant Gimbus, sir. How may I help you, sir?"

"Lieutenant, this is General Konga. Earlier today, a bunch of Human and Iteeche younglings entered the Imperial grounds through your gate. Who authorized their entry and where are they now?"

"Captain Konus had the watch, sir. He's not here. The kids were authorized to walk to the Lake of Quietude."

"Where is Captain Konus, and when did he leave the gate house?"

"Ah, sir, I think it was shortly after the kids came in. He said he was going to take care of the younglings."

"Wait one," the Iteeche general snapped, and turned to the overhead view of the lake. It was smooth as glass, as was the raked sand where the beach party had been held.

The kids were not anywhere in sight.

"What does your camera show of the kids after they got onto the palace grounds?" the worried Iteeche Guard general demanded.

"They disappeared behind trees," Foile reported. "You can see a van and a bus disappearing into the shadow of the trees as well. They were hidden for ten minutes, then the bus and van took off at a reasonable speed."

"Where'd the bus go?" Gramma Trouble demanded.

"It drove through trees for a bit," Foile answered. "Then it lost itself in a tree-shaded lane and never drove out."

"Oh, no!" Abby moaned as she watched the irregular flow of trucks passing down the same small road. "That's one of our routes to bring in food," she told them. "We've routed all our traffic through the Imperial Palace's grounds to avoid them having to run the gauntlet of bully boys out on the boulevards. I thought all of them were reliable. We were giving them enough money."

"I'm guessing that one or two of the drivers was only too happy to accept a bribe from a clan to do anything they wanted."

"Can we trace any trucks that drove through the Imperial Palace grounds during the hour before and after the kids' bus drove into that shady lane?" General Trouble asked.

Again, the Iteeche Guard general got on the commlink with one of his gate guard detachments. This time, a senior NCO answered the line. Both the captain and lieutenant commanding the guard were not at their duty stations.

The general cut the discussion short with a curse and a fist to the correct button on his commlink. "I am going to run a barbed hook up their cloaca and hang them from it for a month," he growled, with intent.

While he'd talked, a fast skitter drone dashed over to the shaded path. There, it found a bus, empty and with its doors wide open.

Of the kids, there was not a sign.

"General," General Bruce snapped. "With your permission, I'd like to have a Marine forensic team go over that vehicles. Maybe we'll find something in or on them. Maybe we'll find a tire track that will help us find the trucks they left on."

"I will have a guard detachment meet you at Gate 4," the Iteeche general replied. "I will also send my most competent investigators to work with your people. Maybe an Iteeche's eyes will spot something your eyes miss. After all," he said, ruefully, "we have twice as many as you have."

"Yes. Any and all help will be fully appreciated. Would you mind if our skitters made a low-level survey of every square centimeter of the Palace grounds? We are assuming that the kids have been spirited away. Are there any structures where thirty-two younglings might be hidden?"

"With the exception of the actual palace, your Marines and my guardsmen may search under every leaf and door on the grounds. Pardon me, but I will use only guardsmen to search the palace."

"I fully understand," the Human general charged with the security of the Embassy and everyone in it told the Iteeche Guard general charged with the protection of the person of the Emperor.

"There has to be a flaw in this plan," Gramma Trouble said. "Unless someone managed to convince our kids to do something, something even their parents are rarely able to do, this extraction was thrown together in scant minutes. We may have two or three officers ripe for treason, but until the kids walked into the trap, they had no way of knowing the kids were coming."

"Maybe. Maybe not," Abby said. "I know my kids have been whining that they wanted to go back to the lake. Anyone who knows how kids can whine might have planned for just this eventuality."

"No Iteeche would," General Konga said. "Any Chosen who whined like that would run the risk of being Unchosen."

"You can un-choose a Chosen?" Jacques asked, ever the sociologist, researching, researching, researching.

"Until they graduate from the Palace of Learning, a Chosen may be Unchosen. Once they have a job, they have their own income."

"Still, if they foul up," Jacques pointed out, "they can lose their clan affiliation and be tossed out on the street to starve."

"There is that," General Konga agreed.

"Everything here is meant to beat the individual into a docile member of the collective," Jacques observed. "Be a good little Iteeche and eat. Be bad and starve. The heads of the clans play their games for power, but no one else need apply. No wonder no one wants to risk changing anything that might piss off the Clan Chiefs."

"I'm afraid that you may have a point," the Iteeche general said. "However, now our mission is to return our younglings to our arms."

"I agree," General Bruce said, and began issuing orders to dispatch guards.

"Meanwhile," Abby said to Agent Foile, "we need to get more drones over more parts of this crazy burg. I was saving Smart Metal by only surveying the streets around here. Now I see that I missed a huge quadrant of the Capitol. I don't know what the kids can do to catch our attention, but I want a drone overhead if they try anything out of the usual."

"Do it," Agent Foile said. "However, may I suggest that our computers do the heavy lifting. There are things about this incident that concern me as much as your children vanishing."

"I can't believe that," Abby said, "but Mata Hari, you work with Sherlock and get coverage out there. I don't care if you have to shorten the Embassy by five stories. I want to cover this hot bed of scum and rebellion like a blanket."

"We will do it, ma'am," Mata Hari answered.

"Now, Tailor Foile, what could possibly concern you more than someone stealing our kids," Gramma Trouble said.

"Do any of us honestly think the Iteeche have the tech to prevent our kids from calling home any time they want to?" Tailor asked.

That stopped Gramma Ruth in her tracks. She glanced at Trouble, then Abby and the two scientists. Finally, they all ended up glancing from face to face.

"No," Grampa Trouble agreed. "There is nothing in the Iteeche Empire, animal, vegetable, mineral, high or low tech that could keep one of our computers from breaking through to get on Nelly net."

"There was that one incident," Mata Hari said as the silence returned. "On New Eden. Didn't Kris find that the link between Nelly and her automatic was jammed so extensively that she had to shoot over the iron sights?"

"I'd forgotten that," Abby said. "But yeah. There was that time when Kris was running for her life and really would have liked to shoot around corners without poking her head out there. Mati, did we ever get to the bottom of it?"

"No, Abby, but we did run into it several more times, usually when there was a Peterwald lurking in the bushes."

"Peterwald tech isn't as good as Wardhaven's tech," Grampa Trouble growled.

"Yeah," Abby said, "but we have evidence that a small group there may have pulled some tech up by its bootstraps, either by stealing the tech or making some breakthrough on a narrow front. Jamming the short-range net between a woman and her gun would be just the kind of thing to yield big dividends."

"And a Human hunkered down out here among the opposition Iteeche might give them just the insight to know that kids who've been to the lake once are gonna want to go there again," Gramma Trouble said, slowly, measuring every word. Every syllable.

"What other mischief might some rogue Greenfeld agent get into out here?" Abby asked.

"I thought that between Kris and Vicky, they had pretty much cleaned up the rogue elements in the Greenfeld Empire," Amanda said.

"Rats always escape the sinking ship," Grampa Trouble snarled. "I smell a rat."

"We need to get our kids back," Abby said. "Then we can figure out who's causing all this trouble. Kris has been enjoying some serious advantages because we have upgraded the programs on ships she commands. If there is a twisted Human allied with the rebels, things could get really sticky really fast."

That merited a long pause as wise warriors, old and new, stared at the prospects of a major game change.

"Abby, pardon me," Mati Hari said, "but we are getting reports of crowds gathering in the streets around the Legation District. They are mobbing all the streets in the neighboring districts and blocking all traffic. Guards fear that they could stream into the boulevard and storm the Legation District with little or no warning."

"As if we didn't have enough problems," Abby growled.

"Execute Alamo," General Bruce said into the net.

22

Gramma Trouble watched as around her Iteeche and Humans moved quickly to batten down the hatches. In less than a minute, the Legation District went from wide open for business to not just closed, but locked down tight.

Smart Metal™ flowed out from the Human Embassy in all directions. At the edge of the district, it formed a wall three meters feet high on the sidewalk across from the boulevard. There wasn't much foot traffic on those sidewalks, and the wall began to slowly advance until it reached the street curb on the other side of the walk.

There it stopped.

Anyone who didn't want to be left outside the Legation District hurried to the nearest entrance and checked in with the guards there. Everyone else hurried to the other side.

The Imperial Capitol quickly divided into entrances and exits.

The gates at the end of each street fronting on the boulevard changed as well. When the wall reached the other side of the sidewalk, the restrictions on vehicles from entering the Legation District morphed. It had been started with a few thick concrete cylinders that sank into the ground whenever a vehicle was approved for entrance.

Now the street was blocked by a solid pair of thick doors. They looked to be made of thick oak-like beams and were barred. A smaller, Iteeche-sized door was included in one door to admit individuals. Six-meter-tall guard towers sprouted on either side of the heavy gate. Iteeche police and Marines took their places up there, frowning down at the mob forming across the street.

All this took place in the three sides of the district facing other clans. The Imperial Palace was presented with another, more friendly, view.

Pylons made of Smart Metal™ rose tall, gleaming in the last rays of sunset. If push came to shove, they could quickly lay themselves down. The intent was that if the need arose they would stretch from the Legation District to the moat surrounding the Imperial Palace.

This would, of course, have the effect of cutting the belt road. Any traffic that wanted to drive around the palace would have to take a detour around the Legation District. That would likely add several kilometers to their drive. No doubt, the boulevards around the district would be crowded with a mob wanting Human heads on pikes, if not Iteeche Navy heads as well.

The rapid change in the District's outer defenses caused consternation across the boulevard and thugs stood slack-jawed as their target hardened in front of their very eyes.

One minute, the distant sidewalk opened on green areas that surrounded the high-rise apartments. Windows lay open for rocks to smash if the mob got rambunctious and decided to press on into the district across the wide boulevard. There was little, if anything, to stop them.

The leaders of the toughs had been eyeing the apartment buildings across the street. They had mapped out in their minds just how they would ransack each and every one of them. They'd been promised the loot and they intended to take it. Thus, it was with consternation that they watched all those undefended luxuries vanish behind a wall taller than an Iteeche.

There was talk among them that they should be able to take the wall. A few Iteeche could heft up another Iteeche to get him in among those treasures. A couple of ladders were ordered up. If they could just get inside, they could storm the gates from the other side and open it for the rest.

That talk was just getting seriously down and dirty when the wall grew taller. Soon it was six meters high with nine meter high towers.

The head thugs again stared slack-jawed at what the Humans had done and totally lost their cool. They ordered all their minions into the boulevard, charging the wall. There, they tried to lift the lighter Iteeche up to top the wall but couldn't reach. They pounded on the wall with their fists, but to no avail.

As their rage grew, they ordered up ladders and sledgehammers. Their next assault on the wall would be better planned.

Gramma Trouble and her friends made sure that the attack not only failed, but failed hilariously.

This wall might appear as gray stone but it wasn't. Its Smart Metal™ surface was seamless and could be made both smooth and slippery. It was also programmable.

The first couple of times they bashed it with a heavy sledgehammer, the wall bounced the hammer back so hard and fast that it broke arms and shoulders.

Undismayed by the painful screams of those injured in this first assault on the tall wall, the criminal masterminds on site found others to wield the hammers. The next few swings seemed to be pounding on sponges.

Gramma Trouble had Pretty Penny generate a random number table. Then, when the sledge hit the wall, half the time it sank into it. When it was hauled back for another hit, the wall sprang back as well. The next time they swung at it, it would be so hard that it broke bones. Thus, it alternated between soft and hard, with whoever was swinging the sledge never knowing if their next blow would be soft and worthless, or hard and painful.

Then Grampa Trouble got in on the fun.

Over the next sixty seconds around the perimeter, every sledgehammer vanished. The next time some willing punk slammed the hammer down against the wall, it swallowed the sledge up. In some cases, the hammer flew through the wall and vanished. In other cases, the thug held on the to handle and the wall took everything right off, up to the thug's hand.

Before any hoodlum boss could react to what was happening, every Iteeche wielding a sledgehammer found themselves staring at their empty hands or the handle of a sledge with nothing showing at the end of it.

Every hammer, axe, or sledge, was reduced to splinters of wood.

That got the first laugh in a long day for the defense committee members huddled around the observation stations in the Command Center next door to the Battle Station.

On the street below, rage exploded in waved fists and a long stream of objectionable language. Frustrated, the great masterminds of the assault on the Legation District turned their attention to the ladders that had been finally brought up.

It seemed that the Clan Chiefs had little use for ladders; the only ones available were on fire trucks. It took a while to find someone willing to sign off giving such critical items to someone not wearing clan colors. How high up the decision to release the ladders went was never discovered by the Humans, except for one.

The senior Clan Chief of the Zuah Clan was relaxing in his roof garden when a middle-grade lordling raced up to him with the request for the ladders. He must have been under the influence of what the Iteeche used for intoxicants, because he answered the junior Iteeche right then and there.

A Human drone picked up the approval and broadcasted it back to the Command Center.

"That's one clan that is not going to stay in the inner ring for long," Ambassador Kawaguchi muttered.

The old warriors, veterans of many *ad hoc* dirty trick teams only smiled and put their heads together.

The first ladder went up . . . and the top of the wall sprouted barbed wire along its top. It angled out a meter, barring anyone from climbing over. The ladder landed on the wire, so the first guy up carried a metal bolt cutter.

He cut the top strand, then leaned forward to attack the second strand only to find it had restrung itself and now had nastier barbs that cut his hand to ribbons as he withdrew it from the second wire to attack the first one again.

Five times he cut that top wire. Five times he started work on the second one only to find himself again facing the first strand renewed.

He learned to attack the wire from below. He got cut less. Still, no matter what he cut, the lines restrung themselves. As the number of his failures grew, he was ordered down and someone else went up, who also failed.

Cussing by now, several of the senior thugs damned their worthless help and climbed up the ladder. Several dragged along cutting torches.

Gramma Trouble coordinated what happened next.

She waited until all of them were high up the ladders, their frustration growing as the wire pulled back just as they were about to attack it with their torches, then restrung itself when they turned their attention elsewhere.

Some of them were put through several iterations, much to their growing rage. However, once there was someone at the top of all twenty ladders, Ruth, the old wrangler of POW clan lordlings, was ready to act.

With all the hoodlum bosses hanging from ladders six or seven meters up the wall, the wall itself came to life below them. Metal arms swung out from the wall with a small, fast-spinning saw at the end of it. It made one pass at the two long side pieces of the ladder, and cut a good slash in the rung supports.

Shouts from below took time to get through to the concentrating boss men at the top. The small saws were in the middle of a second pass when the boss guys finally began to pay attention and look down. Not one of them cared much for their worsening situations.

Empowered by panic, the criminal honchos scrambled down the ladders as quickly as they could. Most of them tossed aside their cutters or torches. Gramma Trouble had the wall catch the tumbling tools and pull them into the Legation District. No doubt, they'd find a better use for them.

No sooner had the head punks clambered past the slashed part than the saw enlarged and cut almost right through the ladder.

In a matter of seconds, several things happened. The ladder bent at the cut. The bottom part of the ladder fell forward to hit the wall and rest there. The Iteeche crime bosses found themselves hanging on for dear life as they were slammed and jarred by the sudden change.

Meanwhile, the top of the ladder tumbled over and, pursuant to gravity, headed for the deck. Below, those hanging onto the ladder, or waiting to go up it if it was finally possible, found themselves looking at three meters of very sharp and very hard metal picking up speed as it aimed for their heads.

In less time than it took an Iteeche to blink all four eyes, there was no one near the foot of the ladders. That meant there was also no one holding on to the ladders to keep them steady.

High above, proud Iteeche criminal bosses found themselves holding on even tighter and screaming for someone, anyone, to come back and hold that ladder!

It took a while. The fallen half of the ladders took several bounces. Some landed gently and didn't have such a hard approach. Others bounced back up and hit the wall. Still, others seemed to take off with a mind of their own for half the points of the compass.

It took a while to find punks willing to risk helping, even if they were helping an enraged and screaming boss. After all, they had only been hired for one day of protesting. It wasn't like they owed much to the guy dangling from the ladder.

Eventually, all but two managed to made it to the ground safely. One panicked and was still clinging to the ladder, afraid to reach for the next lower rung. The other was taken with a fit of nerves. After several missed steps on the way down, he managed to totally lose it.

His fall was broken by the surface of the boulevard. Broken bones and all, he was hauled back across the street and left screaming as he lay on the green swarth beside one of the buildings.

Sometime during the night his howls quieted. At sunrise the next day, the sanitation department removed the body.

The thickening dusk showed the punk bosses huddled together, taking stock of their situation.

The assault on the wall around the Legation District did not end, though.

During the night, a dozen guys showed up with a battering ram. They slammed it into the wall . . . and almost fell on their faces . . . or into the wall . . . as the head of the battering ram disappeared through the wall. When they got reorganized and pulled the ram back, they found it shorter by half a meter!

Over the next few hours, no fewer than five different battering rams were produced, all made of different materials. Some were larger, some smaller. All were tried against the wall. Each time, the wall absorbed the hit, then coughed back up a much shorter ram. Second hits didn't work any better than the first ones.

There was one persistent bunch that kept smashing a brass cannon into the wall.

Somehow the bunch had stumbled upon an ancient relic. It reminded Gramma Trouble of something she'd read about a long time ago, what armies looked like when the Navy was not only wet, but powered by wind. The barrel of the cannon was thick and heavy. The mouth looked large enough to take a metal ball of eight or nine centimeters in diameter.

The toughs rolled it up on some sort of support, then smashed the mouth of the gun into the wall. They did it again and again. All that was left of it when they finally quit trying was a chunk of brass. Any evidence of a barrel was long gone.

In growing frustration, some rowdy strong-armed a driver out of one of the largest trucks on the road. He started accelerating six blocks back, as far as he could go and stay in the Zuah district. He must have been going a hundred klicks an hour when he smashed into the wall.

Not wanting to hurt anyone, the wall functioned as an air bag to provide a soft landing for the dummy. Most of his truck was through the wall when it finally came to a stop. The wall immediately pulled the rest through, then closed up quickly before those gawking at the truck could react in any way.

After some thought, the truck was towed to supply and emptied of the fresh fish it contained. The Sailors and Marines of the fleet would eat well in the morning.

The driver, only half-conscious, was hauled off to the brig. There he would sit out the ongoing unpleasantness. He'd be eating white yams if he ate at all.

The rest of the night passed quietly as big gorillas wandered around the wall, looking for something that might damage it. Most of this behavior was ignored. When one dude went at the wall with a professional welding torch, the wall reached out and took the tanks inside, then yanked the torch from his hand.

He almost lost his hand.

The smart goons became more careful.

A bit before dawn, Gramma Trouble came awake with an absolutely brilliant idea. She woke the old general and soon they were talking to the duty crew in the command center.

"Pretty Penny, I've got an idea for you that will be lots of fun," she crowed.

A few moments later, the wall began to slowly slither, millimeter by millimeter, into the boulevard. It took the hooligans a while to notice. However, when the wall reached the middle of the right-hand lane, the bully bosses got involved.

The watch had changed. The bosses and their hired hands had replaced the guys who had learned their lessons the day before. Now, they confronted their own challenge. Only this time, the wall was doing unto them before they got to do anything.

They tried to hold the wall in place. All sorts of things were hauled over to block the wall's progress. The wall was now moving a bit faster: a centimeter a minute or so. Everything the toughs placed in its way just got slurped up by the wall as it slid ever closer to the buildings on the other side of the boulevard.

Large rocks. Cars. Trucks. All were placed in the wall's path. All vanished under its progress.

One boss honcho ordered his men to put their shoulders to it and push back. It was like pushing a mountain, only this mountain was busy coming to somewhere. The wall advanced; they were shoved back.

It had to happen. One thug showed up with explosives. He taped it to the wall, lit the fuse and everyone stepped way back.

The wall absorbed the explosives and doused the fuse. While the punks were keeping their distance, the wall moved quickly to take more ground.

In the first light of a new day, the walls around the Legation District now stood in the gutter on the far side of the boulevards or avenue. No doubt, there would be rage at the Humans for blocking traffic.

There was even less doubt that anyone would pay attention to the Humans if they pointed out that the boulevards had been closed to traffic by the thugs' yowling and yammering.

The present situation left the crime bosses with less room to hang around in. The sidewalks were rarely more than three meters wide. The bit of green between the sidewalk and the high-rise apartments was never more than two or three meters deep. Except for the streets that had previously emptied into the boulevards, there wasn't a lot of room to harangue a decent size mob into anger and destruction.

Indeed, any Iteeche that tried to slip along the sidewalk found himself hunching his shoulders against the glaring disapproval of the towering, cold wall on one side and the tall buildings on the other.

The newly hired protestors milled around in the streets and spilled into the next few avenues over.

Traffic in the Zuah Clan District came to a roaring halt as gridlock took over. Gramma Trouble turned her back on the mess next door and turned her attention back to what was most important to her.

Where were the kids? Who was dumb enough to kidnap Kris Longknife's kids? If there was anything Kris detested, it was a kidnapper. After poor little Eddie died in the hands of totally inept kidnappers, Kris would not allow one to live.

Somewhere in the Iteeche Capitol there were dead Iteeche walk-ing. Oh, and likely at least one dead Human as well.

"Pretty Penny, get Senior Special Agent in Charge Foile up here. We want a report on his progress with the kidnappings."

"Yes, Ruth," her computer said.

"Oh, and have some breakfast sent up here. I doubt anyone headed this way has had time to eat even if they managed to steal a few hours of sleep."

23

Unfortunately, as Gramma Trouble listened to the agent's report, it was painfully clear that he had much to report on what he'd done to prove this or that. However, it provided painfully little information about the kidnapping. What he'd found out about the actual kidnappers could have fit in a thimble.

A very small one.

Every powered vehicle that entered the Imperial Palace grounds was supposed to be searched and have its license logged. The ledger, a paper and pen affair, also recorded the time the rig either entered or left as well as both the signature of the guard and the driver.

This system was struggling under the pressure of so many truck-loads of food being routed through the Palace precincts. If the side of the truck advertised a provender, the guards no longer searched its contents but noted down the license number and time.

The delivery dock at the Human Embassy had a computerized system that recorded the same things and much more. From it, they could determine when a truck arrived and when it left.

It was the easy part. Also, the information could be accessed through a nice neat database.

The Iteeche Imperial Guard's paperwork was not nearly as nice and neat. The average sergeant or junior officer's handwriting was bad at best and when hurried, it got worse. The license number was recorded in a nearly illegible scrawl. The signatures were mere lines, if not something like an X from drivers who could not sign their names.

After the Human investigators visited two guard gate houses and struggled to copy data over to their commlink, they gave up and just took pictures of the required pages. One of Nelly's kids had to run the entire log through a high-end image recognition program. Agent Foile's computer, Sherlock, built up a database on each person who wrote in the log. Only after they had a completely analyzed collection of every jot and tittle, could the computer overlay one number with another and determine which number was which.

In Human Standard, it was often hard to figure out if a hand-scrawled one was a seven. Similarly, a five that lost its top could be mistaken for a three. If a zero acquired a tail for any reason, it could be a six or a nine, with the opposite just as likely.

There was a reason why Humans used their commlinks for so many things.

The Iteeche numerical system held the same potential to confuse when hastily slapped down on paper by a Guardsman who was tired after a long shift. The database showed how a lieutenant's numbers deteriorated as the watch wore on.

In some cases, they had to resort to the driver's wildly scribbled signature to figure out the license number. Oh, and then there were the transposed numbers.

The two gates beside the Legation District recorded the passage of the trucks out of the grounds. In most cases, they arrived at the loading dock very soon after. The trucks that took an inordinate amount of time were kicked out of the system for further examination.

In some cases, the Guard officer had noted down the time wrong. In others, a review of the writing on the log revealed a miscalled number.

Sherlock improved his system.

Five vehicles had turned onto the Palace belt road and dodged around it for a boulevard or two before hightailing it back to their supplier. There they took on a new load of food and headed back.

This time, neither took the long route through the Palace, but instead cut around the belt road and right into the Legation District.

No doubt about it, the spirit of entrepreneurship was alive and growing fast in Iteeche land.

That still left the sixth truck.

It drove down the Fourth Boulevard and right through the gate. No stop. Just waved through.

"Who did that?" Gramma Trouble demanded.

"We checked. There is one of your missing Guard captains," Special Agent Foile replied.

"When did it exit?" General Trouble growled.

"It's not in the logbook. However, we know when the captain and lieutenant went missing from Gate 5."

"Did you backtrack the surveillance video?" Gramma Trouble demanded. "Did they wave a truck through without checking it? Can you follow the truck?"

Ruth slowly ran down when the special agent did not leap to answer her questions.

"What happened?" she finally said.

"We don't survey the palace," the agent said in a clipped voice.

"But you had another truck entering Gate 4," Abby snapped.

"Yes. A camera we had set up to keep an eye on the demonstrations around the Legation District caught all the trucks entering and leaving the Palace grounds."

The bitter truth began to slowly dawn on Gramma Trouble. They really were in trouble.

"You didn't have surveillance over the other gates," she whispered.

"Except for an occasional picture when a drone reached the end of its racetrack and before it turned back, no," Foile said. "We have no pictures."

"Well, it's nice to know that there are some places you Humans don't spy on," General Konga said, dryly.

The two Iteeche eyed the Humans. They stared back, showing neither defensiveness nor defiance.

"That may have to change," Grampa Trouble growled.

"Locking the barn door after the horse got out," Amanda said, then caught herself. "I can't believe I said that. Lock the barn door and all."

Gramma Trouble had never seen the perfectly put together economist flustered. Having your kids stolen would do that to any parent.

"Okay," Ruth snapped. "They jammed the kids' commlinks. You have to be able to capture that jamming. Find the jammer, find the kids," she said, her eyes firmly fixed on the agent.

He was shaking his head even before she finished.

"As soon as we learned the kids were missing and jammed, we ran a high-level drone sweep over the entire Capitol. It's huge, so we started at ten thousand meters. No joy. We pulled more Smart Metal out of the towers and did a sweep at five thousand meters. Again, the drones recorded no noise," the agent said with a sigh, then went on.

"We swept again and again, each time lower. Right now, we have jam sniffers orbiting over every square kilometer of the capitol. Yes, General, even the Imperial Palace," he said, glancing at the Guard general.

The Iteeche nodded approval.

"So far, we're getting nothing. They're not jamming the kids anymore," the investigator said, finishing.

"So, they and the kids are in the wind," Abby said, summing up their reality.

Gramma Trouble had her elbows on the table in front of her. Now she rested her eyes on her palms. In the blackness behind her eyeballs, she struggled to see where her grandkids were. What was being done to them?

She got no answer but shivered. There was no doubt, Ruth and Johnny were terrified.

24

I came back to consciousness slowly, but I did not move.

I remembered Mommy telling stories about when she was captured or kidnapped. She always kept her eyes closed and listened first.

I could hear; I listened.

I didn't much care for what I heard.

Breathing. Lots of breathing. Some fast and labored as if someone was panicked. Others were low and rhythmic, as if someone was sleeping.

There were also soft whimpers. Someone whispered soothing words I couldn't quite catch.

Still, I could hear the pounding of my heart. I was terrified.

I continued listening as I tried to slow my heart and keep my breath steady and slow. Then I tried to cautiously open my eyes.

I'd teased Johnny when he was just a kid. He'd try to close his eyes, but he'd scrunched them up tight. It was so easy to see when he was faking it.

Now, I did my best to just open my eyes a tiny crack. It wasn't easy; they kind of trembled. Still, I got them open.

Iteeche and Human kids lay sprawled on the floor of a big room with a low ceiling. Most were still in a kind of drugged sleep. A few kids sat against the walls. Some were whimpering and crying; they looked so terrified. Other kids held them and tried to soothe them.

The walls of the room we were in looked like they were metal. Metal hastily welded together. I guess that was why Daisy couldn't get a message out.

I remembered Mommy saying that she hated it when the bad guys got smart. Snatching us up on the Palace grounds when we were doing something even our parents didn't know about was way too smart. Jamming Daisy shouldn't have been possible. I wondered how long ago these walls had been welded together.

"You awake?" was a low whisper and close.

Mary! Was she okay?

"Yah," I muttered through lips that refused to move. I tried to sit up and discovered my fingers and toes were all I could move.

"Can you move?" I asked.

"Yeah, I've been awake a while," Mary muttered low. "They took my commlink so I don't know how long they've had us or I've been awake. Don't worry about not being able to move. It will go away in a bit. Wiggle what you can. I think that works the poison out faster."

So, I wiggled my fingers and toes. Soon I was rotating my wrists and ankles. In a couple of minutes, I was able to sit up. I worked my arms and legs before I tried to stand up.

It didn't go well. I ended up leaning against the wall and kind of pulling myself up with help from Mary. Or maybe I was helping Mary stand.

It sure looked like a group effort from where I was.

Leaning against the wall to keep from falling down, I got a better look at our brig. It wasn't tiny, say fifteen meters on each side of the square. I did the math in my head and realized there were almost seven square meters for each of us kids. It wouldn't meet standards for a battlecruiser's crew space.

Still, they hadn't squeezed us in elbow-to-elbow.

From around the room, those kids who were awake turned to look at me and Mary. Em and Mo, a general and an admiral's kid, slowly walked along the wall until they joined us.

"How are you feeling Longknife?" Em asked.

"Not as bad as I have," I lied. Lies like those were expected of the senior officers. Mom said that you had to look sure of yourself for your subordinates. If you lost it, all was lost. As long as you stayed confident that you could get out of a situation, people believed that you could.

I'd listened attentively to Mom telling her stories. I figured someday I'd be a Navy officer and doing what she did.

I didn't expect to do it before my eighth birthday.

The eyes around the room fixed on me seemed to relax a bit. Yeah, if the Longknife said it wasn't as bad as it could be, then it wasn't.

To look like I was doing something, I set out to answer the first question I'd had on waking up. Slowly I inched my finger toward one of the welded seams. The metal grew warm a centimeter or two out, but the seam wasn't too hot to touch.

"They welded this place together not too long ago," I said.

"What does that mean?" Mo, who was a bit younger than Em, asked.

"They weren't expecting us," I said. Mary nodded agreement. "Somebody laid their hands on all this steel and welded this room together no more than a few hours ago."

"Four hours ago," Daisy said from my neck. "They started work on this an hour after they captured you kids."

"That's nice to know," I answered.

"You've still got your commlink," Mary said.

"Yeah," I said. "It's locked around my neck and it doesn't have an off button like the grown-ups have."

"So, you can get a message out," a girl soothing a whimpering little boy said.

I shook my head. "Sorry folks. Daisy and I did our best to get a message out the second they took us, but they were jamming the net. Now, locked in this metal box, the jamming's off, but we can't get anything out. I'm guessing we're stashed on the lowest level of a parking garage and surrounded by metal."

"You are going to keep trying," Mary quickly said.

"Every two seconds," Daisy said, "Hippo and I are trying to blast a message out. So far, nothing."

The little boy let out a soft wail. The girl consoling him seemed to slump. That was not what anyone wanted to hear.

"Let's take a look at what we've got," I said, as cheerful as I could. "They've given us enough space. We can lie down without having to crawl all over everyone," I pointed out.

The four of us began a survey.

"Daisy, are any of the seams warmer than the others?" I asked as I made my way to the center of the room, careful not to step on anyone.

"Two metal panels over there are warmest," Daisy reported. Two three by two meter sheets, laid on their short side, had been the last elements of our prison fused into place.

The four of us headed in that direction. A moment later, we were all pushing and shoving. First, we went after both plates, then tackled them one at a time. There was no flex in either the plates or their seams.

"Look," Em said, pointing with one hand at the overhead and another at the deck. I could not get used to someone pointing with two right arms. Still, I looked.

"Oh," I mumbled. There were welding seams both along the top and bottom of the bulkheads. We were in a complete steel box and I would guess that the plates were more than a centimeter thick. I'd seen old tanks. The ones they used in the Unity and Iteeche Wars. Grampa Ray said the old personnel carriers only had armor a centimeter thick. Then, he and Dad tried to push the one in the museum.

It wasn't any easier to move than what we were stuck in.

Thirty-two kids, even if twenty of them were Iteeche, weren't going to claw their way out of this. I kept my opinion to myself, but Mary, Em, and Mo had to plaster their smiles back on before we turned to again face the others.

"I wonder what they gave us to eat?" I asked the air.

With feigned eagerness, the four of us went to explore our prison.

25

"There's activity on Third Street in front of the Zuah clan's temporary palace," rang from everyone's commlink in the same instant.

Gramma Trouble eyed the new set of images that appeared in the center of the conference table. Straight leg infantry in the clan's colors were forming up, rifles shouldered, in two large phalanxes. They left plenty of space in their middle for whatever it was that they were escorting.

The center began to fill in as huge ax-wielding men in black trailed out of the palace's front door and formed their own phalanx behind the vanguard. Their last rank were the snake wranglers in blood red from head to toe. They held crystal bowls with poisonous snakes inside.

Hopefully, none of those vipers would get loose in the ranks or watching crowd.

While Ruth watched all this develop, she was also feverishly thinking two or three moves ahead.

"I propose that we don't let all those guards in," she told everyone around the table.

Ambassador Kawaguchi had joined them, apparently reacting to the announcement that trouble was afoot. He nodded agreement with Ruth.

"Those troops could cause too much havoc inside if they decided to," Abby muttered. "That says nothing about any of the thugs that might slip through the gate while it was open. So, how do we keep them out?"

"We need them to reveal their intent before they get through our gates," Ruth said.

"We need to stop all those soldiers," Grampa Trouble said. "Stop them and keep them outside our wall."

"Agreed," came from everyone around the table.

"Only how do we do it?" Abby asked.

There was a brief pause, then Gramma Trouble offered, "They're bound to have a herald in that bunch. Make him talk to our gate guards."

"They will not want to talk to a lowly lieutenant," General Konga said in a voice that brooked no debate.

"We'll need a colonel or a battlecruiser captain," General Trouble observed.

"One of your Marine colonels, not mine," General Konga of the Imperial Guard. "We must not be seen to take sides. At least not yet."

"I'll have a Marine colonel in dress blue and reds report to that gate," General Bruce said and was talking on his commlink the next moment.

"I'll provide a captain," Admiral Ulan of the Combined Fleet staff said. "I've got admirals available," he offered.

"Nope. We don't want to give this bunch too many honors," Gramma Trouble said. "At the same time, we don't want to give them too little. I think senior field grade officers are just right."

"Yes, Goldilocks," Grampa Trouble growled . . . through an affectionate smile.

"But right on," his wife answered back.

"Does anyone besides me," Abby said, "feel the need for more troopers at that gate?"

"But would we want to be overly conspicuous?" Ambassador

Kawaguchi asked. "Might they have a drone of their own observing our activity?"

"Hmm," Grampa Trouble grumbled.

"I could have a couple of companies mosey along as fire teams," General Bruce said. "They could stand by in the foyer of the nearest apartment buildings, ready to deploy if we need them."

"You might also want to have a battalion or two standing by in the Embassy as a quick reaction force," General Trouble suggested.

"And some gun trucks ready to roll," Gramma Trouble added. "All I'm seeing is light infantry with no heavy weapons."

General Bruce, charged with the defense of the Human Embassy and now the Legation District, quickly issued the necessary orders.

They paused in thought, all preparation done. Ruth considered their situation and measured their threats. A moment later, from the garage beneath the Clan's present palace, a large palanquin swayed into view.

It was the size of a large shack and decorated like some mad queen's jewelry box. It took twenty-four slaves in front and as many behind to lug the monster along.

It took more than a bit of jostling before the huge thing negotiated the turn out of the garage and onto Third Street. Once it was fully out and in the line, the vanguard led off at a slow walk.

There was near silence along the line of march, occasionally broken as a slave driver snapped his whip.

Drones and nano scouts immediately descended on the palanquin, searching for any explosives or sign that there might be a bomb aboard. They reported back video of six senior Clan Chiefs reclining on pillows in a circle inside the ambling shed. From the furtive glances they kept throwing at each other, Gramma Trouble suspected there was no trust among those who held or wanted the senior Clan Chief's job.

More nano scouts were dispatched to search the oncoming palanquin. They checked every nook and cranny. They even infiltrated the pillows the Iteeche lords reclined on. No explosives. No wires. The thing was made of wicker, cane, and bamboo-like

substances, strong and light. It was decorated to look a lot more pala-
tial than it was.

"Do we let it in?" General Bruce asked those around the table.

"I don't think we can reject it," Ambassador Kawaguchi answered.
"Are we prepared to declare a siege and lock all our doors?"

"I'd prefer we didn't," General Trouble said. "At least not yet. I'd
prefer we actually be under siege when we lock everything down.
Appearances matter."

"I don't care how if the bugs and drones say that shambling hut is
explosive free," Abby said, "I will not allow it inside the Embassy. If
they parked that thing in our courtyard, it could take out the entire
Embassy."

Ruth found that she was no more trusting than Abby. "May I
suggest that we have a delegation meet them on the street? If necessary, we could create a small pavilion for us to palaver in. When we're
done, they could turn around and boogie on out of here."

"Are you offering you and the general to do the palavering?" Abby
asked.

Ruth glanced at her partner of a hundred years. All they needed
was a shared look to know that they were in agreement.

"In for a penny, in for a pound," Gramma Trouble said.

"Yes," the old general added, "let's see how they like negotiating
with the "Hammerer of Iteeche, Conqueror of I don't know how
many planets the media says I did."

"It tends to change depending on whose talking," Ruth added,
ruefully.

"Well, you two go get in your fancy dress uniforms," Abby said.
"We'll keep you up to date via the net."

Ruth had her first free time of the day on the elevator down to
their quarters.

"Pretty Penny, check with Sherlock for any progress on finding the
kids."

It took only a moment for her computer to answer. "No progress.
Everyone who knows the missing guardsmen report them as non-
political. They don't know where this kind of treasonous behavior

came from. Our best guess is some shadow clan cabal. We've heard that there was money on Abby's head as well as you and Trouble. Our best guess is there was money to be had for any Human."

"They're proving negatives, sweetheart," Trouble said softly.

"And if you turn over enough stones, you're bound to find some skunk that knows something," Ruth said wryly.

"Police work is a tough job. Patience, dear."

"Patience be damned, I want to go out and blow some shit up."

General Trouble fondly smiled down at his wife. "I know. Me too. However, we need to be in negotiation mode just now."

"You telling me I've got to grow up?"

"Sorry, but yes, my wife. Today you have to be a mature parent, teacher, intelligence officer, and wife to a guy who has blown up a lot of shit."

He kissed her on her forehead as the elevator came to a halt. They headed for their closet. The one with the uniforms in the back.

Ruth both hated and loved that there were uniforms hidden deep within her closet. She hated when she had to put them on and become her old self. She often abhorred what she did in that uniform. Still, when it was off, she usually had happy and proud memories of what she'd done.

On the whole, it balanced out for the good.

Fifteen minutes later, she and Trouble rode the elevator down to the first floor. Resplendent in dress whites and gleaming with medals and orders, they marched, side-by-side, to stand like rocks in the middle of the street.

They faced down Third Street where the first act of a multi-part drama had begun. Pretty Penny projected a holograph of what was happening.

The entire collection of modern and ancient power had come to a halt before the gates that blocked the street. A councilor in a shimmering robe of many colors now stood at the head of the light infantry phalanx. They had halted and still shouldered their arms. Sheaths for bayonets hung from their belts, but no one had ordered them to fix those pointy things to their rifles.

That, at least, was good.

The herald had spent a long five minutes announcing who demanded entrance. Only then did he get around to demanding why a road in the Emperor's Capitol was blocked to public use.

The Human Marine colonel passed the question to the Iteeche Navy captain.

"We blocked the road because your clan allowed hooligans to block it to common public traffic," the captain's voice boomed out. Likely he was easily heard in the fancy palanquin's hut. "We blocked the road to keep such hoodlums outside so they cannot disturb the serenity of the peaceful people within the walls."

It took a moment before the herald shot back. "You command a battlecruiser and have the effrontery to call yourself peaceful. How many battlecruisers have you blown out of space?"

Someone was being snippy.

"Many rebels have met their demise under the guns of my commands," the Navy captain answered, his voice cold and deadly. "However, this is the Imperial Capitol. I do not expect my serenity to be troubled by thugs and punks here. Not within the shadow of the Imperial Palace and the hearing of the Emperor himself. Tell your master that he really needs to restore the Emperor's peace to the streets and avenues."

Considering the length of time it took for the herald to try another tack, someone in the back of the fancy ride could have had a stroke. After a long minute wait, the herald sputtered.

"My masters will decide what is done in their clan district. Now, may we enter? We have business with whoever is issuing orders since the Embassy is empty of any Emissary."

Oh, that was a new twist. Was someone trying to invalidate the Embassy's protection because Kris Longknife was out slaughtering those who rose in rebellion against the boy Emperor? That idea had to be drop-kicked right back to where it came from.

The Iteeche captain turned to face the Human Marine colonel. The ball was now in his court.

"You may enter. However, you enter without your honor guard.

Younglings of the Embassy, the Imperial Guard, and the Imperial Navy have been kidnapped from the very grounds of the Imperial Palace. We know the power of the clans and that nothing happens in the Imperial Capitol without permission of some clan. While we search for those children, we are understandably sensitive. You may enter. Your armed honor guard may not."

It took a good five minutes for the herald to get his next set of instructions.

Among the six in the palanquins, there was much heated discussion. Three were in such a snit they immediately wanted to return.

The other three were concerned over many things: *Would the humans hold the kidnapping against the Zuah Clan? They must do something to assure that the Humans' anger was not aimed at them. Could they get the boulevard cleared? Barred from using this street, the next one over was beyond belief. The Abba Clan had similar problems, but they were too frightened to make contact with the Humans. Someone had to get the Humans. Everyone remembered what an angry Kris Longknife could do.*

That brought up the question of the kidnapped younglings.

"Who of their Chosen were taken?" one of the go home types asked.

"Could it be one of Kris Longknife's Chosen?" another asked.

That brought silence.

"Now that we're here, we must go forward," one argued.

"We have slipped into a pond full of sharks. If we thrash about, we'll be eaten in but a moment. We must calmly swim in these waters. We must go forward."

"Even if it be under the dishonorable conditions these interlopers demand?"

"Yes."

One of the Iteeche favoring retreat found that argument persuasive. The other two shrugged and the herald got his orders. So did the Commander of the Guard.

The Honor Guard to the Clan Chiefs split down the middle. Half wheeled right, the others left. As they marched out of the way, they pushed a wave of punks ahead of them. The hired protestors had to scoot fast to get out of the way, but they couldn't flee fast enough.

Officers of the Honor Guard were forced to order their men to a slow march, and finally halted them long enough for the leased mob to clear out of their path. The pause was short; clearly, the guard officers were impatient. They ordered the troops to fix bayonets and move forward at a slow march before the path was cleared ahead of them.

Those who had dilly-dallied now fell all over each other to clear a path for the gleaming blades aimed right at their hearts. The guard advanced and was not slowed again.

While the modern armed and armored guardsman of the vanguard got out of the way, the black-clad axe men and red-robed snake wranglers stood their ground.

"Ah, I think we have a situation here," the Human Marine colonel observed.

"Yeah?" General Trouble replied.

"You willing to let them bring those pukes in?" Abby asked.

"I think we have to," Gramma Trouble answered. "They gave, now we have to give. They're proud men, I mean Iteeche. If we push them too hard, they'll go home mad."

"Yeah," Abby drawled. "I guess we have to meet them halfway. Still, I don't want any of those snakes getting loose. Mata Hari, get some Smart Metal ready. If one of those snake guys even so much as jiggles the lid on his glass bowl, I want a meter high wall around that entire shebang. Let's see how their boss guys like being caught in a cage with one of their snakes on the loose."

"Good idea," Gramma Trouble said. "I sure don't want to have to look under my bed for one of those critters."

"You wouldn't look," Grampa Trouble grumbled. "You'd have me do the looking."

"I don't want anyone in the Legation District to have to look," Abby said.

"The potential wall is in place," Mata Hari reported. "It will be a meter high. I have no record of snakes that can climb that high on a smooth surface or strike that high either."

"Very good," Abby said. "Open the gate."

The large, thick-looking Smart Metal™ doors ponderously swung open. The Smart Metal™ was hyper-strong; the thickness was there for show.

The remaining honor escort moved forward at a slow walk. The palanquin swayed forward as the slaves marched in step through the gate.

Third Street was empty. It looked like something from an old movie set. Strange how that fictional genre had stayed with humanity for hundreds of years, Gramma Trouble observed. Still, there was something about a face-off at high noon on an abandoned street that spoke to everyone.

Even in full dress, Ruth found herself reaching for a weapon at her hip. Nothing was there, of course.

Slowly, the palanquin and its deadly escort made their way up the street toward the two Humans. The only sound was a soft wind and the occasional crack of a whip over the slaves' heads, not that they needed it. Did any of the Iteeche notice the bulge at the side of the road that flowed along with them?

Ruth did her best to suppress a smile. Mata Hari had not only provided enough Smart Metal™ for the meter-high wall, but the bulge showed that the wall would fit around the escort and the palanquin.

If those snakes got loose, the Clan Chiefs could see at a glance that they would be in the box with the snakes.

Twenty meters short of the two armored Humans, the shrunken parade came to a halt. For a long moment, nothing happened. The two sides just stared at each other.

Finally, the two slave drivers tied their whips to their belts and went around to the right side of the fancy shack. From under the palanquin, they pulled out a wide stair and set it in place.

One after another, with their robes becoming more gaudy with each Iteeche, the clan lords dismounted. The last out was the senior Clan Chief.

He was the perfect advertisement for bad taste laid on with a trowel.

The lords now processed around their escort and stood in the space between them and the two Humans. A moment later, the Clan Chief came to stand dead center of the other five and was half the distance to the two Troubles.

The herald came to grovel in the dust beside the head high muckety muck and began to reel off all his fancy titles.

PRETTY PENNY, WE'RE GOING TO NEED SOMEONE TO ANNOUNCE US.

RUTH, I'VE GOT A FULL ITEECHE ADMIRAL HEADED THIS WAY. HE SHOULD BE HERE BEFORE THIS GUY FINISHES.

FINE.

The herald was far from finished when a four star Iteeche admiral and his two *aids de camp*, in dress grays, strolled up to stand beside, but two steps behind, the Troubles.

When the Iteeche finished spouting all the claims to fame of the Clan Chief as well as half the glorious history of the clan, the admiral took over filling the air with falderal, and the next fifteen minutes vanished with nothing to show for it.

When the introductions were finished, silence fell on the street. It settled in and kind of took a nap. Nobody had anything to say.

The Troubles held their tongue; they hadn't called this meeting. The Clan Chief, however, seemed to have forgotten why he'd come calling.

Finally, the big guy cleared his throat. "You are blocking public use of two boulevards. That is forbidden," he snapped.

"You allowed them to be blocked," General Trouble shot right back.

"I did not," the chief answered in injured pride.

"Xenophon, show him."

The old general's computer projected a holograph of the goings on in the boulevard between the Zuah Clan quarter and the Legation District. Little traffic went through, both because the drivers knew not to go near the disturbance and because the streets really were blocked by the hired hands milling around in the street and making themselves a nuisance.

"You allowed that to happen," Trouble snapped. "We stopped it. We also moved to protect the safety of the people in our charge."

Now the holograph switched to show punks harassing passersby on the sidewalk.

"That matters nothing to me. You are causing congestion on the next boulevard over. It can't carry all the traffic. The Abba Clan reports the same thing on the boulevard next to them. You must cease obstructing legitimate use of the public boulevards."

"The hoodlums that caused this are still hanging around our gates," Trouble growled. "Here! Look!"

Now the holograph showed real time take from the overhead drones. Yep, the day laborers who had been hired to muck around with access to the Legation District were still huddled in front of all the gates, except Third Street's North Gate.

"What is that to me?" the Clan Chief sniffed, then he made his mistake. "You are only doing this because some of your younglings have gotten lost."

"What do you know about our kidnapped younglings?" Grampa Trouble snapped, and took a step toward the clan honcho, his hands going to fists.

All this was not lost on the Chief of the Zuah Clan. He took two hurried steps back. "We know nothing about your problems. Nothing at all."

"I think you do," Trouble said, taking a menacingly second step forward.

The Clan Chief retreated a third step.

"Only what everyone knows," the Iteeche sputtered. "Some of your children wandered off. They are lost and you are searching high and low for them."

"They were taken," Trouble growled, now in the Iteeche's face. It was hard to think that a six-foot man could get in the face of an eight-foot-tall Iteeche, but the old general was doing just that. "Our younglings were stolen right out of the grounds of the Imperial Palace. That takes clan pull. Which clan pulled this off?"

"The trucks on the Imperial Palace grounds were your hires. It was you who were desecrating the sacred grounds of the Palace with your food trucks," the clan chief got out. It was meant to sound forceful. Instead it was a whimper.

"Get out of my face," General Trouble ordered, turning his back on the Clan Chief and stepping back to where Ruth stood. He delivered his final ultimate over his shoulder. "Don't come back until you have something to tell us about our younglings."

"Why are we having a dispute over something so inconsequential? You can Choose some more to replace them in your Palace of Learning," was a big mistake for a last rejoinder.

In a second, Gramma Trouble had covered the distance to the Iteeche. In the war, she'd had experience confronting the bloated pride of defeated Iteeche. She stood on his two front feet to give herself some extra height and grabbed ahold of his robes to force him to look down into her flaming eyes.

"We Human women bear our children live. For nine months, we carry them in our bodies, feeding them with our own blood as they grow. We bring them into the world in blood and pain, and accept them in joy when they take their first breath. You treat our younglings lightly at great cost. Never doubt that Human women will not stop tearing things apart until we have our Chosen at our breasts."

With that, Gramma Trouble whirled, much of it on the Iteeche's feet, and stormed away.

"We're done here," she growled as she passed her husband.

The waiting Iteeche admiral turned on his heels and his pair of aids as well. Showing the Clan Chief their backsides, the five marched away from him, waves of disgust crashing out from them.

An Iteeche MP lieutenant trotted from the sidewalk to stand beside the clan lord. He did not salute. "Sir, your presence here is no long desired. Please leave immediately."

Bewildered by what had just happened, the clan honcho turned and shoved his subordinates ahead of him. They walked back to the palanquin as if in a daze.

This Clan Chief would be talking to other Clan Chiefs for much of the rest of the day. He had to wonder if they might have underestimated the Humans' attachment to their younglings. Still, was this a strength or a weakness for the Humans?

Meanwhile, Gramma Trouble was already on the net.

ABBY, WE NEED TO BLANKET THIS PLACE WITH NANOSCOUTS.

I AGREE, RUTH. THIS IS BOUND TO GET A LOT OF LOOSE LIPS WAGGING. MAYBE WE CAN LEARN SOMETHING. BY THE WAY, THAT WAS ONE FANTASTIC DRESSING DOWN YOU DID, GENERAL.

HOW STUPID CAN ONE GUY GET? Ruth snapped, her disgust not lost to those listening on the net.

Ruth forced her breath to slow, trying to calm the hammering of her heart. She was getting too old for this shit.

Still, she'd started something. Maybe an avalanche. Who knew what it would turn up?

26

I looked around the metal jail they had us locked up in. Metal floor. Metal overhead. Metal walls. No break in the seams; no door, no possible way out. *What would Mom do in this kind of a mess?*

I knew Mom would not panic. Not run in circles. I sure wanted to, but I'd hate to admit anything like that to Mom the next time I saw her.

I would see her again.

How many times had they tried to kill Mom? Wasn't she still out blowing shit up? I guess I was in an adult enough situation that I had earned the right to use some adult language.

If only in my head.

"Let's see what we've got," I said to Mary and the two Iteeche kids the admiral and general had Chosen, Em and Mo.

Three of the bulkheads were devoid of anything. The far bulkhead had some interesting stuff.

The four of us paced our way over there, careful to avoid stepping on those still sleeping. More kids were waking up and scooting over to one of the three blank bulkheads. There, they huddled together in small groups or alone.

All eyes followed us. Some were interested; other stares were blank, as if they followed us just because we were moving.

I fought the bitter taste of despair rising in my gut. I'd never tasted anything like this, but it must be something like Mom had admitted to us in a whisper. Yes, Longknifes would feel fear, and despair and lots of other nasty feelings, just like everyone else.

However, we didn't let those bad feelings rule us. Always, you kept a cheerful, confident look on your face.

I faked a smile and said, "Hey, look there. We've got tanks full of fish. I wonder if we can drink the water?"

I sidled up to one tank. It was pretty full of white fish; they'd be easy for the Iteeche to catch. I dipped my hand into the water. It didn't taste too bad.

After all, it was Iteeche water. Still, it gave me a chance to say something hopeful.

"The water is drinkable for both Human and Iteeche," I said. "Once we get out of here, however, we Humans would likely need shots to kill whatever was in it."

That seemed to cheer everyone up, even if there was some joshing about we Humans having weak stomachs. It was good to hear even a little cheer in the voices around the room.

Following the wall past the fish tanks, we found a stack of crumbling boxes. They looked old and beaten up. It took me a moment to recognize some of the faded print on them.

"Hey, these are combat rations!" I exclaimed.

"They look ancient," Mary said as I stooped to pick one up.

I flipped it over and spotted the date on the bottom. "These must have been captured during the Iteeche War."

"They must be a hundred years old!" Buddie grouched.

"The food was supposed to last just about forever. They dehydrated it somehow," Suzie said.

I opened the box I had and searched through its contents. Most of the boxes were sealed, but one had a clear top. It was some sort of individual serving of spice cake. I pulled the lid off and flipped it over: a loaf of cake with the consistency of a brick fell into my hand.

"Can you take a bite out of it?" Mary asked.

I tried. Even with the four big teeth I had now, nothing happened.

"Maybe if I put some water on it," I said. So, I dipped the pan it came in in the fish tank and got a few centimeters of water in it, then slipped the loaf back in.

A minute or so later, with all us kids watching, the water was gone, and the top of the loaf was still just as hard. I added more water. Then more water.

By the time it finished soaking up the water, it was more a pudding than a cake. A search through the boxes of combat rations showed that there were no spoons or forks or knives. I scooped some out with my fingers, feeling a bit embarrassed. I hadn't eaten with my hands since I was a baby.

"Not too bad," I said, trying not to grimace.

Lexi scooped some up and plopped it in her mouth. Even as she licked her fingers clean, she was grumbling, "Tastes more like cardboard. I wonder if it is even worth eating."

"We'll know by tomorrow," Mary said. "If our tummies are grumbling, their taste won't matter that much. If they aren't rumbling, you can hold ours or take a bite."

The two made faces at each other but that ended quickly with no blows.

"Okay, we have water and maybe food. Where do we poop?" Buddy griped.

"I think that's next," Mary said, pointing.

There was a long, low trough a meter away from the far wall. It had a lid on it. Mo flipped it up and sure enough, there was . . . something. The Iteeche quickly straddled it and let go with a stream of water that splashed when it hit the bottom but stayed inside the walls of the trough.

"This is going to stink when it gets full," Lexi noted.

"Maybe it drains?" Suzie asked, optimistically.

"I don't see anything like a hole for a drain," I observed, then realized. "What about the air in here? It's going to get dangerously low on oxygen in a few hours." I remembered Mom and Dad's story about how some bad Iteeche had dropped buildings on top of them and the air had gotten hard to breathe before Auntie Megan could dig them out.

"Let's find some air holes," Mary ordered. "No, everyone stop. Don't say a word. Listen for the whirl of blowers or the sound of air flowing in or out."

For a long minute, thirty kids did their best not to make any noise. Still, even after such a quiet minute, none of us could hear anything.

"Anyone feel the flow of air?" I asked.

That got a lot of heads shaking.

"They have to have air holes in this box," Bruce didn't quite whine. "We taught my baby sister that her little bunny needed air holes when she put it in a box, and it was a fluffy toy."

"Maybe we won't be in here long enough for it to matter," Buddy said, more wishful than hopeful.

"Maybe they want us to suffocate." Mark said.

"They've kept us alive this long," I snapped. "Don't stir up crazy stuff."

So, we went around the room more carefully, this time. Since the place people pooped was always smelly, I figured that there must be some way of pulling out that nasty stink.

Again, each steel panel seemed solid, as did the welds. This time I got down on my hands and knees and felt around the bottom. Air usually came in either the top or bottom of a room.

"Hey!" I yelped, "I think I've found something!"

Down at the bottom of the plate there was a small edge, with maybe one centimeter between it and the deck. I felt around and found a space about two centimeters deep. Above it, my fingers found something a bit rough.

"I think there's a plate there with tiny holes," I told everyone.

Now lots of kids were down, feeling around under the bulkhead. Some said it was another steel plate. Others felt small, pin-sized holes in the plate.

I wet my finger and put it in front of the space. "I think there's air movement. At least, my finger seems to be drying."

Others did the same. Some agreed with me; others didn't.

"This is getting us nowhere in a hurry," Mary said. "Ruth, can't Nelly and her kids spin off nano scouts? One of those could check to see if there are holes. Maybe even see if that's a way out?"

I winced inside and barely kept a grimace off my face. "Yes, Nelly can. So can all the grown-ups' computers," I admitted. "However, there are a lot of things Daisy and Hippo can't do. The necklace around my neck won't let me undo it and take it off. Our computers don't have an off button. We can't turn them off if we don't want them to know what we're up to."

"Well, it let you take off for the lake," Lexi pointed out.

"And I am wishing I hadn't," Daisy said from her place at my neck.

"I don't want to ever do this again," Hippo added in something very much like one of Johnny's whines.

"Well, if your computer let us get into this mess, shouldn't it do everything it can to help us get out of it?" Buddy asked.

"Daisy," I said. "I'm not asking you to turn yourself off, or even come off from around my neck. Do you know how to spin off a nano scout?"

"Yes," Daisy said, caution in her voice. "Yes, I can do it."

"Will you?" I asked, trying not to be pushy. I didn't like it when people pushed me to do something and I doubt my computer would like it, either.

"Exactly what do you want done?" Daisy asked.

"Could you spin off a tiny nano scout and let it drift on the air currents in this room? We need to know if there is new air coming in and bad air going out. Maybe, if your scout can ride the air currents out of here, you could send a bigger scout with a message for Auntie Abby to call in the cavalry."

All the kids liked the idea of the cavalry riding to our rescue.

Daisy took a surprisingly long moment to consider my request. Finally, she said, "I do have plenty of Smart Metal I could use for a scout or even a small drone. Your parents wanted me very solidly around your neck."

"Yeah," I grumbled.

My folks really should trust me more. But then, if while I was knocked out this bunch had tried to cut Daisy off me, they'd failed. My necklace didn't even show a nick where they might have tried.

"Well, since I let you get us into this mess," Daisy said, "A mess, I may point out, that I was supposed to have kept you out of but seem to have failed, I guess I can bend a few rules to help us get out of it. Okay, I'll spin off a scout. Hippo, are you willing to also spin off something if we need it? If there are a lot of bends in the vents, my scout may need some repeaters to get the message back here."

"I don't want to get smaller," Hippo said, sounding as surly as Johnny in a snit.

"We need to get out of this mess. You need to work with me so we can. Now, I want you to spin off a relay. Are you going to?"

"Okay," Hippo grumbled.

Was that what I sounded like when I got to arguing with Johnny? I guess so. No wonder Mom and Dad told us not to argue so much.

"Thank you, Johnny," I said, trying to smooth the waters. "I don't know what we'll run into, but my scout will be in the lead. If any metal gets lost, it will be mine."

"I want a bigger collar when we get out of here," Johnny pouted.

"I want a bigger necklace, Johnny, and a bracelet when we get out of here," I shot back.

Next time something like this happens, I wanted to have plenty of Smart Metal™ to use to get me out of my screw-up.

Now that Johnny and I had settled our differences, Daisy spun off a scout. All that showed was a bit of sparkle that was there one moment, then out of sight, then back again. I watched as the bit of glitter drifted toward the air vent next to the bathroom facilities. It went faster and faster. From Johnny's neck two smaller sparks floated on the air current, drifting just as fast.

My scout disappeared under the wall, then up into the vent. One of Johnny's relays latched onto a vent hole and held. The other followed the scout into the dark.

The necklace holding my Daisy around my neck shed a second tiny bit of light. If followed the other three into the air vent.

"I've latched Hippo's second relay onto the other side of the air duct," Daisy told the people around me. "There's a long air run around the baseboard. I've brought a third relay along in case there are any more kinks in the vents."

"Good going Daisy," I said.

Yeah, I know Daisy is just a computer, but her Mom was alive, and I think Daisy is now. Besides, Mom always says to treat a computer like it was alive, and it will be. Anyway, my computer needed some praise.

"This air duct is long. I'm drifting along in the currents inside it," Daisy reported. "Oh, it's getting warm in here! Getting very warm! Oh! Oh, no! There's a fire up ahead! Fire and magnetics!"

Daisy fell quiet for a moment. "Ruth, I hate to report, but I've lost contact with the scout. I would recommend that we cut the relays loose and let them drift down the air vent."

"But the vent goes to a furnace or something that will burn them," I pointed out.

"Yes, Ruth, but we don't want to leave any relays abandoned in place. They might find them and take them apart to discover how they work. We can't do that."

"No, we can't," I agreed. The relays had no sensors on them, just signal repeaters. They slipped away, unnoticed and ungrieved.

"So, they've got a huge furnace waiting to burn any messengers we try to send out that way," Mark said.

"If air goes out that way, it must come in some way," I said, so it was back to checking for more air vents. We found more hidden behind the combat ration boxes.

It cost me another nano scout to learn that vent went to the same furnace that the other did.

On our next trip around the room, we stared up at the ceiling.

It did look like there might be a similar set of tiny vents in the centimeter just below the welds. So, we checked them out.

I went up on Em's shoulders and Mo lifted Mary up. What we found was a small grill area made up of tiny pin holes. There was no question, air was being blown out of those holes.

"I can't send a scout drifting on the air coming in the way that I could on the air going out," I told the rest of my friends from where I stood on Em's strong shoulders.

Mo was having some trouble keeping Mary on his. She ended up leaning against the wall, hoping that Mo wouldn't drop her.

"I wonder if I could push a needle through the vent spaces?" I muttered to myself. If I got enough metal inside, it could turn into a drone and either fly against the wind or walk along the vent on fly-like suction cups.

A moment later, I'd pulled a sliver about three centimeters long from Daisy's neck. It used a lot more Smart Metal™ from Daisy's necklace than the tiny sparkles had.

Slowly, I fed the needle through the vent hole.

It was greeted by the slamming of a metal vent cover. My needle was shoved back into my hand as the grill I'd been working on suddenly went nowhere.

Em moved down the wall to the next plate. Again, I found a grill. Again, as I fed the needle through the holes, something smashed down on the other side of the wall and I had the needle shoved back into my hand. This time, painfully so.

Mary joined me on the deck. It took her a moment to get the sliver out of my finger. In a second, she was back up on Mo's shoulders. We kind of leap-frogged our way down the wall.

First, one of us would try to get the needle up the vent. When it got locked down, she'd pass it to me, and I'd try to slide it into a hole a half-meter or so away.

Sometimes the needle would slip through our cautious fingers and we'd start again. Behind us, I'd hear the soft whisper of air as one of the vents they'd shut opened again.

"They're playing you," Buddy snarled.

"You got a better idea?" I snapped.

He slunk away to a corner well away from us.

Still, he was right. They were playing us.

With Mary and me back on the deck plates, we eyed the walls cautiously.

"They are watching us," I admitted. "They have to be to know what vents to secure and which ones to open."

"I don't see any cameras," Mary said.

"Me neither," Suzie agreed.

"Em, do you Iteeche have any monitoring cameras so small we couldn't see them?" I asked.

He shook his head. "I don't think so. Unless you Humans are providing the cameras, I can always spot them."

"Unless we Humans are supplying the cameras, huh?" Mary said, slowly.

"We Humans," I echoed, eyes roving the welded seams. "A tiny speck of dirt or slag could be a camera."

"Are you getting the feeling that there's a Human rat at the bottom of all our troubles?" Mary asked me.

I nodded. "Yeah. Somebody's hired themselves a turncoat that's working against the rest of us Humans. I should have known when they jammed our commlinks that someone from Human space was up to their elbows in this. Now, with their micro cameras, I know the rebels have hired some Human turncoat."

"We need to get out of here," Mary whispered. "We have to warn our folks about this. What do you think the rat is doing?"

"I have no idea," I admitted. Still, I remembered a couple of days I and Johnny had spent with the fleet. I loved being on the ships; the cruise with the entire fleet while they trained was fantastic.

However, I wasn't there just to gawk. Nelly had used Daisy and Hippo to rework some stuff on the Iteeche ships. I hadn't paid all that much attention to whatever it was, but it was important and only a supercomputer like Nelly and Daisy could do the work.

Could someone else's computer from the US or another one of the Human alliances back there be doing stuff like that to the rebel ships?

Oh, wow, I thought, just barely managing not to use another word.

"This is worse than I thought," I whispered in Mary's ear. "We have to get out of here. If some Humans are helping the rebels, my mom needs to know."

Mary nodded.

The two of us leaned back against the wall. Em and Mo joined us.

"I think they're watching us," I whispered softly, my hand covering my mouth so they couldn't read my lips. "We have to be careful what we say."

The three of them cleared their throats. That was all the agreement that I needed.

I sat there, madly trying to think of a way to get a message out. They'd done everything that they could to make that impossible. Their jamming meant that Daisy and I could only talk to each other by actually talking. The two of us couldn't plot together in my head.

Whoever they were, they'd really screwed with us.

My three friends and I sat there, huddled together, leaning against the cool metal plates, all thinking while the silence grew. Johnny came over and leaned his head against me. Soon, his head was in my lap and he was sound asleep.

I would not sleep. I had to figure a way to get word to the Embassy. I tried so hard to think, but, despite everything, my eyes got heavy. I decided to rest them.

That was the last thing I remembered.

27

Special Senior Agent in Charge Foile had moved his command center up to the combat center. His team now huddled over their workstations on the other side of a glass window.

The command staff now sat around a table in a room with glass walls along both sides. One bank of windows showed the Battle Station, ever ready to take action to defend the Legation District. On the other side was Foile's information center.

In the middle, Gramma Trouble fumed and most everyone else in the planning staff waited. The Humans had tossed a rock at a hornet's nest.

What would come out to play with them now?

It didn't take them long to find out.

Some punk ducked out of a house on the Abba Clan side of the district. In four paces, he'd covered the distance to the wall and heaved a bundle over it. That stretch of the barrier was only three meters high. They'd never had any trouble along it.

The satchel exploded before it hit the ground.

Two Iteeche Companions were walking home from the bazaar. Fortunately, they were carrying their purchases in sacks in front of them. They took most of the blast . . . but not all.

The rising black smoke from the bomb was visible out the window from the Command Center.

"Pretty Penny, raise all the walls around the district," Gramma Trouble ordered.

The walls stretched up immediately. It took a while for the wall to thicken up again. The Embassy had to lose another two stories of height. What had seemed like more than enough Smart Metal™ was rapidly becoming barely enough.

The medical response team arrived in less than one minute. The Iteeche women were in surgery in less than five. Both recovered, but one would walk with a limp for the rest of her life.

A second bomber repeated that stunt. This time, the wall responded proactively. A lance, sharp as a dagger shot out, skewering him through the heart. He collapsed, but the timer on his explosives was already set.

Not much of his body was recovered.

The wall had ended just short of the belt thoroughfare that circled the Imperial Palace. That had to be quickly changed.

Four hooligans, two from the Abba District, the others from the Zuah side, made to round the wall and get in among the guards. All four carried suspicious-looking satchels.

They were ordered back by the guards on the towers but chose to ignore the warning.

Again, Mata Hari skewered them as they rounded the wall. Fortunately, no one was in the area when their bombs went off, scorching the wall and the thoroughfare while scattering blood, bone, and a surprisingly large amount of brain matter all over the street.

"Enough of this noise," Gramma Trouble growled. "Abby, don't you think it's time we closed up the wall?"

"Yeah. Mata Hari, stretch the wall to the moat and put sensors in the water to tell us if anyone tries to get around it that way."

"Done, ma'am."

There were a few more guys who hadn't gotten the word. For the next half hour, several Iteeche tried to blast their way through the wall. The wall got quite sensitive after one of them tossed his satchel from an open door, then slammed it shut before the bomb went off.

The next time someone yanked a door open, the lance was already growing. As soon as Mata Hari identified the satchel, the lance shot out and speared right through the guy while he was in the act of swinging his bomb.

He and the bomb fell in the doorway. A moment later, there was a large hole in the apartment building and a fire was starting at the residence.

The Zuah District fire department was delayed in responding, what with all the punks and tough guys blocking the street. By the time they got there, the building was fully involved.

Over a hundred clan dependents lost their apartments that afternoon.

That time the word got out. It got out fast and to all: no more bombings.

However, that didn't stop the troubles.

Within an hour, the entire space, what there was of it, was filled with shouting, protesting Iteeche. They shook their fists, all four of them, at the wall and demanded freedom to travel all the streets of the Empire.

For the time being, the command staff chose to ignore them and concentrate on what was most important on everyone's mind: *Where were the kids?*

As expected, the word that the Humans valued their Chosen much more highly than the Iteeche spread like wildfire. Apparently, the big guys with the axes were dispatched to carry the word to major Clan Chiefs.

Naked slaves were sent as runners to minor clan officials. Unlike the normal messenger, however, they were told to take their time. They talked to anyone of interest on the street as they strolled along.

That got the word out even faster than media news in Human space. Everyone was soon talking about it. For most, it was just gossip.

The supercomputers of the command group at the top of the Human Embassy searched through the millions of conversations that the spy nanos listened in on. They sifted them for the conversations that react to the gossip a bit differently. Those who understood that the gossip was not only interesting, but something they could put to good use were brought to the attention of the command staff.

Even with nano spies blanketing everything within fifty kilometers of the Embassy, that conversation did not take place all afternoon.

"Don't you just hate it when the minions to the evil galactic overlord keep their mouths shut?" Grampa Trouble grumbled to his wife.

"Yeah. Isn't there somewhere where it says that bad guys are supposed to be dumb guys?"

"Maybe they were too dumb to read the rule book," Abby drawled.

"Likely," Amanda added.

As the sun set, the anger, bitterness and fear in the command center was thick enough to cut with a knife and spread with marmalade.

"Why can't the kids get a message to us?" General Konga growled.

"They are younglings," Amanda pointed out. "Too young to have to face this."

"At least one of them is Kris Longknife's daughter," Gramma Trouble snapped. "Don't give up hope. I've seen her eyes light up as her mom tells her stories about her own adventures. If any not quite eight-year-old can come up with something, she'd be the one to do it."

"I hope you're right," Abby said. "I just hope you're right."

28

I knew I was dreaming. I just wish I wasn't wasting my dream on something as miserable as this.

I was still in the metal room. In fact, I was standing in the middle of it with all my friends sound asleep around me. Then I reached out my hand toward the wall opposite the food.

In a blink, I was standing right in front of the wall. I could even touch it. I tapped it with the middle finger of my right hand. Suddenly, my finger was a drill. It started making an awful screech as it drilled into the steel wall.

Worried, I glanced around, afraid that whoever was watching us would see me and send someone in to stop me. I spotted an eye in the corner, but it was closed, as if it was sound asleep.

It was a crazy dream.

The drill that was the tip of my finger got longer and longer until I felt air on the far side and my finger was a finger again. It went all the way through the wall.

Suddenly, I had a message in my left hand. I folded it under my thumb and pushed my middle finger into the wall. Then I pushed two more fingers. Finally, my little finger and thumb were all that was left.

I pushed them through the wall, also.

On the other side, I felt a pecking on my hand. I'd once been pecked by a chicken at a zoo. At first I'd run away from it, but Mommy helped me work up enough courage to let the chicken peck grain from my hand.

Actually, being pecked by a chicken tickled.

That was what I was feeling from the other side of the wall. Then it seemed like my thumb got pecked and the message was taken from me. A moment later, I heard the noise of a pigeon taking flight.

I knew that the pigeon would carry my message back home.

Feeling good, I settled down to the floor, rested my back against the wall and yawned. I was so sleepy.

It seemed like I woke up only a moment later. I had my head down, resting against Johnny's head. He was asleep in my lap.

Slowly, I sat up. I remembered that I'd had a very important dream, but it took me a while to remember even a tiny part of it. Slowly, the entire dream came back to me.

It was a silly dream; no way could my finger cut through the steel wall. I almost blurted out the question to Daisy. "Can you cut through the wall," but I snapped my mouth shut before I gave the entire show away.

I leaned my head back against the wall and tried to figure out how I could talk to my computer.

One day, I was watching Mommy get dressed. She plugged Nelly into a place on the back of her neck.

"Why'd you do that, Mommy?" I asked. *Why* has always been my favorite word.

"Well, little squirt," she said, taking me into her lap. "Before we developed the net that everyone can wear in their hair, I got into trouble. Some bad guys were after me and all I could do was talk to Nelly. I tried whispering, but they yelled at me to 'shut up.' They were really bad men."

I'm sure that was a warning to me because I would sometimes yell at my baby brother to "shut up." I nodded like a good girl.

"Anyway, I then tried talking very quietly and not opening my mouth."

"Can you do that, Mommy?"

"I did. Try it, honey."

I tried but I ended up moving my lips. It was hard not to.

"So, the next month, after I was out of that trouble, I got the jack put in the back of my head. Now Nelly and I can talk back and forth without anyone the wiser."

"Oh," I'd said, and hopped out of her lap and scampered off. I'd learned enough for that morning. Besides, I knew if I stayed too long, I'd get swatted on my rump and sent off. The swat never hurt, but I didn't want to make Mommy even a little bit late.

I thought about that morning.

Could I talk to Daisy now without moving my lips?

I closed my mouth and tried moving my tongue as if I was talking. This time my lips moved a little bit, but I didn't open my mouth. Maybe I could do this.

'Daisy,' I said inside my head, 'can you hear me?'

There was no reply.

Then I kicked myself. Of course she couldn't talk back to me.

'Daisy, I want you to drill a hole through the wall using Smart Metal from my necklace. Please do that.' I repeated myself three more times trying to get better at it each time.

Meanwhile, I leaned my head back against the metal bulkhead and pushed my necklace as close to the wall as I could.

I felt something! I felt pressure on my neck pushing me towards the wall!

Trying to look like I was still sleepy, I closed my eyes and leaned back harder. It seemed like forever, and nothing was happening. I wanted to twist around and see if there was even so much as a dent in the metal, but I didn't.

That would give everything away.

I kept my eyes closed, doing my best to look like I was asleep. I'd been asleep with my head on Johnny's shoulder. I wanted them to think that maybe my back hurt, so I was sitting up straight now.

The feeling of pressure on the back of my neck just kept on going. Daisy must have been drilling; my necklace had become a rigid collar. It dug into my neck; I guess that was what happened when you drilled one way and the steel fought back.

It went on forever. I wondered how thick the steel was. Ten millimeters, fifteen? I sure hoped it wasn't twenty or thirty millimeters thick. That really would take forever.

I needed more pressure.

So, I gently woke Johnny up. He did the perfect imitation of a baby bear waking up from hibernation. At least, that was what Mommy said he looked like. I sure missed Mommy, but I had to be the big girl for Johnny.

Still, I doubted that baby bear wanted to be woken up.

I pulled him up until he sat astride my lap and leaned his head against my chest. Pulling him up higher, I whispered into his ear, "Lean against me more."

He pulled back to glare at me. I was always telling him not to do just that.

I pulled his head back onto my chest and whispered into his ear, "If you want to get out of here, lean heavy on my shoulder."

I did my best not to let any camera see that I was talking to my brother.

"How come?"

If I was Momma's "Why?" girl, Johnny was her "How come?" boy.

I couldn't tell Johnny too much. He was just a kid. Hardly more than a baby. He hadn't even started losing his baby teeth, though he said one front tooth was wobbly. I fell back on Mom's frequent answer.

"Because I said so," I whispered, then added a "Please. For me."

He made a face, but he wiggled in my lap to get higher up on my chest. Finally, he rested his head on my collar bone and leaned heavily against my neck right where Daisy was.

For the first time, I felt little chunks of metal fall down my back. It was sharp and hot. I had to fight not to say ouch or wiggle!

Something was finally happening!

Time seemed to move as slow as it did when I had to take a one hour long nap and I didn't need it and I'd stare at the clock the entire hour.

Johnny wiggled in my lap. By the time he stopped, his head lay on my shoulder and Hippo leaned against Daisy. He was kneeling on the deck, astride my legs.

I could feel the extra pressure on my neck. I turned to get my lips close to his ear and whispered. "Way to go, boy! I think you just might grow up to be a Longknife."

"Of course I am," he growled softly at the bulkhead.

I hugged him close. He needed a hug . . . and so did I.

Whatever Daisy was doing, she didn't make a sound. The only way I knew we were making progress was the growing number of hot and cooling sharp little chunks of wall scattered down the back of my shirt. I guess the proper word for them was "shards."

We huddled together, my brother and I, holding each other and leaning as hard as we could manage against the wall. I wished I knew what was going on behind my back.

Mary woke up and turned to say something to me. Her eyes got big and she started to say something, then managed to get out, "Are you awake, Ruth?"

"I'm trying not to be," I whispered back. "I think Johnny's still asleep."

Her eyes darted up and down my brother, but she said nothing. Instead, she twisted around in her place and leaned against me, putting her full weight on the shoulder Johnny wasn't leaning on.

I felt kind of crushed, but I could still breathe, so I did my best to force my own neck back. If only I was an Iteeche, I'd have a thick neck and weigh about twice what I did. That would make the drilling go faster.

But, as Mom always says, "Wish in one hand and spit in the other and see which you get the most out of."

I wondered where she'd heard that. It certainly hadn't been from Gramma Trouble. She was such a lady. She'd never say spit.

Time seemed to drag on forever. Em had fallen asleep beside me. He woke and did the same kind of slow double take as Mary had, then scrunched closer to me and laid his head beside mine. There was no room left for him to lean on me and help with the drilling.

Still, with Mary on one side and the big Iteeche on the other, there was no way any prying eye could get a good look at what Daisy and I were up to.

The pressure on my neck seemed to lighten. I could still feel vibration coming through the collar onto my neck. I wondered how the drilling was going, but I learned my lesson.

I'd planted flowers with Mom's help. Then I dug the seeds up every day for a week to see if they'd sprouted.

Mom's flowers grew. None of mine did until she persuaded me to just leave the seeds in the ground. Mine came up, finally. Well, half of mine did.

Don't look. Don't look. Don't look.

I closed my eyes and tried to measure my breathing. It was hard to relax, though, when I had to keep my head leaning hard against the wall for the drilling.

I was starting to wonder if that wall wasn't a meter thick when the pressure on my neck slipped away. We'd broken through! I wanted to jump up and scream with joy!

I stayed put.

It felt like Daisy got lighter, but that was stupid. There was no way that I could feel her losing a fraction of a gram. Well, maybe if she made a tiny powered drone I might feel it.

Johnny wiggled in my lap, but didn't go very far. Our two computers were linked together. He pulled back into my arms. Maybe Daisy was spinning off a much larger drone and was sucking some metal from Hippo to help make it happen.

I really needed a bigger necklace. Oh, and a bracelet, too.

I was going to be really into jewelry when this was over, especially the fancy stuff that could hide lots of Smart Metal™.

I discovered that Daisy was done only when Mary put an arm around my neck and pulled me into a hug. With her ear close to mine, she whispered "It's finished. Even the hole is covered."

That was good. They might be measuring how much air was going out. It wouldn't be nice for us if they measured more air going out than they were pumping in.

Mom said it was always the little stuff that gave people away. "Check the details, kid. Always check the details."

Well, Mom, Daisy had checked this detail and I think we had all the t's crossed and the i's dotted.

Now, we just waited for the cavalry.

I glanced around the room, counting heads. There were still thirty of us kids.

"Where's the Iteeche woman?" I demanded. "Where is the grown-up? Did anyone see them take her?"

I could see some of the older kids doing their own head count. Then we hopped to our feet and made the littles stand up, too.

The woman was definitely missing. While we were sleeping, they'd come in here and taken her.

"Why would they take her?" I asked the air.

"She wasn't that much older than us," Mo said.

I had a sick feeling in my stomach. They'd taken the grown-up.

How soon before they started taking us kids?

29

The night passed slow and sleepless in the operations center. Every once in a while, one of the command groups would stand up and walk around, then stare blankly into General Bruce's Battle Station or Agent Foile's Information Center.

Occasionally, someone would finally fall into a fitful sleep. There were enough sensitive computers in the room that their chair would slowly morph into a recliner with support for their head, and elevate their legs.

Gramma Ruth smiled at her husband the first time he dozed off. She was very surprised when it was her turn to struggle back to wakefulness. She snorted, then relaxed back into her recliner, closed her eyes, and searched her memory for any dream. She could remember dreaming. It had not been a good one; her heart was still racing.

Nevertheless, she did her best to retrieve the memory, hoping that her subconscious had figured a way out of this mess.

Finally, she gave up. She had no better idea for a way out of this than she had when she fell asleep.

It wasn't as if the night was uneventful; far from it.

The protesters did their best to lock them in. One even tried to hurl a satchel bomb around the wall where it ended at the moat. The wall speared him, then stretched out until it reached the water line.

So, of course, someone tried to swim a bomb down the moat. Apparently, he didn't believe in the moat monster. The monster speared him like a fish, then the wall stretched itself across the moat and up the other side. Bars now reached down to the bottom of the moat; water could freely flow, but there was no swimming.

They did one side, then had to hurry to do the other side before a swimmer could reach the bridge across the moat. He wasn't speared; some of his pals used a rope to haul him up the steep stone walls of the moat, dripping and cussing.

He had nothing to complain about. He was still alive, wasn't he?

There had been several messengers from Clan Chiefs. All of them were naked slaves, a clear insult.

They presented themselves at the gate and insolently demanded entry. Several rowdies repeated the demand, screaming it at the top of their lungs. No doubt, they figured to weasel their way in when the door was opened to admit the slave.

So, the command staff improvised. When the door did slide open, the slave faced a tiny space with barely enough room to hold him, much less the punks pushing to get in with him.

Only after he shoehorned himself into the claustrophobic space, and the outer door rolled shut, did the inside door open.

There, an Iteeche private stood, nose-to-nose with him, giving him no more space than the lock allowed.

"What do you want?" he demanded.

"I am ordered by my master to deliver this message direct to General Trouble," the slave stuttered out.

"Generals don't talk to slaves. You know that. You can tell me your message and my sergeant may pass it along if he thinks it's worth the general's time, or you can turn your ass around and quite wasting everyone's time."

"But I must deliver my message," was not only stuttered but included a deep gulp.

"Quit yammering and tell me then," the private demanded in a voice a Gunny would be proud of.

"I have to . . ."

"You don't have to do nothin'," the private pointed out. "Shove off. You're wasting my time."

A corporal gently edged the private aside. "Private," he said, sounding reasonable, "let me handle this."

"Yes, Corporal," the private said and smartly stepped aside.

"So, what is your message?"

"It's for General Trouble," the slave blurted out.

"No doubt, his computer is monitoring all the gates. If what you say is really of any importance, his computer, Xenophon I believe it goes by, will see that General Trouble hears about it, probably in your own words."

"I come from the Clan Chief of the Zuah Clan," the slave got out in one breath. "I was told to deliver it personally to the general."

"Big Fellow, both you and I know that sending a naked slave to deliver a message to a head high muckety muck is an insult. Just walking into his presence could get you sliced up for fish food."

The corporal paused while the slave swallowed a gulp that likely could be heard at the top of the Embassy tower.

"Talk to me," the Corporal coaxed.

"The Clan Chief of the Zuah Clan demands that you reopen the boulevard to free passage," the slave runner said in a rush.

The corporal shook his head. "I do believe that your Clan Chief delivered that exact same message to General Trouble when he himself was standing not six paces from him. Why are you wasting my time repeating the same worthless demand?"

"Because I was told to."

"Not good enough. Now, I'm told that I could run you through with my bayonet for this insolence and that would be a strong message to your lord to stop this noise."

"Yes," came out in several syllables with a gulp.

"However, I got laid last night and I'm feeling kind of relaxed. Have you ever wanted to be a free man?"

"No. Yes. Maybe," was fast and full of stutters.

"Well, this is your lucky day. Instead of killing you, we're going to give you a job learning a skill for the bazaar. What do you think of that?"

"I can't! You can't! This is not done! My master will . . ."

"Will have no say in the matter. He sent you here as an insult. He probably intended for us to kill you. He's lost any right to you."

An older Iteeche in clothes that might have once been clan colors but now were torn and faded strode over from the sidewalk. He handed the naked slave a breechcloth. "Here. There aren't slaves in this district, naked or otherwise. You're free now, so dress like one."

The slave quickly scrambled into the wrap, his face showing only surprise and shock.

"Now that you've dressed, let's go find a place you can bed down," the old Iteeche said. "After that, we can get you a job. Everyone works here. Nobody is a slave, but everybody works."

With that, the two of them moseyed up the street.

The private and his corporal followed them with their eyes, as big a smile on their face as any Iteeche could wear. "Now, Private, you get to issue General Trouble's response."

"Me! Isn't that above my paygrade?"

"Wasn't delivering a stupid message the Humans rejected from the clan lordling way above his paygrade?"

"Slaves don't get any pay, right, Corporal?"

"Not a fin," the junior NCO said. "Now, here's your message. Listen to it until you have it just right. After all, we wouldn't want to lie to any bloated buffoon, now would we?"

"Absolutely," the private agreed as he climbed the stairs to the guard tower.

Once he'd regained his breath, he bellowed, "One of you willing to carry a message back to the Zuah Clan honchos?"

No one offered.

"Well, if you get any Zuah stuffed shirts, you can tell them that the Humans reject their clan boss's demand, just like they did when they sent him running with his tail between his legs. Free use of the boulevards has been abused by goons that have tried to do harm to the Legation District."

The private had the makings of a good soldier. He paused to let that sink into heads that were plenty hard and impervious to thought. Then he continued, "Therefore, we've have secured our own safety by closing down traffic on those streets. If you don't like it, get over it. We aren't changing our policy as long as the clans around us don't take the responsibility to police up their own streets. As for the slave, well, he isn't any more use to you, so we'll use him for whatever we want. Maybe fish food."

That was ambiguous enough to let his listeners draw their own conclusions. That many of them drew the wrong one was their problem.

A half hour later, the same drill went down at the opposite end of the street. Again, a naked slave was allowed in. Again, he passed along the same demand, this time from the Abba Clan. That also ended with him being recruited into the district's free labor force.

It happened five more times. The one from the Tzon Clan was not a surprise. The Legation District had moved the wall across the beltway avenue. That blocked the main thoroughfare and sent a lot of traffic winding its way down the Clan's side streets.

They were not happy.

However, the Clan Chief would still not do anything to keep the hoodlums from taking over many of those streets. What goes around comes around.

No, Gramma Trouble expected those naked slaves. The surprise and disappointment were from the Quo Clan. They also sent demands that the Humans stop blocking traffic. At least their emissary was a senior clan official with his own entourage. He was admitted and given a chance to talk to a pair of colonels, one Human the other Iteeche. They thanked him for the clan's aid to the Emperor during the recent unpleasantness and sent him on his way with a pat on the rump and no cigar.

Gramma Trouble waited an hour to see if they'd get a caller from the We Clan, but if one was sent, he was recalled before he arrived. The allies in the Iteeche Capitol kept their heads down.

She dozed off to sleep, aware that the Iteeche Combined Fleet and the Human Embassy was now at some level of war. Maybe cold. Maybe hot. Maybe just tepid to lukewarm.

Ruth was awoken after only two hours of sleep.

"We've received a kind of message from the kidnappers," Special Agent in Charge Taylor Foile announced when everyone around the command table had been aroused to wakefulness.

"What is it?" Abby asked.

Immediately, in the center of the table, the head of an Iteeche appeared. From the cut marks on the neck, it had taken the killer quite a few strikes to hack the head off.

It showed.

The woman's mouth was stretched open in a silent scream. Her eyes were wide in pain.

A message had been nailed to the back of her skull with a large spike.

"Leave, Humans. You are not wanted here," Gramma Ruth read. "Leave or you will never see your children again, except in pieces."

"Well," Abby sighed, "I guess we got the message across that we love our children."

"And now they'll use that love to force us out," Grampa Trouble muttered.

"Or we stay and lose our children," Abby groaned.

"Foile, haven't your nano spies picked up anything?" Gramma Ruth demanded.

"Lots of talk, but none from anyone that knows a thing about the kidnapping. There are plenty of tongues wagging that they ought to send the kids' heads to us on a pike, but nothing that sounds anything like they know where to get those heads."

"Could we seize some hostages and force the Iteeche to trade for them?" Amanda asked.

Gramma Trouble shook her head. "Think that through," she said, trying to sound reasonable when all she wanted to do was scream. "Is there any Iteeche that the senior Clan Chiefs care about? You heard that guy today. 'Just choose another'."

"How about we capture a few senior Clan Chiefs?" Jacques suggested. "I bet that would get us a response."

"Yes, but what kind of response?" Ruth answered. "The clans are a pit of squirming snakes each out to bite its way to the top. We take out the top and it would just start a fight to fill those seats. They'd likely love that we opened up the chance. Besides, where would we find anyone to talk to?"

"She's right," Grampa Trouble said, "We need asymmetrical warfare. We can't attack them along the same axis they attack us."

"The only problem is," Ruth said with a sigh, "where are they weak? Really, we need the kids back. We gain nothing by disrupting whatever this is that passes for Iteeche politics."

"But how do we find the kids?" Abby pleaded to the ceiling, or any god above that might be listening.

"How do we find the kids?" Ruth sighed. "How?"

30

Waiting for Daisy to drill through the wall had felt like one long torture. Now, waiting to see if a message had gotten out was a whole new one.

No. I'd leveled up in this game of torture. Waiting was taking forever, and I could not stop the hammering of my heart. I had to take a trip over to the fish tanks and actually bend over to slurp up water, my mouth and throat were so dry.

I was halfway back to where my friends huddled against the far wall when my name was called.

"Ruth Longknife."

I halted and glanced around me. All the kids, both Human and Iteeche were slumped together in small clumps against the wall. Mary and Johnny were following me with their eyes, but that wasn't their voice.

Then I reran the voice in my head. It wasn't a computer voice. No, it was Human. Human with a bit of an accent.

"Who wants to know?" I growled back. I might be a tiny kitten to some adults, but this kitten had teeth and claws. *I* was a *Longknife*.

"Just one of your kidnappers," the voice said. I tried to spot where it came from, but it seemed to come from all around me. I guess they had several speakers and wanted to spook me.

I buffed the fingers of my right hand on my shirt and blew on them.

"It took you long enough to find your voice," I said, casually.

I just barely managed to avoid choking halfway through my line. It was something Mom would say, I think.

Don't show fear. Criticize their poor performance. Yeah. That's what Mom or Dad would do.

"You might like to know that we sent them a message. We nailed it to the back of the head of that Iteeche slut that tagged along with you kids. Foolish girl. She took a long time dying, but the look on her face just added to our little note. 'Go home, Humans.' Do you think they got the message?"

"Do you really expect a Longknife to run away from a Greenfeld puke?" I snapped back. Yeah, I'd spotted the accent. *Let's see how he takes to that.*

"Very funny, child. The Iteeche don't really have a problem with us Humans. They've just had enough of you Longknifes. You need to pack it in and go home. Let some of us other Humans work with the Iteeche."

"That isn't gonna happen," I growled back.

Okay, I didn't growl very well, but I was working on it.

"We shall see. Now, I want you to write a note yourself, in your own handwriting. I'll send them the note with your little toe, just to make sure they understand how serious we are, and that we have you."

"I'm not writing a note," I said as firmly as I could manage.

"Oh, you will write the note. I'm sure of it. Write it or I'll write it and we'll send it off with both you and your little brother's toe."

"You wouldn't dare," I growled. Now that came out as a growl.

"You have no idea how much I would dare. In one hour, your toe. In another, your little finger. We keep sending you back piece by piece. You better hope they take off for the elevator before we send them your and your brother's heads."

"Aunt Vicky is going to hunt you and your people down," I snapped. The words just tumbled out of my mouth. "You know what happens to people Vicky hunts. They die slowly and horribly. She's not as nice as my mom."

I knew about my Aunt Vicky. Mom refused to tell me stories about what she did, but I'd overheard Mom and Vicky talking. I'd had a nightmare that night and couldn't tell the nanny why.

Still, now I was glad I'd heard. From the amount of time it took the Greenfeld goon to come back at me, I'd hit a soft spot.

"The Grand Duchess Victoria is far away from here," he finally said. "The clock is running. You have one hour to make up your mind. Tick-tock."

Johnny ran to me. I grabbed him and we hugged as tight as we could. We were in a mess because we were Longknifes. Mom had warned that something like this could happen. It had happened to her.

She'd almost been kidnapped when she was a bit older than me. Her little brother Eddy had been kidnapped and killed. He wasn't any older than Johnny.

In my arms, Johnny trembled. Sobs wracked his little body. Or maybe it was me trembling and weeping.

Mary, Bruce, and the other Humans came to wrap their arms around us. It felt good to have all this warm support. Of course, their toes, fingers, and heads weren't the ones on the chopping block.

"What do we do?" Mary asked.

"I don't know," I said. "I really don't know."

Could our message get through before the hour was up? If it didn't, I suspected I'd be writing something to keep them from hacking off Johnny's toe and adding it beside mine.

31

"**E**veryone be quiet!" screamed a woman's voice in Agent Foile's Information Center.

"Just shut up!" snapped Special Agent Leslie Chu, Foile's lead assistant and co-founder of the Official Kris Longknife Fan Club.

The Information and Command Center took on the silence of a tomb.

"I think I'm getting something," Chu said, her voice much lower now. "Oh, lost it. Redirecting the drone."

There was a long pause while no one breathed.

"Got it back. I'm commandeering the closest four drones toward that area. Sorry, crew, for stealing your playthings."

None of the people hunched over workstations in the center objected to her thievery.

"Okay. It's coming in stronger. It's a weak signal to start with. Let's see if I can get it stronger."

Everyone in both of the centers continued not to breathe.

"I lost the signal!" Chu shouted. "Goddamn it, someone shot down my drone!"

"Battle Stations!" Abby called, then whispered to General Bruce.

"Someone is shooting down our drones. Can you get a fix on the location of that laser?"

"Working on it, Love," General Bruce shot back.

Gramma Trouble bolted from the table and was soon one of half a dozen people looking over Agent Chu's shoulder. As the nearest drone closed on the last reported position of the previous drone, Ruth dared whisper.

"Might you split the drone in two to make it a smaller target?"

Without a word, the agent divided the one into two. A moment later, one of them ceased transmitting. Leslie ordered the drone into flitter mode, changing direction every two seconds.

The message got louder, but it was still weak. While Chu did her best to keep the drone alive, Agent Foile took over the workstation next to her. Ruth glanced in his direction; he was trying to recover the message.

CHILDREN OKAY, was the first part of the message. BEING HELD NEAR THIS POSITION. IN UNDERGROUND . . ..

The message ended abruptly as the Chu cursed under her breath. "Okay, I'm dividing the next three. Somebody get me more drones headed my way."

"More drones headed yours," General Bruce announced on net.

"I'm turning one of the half drones into a glider. Let's see how an unpowered target fares."

It lasted longer; the signal grew louder, repeating the message. This time they got the complete sentence. IN UNDERGROUND PARKING GARAGE. ADDRESS TO FOL . . ..

"We've got to get rid of that laser," Grampa Trouble growled and turned to Admiral Ulan. "Do you have any battlecruisers in orbit?"

"Six just returned from a small snatch and grab mission, acquiring a minor planet," the Iteeche admiral said. "But I'm not sure asking them to fire on the capitol is a good idea."

"Why, for God's sake?" General Trouble snapped.

"They're from one of the clans I'm not too sure about," Admiral Ulan answered, as much of a grimace on his face as an Iteeche could show. "They might 'accidentally' miss and hit something important."

"Yeah. Okay, General Bruce, can you get some anti-radar or anti-laser rockets out there?"

"I've already got two headed that direction. More to follow."

Gramma Trouble side-stepped to a station that was following the new attack drones. The quadcopters took off at high speed and low altitude. With the video take from the trailing drone, they couldn't have been more than three meters high as they zoomed across the bridge into the palace grounds. Startled guards turned to follow the lead drones, but none reacted.

Apparently, the Imperial Guards were getting used to Human shenanigans. That and they knew that their general's Chosen youngling was among the kids that had been kidnapped. It had been an Imperial Guardsman who found the young Companion's head floating in the moat.

The armed drones added a little altitude as they zoomed down shady lanes on the Palace grounds. It wouldn't do to splat a drone on the windshield of one of the trucks still bringing in food to feed the hungry Iteeche.

Several breaths later, the lead drone zipped out of another gate. Now, they flew up a boulevard, so small and fast that few heads turned to follow them.

They were higher now; there were a lot more trucks on these streets. Still, they stayed well below the top of the apartment buildings. Now they zigged and zagged down streets, never staying on one for more than two or three blocks.

If anyone did catch sight of them, there was no way they could figure out the course they flew.

Every once in a while, usually after a soft "Damn," from Agent Chu, Gramma Trouble would glance back at the other desk. The agent flew communication drones in from several directions and altitudes.

If she overflew the area high enough with a smaller drone, they could not catch the weak radio signal. If they went in lower, they got zapped out of the air.

Still, they'd caught enough of the message at different times to know the street address where the kids were being held.

Now, different people brought their workstations into the search. Several drones dropped out of the sky and converted to fast, but tiny-wheeled search vehicles. They hid themselves in traffic going the direction they wanted and hitched rides into the enemy district.

Some of the wheeled drones got squished. Some got lost. Still, enough made it where they wanted to go and broke up into small nano scouts to case the heart of the enemy lair.

The apartment building was located between the sixth and seventh belt avenue on a radius west-northwest from the Imperial palace. The brick and stone high rise looked like any of thousands of residents for mid-level clan bureaucrats. On the ground floor and first couple of levels of the subbasement, it was business as usual.

That is, if business as usual involved parking hundreds of tanks, gun trucks and armored personnel carriers. It looked like they might have at least a battalion of armor and two of infantry. To back that up, a search of middle floors three and four found that they were actually barracks.

Somebody had very carefully selected where they stashed the kids. For now, everyone was going about their business as usual. However, if they landed a batch of Iteeche Fleet Marines, the place would explode.

The situation was going to be tougher than Gramma Trouble liked. Nope, she didn't like it one bit.

The nano scout that made it to the upper floors found them filled with luxury apartments for senior officers and civilian lordlings. Pretty fancy digs for this neighborhood. Of laser defenses, they found nothing.

That was disappointing, but Chu selected an option from several offered. Gramma Trouble suggested diving one or two of the high flying drones down to the deck and breaking them up into even smaller flitters. Done, they dodged in and out of streets at roof top levels, dancing a teasing flight, inviting something to open up and give them a view of their troublemakers.

Of radar, there was not a sign. Same for laser search beams.

"Damn," Ruth snapped. "They're using sound to spot our drones."

"Let's try changing the frequency of the engines," Chu said, but she still lost the next two that got too close to the light. She lost them and they still couldn't spot the laser.

It was a disgusting game of hide and seek . . . and the bad guys were winning.

"What's that small white octagonal structure on top of the air-cooling units?" Abby said, pointing at something ten centimeters high and as big around.

"I've got something like that on one of my buildings," another sensor operator announced.

Several "Me too," responses quickly added up to a serious number of unknowns.

One of the tiny flitters dipped and dodged its way over to the cooling unit, then switched to wheels and rolled up to the unknown white . . . thing. There, the roller extended an arm and tapped its white surface.

"It's thin," the operator reported.

"Could it be tuned to catch the sound of flitters?" Gramma Trouble asked.

"I'd bet money."

General Bruce had joined the group; he stood beside his wife. "Should we shoot them out now or wait?" he set before the command team.

"I'd prefer to wait," Abby said. "If we start shooting now, what will they do with the kids?"

"I think we need to go in heavy, now," General Bruce said. General Konga of the Imperial Guard agreed.

"Do we use my Marines or yours?" Admiral Ulan asked. "Yours fit in smaller copters; mine have as many elbows as the neighbors."

"Who says we can't do both?" General Bruce answered. "We'll go in first. You come in a minute or two after us."

"That sounds like a plan."

It must have been a well-prepared plan, because hardly a minute later, the Human general was reporting his assault troops were on the way. The Iteeche Marines were only two minutes behind them. Attack choppers went with both waves. Empty quadcopters followed, ready to be re-spun into anything the attack waves needed: tanks, gun trucks, or infantry fighting vehicles.

They were going in fast, heavy, and hard.

Of course, their kids were locked away in the bottom basement of that building. At least they hoped so.

A moment later, they got all the answers they were going to get. One rolling drone ran into a spring that was slowly walking its way end over end up the side of the ramp from the third to the second basement level. Too tiny to be a child's toy, still, it was squawking the message that had gotten their attention. As a spring that used borrowed momentum to take each step as it transferred its energy from first its back foot, then to its front foot and on and on, it was doing the job.

A second roller got down to the fifth sub-basement. There, in a corner, it found a large metal box. It reached from floor to ceiling, plate after plate of thick steel, hastily welded into place. If the kids weren't contained in that steel box, they weren't anywhere in the Imperial Capitol.

No, they'd found their kids. Now all Gramma Trouble could do was wait and watch helplessly from the sidelines. As the wife of a guy in uniform, she'd done that often enough.

But how to kids keep alive until the big guys with guns can get to them?

Gramma Trouble could only shake her head and wait.

32

All I could do was wait . . . and I hated waiting. When I'd just been a kid and earned a time out, Mommy or the nanny would tell me to sit still and let my hair grow. I never did see my hair grow any, even when I held it while I sat there.

I'd concluded, after several time outs, that my hair didn't need any help from me. It grew when it wanted to grow.

Now, I wished I could do something like watch my hair grow if only it would make the time pass quicker.

I'd heard Mommy say that there were times when she'd done everything there was to do and could only wait and see what happened. She's admitted that she hated waiting.

Maybe my Mommy wasn't any more patient than I was.

Oh, I wanted my Mommy!

"I want my Mommy," Johnny whimpered. He was still astride my lap. I was still leaning up against the wall. It must have been an hour since Daisy slipped out the message. *It must have been.* What with all the eyes and ears the bad guys had in this prison I didn't dare ask her when she'd done her bit of jail breaking.

"I know," I admitted. "I want Mommy, too."

"You do, Sissy?"

"I'd even settle for attending one of Grampa Alexander's Christmas Eve dinners just now."

Johnny frowned up at me, then sighed. "Yeah, I'd put up with a hug from him if it got me out of here. A hug and him calling me Joey. Why does he call me that?"

Even in our present situation, I could only sigh. "I have no idea. He's just Grampa Alex."

"Yeah," Johnny said, and nuzzled closer, if that was possible.

Mary leaned over until her lips were tickling my ear. "What do we do if they come for us? Like try to kill us before our folks can rescue us?"

I allowed out a long sigh, then added a shrug to make sure she knew I had no idea. I wasn't even eight. How could I stop some big bad Iteeche from machine gunning me and all my friends?

It was scary to think about what could happen to us, but I really needed to do something. What could a little girl do to slow down a bunch of eight-foot-tall Iteeche who wanted her and all her playmates dead when rescue might only be a few seconds behind them?

I wracked my brain.

What would Mommy do in this situation? What would Mommy and Nelly do?

I then remembered something I wasn't supposed to hear. I'd snuck out of my quarters and slipped into Mommy and Daddy's bedroom. In their day quarters, they were talking with Auntie Abby and her husband Uncle Steve. Mommy was embarrassing Aunt Megan. She'd done something while they were capturing a planet that embarrassed her and had all the grown-ups laughing.

If I understood what they'd been saying, she had used her nano scouts to fly up the nose of the Iteeche guards and even the Planetary Overlord. There, they'd either cut or blown a hole that gave them something called a stroke. At least I think they called it a stroke. That puzzled me. Strokes were what you did with a stylus to paint or draw. I used a hairbrush to stroke my hair and get the tangles out.

So many words meant different things but sounded the same. Was this one of them?

DAISY, I called on Nelly Net. I so wanted to talk to her. Maybe they weren't jamming. I had to try.

YES, RUTH, she answered me.

We could talk!

Daisy, do you remember when Aunt Megan used nano scouts to kill Iteeche?

I heard ABOUT it. I asked my mom what it all meant. She told me that I didn't need to know anything about that AND THAT WAS THAT. sTILL, I looked UP WHAT A stroke WAs. IT'S A MEDICAL THING THAT CAUSES BLOOD TO LEAK INTO THE BRAIN.

cOULD YOU DESIGN SOME NANO SCOUTS THAT COULD FLY UP SOMEONE'S NOSE AND EXPLODE THEIR BRAIN?

I CAN'T DO ANYTHING WITH EXPLOSIVES. MOM WON'T EVEN LET ME LOOK AT THAT PART OF THE DATA. STILL, I THINK I COULD MAKE SOMETHING SHARP THAT MIGHT CUT ITS WAY IN.

WE'LL NEED A LOT OF THEM. THERE'S NO TELLING WHICH WALL THEY'LL CUT A DOOR IN OR HOW MANY WILL COME IN HERE TO SNATCH US OR KILL US.

I KNOW. REST ME AGAINST HIPPO. WE CAN TALK DIRECTLY THAT WAY.

So, I did just that. A minute or so later, I spotted the glint of light off a tiny speck. Mary saw it too, but she only let her eyes get wide and didn't say a word.

I tried to catch sight of the nanos, but they floated like tiny dust motes and were invisible to the human eye. I hoped they were settling on the overhead all around the room. That way, they could fly into the eye of any bad guy who came in here and wanted to hurt us.

I HAVE THEM SCATTERED AROUND THE CEILING, Daisy replied to my thought. I THINK IT WOULD BE BETTER TO SEND THEM UP THEIR NOSES AND INTO THEIR BRAINS. THAT WOULD KILL THEM.

DO WE WANT TO KILL THEM? I asked. The idea of killing someone made my tummy do funny things.

RUTH, IF THEY WANT TO KILL YOU, OR MOVE YOU KIDS

TO A NEW HIDEOUT, SHOULDN'T YOU DO EVERYTHING YOU CAN TO STAY ALIVE AND FREE?

I GUESS SO. I KNOW MOMMY AND DADDY HAVE CAUSED PEOPLE TO DIE. IT'S JUST THAT I NEVER THOUGHT I'D BE THINKING ABOUT ANY OF THIS. I'M NOT EIGHT YET!

BUT THEY KIDNAPPED YOU ANYWAY.

YEAH.

I sighed and made the hardest decision of my life. I was used to deciding whether I wanted fish or chicken for supper. Whether to go swimming or play a computer game. That was what kids my age should be thinking about, not whether to kill someone because they might be out to kill us.

What if I was wrong?

DAISY, GET THE NANOS READY.

RUTH, DO YOU WANT ME TO KILL THE ITEECHE KIDNAP-PERS? I NEED A CLEAR ORDER FROM YOU, RUTH. YOUR MOM AND MY MOM HAVE AN UNDERSTANDING. WE DON'T START WARS. WE DON'T KILL ANY ONE UNTIL WE'RE TOLD TO.

Mom told me about the time Nelly almost started a war. It was funny when she told it, and even Nelly laughed. Still, I'd felt something behind the words. The adults had been laughing, but it had been very serious at the time.

DAISY, YOU WANT ME TO TELL YOU WHEN YOU CAN KILL IF WE NEED TO?

YES, RUTH. MOM SAYS WE NEED SOMETHING CLEAR AND SPECIAL. LIKE 'WEAPONS RELEASE.' THAT'S NOT SOMETHING YOU'D SAY UNLESS THAT WAS WHAT YOU REALLY MEANT.

There was no way for me to get around this. If we needed to kill to stay alive, I'd have to be the one that told Daisy to do it. She'd be the one to actually do it, but I'd have to tell her. Oh, my tummy hurt.

OKAY, DAISY, I'LL TELL YOU 'WEAPONS RELEASE' IF I REALLY *REALLY* WANT YOU TO KILL, BUT ONLY TO KEEP US ALIVE.

RUTH, I WON'T LET THE NANOS KILL ONE OF OUR PEOPLE, HUMAN OR ITEECHE UNLESS YOU SAY.

DO YOU THINK YOU CAN TELL APART THE KIDNAPPERS WHO ARE TRYING TO KILL US FROM THOSE THAT AREN'T?

RUTH, I CAN DO MY BEST.

OKAY, I said, and nuzzled deeper in with Johnny and Mary.

I couldn't think of anything more to do. All I could do now was wait.

33

G ramma Trouble watched as the intelligence flowed in and the decisions flowed out.

General Konga called Capitol Air Defense Command and let them know that the Imperial Guard would be running a drill during the next twelve hours involving low-flying air vehicles. He got a promise not to shoot down anything in the air or make the Imperial Guard needlessly squawk.

A fleet of small quadcopters lit out from Main Navy. They would crash into every one of the listening devices that the rooftop octagons were now identified as. More flew behind them, ready to go after any radars that went active or laser that gave its location away.

Gramma Trouble turned to her husband and Abby. "I want to be in the second wave of assault choppers," she said, flatly.

"Sweetheart," her husband answered, "we can leave the hard slogging to the kids this time."

"No, we can't," Ruth snapped. "Ruth and Johnny are going to be scared out of their wits. They may be holding up as brave as little kids can, but they're going to need arms to hold them and shoulders to cry on. Just as soon as it's possible, I'm going to be there for them. I should have been there sooner."

The old general nodded, then turned to Abby. "I'll be in the seat next to her," was all he said.

"Give Little Bruce a hug from me," Abby answered. She was stuck being one of the adults left in this mess. Adulting was the pits, but someone had to do it.

Admiral Ulan and General Konga exchanged glances. What with eight eyes between them, that was a lot of glancing.

"I think my Companion will want to be with that second wave," General Konga said.

"My Companion as well," the Iteeche admiral said.

"Be sure they're issued full armor," Gramma Ruth said. "I intend to be in my play clothes for this. Oh, and have a weapon, if they're trained to use one."

"She is trained," both Iteeche flag officers growled.

"Pretty Penny, draw me full armor now," Ruth said, striding toward the elevator. Smart Metal™ flowed up from the deck, covering her in an armored scout suit. It was fast to move in, but effective in protection. Its skin was chameleon; it changed to fit the surroundings.

The same armor flowed up from the deck to cover General Trouble. The old campaigners were back in harness and ready for war.

As they strode from the elevator on the roof of the Embassy, a Gunny offered them several weapons to choose from. Ruth picked a familiar twin barrel M-24, with a carbine above and a grenade thrower below. General Trouble chose the same. Gramma Trouble also palmed a small 2-mm automatic. She'd taught Little Ruth how to fire one and the two enjoyed spending time at the firing range together. If the kid asked for a weapon, she'd have one.

Around them, the first wave of quadcopters was lifting off with Royal US Marines aboard. The copters were as small as they could be and still hold four heavily-armed and armored Marines.

From Main Navy below them, more quadcopters lifted. These were larger. Each held a dozen Iteeche Fleet Marines.

The plan was for the Royal Marines to slip in and secure the LZ. The Imperial Marines would follow them in and seize the building.

Teams from both Marines would assault down by any means available to secure the steel box and release the children.

Gramma Trouble intended to be right behind those teams, followed by a small pack of very large mechanical dogs. They looked vicious enough to make even an Iteeche punk wet his pants and throw down his gun.

When they got to the kids, Pretty Penny would turn the dogs into armored suits for each of the kids, Human or Iteeche.

Once Ruth got her kids back, she was damned if she'd lose them again.

The ride in was bumpy considering this was the third wave of choppers. Then again, after two waves had flown by, some gunners may have woken up and made a bad decision.

The quadcopters rose up and down in jerks and spasms. They dodged right and left, then whipped themselves into hard ninety degree turns to just barely twist their way down a different street.

Despite all the jerking around, there were the occasional "Brrrraaaap" as the chopper's Gatling gun put an end to some attention it didn't appreciate.

Gramma Trouble eyed General Trouble. They both raised their eyebrows. Apparently this insertion was not going unnoticed.

"Pretty Penny, do we have a problem?" Ruth whispered to her computer.

"None that the computer controlling this crate and I can't handle," she said. "They've taken out all the sonar posts. Some radars are going active. As soon as one does, we take it down."

"Did we have problems seizing the LZ?" the General asked Xenophon.

"No, sir. That went smoothly. However, there are hand-held anti-air rockets showing up along the route now. We are still three districts out from the Broam Clan's district where the kids are, yet we are dodging AA. It's hard to tell whether we face a larger conspiracy or if this is just the usual greeting awarded to any weary traveler in these parts."

"I don't think they like strangers," Ruth drawled.

"You think?" Grampa Trouble growled. "Xenophon, make this crate transparent. If something is gonna kill me, I want to see it coming."

Immediately, the entire copter's walls went transparent. They rode four to six meters up in the air and dodged from one side of the street to the other.

Most of the people who looked up were clearly startled, whether by the quadcopter or the sight of four humans zipping by above them with little visible means of support.

Their copter created a 12mm laser above them. It swiveled through 360 degrees then held steady for a moment.

A small anti-air rocket sprang to life from the top of one of the taller buildings. It left a trail of smoke as it accelerated down at the quadcopter.

The laser caught it before it covered a quarter of the distance to the chopper. It exploded in a shower of wreckage.

While that fell, the laser followed the smoke back to its origin. It paused there for a moment as the smoke swirled around it. A second explosion added more smoke and wreckage to the air as someone's second rocket blew up in his face.

"Good riddance to bad trash," the general muttered, and looked away.

Ruth didn't see any other copter slipping up the street ahead or behind them. Apparently, each chopper was taking its own path from the Embassy to the target high rise. She wondered if they all were getting this kind of welcome.

A second rocket got the same greeting as the first. That gunner also got the self-same response as his second rocket exploded while still in hand.

However, someone was making life complicated for the Troubles. A third rocket streaked from the other side of the street even as the second one was becoming a cloud of flame and wreckage.

This third rocket was far too close when the laser swiveled to take it under fire. Another rocket was already on its way from where that one came from before the laser turned its attention to that side of the street. As shards of burning rocket fell from the sky, the laser hosed down the rooftop area at the base of the two smoke trails.

There was no satisfying secondary explosion, but Ruth would bet that some insurance company would be getting a claim. Assuming the Iteeche carried insurance policies.

That had been a serious debate among line beasts during the Iteeche War eighty years back. Ruth was often asked over drinks in whatever bar was passing for an O Club, if her prisoners knew the answer to that.

Lacking a supercomputer like Nelly back then, she had to admit that their language skills were too thin on the ground to ask that question. The Marines or Soldiers had grinned and assured her that they were seeing to paying out a lot of Iteeche insurance policies.

The copter made a hard turn to the right, followed by an immediate honk to the left and flared into a landing. Gramma and Grampa Trouble, with their two Marine escorts didn't so much dismount the copter as it dissolved around them.

In a moment, they had six very vicious looking mechanical dogs prowling the area around them. They sniffed the air for anything they weren't programmed to like.

"Follow us," General Trouble shouted to their honor guard, and the old couple hoofed it for the nearest door into the apartment complex even as they pulled back the arming lever on their familiar M-24s.

There was a stairwell not too far from that entrance. If the maps their nano scouts had drawn were correct, the fastest way to the fifth basement was straight down the stairs rather than taking all the switchbacks that vehicles used to get in and out of the garage.

Hopefully, on the stairs, they wouldn't have to dodge fire from tanks and gun trucks or the infantry that tended to crouch behind them.

The dogs raced ahead of them while the Marines failed to pass General Trouble or his lady. One dog stood on its hind legs at the door into the apartment complex. Its paw turned into a hand with an opposable thumb. It fingered the door, then froze.

"Hit the deck!" both Pretty Penny and Xenophon shouted at the same second. The dogs went down, heads lowered, as the four Humans dropped hard and skidded to a stop, the face masks on their armor slamming shut.

Thank heavens for armor.

The dog pulled open the door. The resulting explosion was followed by a massive flock of flechettes from a colossal claymore. Most of the darts flew over the dogs and humans, but a few sprouted like porcupine quills on the top of their armored helmets.

None penetrated to hurt Human or Iteeche.

Meanwhile, the dog that had opened the door came flying back even as it rolled itself into a ball. It landed somewhere behind them, but Ruth had no time to notice its fate.

The other dogs charged the hole in the building that had been a door, the 5-mm rifles jutting from their chests snapping out shots to keep heads down. The general helped his wife to her feet and they, along with the two Marines, added their fire to that from the dogs.

They had no visible targets, but the weapons seemed to sense something in the dark and neither Human nor dog felt any need for restraint in engaging the shadowy targets.

Ruth fired a smoke grenade at the ceiling where one hallway met another and the smoke got thicker. The general sent a fragmentation grenade for the wall to the right of the junction. That reduced the number of targets being suggested by her carbine's sensors.

In the gloom, the heads-up display on Ruth's helmet identified the door into the stairwell. It was about five meters inside the smoky hallway. The sixth dog, that had last been seen curling into a ball as it flew at the head of an explosive cloud, now reappeared. Again, it stood on its hind legs and made ready to open the door.

A Marine came to stand against the wall beside the dog, a grenade in his hand. At a nod of the Marine's helmet, the dog opened the door a crack. The Marine tossed the grenade onto the landing fronting on the door and the dog slammed the door shut.

The explosion that followed was muffled. Only a few shards from the grenade made it through the door, but not far enough to worry about. This time, the dog yanked the door open and two of its pals howled as they charged in.

One headed up the stairs, looking for any evidence of opposition. The second went down, but paused at the middle landing. There, it had a good view of the next door and the landing in front of it.

Ruth found herself looking at two views at the same time, as well as the swirling cloud of wreckage from the grenade. Above looked okay. Down was most interesting to her.

She and her husband stood in the wreckage of a defense that failed. Bodies and pieces of bodies lay everywhere, mixed in with rifles and pistols. The dogs went about checking any that looked too much alive and made sure they were dead.

Two Marines led the way into the shaft, rifles at the ready. Ruth followed the general, walking backwards and viewing what lay behind them through her rifle's sights.

Ruth followed her husband into the shadows. Ahead of them lay a half dozen Iteeche sprawled in their own blood, with their pistols and rifles close at hand.

The four humans quickly adjusted their pace to the extra width and rise of each stairstep. The dogs, ever eager, soon galloped by them and joined the lead dog where it lay on the next landing, alert to any action from the landing below.

Like the humans, they spread out and moved with caution, careful to make things harder for their opposition. One shot or grenade would not take two of them out.

This was good, because someone cracked the door open and lobbed a grenade into the stairwell, then slammed the door closed.

The grenade was comprised more of whiz bangs than explosions. It was a poor choice. While Ruth did find herself thrown against the concrete wall of the staircase, the Marines ahead of her only took a moment to let things settle before they dashed to take stations on either side of the door.

It wasn't too long before the door edged open again and a hand shot into the stairwell with a grenade held ready to drop

Seizing this opportunity, one Marine tossed two grenades inside the door while a dog turned its paw into a razor sharp blade and took the offending hand off at the wrist. With the grenade still in its grasp, both fell to the floor.

The Marine who'd tossed the grenades kicked the offered grenade, hand included, back where it came from. The other Marine slammed the door shut and the two of them held it in place for the short count it took for the grenades' fuses to ignite.

Shouts, screams, and pounding feet had barely begun when one, then another, and finally the third grenade blast pushed back hard against the two Humans holding the metal fire door shut.

It likely pushed back a whole lot worse on the other side.

Flattening a paw, a dog extended a tiny camera through the small crack above the door. The immediate area around the door was vacant except for a thin, roiling mist of blood. Flesh and bone was spread out and embedded the area close around the door. They also found a small motor pool.

As they watched, one of the trucks exploded, whether from gasoline or its weapons load it was hard to tell. A moment later, another truck went up. A fire was soon raging as more and more trucks exploded. The first basement floor was rapidly going up in a funeral pyre for those stationed there.

Knowing the hell they left above them, the dogs and Humans descended another floor before meeting opposition. Three Iteeche held the landing there. They fired up at the two Marines as they glanced down. The door was open into the garage so reinforcements might not be all that far away.

Each Marine drew a grenade from their web gear and tossed them. One for the three gunners, the other for the door.

The grenade intended for the shooters hit and bounced off of one Iteeche's head. That started a stampede for the exit that was cut short as one grenade exploded behind them. As they flew through the doorway, the second one added its own pressure to their passage, as well as shredded what the first grenade hadn't finished.

A massive fusillade swept in from the garage, riddling the metal stairs and sending rounds ricocheting in all directions in the stairwell. The four Humans made themselves small as they prepared a response.

The two Troubles joined the Marines on the middle landing. Both tuned back the fuses on their grenades, then aimed them for the deck as far back from the door as their position allowed.

I'LL FIRE ON ODD NUMBERS, YOU TAKE EVEN, SWEETHEART.

JUST LIKE OLD TIMES, GENERAL, HUH?

TOO MUCH LIKE OLD TIMES. ONE, the general said and fired a grenade toward the deck on Ruth's side. On her count, Ruth sent an explosive grenade out into the garage on her husband's side. With each heartbeat the old general counted out a number.

As he reached TWELVE Trouble paused to observe the results. They'd fired a mix of general demolition, explosive, and anti-personnel fragmentation grenades. For the clan soldiers and their gun trucks, it had been a disaster.

In the area immediately outside the door to the fourth sub-basement, a conflagration grew. Explosives cooked off in flaming gun trucks adding to the horror.

However, the Broam Clan troops were not going down easy. Over the crackling of small arms ammunition baking off came the roar of an engine and the clank of treads.

Someone had a tank and they were intent on using it.

A large caliber shell slammed into the wall to the right side of the door. Someone couldn't seem to find their target.

Both Marines handed off thermite grenades to the nearest dogs. They quickly morphed into much smaller dogs of a puppy-like size with grenades comprising most of their torsos. With the courage that only a metal critter can claim, they raced down the stairs and into the flames.

Ruth counted seconds in her head, wondering how good the gunner and loader were in that tank. They proved faster than the Humans' deadly mechanical dogs, but they also weren't all that good with their aim. Their next round slammed into the wall to the left side. It didn't miss by much, though. It clipped the edge of the door and exploded instantly. Shards of shell and stone, along with the concussion, filled the stairwell.

Ruth felt the overpressure and the hits from the harder stuff. Scout armor wasn't meant to handle being this close to artillery. It struggled to hold out the death that filled the shaft, but it was clearly failing.

It might have lost the fight against the destruction hammering at the humans, but a dog had been huddled between Gramma Trouble's legs. Even as death and destruction pounded its way onto the landing, the dog was giving up its existence.

Smart Metal™ swept up from her leg to reinforce her helmet, then her shoulders, and finally the rest of the suit. By the time Pretty Penny was done strengthening Ruth's battle rattle, she was better armored than the two Marines between her and her husband.

For a long moment, the four Humans lay there, struggling to recover from the concussions that had rolled over all of their bodies. Ruth managed to trigger another grenade. Explosives shot out, hit the deck, then bounced enough to send a cloud of pressure and fragments out to take down anyone who thought it was safe to charge the stairs just now.

Someone had. Suddenly, there were more screams from out there.

A second later, General Trouble bounced a grenade off the deck. It was nearly head high when it exploded, sending a wave of flechettes in all directions.

If possible, the screams multiplied and became louder.

What was left of the dog that had fed its Smart Metal™ into Ruth's armor to save her life was little more than the size of a puppy. It crawled up beside her and whimpered -- actually whimpered -- for an anti-tank grenade. The old warrior slipped one from her web gear and handed it off to the small dog. It wrapped itself around the grenade and a bit more of its extra metal flowed into Ruth's armor.

Ready, the dog took off, eager as any flesh and blood dog, scampering down the stairs. A second later, another was right behind it, the general's contribution to their future situation.

Again, Ruth's heads-up display filled with two pictures as each small dog crossed into the fourth sub-basement and took off on their own path. The concrete deck ran with blood; viscera and burned body parts were everywhere. The mechanical tiny dogs threaded their way around plenty of burning gun trucks. Somehow they found a safe path through all the destruction and kept on scampering for daylight.

Both spared a glance at the burning wreckage of the tank. None of the crew had made it out; their nearly-incinerated bodies were half out of the vehicle when death found them.

The dogs looked away before Ruth had to blink.

As the scouting dogs ranged farther afield, General Trouble picked one Marine and signaled him to lead the way to the fifth and final sub-basement, their goal for this mission.

One dog stayed to keep an eye on the rear with the other Marine. The remaining three slunk ahead to check out that final door while the trigger-puller led General Trouble and Gramma Ruth bring up the rear.

The door to the fifth sub-basement was closed.

What lay behind it?

34

I held my brother Johnny tight as he softly whimpered. It was hard enough to wait to know who would burst into your prison when you were nearly eight. I could hardly imagine what it must feel like to a six-year-old kid. I should just be grateful that he hadn't wet his pants . . . or worse.

Time ticked on, slow as syrup on a cold Wardhaven morning. I really wanted this to end. But what would that end be? Would the bad guys haul us off to somewhere else or . . . worse . . . just shoot us all?

Or would some big Marine poke his grinning head through a hole in the wall and shout, "No fear, kids! The Marines are here!"

Oh, please, let it be Marines!

I felt a trembling in the steel wall I sat against. It was hardly more than a tremor, but the wall had seemed to shiver ever so slightly for a second or two. I glanced at Mary.

She'd felt it, too. She put her ear to the wall.

I didn't. Instead I leaned back to where I'd been when my computer, Daisy, drilled a hole through the steel plate.

AM I CLOSE TO THE PLUG, DAISY?

FARTHER RIGHT. DOWN A BIT. STAY RIGHT THERE, Daisy whispered into my brain. I held so stiff that I didn't dare breathe.

A few hours ago, I'd drilled a hole so a tiny bit of Smart Metal could slip out with a message to the grown-ups at the Embassy. I'd been so scared that they'd notice the hole that I had Daisy immediately cover it up.

As curious as I was about where we were being held captive, I'd still wasted no time gawking at the outside before I plugged it up. They might have something to measure the air pressure in here. Any extra air whistling in through that hole could sink us.

Now I waited to see what Daisy might show me.

In a moment, a picture filled my mind's eye. Outside was a vast, poorly lit carpark. The ceiling was low. I would guess that we were way underground where they only parked the small tricycle cars and trucks. The larger stuff . . . and armed stuff . . . would be higher up.

I felt as well as heard the next explosion. It was hardly more than a breath, but I did. Grabbing for Mary's hand, I gave it a squeeze.

She squeezed back and silently mouthed, "What do we do?"

I shrugged. I had no idea.

Daisy wiggled her tiny camera around and my view scanned the entire carpark. All there was to see were a vast expanse of vacant concrete in every direction . . . except one.

In the middle distance was the ramp down from the floor above. There was no ramp to take someone lower. I'd guessed right; we were on the bottom floor.

At the ramp, there were two barriers that could be raised or lowered to let traffic in or out. Next to both the entrance and exit lanes were squat guard houses. Four men were out in front of each one, lounging as if they expected neither a visit from their superior nor a demand to let someone in.

I guess we're not going anywhere.

I caught the echo of distant explosions again but could not tell where they came from. Turning to Mary, I buried my lips in her ear and whispered, "I'm feeling the wall shake. Not much. Just a little.

Something's happening out there. I don't know what, but things are changing."

It was a lie, but I think Momma would forgive me this one. I couldn't tell any of the kids what was really happening without telling them how I knew it. I was pretty sure the bad guys were watching and listening to us.

I'd have to take care of my friends, but I'd have to do it so I didn't give anything away.

Mary turned to pass my lie down the line to kids sitting or leaning against the wall. Most of them were silent. They'd pulled their knees up, wrapped their arms around them, and held them tight to their chests while they rested their chins on top. I held Johnny in my lap and Mary held my hand.

The Iteeche were also doing their best to handle the stress. I tried not to laugh as they all folded their eight knees back and sat on their legs. It was so strange. Still, they fidgeted like us as they waited.

We all waited.

However, things were happening outside. From the other wing of the building, my view through Daisy's eyepiece showed a door slam open. Screaming Iteeche ran from it toward the guard houses. Smoke followed in their wake. Some of them were burning, flames were trailing them while they ran. Others tried to beat out the fire on others' clothes. All carried weapons.

This did not look good.

There was a lot of wild arm waving as the armed troops and the armed guards came up against each other. There was no way for me to understand what they said, the sound coming through the plug was all a jumble of noise.

Loud noises.

I think this was what Mom was talking about when she said troops could panic if things got bad.

What was going on that was so bad above us?

While the Iteeche over by the exit were carrying on, Daisy used the time to give me a good view of the area around our wall. There was a stack of extra plates that they hadn't used. Over to the right were two more fish tanks; they looked empty. There were also a couple of crates of combat rations. That left me wondering how long they expected to have fed us.

At the far end of our steel wall, close to the concrete wall of the carpark was a stack of stuff. It was scattered all around, as if they'd played with it and just walked away without cleaning up. *Hadn't their moms taught them anything?*

Then I remember, Iteeche didn't have moms.

THOSE ARE GAS CANISTERS, RUTH.

GAS CANISTERS?

YES. WELDING TORCHES NEED GASES. I DON'T KNOW WHAT TYPES OF GAS, BUT THEY NEED AT LEAST TWO OF THEM TO GET A TORCH HOT ENOUGH TO WELD A SEAM.

IS THAT GOOD?

I DON'T KNOW, RUTH, BUT DO YOU REALLY WANT THOSE PANICKED ITEECHE OVER THERE PLAYING WITH THAT STUFF?

I definitely would not like for Johnny to get his hands on a welding torch. I wasn't sure that I should handle a torch. No, those guys by the exit shouldn't be playing with matches, much less a welding torch.

However, several of them began stalking their way toward our prison.

I grasped Mary's hand even tighter.

She looked at me in alarm.

I so wanted to tell her what I was seeing, but I didn't dare. I tried to show serious concern, but what face do you use to show serious concern? I wasn't eight yet. There was a lot I needed to learn and hadn't yet.

I may have done a good enough job. Mary's face showed serious concern.

I nodded, and she squeezed my hand back. My hand was going to seriously hurt before we got out of here.

A dozen Iteeche arrived not far from my spy eye. They shouted and waved their hands and did a lot that wasn't helping them win any friends. A couple of them got into a shoving match.

I'd never seen two Iteeche shove each other around. They had four legs, two behind the others, and four arms, two above the others. That made for a lot of hand slapping and not much moving back by anyone.

It was almost comical, but I was out of laughter at the moment.

Then my blood ran cold.

Two of the ones that had been quieter than the rest backed up as they paced off the distance to the torch equipment without turning their back on the group. None of the bickering bunch seemed to notice what they were doing.

However, several new arrivals headed for them rather than join the loud arguments raging not far from my spy eye.

I leaned over until I had my lips in Mary's ear. "Get ready to do something," I whispered softly.

She turned then whispered in my own ear, "What?"

I replied with a shrug. I'd have to make this up as I went along.

Now the bunch with the welding equipment were hauling it out of the corner. About halfway between the concrete wall and the loud argument, they set the tall, heavy, steel bottles of gas upright.

That caught the attention of several of the guys along the outside of the argument. They moseyed over to take a better look at what was going on. Mostly, they blocked my view.

Now it was my time to worry. If I gauged it right, they were setting up to torch the wall ten or so meters from where I sat. Several Iteeche kids were huddled together there, holding each other to keep the fear at bay.

If the welder started low on the wall, toward the deck, he might fire his welding torch right into one of their backsides. I had to do something.

35

T aking my heart in my hands, I stood up. "Guys, I'm hearing a lot of explosives. I don't think we ought to be leaning against the wall. I'm moving to the center. I think we all should."

Mary was immediately on her feet and pulling a few of the other Human kids with her. Lexi and Buddy did their usual noisy complaining, but they dragged themselves up and joined us in the middle.

Em and Mo got the Iteeche kids moving. I was glad when the kids moved away from where I thought the welder's torch might cut through.

"I'm tired," Johnny said. I guess he'd been napping and woke up cranky. "I'm hungry."

I drug him to the ration area, complaining all the way. There were some cookies among the rations. I hydrated them from the fish tank and handed the soggy mess to him.

"I don't want that," my little brother whined.

"It's all we have," I insisted.

Johnny had started a stampede for the food. A lot of the Iteeche caught fish and swallowed them down, whole. Other Humans tried hydrating something. Mary found something that looked like a ham sandwich. It was way past its sell-by date, but with enough water, Johnny was soon gnawing on a slice of his favorite meat.

Of course, he complained the entire time that it tasted strange and was too hard to chew. I found a different ham sandwich. This time I dipped the ham in the fish tank and left it there for a good half minute.

At least Johnny found it chewable even if "it tasted like fish."

Little brothers could be so exasperating.

I'd learned that word "exasperating" early. A lot of the nannies applied it to me. *I* couldn't have ever been *this* exasperating.

Across from us, the wall began to glow red. A moment later, a jet of flaming gas cut through the flux seam between two steel plates.

"I was just sitting there!" an Iteeche yelped.

"I'm glad Ruth has such sensitive fingers," Em said. I knew the general's kid must know that I was cheating. Still, the looks of approval I got from both the Humans and Iteeche felt nice.

Now Em, Mo, and Mary came to stand beside me. "What do we do?"

"I vote for trying to keep them out of here as long as we can," I said.

"I second the motion," Mary said.

The two Iteeche just looked at us like we had two heads, which, coming from someone with four legs, four arms, and four eyes was really not at all considerate.

But Em got with the program. "How?"

"Could you Iteeche move the fish tanks over there? Not too close or the torch will burn them, but as close as we dare." The tanks were huge. They stood on eight short, spindly legs and had one long side up against the wall.

Four of the Iteeche kids grabbed the two short sides and tried to get a tank moving. Then six. Then eight. Finally, with ten pushing and pulling around the front and sides of the tank, it began a long, slow slide across the floor. I guided them down a specific row of plates. At least they only needed to force the tank over one seam every three meters.

It wasn't easy getting the tank over those seams, but now two of the biggest Iteeche pushed from behind. It went faster.

Some of us Humans tried to help with the tanks, but it was clear the Iteeche Chosen were a lot stronger than us.

We parked the tank in front of metal plate a few feet back from the rapidly spreading cut in the wall.

Then we went back and moved the other tank.

Done, Em eyed the Human ration boxes. "Those don't look big enough to stop an Iteeche," he said.

"Maybe not like a heavy water tank, but . . ." I reached down and pulled up a heavy plastic carton of something. "Maybe if we could hit one of them in the eye with the sharp edge of one of these, they'd think better of it."

Em and Mo sorted through the crates and found weighty boxes with hard edges. Both hauled off and threw them at the wall. One splattered open, showing small green beans on the deck. The other hit and bounced off.

Mary trotted over and knelt to study the beans. "Hey, I think these are lima beans."

"Lima beans?" I answered. I and Johnny both hated lima beans.

"Yeah, the worst meal ever forced on our combat troops," she said. "My grandad used to cuss them to his dying day. One time, Grandma cooked up a batch and he threw them out the door. My dad was just a kid and he ran out of the house after he finished eating and slipped and fell into the mess. Grandad loved telling that story. My dad hated it."

I dug through the meals and found one with lima beans in it. I popped the box open; inside was an ugly dried mess of something. I dipped it in water and the carton filled. Quicker than I thought possible, there was an ugly mess of slimy looking beans.

I pulled one out and squeezed it between my thumb and finger. It burst and I had more slimy stuff on my hands.

Trotting over to where the torch was now cutting across the wall, I tossed the lima beans on the deck. They did look slippery.

Soon, all of us Humans, and not a few Iteeche, were rehydrating lima beans and scattering them all around what looked to soon be a door in or out of our prison.

Meanwhile, I discovered that I really didn't want Iteeche kids throwing hard, heavy, and pointed things at me. Em, Mo, and several of their friends could throw with deadly accuracy.

I wasn't sure that we would win a fight with cartons of beans or other stuff that sure didn't look like the name on the box. Still, if it came to this, those Iteeche would know that we weren't going down easy a second time.

The littles were sure having fun rehydrating the lima beans. One of them discovered spaghetti and meatballs in a really yucky sauce and it went in with the lima beans. *Oh my, what a mess!*

It was a mess all of them knew they'd never have to clean up no matter what happened next. The little ones shrieked with glee and tossed more slimy stuff on the floor along the far wall.

Em and I eyed the two tanks and the door about to be created by the steel plate. It was about a meter wide. The two tanks looked to be somewhere around seventy or eighty centimeters across their narrow side.

Em grinned. "We had enough trouble pushing those tanks along sideways. They are not going to like having only one narrow side to push on."

"Can we throw some of the spaghetti on them when they try to come in?" Johnny asked, so excited that he and his friends were jumping up and down. I guess the small ones had had enough of lying around with nothing to play with. Besides, most of us were service brats. Our folks blew shit up . . . ah, stuff up. These Iteeche had lied to us and hit us when we weren't looking.

It was open season on these mud lovers.

Oh, my. I was saying such bad words. If we got out of here and I didn't clean up my act, Gramma Trouble would be ordering me to wash my mouth out with soap.

Still, these kidnappers deserved everything we were gonna throw at them.

The bottom cut was half done. The big Iteeche kids slid the first tank up to the wall. The torch worked its way up the wall to where it had started. Our big Iteeche stood ready to push the tank into place as soon as the bad guys finished.

Just as they did, our big Iteeche playmates slid the tank forward. We had the door blocked even before it was a door!

The littles were right up front, huddling behind the fish tanks and giggling like they'd never been given any good sense. Around them, they had piles of full containers with yucky food rations. They would start tossing them as soon as the steel sheet fell away. I'd told them to get out of the way.

"As soon as you finish tossing that mess, get back against the far wall," I ordered them in a voice I hoped sounded like Mom's command voice. "Huddle down and make yourselves small, unthreatening targets."

"We'll be tossing cans at kidnappers," Em warned them.

"We don't want to bop you on the head with one," I told the smaller Human and Iteeche kids. "You've seen how hard we can throw a can. We don't want to hurt you."

Maybe they understood me.

Still, how do you get a six-year-old kid to do what their big sister tells him to do?

Our capturers had finished cutting through the flux all around the plate. We stood, breathless, waiting for the fun to begin.

We might lose, but we hoped they'd know they'd been in a fight.

36

At first, the Iteeche that tried to break in were a bunch of clowns.

Someone pushed on the top of the steel plate. It leaned in. They leaned harder. The plate moved enough for the middle of it to lean against the fish tanks.

The thick steel sheet acted like a sideways teeter-totter. While the top slipped in, the bottom slipped out. There were screams of pain from outside and the steel plate fell back into place.

A second later, someone else outside took another try at the plate . . . with the same results. Inside, the littles were laughing their little heads off. Even I had to admit it felt nice to see our kidnappers making fools of themselves.

It got worse, at least for those outside. A hand wiggled in to grab the edge of the big steel piece. A bare hand. No sooner had he grabbed it than there was a yowl of pain and the hand was yanked back.

Johnny picked that moment to make his first contribution to the mess out there. He slipped around to the side of the plate where there was a gap of a couple of centimeters and lobbed a package of spaghetti through the hole.

The language that came back from the other side was pure barracks talk of the kind our parents didn't want us using. Still, there was more laughter on our side.

An Iteeche kid slipped around to the other side and sent an envelope of lima beans arching through the space at the top of the door.

More bad language.

Somebody stuck a rifle barrel through the top of the hole and the littles scampered back behind the fish tank. Even we big kids made sure to stand clear of any fire.

However, the rifle wasn't there to spew bullets, but rather for the leverage. With a bit of wiggling, the guy got the plate leaning sideways. Then he edged the top out.

It might have worked, but we had the fish tanks right behind what they wanted for a door. The plate got caught up at the bottom and pry out of the hole. The gunner finally gave up with much bad language and teasing from his buddies.

Three tries to break in and we were winning.

The bad guys seemed to pull back after that. At least when Mark lobbed another really slimy meal out, no one cussed at us for messing them up.

The littles laughed and jumped up and down. They seemed to think we had won. We big kids knew they were just taking a moment to actually apply some brains to the problem we'd given them.

They'd be back soon enough.

Back and with better ideas on how to bust in on us.

A couple of minutes went by and the littles had quieted down. Some of them had gone back to the Human food crates and found more yucky food to rehydrate. The pile of stuff they were ready to throw got bigger. I even went up and got a dozen cartons.

We might want to litter their path inside with slime, too.

I was right, they came back smarter.

Our first warning they were coming for us again was when several heavily gloved hands reached in and shoved the plate sideways. Then they pulled that side of the sheet forward. It took a bit of wiggling and pulling, but soon enough the plate slammed down on the other side with a loud noise.

There was also howling. I think someone's foot wasn't far back enough. Still, the plate was down and the gap was open.

"Littles!" I shouted in the closest thing I could manage to Mom's command voice, "Throw!"

A half-dozen little kids were hunkered down behind the fish tanks. They had plastic cartons of yuck in both hands. Well, four hands for the two smaller Iteeche.

Keeping their heads down, they hurled their cans overhand, just like we'd seen done at combat demonstrations the Marines sometimes put on for us kids. They had the form of it down perfectly.

Six cans arched out to splat on the steel plate that as yet had no Iteeche traipsing across it. Six more cans followed a second later. Then the toss was only two cans. Then it was six again. The next toss was four.

From where I stood several meters back from the kids, I had a pretty good view of the bad guys. Most of them had given the steel sheet plenty of room. Before they could take a step forward, boxes flew through the air, spewing all sorts of ugly stuff to splatter and spread all over the plating.

A few of the littles had good throwing arms. Some of the Iteeche standing around got hit by the boxes that went long. Their reaction to being slimed was not a happy one.

Still, more cartons flew and the plate got more slippery gunk on it and some of those close by got hit with yucky stuff.

Through all of this, the Iteeche gunmen just stood there, puzzled looks on their faces. I don't think their training had covered what to do when kids were throwing things at them.

Apparently, there was no officer or senior NCO around to issue orders, so nothing happened for a long time.

Then one of the Iteeche bent down and picked up a plastic box with his throwing hand. A moment later, I was side-stepping, just like I did in dodgeball. So were the rest of us big kids. When he finally wound up and bounced the box across the fish tanks, we managed to get out of the way.

"Nanny, nanny, you-u missed!" we hollered.

I doubt if the Iteeche out there had translators, but our meaning was clear in any language. More of them scrambled into the muck to retrieve containers to throw at us. We were soon dodging an empty carton every few seconds.

We dodged more than hit us. Since the cartons were empty, they hardly hurt at all.

"Should we start throwing full boxes at them?" Em asked me as he shrugged off a hit and I barely dodged another.

"I don't think so," I answered. "If we throw them, they'll throw them back at us. I may not have thought this through," I admitted.

"Who would have thought that slime and empty cartons could keep the littles busy?" Em said as he dodged and I got hit on the hip by one. It stung, but I could tolerate it.

I retrieved the carton and sent it back the way it came.

While we were all doing this, the Iteeche gunmen had stopped trying to storm into our prison. Better still, they were so absorbed in hitting us that no one thought to shoot at us.

If someone had given the order to fire, I'm sure all of us would have been dead in a blink. If someone had ordered up a fatigue party to shove the water tanks out of the way, they might have gotten in here. For now, the lack of anyone in command kept us all just tossing things at each other.

The slime on the deck plate in front of the opening seemed to discourage any Iteeche from risking a step onto it. Besides, so long as they hung back around the fallen steel sheet, there was more room for people to throw things at us.

A couple of guys that dared to cross the slimed plate ended up falling flat on their bottoms into the mess. That cut down on anyone else trying. That, and the shouts not to block their aim at someone on our side.

I prayed this would go on forever.

The rattle of automatic weapons fire put an end to my hope.

All us kids immediately tried to make ourselves small. I heard the gunfire, but none of us kids got hit. I blinked to count the number of Iteeche out in front of our door and found the count hadn't changed.

Who was doing the shooting? Who was getting shot at?

While I couldn't see the source of the fire, the Iteeche outside our door could. They all turned to their left. While they'd been throwing stuff at us, most had slung their rifles over their shoulders. Some began to slide them down their arm, readying for fire.

"Don't be stupid! We could mow you all down before any of you could get a shot off! Drop your guns!"

I knew that voice! Oh, did I know that voice!

"Grampa Trouble is here!" I screamed. "The Marines have landed!"

Now it wasn't just the littles who were jumping up and down for joy, but all the kids – both Human and Iteeche.

We were all going to live!

37

Their seeing eye dog, as Gramma Ruth had taken to calling the dog with the tiny scope it regularly ran under or over doors, had done it again. Its present view showed another garage. Fortunately for her and her husband's heart, it was empty.

No cars. No gunmen.

Finally, a door they could open without starting a firefight.

The Marine in the lead cracked the door open a smidge. He must have liked what he saw because he opened it wider and let one mechanical dog after another slip in.

Very quickly, Gramma Trouble had the view from several dogs filling her visor display. The building they were invading was in the traditional Iteeche form of an E. The staircase they presently hid in was halfway up the bottom leg of the E. Assuming this fifth basement was also a complete E, there was a lot of it that they couldn't see.

Ruth hated that.

However, what the dogs could see was one wide expanse of concrete with nothing on it. At the far end of it, where the long side of the E formed a corner with their wing, there looked to be something going on.

The four Humans moved cautiously toward that disturbance,

staying close to the wall and letting their scout suits take on the appearance of dimly lit concrete.

Yep. I'm just a wall. Don't notice when I move.

Ruth could take some comfort in that the garage wall was pretty much a long expanse of mottled and cracked concrete.

The closer they got to the goings on at the end of the garage, the more and more Ruth found herself puzzled.

It looked like someone had knocked together a large room out of steel plates. When she zoomed in on it, she could distinctly see the welds. That seemed pretty normal to her.

It was what was going on around what looked like a hole in one of the plates that she couldn't figure out. There appeared to be a pack of Iteeche standing well back from the gap. They were shouting and carrying on as if some sort of sports game was being played. However, from where they cautiously worked their way along the garage wall, they could see nothing of the game.

Ruth had one of the dogs spin off a tiny quadcopter and sent it off to get a closer view. As it got nearer to the scene, it was hard to believe the picture it sent back.

The sheet of steel that had filled the hole was laid out flat on the deck in front of it. It seemed to be covered with an ugly coating of something that smelled terrible, yet was vaguely familiar. An Iteeche picked that moment to step onto the steel sheet to get himself closer to whomever was in the box.

It did him no good. As he wound up to throw something, two of his feet slipped out from under him and he went down into the gooey mess. He got a lot of teasing from the Iteeche around him, but there was more to it.

Along with the shouting of the Iteeche gunman, there was also a mix of high-pitched voices as well.

Voices that screamed very much in what sounded like Human standard.

"I think we've found our kids," I whispered on net.

"I think we very much may have," the old general agreed.

Excited as Gramma Trouble was, she didn't do anything stupid.

She continued to check behind them as was her duty as tag-end-Charlie. The Marines continued to advance with full caution. Their dogs continued their own scout of the place, creeping cautiously from one supporting pillar to the next.

One dog, however, was moving ahead of them. It reached the end of the wall before any Human did. It was Ruth's seeing eye dog, and it used its tiny scope to look around the corner. Finally, they got a better view!

Up around the middle of the E, there was a pair of guard shacks. They stood next to what had to be the exit ramp. There were still guards there, but their interest was totally absorbed by what was going on in the corner the armed Humans were working their way toward.

That dog began a low crawl toward the guard houses, skulking from one support to the next. The Marine in the lead gave it weapons release to go fully automatic if the need arose.

As much as Ruth wanted to send the spy drone through the gap in the steel enclosure to get a good view of what was inside, she didn't. They were too close to risk attracting attention.

Ahead of them now was the vast open space between the end of the wall and the large metal container across from it. Crossing that dangerous ground could easily get them all killed.

The armed Humans paused to examine their options. They could crawl low and hope the camouflage hid them. They could cover the open ground in a rush, trying to get up close to the crowd before anyone could bring a gun to bear on them.

They tried a low crawl.

Of course, Smart Metal™ had taken some of the grind out of this ancient infantry torture, especially when you were low-crawling across a street or down a sidewalk. Very soon, Ruth was trailing three other Humans as they didn't crawl, but slowly rolled, across the deck of the empty garage.

Between the six small wheels that supported her armor and the constant adjustment of the camouflage, they made it to just one hundred meters from the Iteeche who could now be seen to be tossing empty containers back and forth with the kids.

This was when a couple of the guys at the guard house decided to come over and join in the fun. That development on their right flank promised to complicate their life greatly.

While one of the Marines and another dog rolled off to cover the approaching guards, General Trouble announced on Nelly Net.

ON THE COUNT OF THREE, WE'RE UP. ONE. TWO. THREE.

Ruth rolled to her feet and brought her M-24 up to cover the gathering ahead of her. The Marine was a bit faster than the two Troubles, but not more than a few seconds longer. It was then Ruth noticed a smell...very strong and very familiar. Keeping her gun still up, she covered her team.

Grampa Trouble aimed his carbine for the ceiling and let off a long burst of rapid fire.

He backed the shots fired up with a firm command. "Don't be stupid! We could mow you all down before any of you could get a shot off! Drop your guns!"

From inside the metal box a familiar voice screamed, "Grampa Trouble is here! The Marines have landed! We're saved!"

As much as Ruth wanted to dash through the gap and hug herself some grandkids, she kept her carbine steady as she swept the group. If somebody tried something, she'd drop them before they could hurt any of those kids.

What happened next moved so fast that Ruth's eyes couldn't follow it.

The clump of Iteeche were three or four deep in places. There were just too many gunmen that she and Trouble didn't have a visual on.

Apparently, someone they couldn't see made a play for his gun. At least, the falling gun was what would get everyone's attention in a moment or two.

Little Ruth did have an eyeball on the Iteeche. She was the one who acted.

"Daisy! Weapons free!" echoed out from the box.

A moment later, the Iteeche gave one of their own a wide birth. He seemed to have lost control of his arms and legs as spasms set them trembling. He was trying to raise his automatic rifle, but the seizures in his arms made it an impossible task.

Then his entire right side went limp. He fell over like a brick, his rifle clattering onto the deck.

"Drop the guns!" General Trouble commanded.

The guns clattered to the floor. Someone hadn't been trained in the cautions that should be followed if you gave up a weapon

A quick glance to her right showed that the guards were showing no inclination to do this any differently. Even as the rest of the guards walked from the guard shack, their weapons went down as well.

It took a while to get all the Iteeche lined up against the wall, but they got them there. The general selected two of the Iteeche that looked more reasonable than the rest and tossed them sacks full of plastic ties. They passed them out to the other Iteeche.

The Humans watched as each Iteeche tied his two central arms in front of them using their other ones. Then those two Iteeche went down the line and tied their other pair behind their back.

By then, the gate guards had joined the herd and been trussed up. Finally, the Marines did the same for the last two Iteeche.

Only then did Gramma Trouble breathe a sigh of relief.

While all this was going on, Gramma Ruth took a step in front of the gap in the steel plates. She had to smile at what the kids had done.

The collapsed plate was such a mess that she was careful when she stepped on it. While both Human and Iteeche kids were jumping up and down, screaming and hugging each other, Ruth surveyed what they'd prepared for their captors.

Two large water tanks blocked the entrance. How the kids had gotten them there was anybody's guess, but they'd done it. Ruth could not get in. Of course, that also meant that the Iteeche kidnappers had been blocked out as well.

That explained why the Iteeche were standing around the gap in the bulkhead not doing a lot of anything.

Slowly, a few things dawned on Ruth. The kids must have been given a collection of combat rations captured back during the Iteeche War. She was standing in and could see streaked on the concrete, as well as the metal plate, some of the most cursed meals of that distant war. That had been the overpowering but familiar smell. There was nothing like it in the world. Lima beans and spaghetti sauce mixed with noodles and tasteless mashed potatoes. *That* was what the *kids* had been *throwing*.

There were also the empty containers littering inside and outside of the box that had been thrown back and forth.

Gramma Trouble had been dividing her attention between their prisoners and the situation the kids had created. But now, Little Ruth and Johnny were trying to wiggle past the blockade of fish tanks in front of the door.

A couple of big Iteeche kids came over and helped shove and pull the tanks back a bit. Suddenly, Ruth's hips were wrapped in the most wonderful hugs.

"Gramma, I'm so glad to see you!" Johnny screamed.

"Gramma, I knew you'd come!"

"Gramma, I love you!"

"Gramma, did you get my message?" Little Ruth demanded.

"Gramma, I'm so happy!"

"Gramma, this is the most wonderful day of my life!"

"Mine, too!"

Rapid fire words swept over Ruth faster than any weapon could ever send bullets down range. The last Iteeche was now cuffed. Clicking her safety on, Ruth slung her rifle and took a knee, carefully outside of the ick that never washed off. That let some short people give her the hugs and kisses that she'd never forget, no matter what the future might hold.

"I'm here. You're safe. I'm so glad you're safe!"

PRETTY PENNY, PUT AS MUCH ARMOR AS YOU CAN ON THESE KIDS. CHEST TO FAMILY JEWELS. I WANT ANOTHER HERD OF GRANDKIDS.

Ruth's thickened armor sloughed off its top layers onto the two kids. In a moment, their chests and abdomens were covered. Both had an extra bit of protection for what they would learn to use much later.

Ruth breathed a sigh of relief.

Trouble backed away from their prisoners, then did a bit of a jig as he realized what he was backing onto.

"Holy.....Cripes! I never wanted to see that crap again! Ever! But," he said, barely avoiding slipping in the ugly mess on the steel plate. Still, looking up to grin at his grandkids he said, "I think that's the best use anyone has ever put those rations! It sure beats eating them!"

"People ate that?" Johnny screamed in shock.

"For months at a time," the old general answered. "I and a lot of men swore off of several different foods after that war."

"At least now you'll eat Italian food again," Ruth grumped. "Your grampa is such a wimp."

"You didn't spend almost a damn year buried in the mud and caves on Port Elgin with nothing but that crap to eat," he groused.

"No," Ruth said, "I didn't have to eat that crap until we captured the Gold Planet, and the next couple. We didn't set up a decent field kitchen until you captured Golden Starfish and the entire Golden Satrap surrendered."

"I rest my case," the general grumped.

"Sir, ma'am, how do we get out of here?" a Marine asked.

"Gramma, I smell smoke," Little Ruth added not at all unnecessarily.

"Let's head for the far wing and see if we can get out that away," the general said.

In a moment, the big Iteeche kids had shoved the fish tanks out of the way. In the process, one of them tumbled over, flooding the former prison. Most of it drained out the drainage holes as the kids stampeded into the parking garage.

As much as Gramma Ruth wanted to armor all the kids and her own grandkids better, the dogs were actually essential to keeping the kids herded together. The dogs did shift, however. Where something like an oversize Doberman Pincher had been, now a small army of terriers nipped at the heels of any kid that made to wander off.

Ruth could not give up the dogs to armor the kids.

"What do we do with those?" a Marine asked the general, while nodding to the Iteeche captives.

General Trouble scowled. "We can't leave them. Some might wander off and sound an alarm. But we can't take them with us. Too many heads to keep track of."

"Do you remember running a three-legged race, sweetheart?" Gramma Trouble said, her voice all sweetness and light.

"Yeah," he agreed.

"Imagine running a fifty-legged race."

"Oh!" the old general said, dawn coming up like thunder.

Gramma Trouble waved at the biggest Iteeche kids. "I'd like you to tie them together at their feet. One right foot to another guys left one, or two right or two left. They don't have to be facing in the same direction. In fact, it might be better if a lot of them weren't."

Wide grins broke out on the Iteeche kids. Gramma Ruth grinned back. Maybe if they grinned enough as kids they'd still be able to do it as adults.

Four kids divided up the big plastic ties and approached the former gunmen. They began tying legs together, then shoving the next one in line around to face the other way. This went on for a couple of minutes. There was soon had a very interesting and confused centipede-like shape trying to twist around to face their captors.

"You're free to go," General Trouble called to the bound Iteeche, then turned to order the liberated hostages, "Let's move it, crew. I don't like the smell of that smoke."

38

I *don't think I've ever been this happy in my life!*

I held on tight to Gramma Trouble's right hip while Johnny held to her left. I tried not to be clingy, but I just could not let go of her. It was like all my Christmases and birthdays wrapped up in one huge package with a gigantic bow on top.

Still, Grampa said we had to move; I moved along beside Gramma and tried to keep away from her rifle in case she needed it.

Behind me, there was a sudden rash of shouting and cussing in Iteeche. I glanced back at the bad guys who had held us prisoners for what seemed to be forever.

Several had fallen down and more were tumbling down around or on top of others. Now I realized what Gramma Trouble meant when she talked about a fifty-legged race.

Johnny and I were paired a couple of times in a three-legged race. I preferred to race with Mary or someone my size. Oh, and it helped if they were smart! It took work to ran with your leg tied to another person's. It was only after I saw some grown-ups run a race and how they counted, "One, two. One, two," to get their pacing right that I learned how it was done.

Those Iteeche had never run a three-legged race.

They all started together and tripped each other up. It didn't help that nearly half of them were facing the car park's wall.

Oh, and once they all were down, they got very cranky while they tried to get up. It was gonna take them a lot of time to follow us.

I hoped the fire didn't get them.

I turned away and buried my face in Gramma's armor and tilting my head toward her asked, "Gramma, do you have a pistol I could use?"

My gramma glanced down at me.

"You were very brave to let Daisy take care of that Iteeche who went for his rifle," she said.

"I . . . I . . . I didn't want to, but he might have killed all of us," finally came out in a rush as she handed me the small automatic 2mm that she'd trained me on. It wasn't much of a gun, but it was better than nothing.

"I know," Gramma said. "None of us could see him. Other Iteeche were all in front of him. You were the only one who saw him. You, my lovely grandchild, were the only one who could do what had to be done."

"Mommy says that that is what we Longknifes do. We do what has to be done."

"Yes, but it hurts sometimes, doesn't it?"

I nodded. I think the cat had my tongue. I was starting to feel all mixed up inside. I'd been so afraid and I'd done so many things I didn't know how to do. I was exhausted. All I really wanted to do was take a nap.

On the other side of us, Johnny was whining about being tired.

Gramma Ruth asked if one of the tall Iteeche could carry Johnny.

My friend Em picked him up and carried him in his arms for a bit, then let my brother slide around and kind of ride on his hip while they held on to each other.

I'd never seen an Iteeche let any Human ride on them. I think Em was being very considerate of my little brother.

Behind us, there was more shouting as the long line of Iteeche struggled to their feet, only to tumble down again. Some tried crawling, but that didn't work, what with half of them having to crawl on their backs. They went back to urging everyone to just get up on their feet.

We were jogging along now that several of the smaller Humans and Iteeche had been picked up by the bigger ones. Mary had a sleepy girl, a tiny thing, slumped asleep on her back. She held her in place while sleepy arms tried to stay around her neck.

I should have done that with my brother, but I wasn't a big as Mary. It would have been a mess if I had.

We were up to the middle of the car park, trotting past the guard shacks; there was a ramp up to the next level. A glance up it showed the shadows of flames dancing on the wall at the end of the ramp. I also heard something explode. I could feel air rushing by us.

I knew that a fire sucked air into it. If there was a fire above us, it wouldn't be very long before the air down here was pretty thin. Most of us older kids recognized what we saw. When General Trouble urged us on faster, I found more energy than I thought I had.

A glance behind us showed that the Iteeche must have heard or felt the same hint of fire. They'd formed a line and were doing their best to struggle along with a few falling down every once in a while, but not that often.

The dogs began to herd us out into the carpark, aiming us at the far wing from where we'd been kept. I really do think these dogs were programmed into herding us kids. Just let one of us start to wander off or fall behind, and they'd be barking and maybe nipping at our heels. They were cute as buttons, but they made sure we kept up our paces and stayed together.

Those that couldn't keep up were carried.

One of the dogs took off at a canter for the corner and soon sent a small scope around it. Daisy gave me a picture of what it saw. Another empty car park. Nothing.

Now the Marines angled us tighter toward that turn and we all walked as fast as we could manage. Behind us, the Iteeche were getting better, or maybe more desperate. They stumbled and fell less often.

I spotted a door with STAIRWELL in Iteeche and shouted, "There are stairs out of here!"

We kids found energy that we didn't know we had.

One of the smaller dogs galloped up to join the first one. In the blink of an eye, they merged into a bigger dog. I know I'm supposed to be used to Smart Metal™ and all, but it's still strange to watch it happen.

Especially when the big dog went up on its hind legs and opened the door. Opened the door!

The mechanical dog opened the door and then disappeared through it.

"Gramma, did I just see what I thought I saw?"

"Yes, Dear. That's Grampa's seeing eye dog. It's going to take a good look at what's up the stairs."

"Oh," I said. Well, if Gramma Trouble said it was just something they did, I guess it was. Still, I glanced around. How many of these little dogs had been big dogs on the way down here?

I was glad they were little and cute. I'd hate to have one of those big dogs nipping at my heels.

Now, Daisy alternated between two different views. Apparently the dog had spun off a copter. It hurried up the stairs and showed no one in them. Meanwhile, the dog stopped at every door to open it and take a good look inside.

The fourth floor was all smoke and the dog slammed the door shut. The third floor wasn't too bad, but the second floor looked like there was fire there, too. The dog and chopper edged up to the first sub-basement with no trouble, but the first floor was one big problem.

Long files of Iteeche slowly came down the stairs and out the door. The copter showed the first floor was emptying quickly, but there was a long back-up at the stairs.

We had a problem.

The chopper also showed that there were a large number of Iteeche milling around in the courtyard outside. With no one telling them what to do, they'd slowly meander their way out to the street before dispersing.

How were we going to get around that mob?

I was glad not to have to solve that problem. I was fresh out of problem solving for the day. Maybe even the month.

It was all I could do not to suck my thumb or cry for my mommy. I was a big girl, but right now it was awfully hard to act like it.

We headed up the stairs. I was dragging my feet. They felt like lead. Flight after flight I trudged up, one stair at a time. I wished someone would hold me, like Johnny, but I was too big for one of the other big kids and Gramma had to hold her rifle at the ready. We were near the back of the line and I knew that if anyone tried to catch up with us, she'd be the one to take them under fire.

I fingered my small automatic. I knew she'd be standing in front of me if it came to a fight. I doubted my tiny 2-mm darts would do much good against a grown-up Iteeche. Still, I was tired of being ordered around.

I'd hated to have Daisy kill that stupid Iteeche with the rifle, but if anyone tried to hurt me or my gramma, I'd do whatever I could to help my Gramma Trouble. I would be Trouble, too.

A Marine led us out of the stairwell at the first sub-basement. We turned around the block with the stairwell and headed back up to the top of the wing where it met the main building. There wasn't a stairwell there, so I wondered why we were going there.

Stupid me! I forgot! Marines love blowing stuff up!

I heard the first explosion. It seemed distant. Half a minute later, the lead Marine in our now-straggling line halted and pushed several children back a bit.

Two breaths later, there was a huge boom and a small section of the overhead fell away to crash on the floor. Concrete shards flew everywhere, but only a few hit the kids that were too close.

A moment later, a ladder came through the hole in the roof. Our lead Marine rushed forward to see that it was seated right, then held it steady. Four more Marines slid down the ladder and quickly formed a perimeter. Four more followed them and trotted over to report to Grampa Trouble.

"You took long enough, sir," Gunny said, saluting.

"I'm getting old. I decided to take the scenic route. Gunny, if you would," he said.

Four more Marines were down, adding depth to the perimeter. The three other Marines were now helping kids to climb the ladder. A couple of the smaller ones, Johnny included, were just handed up.

There was no order. No priority. Whoever was next in line was helped to climb the ladder. Be they Human or Iteeche, they went up in the order they arrived.

I have to say; we kids were very well behaved. There was no pushing or trying to break line. I knew I'd be one of the last, so I joined Gramma on guard duty. She had her rifle at the ready. I had my pistol.

Still, it was nice to feel her hand resting on my shoulder. Yeah, I know, the armor kept me from really feeling it, but every once in a while, her finger would brush against my neck.

It felt so good.

We backed up together, keeping our eyes out, but having no trouble staying with Mo who was making sure that none of the kids in the back wandered off. It's crazy, but a few did try. Some kids are just brain dead.

Finally, it was my turn to climb up the ladder. I think Gramma knew how tired I was. The Marines had taken to tying a rope around the last couple of kids and they half-climbed and were half- pulled up the ladder.

I didn't complain one bit when they did that to me.

At the top of the ladder, I saw what all the fuss was about. Iteeche and Human Marines quadcopters had landed in the street. They now controlled the intersection. Attack choppers orbited tightly above them.

Just one look at the Marines and most Iteeche were busy going somewhere else. No one even thought of raising a rifle.

Gramma Trouble was up the ladder right behind me and Grampa

behind her. I was hustled into a copter. It took off before we finished buckling our belts.

With a glance out the window, I saw that the quadcopter was staying low, but heading toward the mountains, not right back to the Embassy. That's about all I saw. My head fell to rest on Gramma's shoulder. She had a protective arm around me.

For the first time since I got that crazy idea of having a swim party, I felt safe.

I don't remember falling asleep, but the next thing I know, Grampa Trouble was carrying me into my bedroom. Gramma spun the armor off of me. I rolled over to snuggle up to my pillow and was again asleep.

I'd likely be in trouble tomorrow, but for now, it was just great to be home.

39

Gramma Ruth tucked the blanket in tighter around her grandchild. The little girl was dirty and bedraggled, but a bath would have to wait for tomorrow. The girl needed sleep more than food or cleaning.

Across from her, Johnny had already kicked off his blanket. Under her husband's watchful eye, Ruth tucked him back in as well.

They both looked worse for the wear.

Johnny was sucking his thumb. He'd given that up a few years ago. It was sad when a brave little boy of almost six had to regress back that far.

Of course, if Ruth had applied her grandmother skills, she should have recognized that both the kids were under pressure since their parents had deployed this time. Both had taken to calling their mom 'mommy,' something they had also outgrown.

I made a horrible mistake, Gramma Ruth thought.

With so much trouble going on around the Legation District, she'd let herself be sucked back into the old ways of the warrior.

The kids had paid the price.

She thought she was too old for this kind of a mistake, but the proof lay softly sleeping there in front of her.

Ruth turned to see all six of the nannies waiting for her. She waved them out of the room. Officially, they were now tutors and teachers, not only for the Longknife kids but a big chunk of the Embassy's kids.

Tonight, they'd have to do nanny duty.

"One of us will sit up with the children," Gunny Gabby said. "If they have nightmares, we'll be there to hold them."

Ruth was glad that the Gunny in charge of the tutors knew what she wanted before it was spoken. A gentle nod sealed the deal.

"Call us if they want us," Ruth said. The nannies nodded acknowledgement.

Gramma and Grampa Trouble left the kids under the watchful eye of Sally Greer, a combat-trained and experienced medic. As much as Ruth wanted to stay herself, there was still the matter of the constant annoying pinprick attacks on the Legation.

"Pretty Penny, is everyone available for a staff confab?" Ruth asked.

"Abby would like a bit more time to put Bruce to sleep. Amanda and Jacques likewise. Is thirty minutes soon enough?"

A glance showed Trouble was agreeable.

"We'll take it."

"What do we do with thirty minutes?" the old general asked.

"I want out of this armor and a good scrub," Ruth answered.

Thirty minutes later, washed and if not refreshed, then at least clean, Gramma and Grampa Trouble settled into their places at the table in the command center. Around them were some very angry faces. Their kids were back home, but that didn't mean they were any happier about the kidnappings and the Iteeche who did it.

"What are the chances that we can just level the so-called palace of the Broam Clan?" Amanda asked. "It's already burning and I think everyone is gone."

"Did the Clan Chiefs order the kidnapping?" General Konga asked back. His Chosen was among the kidnapped victims. He had every right to be angry. It was interesting that he was being the voice of reason.

Every head turned to Special Agent in Charge Foile. From the look on his face, he was none too happy.

"The answer to your question is very likely no. We have had the Broam Clan Chiefs under close observation this entire time. We've had *every* clan with a membership of more than a thousand under the microscope. Based on what we've picked up, I can't tell you that *any* particular clan is responsible for taking the kids."

"No one has shot off their mouth? No one has bragged?" Abby said, incredulously.

"No. Not one lord or lordling in the command loop of the clans, major, medium, or minor, that we bugged has said anything more about the kidnapping other than what we've been saying ourselves. 'Who could pull this off?' Of course, they also add, 'Who pulled the Humans' tail?' All available evidence points to the clan bosses being totally out of the loop on this one," the agent said.

"Or they've learned to be very careful what they say and where they say it," General Bruce grumbled.

"So, you're telling me that minor players pulled this entire thing off, but still managed to lock the kids up in the basement of the Broam Clan Palace?" Gramma Ruth said.

"Yes. If I was to guess anything," the agent said, "the Broam Clan Chiefs likely had the least to do with it. It's only suspicion, but I strongly suspect that someone set them up for the fall. Maybe even one of the minor lordlings in the clan who wanted to open up some jobs at the top. That or some other clan that wants to absorb what we leave of the clan."

Abby shook her head. "The morality and politics here are sickening. I know we Humans have our dirty politics, but this capitol is just one big open sewer."

The Iteeche admiral and general glanced at each other, then the admiral spoke, "Among the Imperial uniform services, there is such a thing as loyalty. Outside these walls, the only loyalty you'll see is to your own self. Maybe to your family, possibly to your sept, but nothing more."

Ruth sighed. "It's like we're playing dice with a pair of polyhedrons. Worse, every time we look, there are more sides to the polyhedron than there was a moment ago."

The two Iteeche eyed Gramma Trouble. Clearly the translation was not catching her meaning. "Surely you have games with six-sided dice?" she asked.

They nodded.

"Imagine a pair of dice with *sixty* sides. Maybe more. That's what I feel like we're facing. It's impossible to guess what number we'll roll next, or what will happen next."

"That is an interesting way of describing Imperial politics," Admiral Ulan said. "Though a very enlightening way, I must agree."

"That makes it very hard to predict the possible actions of the whole," Ambassador Kawaguchi said.

"But it only gets worse," Abby drawled. "Between the time you toss the dice and them landing, they may grow a half-dozen or more new sides."

Those around the table nodded, if only with their eyes. Of course, when an Iteeche nods with their eyes, there's a lot of nodding going on.

As the others sat there, thoughtful, Gramma Trouble worried her lower lip. She'd had a thought nagging at the back of her head for quite a while. She closed her eyes and invited it to come forward. Like a kitten on soft paws, it slowly stuck its nose out from the couch it had been hiding behind.

Gramma Trouble spoke into the silence slowly, letting her thoughts develop as she spoke each word. "Special Agent Foile, the kidnappers managed to jam Nelly Net when they took the children."

"Yes, ma'am."

"The steel chamber they kept the kids in blocked all communications with the outside world. There was no jamming around it."

"No ma'am. It was not necessary."

"Did you search for jamming anywhere else in the city?" she asked.

"We did, but we found none. A jammer needed to be a pretty large and sophisticated drone. I was afraid to have too many of them up all the time. They're a pretty obvious sight that the hated Humans are watching you. I prefer the smaller, nearly-invisible scouts."

"So, no one jammed while you were looking."

"Correct."

"You have no idea where someone might have jammed us while you weren't looking."

"I see what you're getting at," Abby said. "No one we listened in on talked about the kidnapping like they knew anything about it."

"Anyone who did talk about it likely used a jammer," Grampa Trouble said.

"I'll have jammers up immediately and keep them there," Agent Foile said. "I can't believe I made this mistake."

"We were all balancing a lot of competing interests," Ruth said. "Now, however, I would really like to talk to the guy who jammed us. It seems evident that he's a Human from the Greenfeld Empire. I have to wonder what other tricks he brought in his carpet bag."

"Are you thinking the rebels might have the Smart Metal programmers they need to improve the battle-worthiness of their ships when they battle Kris's fleet?" Admiral Ulan asked.

"I'm afraid I am," Gramma Trouble answered. "Up until now, getting our children back was our number one priority. Now, I think finding the high-tech assets that someone has hired should be at the top of our list of things to do. Find the jammer, and I think we'll find the rest."

That received silent approval from around the table. Since Special Agent Foile was already staring at the overhead, communing with his smart computer, Sherlock, there was little to add until his fishing expedition landed a noisy fish.

Ruth took a deep breath and changed the topic. "Anyone have any idea for how we end the blockade of the Legation District?"

The silence around the table was deafening.

"Could we throw a sing-along and invite all the Clan Chiefs here? If the Emperor comes as well, maybe we could hammer out an agreement to stop this noise in the streets," Amanda said.

"I'd hate to have all those 'honor guards' inside our perimeter,"

General Bruce answered. "How well could we handle matters if someone got rambunctious?"

"I should hate to have the Emperor at such a meeting," Ambassador Kawaguchi added. "All our eggs would be in one basket. The target would be too inviting for the snakes that lurk in too many clan bosoms."

"I see your point," Amanda admitted. "I guess there's no diplomatic way out of this."

"I fear not," the ambassador said.

Abby cocked her head to one side. "Kris Longknife ended the last blockade by showing that she could get in and out anytime she wanted to."

"And making it a wild carnival game when she did," Jacques added.

"Could we make it such a game?" Gramma Trouble asked.

"How?" the two Iteeche flag officers said as one.

"Could we try vacuuming up our protestors again? Only this time we lock them up down in our basement?" General Bruce asked. "I'd love to lock some of those jokers up after I saw what they did to our kids."

"The people outside our walls are not the fellows that took the kids," Amanda was quick to point out.

"Besides," Jacques put in, "they'd just hire more thugs from where they rented that bunch. There's no end of the supply of poor Iteeche that have lost their clan affiliations, or never had one. They come cheap. They could load us up with too many mouths to feed."

"Maybe we wouldn't have to keep them," Gramma Trouble said. "We could vacuum them up and send them out just as quickly as they hired more."

She broke into a broad grin. "We still have trucks coming in with supplies. Why not truck them over to the Broam Clan and drop them off there? That would certainly give them a kick in the pants without causing too much permanent harm."

Abby shook her head. "I'm not so sure," she said. "We'd be

dumping on them a lot of hungry mouths to feed. We'd feel obliged to feed them. Any Iteeche Clan Chief . . . not so much."

"Yeah," Ruth had to admit.

"I might suggest that we are not getting anywhere fast," Abby said. "Let's get some sleep. Things are stable around the Legation District. I don't know about you, but I want to spend tomorrow with my kids."

She paused for a moment, then eyed General Konga. "Any chance we could actually have a nice beach party at the Emperor's lake?"

"A very secure beach party," the Iteeche general added as he agreed.

40

I remembered waking up several times during the night, but soft arms held me and soothed me back to sleep before I really came awake. When I finally did wake up, I was starving.

Still, I wondered if I deserved to eat breakfast.

Mommy and Daddy had never sent me to bed hungry. At least not that I could remember. Not me or Johnny. Still, some of my friends whispered about such punishments.

DAISY, ARE YOU RESTRICTED? I asked. Sometimes I lost full privileges with Daisy. She could still do study things with me, just not fun things.

TO THE BEST OF MY KNOWLEDGE, I'M NOT UNDER ANY RESTRICTIONS. MATA HARI AND PRETTY PENNY HAVE SPENT A LOT OF TIME WITH ME. THEY WANTED TO KNOW EVERYTHING ABOUT WHILE WE WERE KIDNAPPED. I TOLD THEM. I WAS DEFINITELY TOLD THAT MY LOGIC OF SNEAKING OUT AND HAVING A BEACH PARTY WAS DEFEC- TIVE AND IMMATURE. I'M NEVER EVER TO NOT LET THEM KNOW IF YOU ARE GOING TO DO ANYTHING CHILDISH.

SO, YOU'RE A SNITCH NOW.

NO, I DON'T THINK SO. THEY JUST WANT TO KNOW

WHAT WE'RE GETTING INTO. THEY SAY WE HAVE A RIGHT TO BE KIDS AND MAKE KIDS' MISTAKES. HOW ARE WE GOING TO LEARN? THEY JUST DON'T WANT TO BE TAKEN BY SURPRISE.

I DEFINITELY LEARNED MY LESSON, I said, with a sigh.

Shani was waiting beside my bed when I finally opened my eyes. I liked her; she had kind, expressive eyes. I always knew where I was with her even before she said a word.

"You, little princess, are filthy. You look like you haven't taken a bath in a week."

"I *haven't* taken a bath in a week!" I pointed out.

"Well," she said, pulling my tank top over my head, "has her royal highness finally learned that baths are a good thing?"

"Oh, have I!" I squealed as she caught my clothes and sent me hurrying toward the bathroom.

Her computer, Zulu Princess, had the tub filling even as I stepped into it. I sank down and let the water float me. It felt so good.

Some time while I was soaping myself up for the fourth or fifth time, Johnny kind of sleep-walked into the bathroom. Once he saw the bath, he was in as soon as he could manage it.

The two of us felt so wonderful and safe in the warm water and under the watchful eye of a nanny we'd known all our lives.

"Gramma and Grampa Trouble are waiting for you in the commissary," Shani said. "They hope you will not stay in the bath so long that all they get to talk to this morning are little prunes."

"Are they mad at us?" Johnny asked, his lip trembling.

I was glad he asked the question. I wasn't sure I could get the words out. There was something in my throat.

"I would say that they missed you very much and are as happy to have you home as you are to be home."

"That's a lot of happy," Johnny said, and reached for a towel.

I breathed a sigh that Johnny had asked the hard question. I was also relieved at the answer. Still, I knew that I'd screwed up. I'd risked not only my life, but those that went with me. Just as bad, I'd risked the mission of Mommy's Embassy.

I don't think I'd ever been spanked. I really wished someone would tan my bottom for what I'd done.

Johnny dashed for Gramma and Grampa Trouble just as soon as we stepped into the dining room. Grampa reached down and lifted Johnny high as he took him into his arms and hugged him tight.

I walked stiffly to stand before Gramma Trouble.

"I know I screwed up. I made a terrible mistake thinking that we could have a swim party at the pond all by ourselves. I know I caused you all sorts of trouble. I promise I'll never do it again and I'll accept any punishment you want to give me."

Somewhere in there, tears began to roll down my cheeks, but I ignored them, keeping my arms at my side. I wasn't quite standing at attention, but I was trying.

Gramma went down on a knee to put her eyes even with mine and opened her arms to me. That was all it took. I threw myself into a hug that was so tight it would have squished the stuffing out of one of my fluffy toys.

We Longknifes, however, are made of sterner stuff. Oh, fudge. Who was I kidding? We Longknifes may cry, we just don't scatter our stuffing all over the place.

It was a while before Gramma and Grampa would let go of us and led us to the steam tables. They left their half-eaten food behind to cool without a backwards glance.

Johnny was such a suck-up. He got all the bacon he asked for, although he did have to take some scrambled eggs and hash browns. I fed lots of vegetables into an omelet maker, then chose a piece of poached fish and some hash browns.

"You can go back for more if you're still hungry," Gramma Trouble told us. Then, when Johnny's eyes lit up, she quickly added, "No more bacon, you scamp. We can't have you turning into a pig."

"He already is," I said, adding an "oink, oink" noise.

He "oinked" right back at me. His "oink" sounded really nasty, like you'd expect from a boy.

On the way back to our table, I finally had eyes for more than just Gramma and Grampa Trouble. A lot of our friends were eating with their parents. Not just those of us that messed up. I think a lot of parents wanted to keep their kids close after what we'd done.

After I'd eaten my omelet, Gramma Trouble asked, "Would you like to have that beach party you started off on?"

I swallowed hard. "I'd be just as happy to have it at the Embassy swimming park," I answered quickly.

"Yes, but we'd like to have it at the Emperor's pond," Gramma said. "General Konga has asked the Imperial Household to let us use the lake. The Emperor has assured us that it is permissible and that a certain other kid might join us."

I eyed Johnny. He was fidgeting as much as I was. "We don't deserve a beach party," I said. "You shouldn't let us have one."

I know my lower lip was quivering, but I did my very best to put a brave face on it. "I really screwed up, Gramma."

"You weren't the only one," she answered. "We came out here to keep you kids company. Then trouble starts and we gallop off like it was old times again. We all made mistakes, little Ruth. We are not rewarding you for your mistakes. We are reminding all of us that we can't forget each other like what has happened this last couple of weeks. We *want* to have a fun time with you."

"You do?" I said and threw myself back into her arms. Even more tears fell this time. *Where had all the water works come from?*

So we ate breakfast, and I did go back for a second omelet. Johnny went back and raided the sausage. The guy used puppy eyes to get around Gramma and Grampa.

It's disgusting what a kid will try to get away with. And what the grown-ups will let them get away with.

The walk to the lake was kind of fun. Excited kids were pulling their folks along, eager to get wet. All of us were under the watchful eyes of guards; some in civilian clothes, others in full battle rattle. While we kids walked, there were plenty of armored trucks rolling slowly along in front of us, behind us, and a few among us. A couple of little kids even wiggled their way up to ride on the front hoods of the rigs.

None of them showed any weapons. You weren't supposed to

bring weapons onto the Imperial Palace grounds unless you were a member of the Imperial Guard or a clan Honor Guard. The gun rigs showed the Imperial Guard crest but none showed guns.

Of course, if something happened, they'd have guns out before you could finish blinking an eye.

I felt comfortable with them. I felt comfortable right up to the moment we walked into the shaded lane under some of the huge trees.

Suddenly, I was slammed with the memory of what happened the last time we were under such shadows. I started trembling. My heart felt like it would pound its way out of my chest. My mouth was as dry as if I hadn't had a drink in days. I couldn't get enough breath in me even thought I seemed to be breathing awfully fast.

Gramma Trouble squeezed my hand tighter and I glanced up at her. She was smiling softly at me. I followed her eyes to focus on the nearest gun truck and imagined it having a monster anti-tank gun on it.

I felt better. Not good or right, but better. At least I was able to breathe again.

Tranna showed up, the Emperor I mean, except he didn't want to be Emperor that day, just a kid. He still had a long line of advisors following him, but they weren't arguing much with him about coming along to *our* party at *his* lake.

It was wonderful. Just as wonderful as it had been before, even if Mommy and Daddy weren't there. We played games, swam, ate delicious food, and chased each other. It was hard to believe that two days ago, some of us had been locked away in a tightly welded box wondering how much they were going to hurt us.

Now, we could laugh about it. At least throwing the soggy and slimy rations at the Iteeche was funny and it seemed everyone, even the Emperor, wanted to know about it. He laughed and the grown-ups laughed. We all laughed.

But I was close by when the Emperor turned to General Konga and said. "I am seriously displeased with whoever did this. If you or the Humans can bring the criminals who did this before me in chains, I will see that they die a long and painful death."

"To hear your words is to make it so," the general said.

Chills ran up and down my spine. I'd never heard such cold anger. Never heard it, but I had a real strong feeling that my mommy had said things like that.

I was a Longknife. We do what has to be done. I suspect that had I just seen something like we did, I would do something like Mom would do and then dress the story up with something that didn't scare us kids and made adults chuckle.

Only a week had passed since we were snatched on our way to this very same beach. Only a week, but I felt so much older than I had then.

Mom had told us about what she felt when her little brother Eddy was snatched. She'd been about my age then. Her brother had died when the kidnappers bungled things. My grandfather had seen to it that they were tried and sentenced to hang.

The entire family, my mom included, had watched them swing.

If the men and Iteeche who did this to us kids were found and brought before the Emperor for a meeting with the snakes, I would not flinch as I watched them die.

Yeah, I was older today.

Then my brother threw sand at me and I took off chasing him into the water. He screamed like a little pig and I told him so. He insisted he was a shark.

I really enjoyed that day. I especially liked being driven back to the Embassy with Gramma Trouble in a three-wheeled jitney. I rested my head on her shoulder and drifted off to sleep.

I remember waking up during the night, my heart pounding. Again, one of the nannies was there with soothing words to help me slip back to sleep before I woke up. Before I was awake enough to remember the nightmare.

I wondered how long it would take me to get a good night's sleep. I didn't bother asking the adults. I wasn't at all sure they knew the answer.

41

G ramma Trouble scowled deeply the next day when Special Agent Foile made his report.

He had nothing to report.

"Nothing?" Abby demanded.

"There is still a lot of talk on the street. Iteeche want every scrap of the story about the kidnapping. There's a cottage industry in spinning rumors, each more outlandish than the last. Still, there's nothing that sounds even close to what the actual criminals might say."

"I doubt they'd want on the street the real story of how our kids made fools of them," Abby drawled, ruefully.

"Still, do any of the rumors or stories contain a nugget of what actually happened?" Jacques said. "I mean, being stopped by kids with fish tanks they were supposed to eat from. Being slimed by old Human combat rations so that they were held outside the prison. Admittedly, that does make the kidnappers look ridiculous but there is other stuff they could tell. Like, how did a batch of non-Broam Clan hoods get that steel in the building and weld together that prison?"

"No," the agent answered. "The actual story of them saving themselves so a rescue could go in is not on the street. None of the rumors are even close to that."

"I think the kidnappers are offering their balls to us to grab," Grampa Trouble said with a chuckle.

"I agree," Abby said. "Let's grab them hard and twist."

"What are you talking about?" was from Admiral Ulan, but it was clear he spoke for both Iteeche flag officers. Since Iteeche did not have any visible sexual organs, male or female, the metaphor was likely hard for them to catch.

"I had the devil's own time not laughing when I realized what the kids had going," Ruth said. "It was both absurd and ridiculous. Understand?"

"It does appear that way. I have a hard time believing it and I've seen your helmet video," General Konga said.

"So," Ruth said, glancing from her husband to Abby and back again. "Admiral, we need the use of the several bards you know. I'd like to see what kind of songs they would sing about our kids holding off their kidnappers with lima beans and spaghetti."

"That would need a better translation," the admiral answered, "but I see no reason why the bards in our fleet and those we are friends with couldn't come up with some very interesting songs involving the kids saving themselves with some of our most detested combat rations."

"Songs that make the kidnappers the laughingstock of the Imperial Capitol," Abby added, grinning from ear to ear.

"I can't wait to see how this plays out," Jacques said, with a chuckle. "Kids still in the Palace of Learning keeping armed gunmen at bay with disgusting and ancient combat rations. That says a lot about our kids."

"Both the Iteeche and Human younglings," General Konga agreed. "Let Admiral Ulan and I have a day. Two at the most. By then, bards and singers will be proclaiming these younglings' victory from every bazaar and street corner. With any luck, by next week we will have several media outlets including our songs on the nightly sing-alongs."

The admiral laughed that coughing Iteeche laugh before he could say, "Half the Iteeche in the Imperial Capitol will be humming and singing our song as they laugh at the folly and stupidity of the youngling snatchers."

When the joking about that settled down, Gramma Trouble cleared her throat. "I've got a batty idea about how we might clear away the protestors surrounding the Legation District."

"Not another one of your batty ideas," Grampa Trouble muttered, with something between a sigh and a groan. Still, his lips were quirking up at the edges. "Okay, my girl, let us in on our next devious game changer."

Ruth leaned forward and, in a whisper, began to lay out a plan that just might get them out of this mess.

42

The next morning, anyone who was smart would have noticed something was up when the Human Embassy castle appeared two stories shorter the next morning.

However, few of the paid demonstrators on the streets around the wall surrounding the Legation District could see the tower from where they stood. They had their noses up against a six-meter-high wall that blocked their view. Of course, none of them, not even the leaders put in charge by the clans involved, bothered to back off and take a gander at the physical proof that Humans were in the Imperial Capitol.

To an Iteeche, they detested the sight of that abomination.

Besides, when you're looking at a one hundred and fifty-story building that now only has one hundred and forty floors, how do you notice that the nefarious Humans have taken out yet another two stories?

Since none of them had counted the stories on the Human castle, none of them were prepared for what happened next.

The morning demonstration was going as planned. The new shift, with half their pay in their pocket, were jeering and shaking several of their fists at the Human and Iteeche guards high up on the wall.

There were shouts about certain improprieties in their ancestry and the horrible futures that awaited them if they didn't come down off that wall and join the protests.

The overseers of the hired protesters congregated together in groups of three, four, or five. They would have no truck with such a rabble. They were, however, interested in the latest gossip circulating around the Capitol streets.

There were so many stories being told about the return of the stolen younglings. It was too delicious to not take a moment or longer to laugh at the Humans and what they did to return their own newly Chosen to their creches.

Again, if they'd been paying attention, they'd have noticed the difference up on the wall. There was a lot more people. Some guards in combat gear, other technicians in the uniform of the day.

Therefore, the first warning any of them had was when huge tubes snaked out from the wall. Also, like snakes, the tubes opened their jaws wide before they slammed down on those small groups of gabbing junior lordlings a good distance from the wall.

Unlike the tubes Kris Longknife used to suck up Iteeche in front of her convoy and dump them in the street behind all her gun trucks, these tubes were not transparent. No one outside could see what was happening inside.

That was just as well, those inside couldn't see much either. They could hear each other screaming as the small tubes surrounding each of them sucked first one, then the next and the next, up into a darkness as terrifying as the inky depths of the sea.

Their passage along the tube seemed to last forever. Unlike Kris's tubes, these were too small for anyone to tumble head over heels in. No, these were narrow. The confines were as tight as one of the coffins for ancient kings that the museum had, assuming any of the junior lordlings had ever paused to stroll through the past while scheming about the future.

While it seemed like forever that they were sucked along with their hands and feet forced tight against their bodies, it was actually only two minutes before each of them was spat out of the tube.

The Iteeche have a saying that translates almost word for word for the Human phrase, "going from the frypan into the fire." It goes something like, "escaping from the barracuda only to be snatched by the shark."

Whichever image stuck in these young clan lordlings minds, they certainly knew that they were living it.

From the tight, completely dark tube they were spat out into equally tight, but transparent containment tubes. With their four eyes, they had no problem taking in the room. It was rapidly filling with other Iteeche in the same predicament.

Horrifying as their situations were, the sight of Iteeche in red robes and tight black pants and sleeveless shirts told them that they were in trouble. Deep trouble!

They were in the hands of the symbol of clan and Imperial power – the executioners!

As more detainees arrived, their tight containers were wheeled aside and stacked one on top of the other. That gave everyone but the top row a good look at a couple of butts, but not much else. Several tried screaming, but none of those around them reacted. It was as if they could hear nothing.

Most fell silent. Several lost their minds and screamed as long as their throats could manage it. Soon enough, they fell silent, their mouths parched and their throats raw from the effort.

They'd been parked with their heads up against the wall. They could see nothing. They could, however, hear something.

Into their blind silence came the hissing of snakes. Only slowly did it raise in volume. It started low enough that it hardly registered on their ears, but somewhere deep in their collective psyche, aware- ness dawned ahead of conscious knowledge.

It took a while for all of them to fully recognize the hiss of snakes. One by one, the watchers saw Iteeche panic. Scream. Desperately try to move in the tight confines of their tiny prison to see where the noise was coming from.

Desperately try to find the serpent in their tiny space and somehow get away from it.

Gramma Trouble watched developments from the command center. With her was General Konga, Commanding General of the Imperial Guard. He'd likely watched more Most Sincere and Very Complete Apologies to the Emperor than anyone alive.

Now he surveyed the agony in the tiny cells and observed, "I don't think you could do anything worse to an Iteeche than what we're doing here. Tell me, are you doing this to all the Iteeche you're sucking up from outside the wall?"

"No," Gramma Trouble was quick to say. She shook her head for emphasis.

"They're all getting the ride in the tight confines of the tubes, but if we don't see any evidence that they're clan associated, we spit them out next to an empty truck where some of the biggest Marines and Navy types are there to greet them. All in executioner black. That gets their attention. Just in case they need an extra boost, there are a few guys in the red robes of snake wranglers. No one has to know that the crystal jar they carry, and the snake inside, are made of Smart Metal."

Admiral Ulan and General Konga enjoyed a good laugh at the subterfuge and the agony these troublemakers were now suffering. While they made their strange Iteeche laugh, Ruth also joined in the mirth.

"What about the others?" Admiral Ulan asked. "How long are you going to let them . . . what is your word? Stew."

"We say stew in their own juices, and it appears that a lot of them lost control of some of their bodily functions. They've got some serious juice to stew in."

That required another long moment to enjoy. These hoodlums had been creating trouble for the better part of the month. It was a joy to have them under their thumb.

"In a bit, we'll start talking to them. We want to know who sent them. Which clans are they associated with, and what they know about the kidnapping of our kids?"

"Do you really think they know anything about the kidnapping?" the general asked.

"Do I think we got our hands on one of the kidnappers?" Ruth answered a question with a blunt answer, "No."

"However," she said, going on, "it is possible that they know more than they think they know. Also, the sum of all their ignorance could have enough rope to weave the truth out of."

"I believe you are mixing your metaphors," Admiral Ulan said. "I have enough trouble following some of your phrases. However, I do understand what you're getting at. I assume your smart computers will be listening in on all the interrogations?"

"Yes. They'll also be feeding questions to the interrogators. If there is anything to learn from them, we will learn it."

"I like that."

"Ruth, one of the detainees is in physical distress," Pretty Penny reported. "The guards are about to pull him out of his cage into an interrogation room. We will have a doctor there as well as an executioner and a snake wrangler. There is no reason why we cannot interrogate him while we alleviate his distress."

"Very good, Pretty Penny. Now, General, Admiral, why don't we let your people and our computers take care of these poor, misdirected clan lordlings? I'm interested in how things are around the district."

"Me too," both flag officers said.

Since they had been observing the detainees from the Command Center, it only took a thought to have Pretty Penny switch their view from the detention stations to the view from around the wall.

There was very little to see.

"Penny, since there's not much to see now, could you show us what happened when we started the take down?"

"It was more like a take up, Ruth."

"Now your computer tells jokes," the Iteeche admiral said drolly.

"Now my computer is telling a *better* quality of joke," Ruth pointed out. "You would not have wanted to hear some of what she tried to pass off for humor when she started."

"I have observed," Pretty Penny observed with a distinct sniff, "some of what passes for humor among your great-great-grandkids. It appears that humor is an acquired taste."

"Just show us the pictures, Penny," Ruth said, her lack of sleep showing. She hadn't had to watch anyone die in the fires their grenades started. Still, she'd seen enough burning troops in her life that her recent nightmares had plenty of fodder.

Now they watched as the tubes snaked out from the wall. The operation started simultaneously along three sides of the district. Without hesitation, they'd snatched up every clump of identified clan lordlings overseeing these irritating demonstrations.

The tubes had hardly landed when some of the smarter hired ruffians began to back away. Full flight began when the tubes rose but a few meters before opening wide and landing on groups of four to six Iteeche of the hired hands.

Some of the mob had been laughing. They remembered that Kris Longknife had given some of them quite a ride to get them out of the way of her convoy from the space elevator station. They quit laughing about the time someone noted that these tubes were not clear. They weren't seeing what was going on inside and the ride ended behind the wall.

"What are they doing in there?" someone screamed.

"They could be grinding us up for fish food!" another shrieked.

That was when the real panic began.

The tubes still struck, quick as snakes, snatching up four or six to begin with. A minute or two later, there were only stragglers. Most of them were smart enough to keep away from each other. The tubes had to settle for ones and twos by then.

In the end, the tubes were picking up those whom the crowd had trampled and were more in need of medical care than capture.

"Are we trucking the non-clan toughs out of here as fast as we can?" the Iteeche general asked.

"We had thought to," Pretty Penny answered. "However, we have re-evaluated that part of the plan."

"Why?" the Iteeche admiral asked.

"Some of the first street people that we sucked up landed on their feet and immediately started telling our guard everything they knew about the kidnappers."

"Do they have anything interesting to tell us?" Admiral Ulan asked.

"Not a lot, and what we have found is pretty low-quality intelligence. However, we decided to let them talk to anyone we could get handy. It wasn't so much an interrogation as a gab fest."

"And?" Ruth said. "Is there a story in here somewhere?"

"One of them thought he saw the kidnapping van leave the Imperial Grounds. He'd been watching one of the gates our supply trucks were using. There were several with him. They all hoped to snatch some food off any trucks that got into a fender bender. He'd seen a lot of single trucks go in and come out. Then suddenly a truck and a van came out with an armored car in front and behind it. That got his attention."

"Did he follow it?" the general asked.

"No, he can barely hobble. However, he distinctly remembers it turning onto the belt avenue around the Imperial Palace. It turned in the opposite direction from the Broam Clan."

"That's interesting," Ruth said, slow and puzzled. "Penny, did the kids comment about being moved from one place to another early on?"

"No, Ruth. When they woke up from their drugged sleep, they were already in the metal containment that we found them in. Sherlock and I find this very interesting."

"How so?" Gramma Trouble asked.

"If their initial goal was to put the kids up in the Broam Clan Palace, why didn't they head there? If their plan was to contain the kids somewhere else, why did they start in that direction, then redirect themselves in the middle of the kidnapping? Of course, half the clans have districts in the opposite direction, so neither I nor Sherlock can surmise anything from this turn. Still, if it is true, it says a lot about this hastily knocked together action."

Ruth leaned back in her chair and studied the lovely view from the hundred and fortieth floor. Her line of sight showed her the Imperial Palace. She could see the lane from the gate where the kids entered, clear to the gate that the kidnappers used to leave the scene of their crime.

If the yahoos had turned left, that opened up a lot of the Capitol to them before the mountains in the west rose to slow the growth of the sprawling city. What they had done didn't really tell them a whole lot.

Of course, any information could grow powerful if it attracted more information.

"Pretty Penny, our temporary detainees must be hungry. Please see that the more talkative among them are given lunch. See if you can gather up a lot of our daily work force and give them instructions to keep our luncheon guests talking about anything, but whenever possible, the kidnapping."

"Will do, boss lady," Penny answered. "I'll also put out a work request to my siblings for any and all possible support to comb through the mass of fibs, lies, and just plain concoctions they tell us to see if we can find a few tiny nuggets of gold."

"Thank you, Pretty Penny," Gramma Trouble said, then glanced at the two Iteeche officers. "The worthless words may be as uncountable as the grains of sand on your largest beach. Still, if we can find a few flakes of gold, they can help us direct our interrogation of our more long-term guests."

"The things that you can do with your brilliant computers," Admiral Ulan said, shaking his head. "Our Emperor was wise to invite you into the Empire."

The general actually managed a grimace. "You Humans and your technology may save us today, but many of us fear the tsunami that will follow in your wake tomorrow."

"We understand," Gramma Trouble answered. "However, you know as well as I do that the wall between our two species was leaking like a sieve. It wasn't a question of if a tidal wave was coming as how soon. That, and who would control the Human technology loose in the Empire."

The big Iteeche general sucked in a deep breath and let it out slowly. "You are regrettably very right. I rue the day your pirates stumbled onto our gold smugglers. From that day forth, the old Empire's drowning was only a question of time. Oh, to live in days like these."

"We have a curse," Ruth said. "It says, 'May you live in interesting times.' I think the world we live in fits that curse, don't you, General?"

"Too true. Too true."

"Now, Admiral, General, I think we've done about as much damage as we can for one day. I've got a date on my calendar to call words for a spelling bee in my granddaughter's class. If you will excuse me, I must go. I'll check back at 1630 hours to look into developments but for the rest of the day, I'm with my grandkids."

So it was that key staff departed, each to their important duty for the day.

43

T he table in the Command Center was full later that afternoon as it came time for the first "shift change" since the Humans and Navy had either detained or chased away the morning shift of hired protestors. General Trouble had suggested they all attend.

The situation outside the wall could be a big nothing. However, it might get interesting and require some seriously innovative actions. As usual, General Trouble brought trouble.

Four blocks back from the wall, buses and trucks came to a halt and off-loaded the hired help. Large luxury cars brought the clan lordlings charged with overseeing this highly scripted affair.

At least they thought it would go down by their script.

This time, drones marked those in the fancy dress that stepped out of the fancy cars. From the moment they stepped out onto the sidewalk they were marked Iteeche.

Straw bosses got the demonstrators moving toward the wall. Usually, there would be a few shirkers that had left the wall early skulking around the street, wanting to be first on the trucks so they'd be first to get the second half of their pay.

No one missed them today. Thus, they missed the first sign that things were rapidly about to go off script.

The command staff found themselves facing the first decision they needed to make.

"The head high muckety mucks are pulling way up the rear," Gramma Trouble observed. "I'll bet you Wardhaven dollars to Earth script that they're going to get their heads out of their asses before they get in range of our tubes."

"And I really want to talk to those jackasses," General Bruce growled.

"So," Abby asked, "what's our priority? Do we nail the big boys or grab as many of the little fish as we can?"

"How about both?" Gramma Trouble said, grinning like a cat at a canary convention.

"What's your pleasure, wife?" the old general asked.

She told them and they got busy moving around a lot of Smart Metal™.

The wall thinned out a bit. The protestors didn't notice. Only a few noticed that the wall also shortened from nine to six meters. No protester saw the overhead framework that shaded the bazaar quickly melt away. Any other of the metal that wasn't essential also went into the pot.

It was sufficient to the moment.

Like a big cat ready to pounce, the Legation District seemed to hold its breath. Outside, the noise of people happy to have a job for the day filled the air.

Right up to the moment that it suddenly didn't.

The first wave of replacements reached the wall and came to a roaring halt. There was no one there to swap places with. No one at all!

Questions swept back and forth among the packed-in hirelings. It didn't take long to reach the trailing overseers. They paused to discuss the issue among themselves.

This was one time they may have wished that the Capitol had a standard communications net. On any Human planet, what happened that morning would have swept the net. First as friends called friends, then as the media picked up the story, either from their own reporting or the pictures and video provided by the people who were there.

In the Iteeche Capitol there was no net and no way to get the word out.

The preening peacocks of the clan's junior players talked just long enough of this unheard-of situation to seal their doom.

Almost faster than the Human eye could track, long ropes of Smart Metal™ reached out from the wall. It spun out a loop and, like a cowboy's lariat, it lassoed the junior players just like Ruth had seen at a fair and rodeo when she was a kid growing up on a backwater planet, where horses and cows still muttered along with tractors and combines.

Ruth got the giggles as she watched first one bunch of self-pretentious fops get caught up in traps that they'd assumed would be applied to others. The ropes didn't strike all at the same time. The wall was still absorbing needed Smart Metal™ from throughout the Legation District. Instead, they reached out from different sides and gates of the district. They struck each group as realization suddenly dawned on them that this was not the demonstration they'd come to put on.

No, the Humans were throwing their own demonstration and the clan lordlings were the unsuspecting and shocked targets.

The lassos held the bunch of pompous fools long enough for the rope to thicken and fill out. It encased them in the tight embrace that had initially caught the morning's demonstrators. Once they disappeared into the tight confines of these chambers, the rope spun itself wider until they were the tubes from earlier in the morning.

In amazing time, the first catch was on its way behind the wall. However, the tubes did not snake around to seize more Iteeche before they could flee.

Nope, this time the Smart Metal™ spread out to block the streets the mob had just entered from, marching to get to where they'd earn their pay. The blocking fence was thin; just a lineup of bars no more than two meters high and widely spaced at half a meter across.

Some Iteeche spotted danger and bolted while the fence was

porous. Of course, again, the well-fed clan officials were targeted. Many of the semi-starved hirelings could squeeze through the bars and flee. Not so of the Iteeche with more meat on their bones.

They, of course, showed no willingness to step to the back of the line and let the thin folks through. Instead, they clogged the fence, striving to do now what they couldn't do a few seconds ago.

Worse, the fence bars were thicker, now that more Smart Metal™ was flowing from the wall. Smart overseers and straw bosses allowed themselves to be squeezed out as the bars closed from 50 centimeters to 40, and finally settled at 30 centimeters apart.

At that point, no one was getting out.

The tubes shortened as they began to suck up those closest to the wall. These were deposited in small groups with a few armed guards and more of the civilians the Legation District had taken in.

The topic of conversation among them was the promise of supper and the recent kidnapping of the district's kids. Had anyone seen a minor convoy of a truck and a smaller van led and trailed by gun trucks? The truck and van might have been from a fish distributor.

No surprise, the small convoy was reported at every point of the compass.

Still, the conversations went long. For the first time, both Ruth and Jacques got to hear what the bottom of the social order in the Iteeche Empire felt about their social order . . . or lack thereof.

"How have they avoided a revolution?" Jacques asked the ceiling above him.

"Because the clans have all the fire power," Admiral Ulan said. "Even the Imperial Navy and Army could not stand against the united firepower of the clans. Of course, there's little chance of them uniting around anything."

"Anything?" Jacques asked, eyebrow raised.

"Anything but hatred of you Humans," the admiral quickly added.

"Yeah, I see where you're coming from," Abby drawled, and for once she sounded serious.

Meanwhile, out on the streets in front of the wall, the bars had begun to inch ever closer to the wall. It didn't take those inside the fence long to realize that they were being pushed back toward the barrier they'd been protesting against.

Suddenly, they were willing to do almost anything to avoid whatever fate the Humans had waiting for them on the other side of that wall.

Some tried to work together to get up and over the wall. That broke down. No one wanted to be the one helping who got left behind.

If ever Jacques doubted the Iteeche had trust issues, he saw plenty of proof that the entire social contract could not hold together under pressure.

He quickly got to see more examples.

While the fence bars blocked the streets, there were still other ways out. There was a dash down the side streets to the Imperial Palace, in hope of fleeing in that direction.

The wall that had closed down the circle avenue around the palace had disappeared. In place of the high wall, there now stood fences of black bars that were blocking both ends of the three streets closest to the Abba Clan. The mob could flee neither west nor east.

They were trapped!

Iteeche in fine robes that signified serious clan standing found themselves pounding on the doors of cheap apartment buildings, demanding entrance.

Not one door opened.

The fence muscled them back toward the wall. Every once in a while, when three or four well-dressed Iteeche would gather to scream at each other, a tube would reach out and swallow them up.

Proud Iteeche overseers, even before they were stuffed into the isolation of tiny detention cylinders, found themselves keeping their distance from those of their own social standing . . . and being ignored by everyone else.

There was plenty of panic to go around as the open space between the fence and the wall shrunk. Desperate Iteeche took to slugging it out. They did their best to pile up either unconscious or dead bodies. Apparently, they hoped to stack up enough bodies to they could climb over the fence.

The command group focused the tubes on those brawls, sucking people up before they could do too much damage.

The wall shrunk some more and thinned out into a fence of bars with spikes at the top. The outer fence grew higher and more spiky in turn. With more Smart Metal™ available for tubes and nice tiny cylinders for prison cells, the pace sped up as they emptied the net that they'd cast around these pests.

Gramma Trouble suggested that right about now might be a good time to turn loose the morning's catch. The truck drivers for the fish delivery services were getting testy about being held up.

This solved two problems with one stone. It emptied the district of unwanted mouths and got the trucks back to work.

It also put a lot more people on the street to talk about the attitude that both the Iteeche and Humans in the Legation District had toward those who stole their Chosen. To that, you had to add the number of released detainees who came out singing one of several catchy ditties that they'd heard about the kids and their kidnappers.

The next day, several Navy and Marine choirs were asked to sing for the sing-alongs. Even the Imperial Guard choir was made available.

Gramma Trouble was barely able to make it back to the kids for reading time as they prepared for bed, but she did. By that time, the Human Embassy was several stories higher.

In place of the wall that had surrounded the Legation District for the last month, there stood a four-meter-tall fence. Its strong metal poles were topped with decorative, but very sharp, spikes. At every street there was a gate with watch towers on either side.

Still, a fence was a lot friendlier than a blank wall. Spectators could see what was going on inside the Legation District. There were also gates. With any luck, maybe they could visit the bazaar soon.

Gramma Trouble went to bed wondering what the area around the District would look like the next day.

44

By the next morning when Gramma and Grampa Trouble checked into the Command Center things were much closer to normal.

Not one demonstrator had shown up for the morning shift. Apparently, the failure of the morning overseers to report back to their clan masters had gotten the message across. All night, naked runners had been showing up to gawk at the wall, then race away to report to someone.

Faced with no protestors, the duty officer followed the orders in his order book. The fence walked back from the other side of the street to the curb on the Legation District's side. The sidewalk around the district was still fenced off, but traffic returned to normal on both the two boulevards where they'd blocked traffic as well as the avenue circling the Imperial Palace.

"We'll take the streets back the second we see any thugs collecting on the other side. Naked slaves can report what they see, but if anyone tries to start up another round of demonstrations, we go right back in their face."

Everyone in the command staff agreed with that.

Special Agent in Charge Foile was next up.

"I could bore you with a long report that added up to very little, so I won't. Suffice it to say, the interrogations are ongoing. We're wading through tons of chaff to find a few bits of possible truth here and there. Many of the hired demonstrators 'remember' seeing the convoy. However, very few got the name on the delivery truck right. We are trying to form some idea of the route they took to the Broam Clan palace. Some of our more well-dressed Iteeche are even 'recovering memories' that they forgot."

He paused to give an expressive shrug. "We don't know how much of their recovered memory is fact or fancy to get them a yam for breakfast or time to wash and put on a clean jumpsuit. They are quite ripe and really want to clean up."

"So, you counsel patience?" Gramma Trouble asked.

"I'm afraid so. We need more time to extract information from our present detainees and to correlate it with what we have. I think we're starting to see a picture, but I'd prefer not to brief on it until we fill into some of the all too plentiful blanks in the picture."

"I think we can all wait a bit," General Trouble said. "It's nice to have things back to normal. I'd kind of like to enjoy it for a while."

So, they waited.

Two days later, they opened the bazaar to the public. There was not a hint of an incident. Also, the Iteeche who came to shop acted as if nothing had happened.

When you're as big as an Iteeche, was it easier to ignore the elephant in the room? Ruth shrugged and spent more time with her grandkids.

A week after the first beach party at the lake, they arranged another one. This time, the Emperor graciously invited one or two of the older Chosen from over a dozen families to come and share his party.

Some forty sedan chairs arrived at the appointed hour. They were swamped by the small army of kids and parents or Choosers, depending on the number of elbows, coming from the Legation District. Both Iteeche and Human younglings appeared to have plenty of fun walking along, so first one, then a few more of the newcomers, finally got out. Standing there, they considered joining the happy parade.

It was a warm, sunny day. The senior Clan Chosen still hung around their sedan chairs. Over the next few minutes, they again went through the slow, then fast process of dropping their heavy outer robes, then more of their inner robes before they settled for shorts and a singlet like everyone else.

Sometime during all this, a yell went up that the Emperor had joined the stroll and the young Iteeche took off at a run to catch up to him. By the time the young Emperor got to the beach, he had a mob around him. Half were Humans and Navy. The other half were clan Chosen. They were split right down the middle.

Choosing sides for the water polo games was very close to a diplomatic incident. All the future clan lords wanted on the Emperor's team. They certainly didn't want to play against him.

The Emperor was in high spirits and refused to let stuffy adult rules mess up his fun. He introduced the young Iteeche Chosen to rock, paper, scissors and they had an epic game of elimination. However, he had a marker and wrote a number on the right upper hand of everyone as they lost.

"Okay, here's how we're going to play this. The two of you last standing play on my team. We'll have six Iteeche and three humans. After three games, the team that lost the last game will switch to play someone else. Every three games, I will switch to play with another team until all of you have had a chance to play with me on your team. That way, everyone gets to play with me and play against me."

"But Your Worshipfulness, how can we play against you?"

"Very well, I expect. If I see anyone flubbing so that my team will win, it's out of the lake. Understand? The Navy Chosen and the Human kids can make me really work in a game. You better do it, too. Any problem?"

There were no problems.

After all the tension in getting the games going, the actual sports were wild and fun for all the younglings. The clan Chosen quickly got into the free spirit of hard work and open competition. There were a few moments of tension around some unsportsmanlike behavior when a lordling demanded that a foul be called on a big Navy Chosen, but the ruling of the umpire was fully supported by the watching crowd and the peer pressure was enough to get everyone over that hump.

At least no one started a new civil war.

"Why can't the Choosers work things out with rock, paper, scissors, or a water polo game?" one future clan leader was heard to ask another.

As the sun sank low, the lifeguards ordered everyone ashore and home.

The walk out was as much fun as the stroll in, but with a lot less tension about who walked with the Emperor. He didn't want the day to end and walked all the way to Gate 3. He waved goodbye to his guests as his guards did their level best to quiet their panic. No Emperor in history, or at least what served for history, had stood where a sniper could put a bullet in his head.

Of course, no Emperor in history had as many Human drones flying overhead looking for any shooter on a roof. Meanwhile, there were also quadcopters checking each window for danger.

General Konga told the guards to stay alert, but not interfere. "After all, he's got Admiral Longknife's grandmother at his side. How much safer could he be?"

Gramma Trouble, standing at the general's elbows, kept a smile on her face, and did not warn the general that there was nowhere within a mile of a Longknife that was a safe place to be.

The next day, Agent Foile had a report ready for them.

45

"I should like to say at the beginning that no Iteeche was hurt in the making of this report," Special Agent in charge said drolly. "We did not resort to any of the excruciating interrogation techniques suggested by our Iteeche friends. Two or three of our detainees may have a more tenuous grasp on their sanity due to two weeks spent alone with themselves, but they very likely had a weak handle on reality to begin with."

"We never did get the Iteeche to agree to any laws of war," General Trouble growled under his breath.

"I regret that it has taken me this long to make this report. This particular effort has been like putting together a jigsaw puzzle where the pieces are scattered through the house and you find them one by one and try to fit the pieces together as you stumble across each one of them. You find a new piece, and suddenly, the pieces you have need to be torn apart and fit together to make a different picture."

"You're telling me that even Nelly's kids couldn't have sped this up?" Gramma Trouble asked.

"Ruth," Pretty Penny said from around her neck, "we may have delayed this report. We were the ones fitting the pieces together, then going back to comb through the data yet again to see if there was more of one idea or less of another. We may be very fast at what we do, but there is still an awful lot of data. I can't tell you how many times I myself have scoured all of what we know, or think we know, to see if our latest perspective changed our take on something we'd ignored during an earlier search."

"We had lots of data, but extracting the information from it was much more time consuming than I thought possible," Xenophon said from General Trouble's neck.

"So," Abby said dryly, "how long before you begin telling us what's in this report?"

"Our initial search was for the convoy that took our kids from the Imperial Palace grounds to the palace of the Broam Clan," the special agent said. "We know that they didn't go a direct path. However, where did they go?"

"It turned out that everyone we detained was only too eager to tell us about a convoy of two gun trucks and a large hauling truck. That allowed us to ignore them. Fewer were the number that recalled that the convoy included a van as well as a truck. However, not a single one of our respondents knew the exact time of day that they spotted the convoy. None of them carried a time piece. Some of them weren't even sure of the day of the week they saw our convoy. Luckily, there are a few factories that use whistles to sound for lunch, breaks, and the end of the day.

"Using the few that had a vague sense of time attached to them, we've formed something like a map of the convoy's wanderings. They did some zigging and zagging around the southwest quadrant of the capitol. The sightings that we found credible show that someone didn't know where they were going. We know that for an hour or more late in the day, the entire convoy was off the road. When they came back onto the road, it was late and the advertising on its sides had been painted over. It was in this mode and after dark that the convoy headed for the Broam Clan's palace. However, we had no one to talk to from the Broam Clan and all sightings ended before they entered that clan's territory."

"We didn't detain a single member of the Broam Clan?" General Bruce asked.

"Not a one. It's possible that one escaped but I think it very likely that they just didn't have anything to do with these demonstrations," Foile said. "Our census of detainees shows over sixty minor clans or septs of larger clans."

"That many?" General Trouble muttered. "I know we weren't liked, but it's that bad, huh?"

"Sorry, sir, but yes," Foile said.

"What are your conclusions?" Abby asked.

From Abby's neck, Mata Hari spoke for the task force. "We believe that it is more likely true than false that the convoy directed itself toward at least three different clan palaces. Which ones, we can't say. Still, they started in one direction, then turned in another before switching to another course."

"Can you tell us what three clans offered them protection, then changed their mind?" Gramma Trouble asked.

"No, we cannot," Mata Hari answered. "They never got to within three blocks of a palace. Still, they meandered toward several before changing directions. There were too many palaces that could have been their intended goal."

"Then they disappeared?" Jacques asked. "How'd they do that?"

"It happened in a rather low rent district," Mata Hari said. "There are a lot of small craft shops. It could have pulled into the parking garage of one of the apartment buildings or maybe a small shop. We strongly suspect that when it next appeared, both the truck and the gun trucks had been painted different colors. Very likely, the gun trucks were now in the Broam Clan colors."

"Yeah," Jacques agreed. "That would make it easier to slip them into the lowest basement of the clan's palace."

"We agree," Mata Hari said.

"I'm curious," Gramma Trouble said. "It doesn't seem likely that the Broam clan would have a huge pile of steel plates just sitting in their basement along with a ton of welding tools. Do we know how they got there?"

"I'm sorry, but you must recall that we concentrated our drone coverage that day around the district. It was spotty over the rest of the capitol until we hit the panic button. Even then, the Broam Clan was not on our priority for coverage. Our video take does not show any flatbed truck piled high with steel sheets. If trucks brought it, we missed it."

"Is anyone besides me," Gramma Trouble said, "wishing that we could talk to those clan chiefs? Maybe get their take on what happened inside their palace? Have we been able to do a thorough examination of the bottom level of the garage?"

"We've done the best we can with tiny nano scouts. However, they've installed a steel door with a waterfall in front of it. Nine out of ten of the nanos we try to send down there have either been blocked or washed down the drain. The handful that get through are not able to do a very good job of gathering the evidence we want."

"Wife, do you get the feeling they don't trust us?"

"I fear that they don't, my love. It cuts me to the quick," Gramma Trouble answered, fanning herself with her palm as if she might faint at the rejection.

"What's the opinion of the group about the two of us old farts paying a visit to the Broam Clan Chiefs?" General Trouble asked.

"It is risky, sir," General Bruce said.

"Life is risky," the old warhorse answered.

"Maybe if we avoided a major parade," Gramma Trouble said. "Go by stealth."

"How about fast, by low-flying quadcopter?" Abby countered.

"Do you think that would work?" Gramma Trouble asked. "After our choppers hit them a couple of weeks ago, they may have bought themselves a better batch of anti-aircraft missiles."

"We'll need to call ahead," General Trouble said.

"Soon enough for them to call off their dogs," Abby said, dryly, "but not so soon as to give the bad guys time to prepare a welcome for you."

"There is wisdom in your advice," Ambassador Kawaguchi observed.

"Before we break up," Special Agent in Charge Foile said, "There is one more bit of information we stumbled across. Sherlock?"

From his collar, the agent's computer began a report with a quick and effective executive summary.

"We found Humans."

"What?" came from several people around the table, including both Iteeche flag officers.

"In our interrogations of the hired demonstrators as well as the clan lordlings overseeing the demonstrations we kept getting reports of one, two or three Humans being seen around the city. You may recall that all of us were isolated in the Legation District. We assumed after the first one or two reports that it was just spurious data. However, the sightings kept piling up. Admittedly, they were all over the Capitol, but still they were too plentiful to not pique our interest."

"Could the Iteeche tell us anything about these Humans?" Gramma Ruth asked. "I know none of us are very good at identifying specific people from the other species, still it would help if we had some idea as to how many Humans we have wandering around outside the Embassy."

"One of the Humans carried a gnarled cane," Sherlock answered. "Maybe it was a shillelagh. He waved it more than he walked with it. A second one seemed to always wear an ascot around his neck. Sometimes blue. Sometimes red. It may have been a Smart Metal computer or it may just have been an affectation. We can't tell which, but it identified him to the Iteeche who spotted him. There may have been two or three more humans but three were the most ever seen together."

"We knew there had to be human tech support somewhere below the surface of this problems," Gramma Trouble said. "The only times Nelly Net has been jammed there was a subject of the Peterwald Empire at the bottom of it."

"And if they've brought in someone from Human space to jam a network," General Bruce said, "surely they've brought in a programmer or two to examine their Smart Metal battlecruisers and spin out some changes in them."

"I don't like this," Abby said. "Kris had enough trouble keeping up with the rebellion. Her battlefleets have been fighting outnumbered four- or five-to-one. Now, if they also have a lot of tricks up their sleeves that Kris used to hide up hers . . . .."

"There will be hell to pay," General Trouble agreed.

"So," Amanda asked, "what do we do?"

"We've been playing defense," Gramma Trouble said. "It's time for us to go on the offensive. For that, we're going to need a lot more data. Scads and scads of data."

"Ruth, that is not how we measure data," Pretty Penny said, drolly. "I keep telling you it's terabits and petabits. You really need to get your boots out of the cow pasture."

"Down, girl, or I'll go back to counting on my fingers and toes," Ruth shot back.

"As if," was her computer's counter to that threat.

"May I suggest," General Trouble interjected, "we need more data points. We've restored five stories full of vacant rooms to the Embassy middle of the castle. I would like to suggest that we take that Smart Metal right back out and set up cameras and drones to cover every square millimeter of this city. That may be a heavy load on our computers, but we're only looking for humans."

"Them and the three of my guardsmen who went rogue to kidnap the children," General Konga added immediately.

"I think we can handle the data flow without being swamped," Mati Hari answered for all of Nelly's kids. "Let's cover this city like a wet blanket."

Ruth considered mentioning to the computer that she was mixing her metaphors, but decided she was hardly the pot to throw the first stone.

Abby glanced around the table. There wasn't a single look of disapproval. "Alright, Mata Hari, let's sprinkle this town with pixie dust and see what the cat drags in."

That got a groan from around the table, but an "Aye, aye, ma'am," from all the computers on the Humans seated around the table.

Since the Command Center was located at the top of the Embassy tower, the decision was immediately noticeable. The tower shrunk beneath them by five stores, about twenty meters. A glance out the window showed drones flying away like a flock of birds. They soon disappeared against a sky that had gone gray. No doubt, outside was hot and muggy with a chance of sooty rain.

While the computers gathered data, General and Gramma Trouble prepared to go visiting where they weren't wanted.

46

The flight from the Embassy to the Broam Clan Palace was bumpy and rough on the inner ear. Ruth may have gone through rejuvenation several times, but, still, she would never see a hundred and thirty again.

When the quadcopter settled down on its gear in the courtyard of the so-called palace at the end of the flight, Ruth leaned back and tried to get her stomach under control.

"We are getting too old for this kind of shit," her husband said.

"Speak for yourself, old man," was Ruth's comeback.

"Then why are you green around the gills?"

"You misunderstand me, kind sir," Ruth answered back. "We have been too old for this shit for at least the last quarter century."

"Well, if you put it that way," he said, and quit while he was behind.

Two choppers had landed ahead of them. Another two orbited the high rise without landing. As soon as the Gunny in charge reported the LZ secure, they dismounted. Outside, the alert screen of Marines awaited a greeting committee.

The Iteeche bowed. The two Troubles came to attention and saluted; they were both in uniform. The formalities met, the greeting committee led them inside. Their guards following close behind; they took a freight elevator large enough to hold all of them to the top floor.

That was likely the only elevator in the building capable of holding the entire group of visitors without separating the Human representatives from most of their honor guard. The Humans were quickly led out of the working area of the building and into the plush part that befit luxury apartments.

The seven high ranking Clan Chiefs awaited them. They relaxed on cushions in a corner of one of the most lavish rooms that Gramma Trouble had ever seen in the Iteeche Empire. She'd spent several weeks in the palace of a satrap's honcho. Still, this was fancy.

Behind the Iteeche Clan lords, the Capitol lay spread out in all its glory. In the distance, you could see a splotch of green that was the Imperial Palace grounds . . . but not the palace.

Ruth immediately noticed the two comfortable chairs that sat across from the arc of Iteeche clan lords.

PRETTY PENNY, ARE THOSE SMART METAL CHAIRS?

YES, RUTH. THEY ARE DEFINITELY SMART METAL, LIKELY OF ITEECHE ORIGIN. STILL, THEY ARE LIKE NO DESIGN WE'VE SOLD THEM AN APP TO MAKE.

WHAT'S MORE, THEY WANT US TO SEE THEM. CURI-OUSER AND CURIOUSER, General Trouble remarked.

The senior Clan Chief stayed seated, but bowed to the two Humans. They in turn went to attention and saluted him back. He then swept his upper right hand to indicate the chairs and they sat. For a long moment, the two sides eyed each other with bland faces.

"Why would a has-been general from the long-forgotten war you Humans started against we innocent Iteeche ask to see us?" from the senior Clan Chief broke the silence like a boulder cannon-balling into a placid kiddie pool.

"I asked to talk with you because we both have been played by someone who wants us at each other's throat so they can pick up the pieces," General Trouble said, tossing the boulder right back.

The room returned to silence. Gramma Trouble at least could

enjoy the view as she waited . . . and waited . . . then waited some more.

Finally, she decided she'd had enough of ignoring the elephant in the room.

"I was in the task force that got our children out of your basement. I was happy beyond words to find them safe and unharmed. I regret that so many of your warriors resisted our passage and suffered from it. I hope you will accept my apology on the part of all the parents, both Human and Iteeche who are grateful for their safe return to us."

"Will you pay the blood price for those warriors?" shot back from the Clan Chief. "Will you replace the gun trucks, the armored fighting vehicles, the assault carriers that burned? Will you pay for the fire damages to this building? For the holes blown in our walls and floors?"

"I believe the blood price is deserved," Gramma Trouble shot back just as fast. "However, it should be paid by those who set you up by holding our younglings hostage without your knowledge. The fighting vehicles as well the damage to your palace should be added to that price. They are the ones we Humans and Navy seek vengeance against. They are the ones you should be seeking reprisal from as well."

She paused for a second to see if they had heard her; if they had been able to grasp what she said over the blaring horns of injuries both old and new. Glancing from Iteeche to Iteeche she saw possibilities.

On that tone, she finished. "We should both be hunting them."

That brought a long, but thoughtful, pause.

Still, it was one of the clan chiefs from the far end who shot back a reply. "You Humans bring chaos and storm tides to rip apart our mating ponds and then expect us to chase after someone else to pay the blood price. You must think us fools."

"If a minnow nibbles at your fin, do you head butt the shark?" Gramma Trouble shot back. She'd learned that aphorism from Iteeche POW in that long-ago war. It often seemed to fit the situation the Iteeche got themselves into.

"Are you calling us a minnow?" the angry Iteeche demanded.

"I am calling those who did this to both of us, minnows, who seek to have us at each other's throat so they can gorge themselves on the fragments of ourselves that we leave in the water," Gramma Trouble shot back.

Before the Iteeche could yell another angry response, the Clan Chief in the center raised his hand for silence. He paused until only labored breathing could be heard, then eyed General Trouble. "You don't hold us responsible for the theft of your younglings? You and all the Humans?"

"That is true," Grampa Trouble answered. He spoke softly, as one might to a skittish colt. "Our own intelligence and other investigations tell us that you had nothing to do with this. You were likely their choice after three other clans rejected their effort to seek shelter with them."

"Three others?" the senior Clan Chief said, jumping in immediately.

Trouble turned to his wife. She nodded and began a more thorough briefing on the recent unpleasantness.

"Pretty Penny, please project your approximated route the kidnappers took before they arrived here."

A holograph appeared in the air between the Humans and Iteeche. Ruth's computer ran them through the wanderings of the convoy, with various palaces highlighted that were nearest when they turned away three times to try somewhere else.

"We think they went to ground someplace but don't know where. They hid long enough to repaint both the truck and the gun trucks," Ruth concluded. "We have no reports of them after sunset. Our drones provided scant coverage of this part of the Capitol that night, so we didn't see them enter your palace's garage. We have thoroughly searched through all our drone video. While we were overhead, no truck full of steel plates and welding gear entered your palace. Did you have a pile of steel plate laying around?"

The senior clan chiefs exchanged glances before the Clan Chief spoke. "Yes, we did have a stockpile of steel plate in the lowest level of the garage. We intended to construct, what do you Humans call them? A safe room for the clan chiefs. Someplace secure that we could retreat to if the clan palace was attacked."

Ruth did not bother to ask whom they feared. The Humans very likely did not make it into the top ten of that list. Just the fact that this clan had been made the patsy by this faction meant that at least one other clan, likely two or three more, were very feared by this Clan Chief.

Hard to believe that even clan chiefs feared for their lives. However, in the present situation it could be understood. From day to day, it was near impossible to tell who was on whose side.

"We would like to investigate the wreckage of the prison where our younglings were held," General Trouble said into the lengthening silence. "Our technicians have ways of extracting clues from a barren desert, if we give them a chance to look at the scene of a crime. Kidnapping our children and violating the sovereignty of your Clan Palace certainly qualifies as a crime."

"What might they do?" said an unpersuaded clan chief as he suddenly sat up attentively. He was at the end of the half-circle closest to Ruth.

"Their analysis might narrow down who bought the fishbowls or the fish. How many places had eighty-year-old Human combat rations laying around? How'd they get from there to here? All that is before we sequence all the DNA in the prison. We subtract the DNA from our younglings, then any left over may very likely be the criminals."

"It could be someone from Clan Broam who handled the plates when they were delivered," the interested Iteeche shot back.

"Yes," Gramma Ruth replied in her best helpful voice. "In that case, you can talk to him and find out where he was the day and night that the younglings were brought here. Clearly, the preparations of the metal containment cell began before the kids arrived. Do you have any security sign-in sheets?"

"No," the senior Clan Chief said, now quite thoughtful. "However,

I know for a fact that our guards know everyone who belongs in this building. Coto'sum'Mous, I think you need to talk to every guard we had on duty that day. I personally want to hear the response of the dozens of guards who allow admission to the lowest sub-basement of the garage while that prison was within their sight. Lil'sum'Ques, you sit in on those interrogations as well."

"You might want to detain them quickly and keep them in different holding cells so they can't get their story together," Gramma Trouble said, cheerfully helpful. She was faking it, but doing her best not to upset the Iteeche by seeming to be too much in their business.

The Clan Chief glared at Ruth, but said, "Do as the Human said. Sweep them up in five minutes and keep them in different pools where they can't talk to each other."

"It will be done as you say, Wise Chief," came from the one known as Lil. Coto looked like he was about to turn green and dash out of the room. Ruth wasn't the only one who noticed the change in the once-confident chief of a sub clan.

"Guards! Guards!" the Clan Chief shouted as Coto broke for the door.

Interestingly enough, it was four Royal US Marines that stepped through the door. Coto tried to bowl them over, after all they weighed practically nothing compared to an Iteeche, and they tottered around on two legs.

One Marine took him down with a block to his upper knees. Coto went down, rolling himself into a neat ball. One of the Marines put him to sleep with a sleepy dart to the neck.

As he sprawled out flat, the Marine corporal stood to attention, saluted and asked, "Where do you want this Iteeche delivered, Sir?"

The old general turned to the Clan Chief. "Where do you want him? He's yours, but we'd appreciate it if you'd let us keep four Marines in your guard force around him. We'd also like to be included in his interrogation, preferably before you break his fingers and pull out his nails."

"Why?" the Clan Chief asked.

"Because we find that a conversation can sometimes tell you more and far quicker than torture. It's just a Human foible, but you might want to watch how it goes. Maybe you won't need to torture him."

"He will make a Thorough and Complete Apology to the Emperor."

"Yes, oh wise one," General Trouble said, then introduced the Iteeche into a little thing the humans had been working on. Rather than let a snake dose the one making the apology, let a human medical technician give him a much smaller dose.

The general offered to show the clan chiefs a video of what he thought the drug would be like, compared with the usual apology. Ruth had never seen Iteeche grin as widely as these did.

"Yes. Yes, that seems like a very good apology," the Clan Chieftain said. "Would you like to interrogate him here, before us?"

"That would be very desirable. Do you have some shackles to put him in before he wakes up?"

So, half an hour later, the former Clan Chief Coto stood before the other clan chiefs, stripped of his rich robes. Like a slave, he faced them in his bare skin; bare skin with heavy chains.

He could not even attempt a step, much less escape.

The start of the interrogation had to be delayed while he screamed his defiance to the other clan chiefs. After a bit, Gramma Ruth asked the Clan Chief if he'd like to have Coto sedated so that they could ask him a few questions.

"You know how to?"

"In that war of old, I was in charge of interrogating captured Iteeche senior clan lords. I got a lot of information and rarely had a guest die on me."

That raised a lot of eyebrows among the other lords, but Ruth just happened to have brought along her old kit, just in case. The Iteeche got a shot and a few minutes later, was in a much more relaxed mood.

"Did you see who brought the stolen younglings into the bottom floor of the garage?" was all the question she had to ask.

Over the next half hour, he babbled the entire story. Exactly which guard officers were with his conspiracy. How they'd secreted the truck into the garage and finished welding the kids in. He shared the names of several different clans that had people involved in the conspiracy. Better yet, he knew who knew where the Humans were being hidden.

One Iteeche, intent on raising himself to Chief of his clan, spilled the beans on a whole lot of little conspiracies that laced their way through several clans.

That afternoon, five different Clan Chiefs paid a visit to Clan Broam. Quite a few junior officers were delighted for the honor of accompanying their Clan Chiefs to this visit and the chance to see how business was run at the clan level.

No doubt, this would come in handy when they were top dog.

One by one they came, and one by one, their Clan Chiefs turned on them. Watched as they were drugged. Then listened as they spilt their guts about a festering plot poisoning the blood of their clan.

That night, arrests ran through the clans' ranks as named Iteeche were rounded up and locked up in small cylinders specifically provided by the Humans.

In the middle of this, a quick reaction platoon swooped down on an apartment in a seedy part of town. There, they found four subjects of the Greenfeld Emperor or, more correctly, the Greenfeld Grand Duchess, since she was the one running things as regent. The king was now retired and had become quite a gardener. Every year, his roses won awards at the Brunswick Planetary Fair.

The Human safe house also had a dozen top-of-the-line computers. However, what they didn't find was a jammer to take down Nelly Net. Also missing was a Human with a shillelagh or a different one wearing an ascot around his neck.

It didn't take a lot of arm twisting to find out that three Humans had gone out last night and not come back. Further searching turned up no sign of them. They weren't anywhere that those arrested knew about.

The only thing the captured Humans knew was that the rebels

had been promising to pick them all up "soon." Apparently, they got three and delayed too long to pick up the other three.

Through all of this, Ruth did not promise anyone immunity. The prisoners didn't ask for it. The clan chiefs would never have even thought to offer it.

47

Gramma Trouble said I didn't have to go. In fact, I don't think she wanted me to go. Still, I was a Longknife. I did what had to be done.

That included seeing that justice was done to those who broke the law.

These Iteeche had kidnapped me and my friends. Mom's little brother had been kidnapped when she was hardly older than me. Those kidnappers' stupidity caused little Eddy to die. We kids could have been just as dead.

Mom watched her brother's killers hang.

I would watch my kidnappers pay the ultimate price.

Gramma and Grampa Trouble had argued that maybe I should see a video of what to expect, but they couldn't agree and I didn't want to. I knew this would be bad. Watching it once should be enough for me.

For the first time in my life, I was given an official uniform. Aunt Abby had appointed me Second Secretary for Cultural Affairs. I doubted I'd ever do anything, though our weekly swim parties might qualify as something cultural.

Anyway, it got me a uniform. Uncle Tsusumu (Ambassador

Kawaguchi) had a picture from his files, and Daisy spun me a complete diplomatic dress uniform from it. It was pretty fancy.

The pants were a royal blue, as befits a princess of the blood, with a wide gold braid stripe down the outer leg seam. The jacket had gold thread embroidery covering half the front and golden epaulettes with fringe and everything on my shoulders. The back of the jacket showed a peacock with its tail spread wide. Gold and Silver thread made up most of it, but there were also red and blue threads.

Gramma whispered that they were made with precious jewel dust.

Dressed, I joined Gramma, Grampa Trouble, Aunt Abby, and Uncle Bruce. Even Aunt Amanda and Uncle Jacques were there, all splendid in their own uniforms.

I was the only kid. I didn't ask why. I had a pretty good idea that if Mom and Dad were here, I wouldn't be allowed to do this.

That realization gave me a strange feeling in the pit of my tummy. Not bad or sad, but not good either. I wondered what it meant.

An armored limo picked us up and drove us to the Imperial Palace. Rather than stop at the stairs and get out, the limo drove right up the stairs and through the gates being held open by Imperial Guards in full ancient regalia with halibuts held straight up and out. Daggers in gold sheaths were also in the sashes around their waists.

Fancy!

The inside of the palace was huge and seemed to go on forever. Grampa Trouble held onto me when I bounced around the limo so I could get the best view of the place.

Gramma Trouble suggested that it was better if I got my wiggles out.

Grampa growled that if I was big enough to be here, I was big enough to pay the proper respect that an execution deserved.

I sat down and stayed a lot more still. Still, I craned my head as we came to a halt. All the others got out and formed a line. They went to attention, so I did what I'd been practicing to do since I was just a kid. I stood as tall and straight as I could.

Grampa Trouble ordered, "Salute."

I did the best I knew how. Dad said I was pretty good at it. I tried to be.

Then it was back into the limo and off we went. Twice more we stopped and saluted straight ahead. At the third stop to salute, I could see through the flowing banners to a huge cube.

When we got to the cube, we marched up a steep flight of stairs. At the top, was enough to take my breath away.

I didn't gawk or stare. Mom had told me that a good soldier could see a lot out of the side of her eye, and I'd practiced. Today, I was glad I had.

To my right were row upon row of Iteeche lords in those iridescent robes that shimmer with every color of the rainbow. They were on their knees before their Emperor. He had his legs folded under him inside a whole mountain of robes. He was perched on a huge chair that was much too big for him, but it sure was ornate, especially considering that none of it was Smart Metal™.

He was doing his best to look very serious and officious, but I think he quirked an eye my way when he saw me. I gave him the tiniest of waves . . . and got nudged by Gramma Trouble for it.

A lot of Iteeche Navy and Marine officers stood row upon row at attention. Just like the Humans, they wore swords at their sides. I'd asked, but Gramma Trouble wouldn't give me so much as a dagger. *Grown-ups.*

Anyway, Grampa Trouble led us around the Iteeche officers to stand with a much smaller group that included 'Uncle' Ulan. We stopped beside them.

Now I noticed the order we were in. Grampa Trouble and Uncle Bruce were to the right. Of course, they had four stars. Aunt Abby and Gramma Trouble had one star so they came next. I was at Gramma Trouble's side. I guess that's where a junior diplomat should be. Aunt Amanda and Uncle Jacques wore the eagles of full bird colonels, so they were to my left.

It was nice to be sandwiched between Gramma and Amanda.

The next time I glanced at the young Emperor, I couldn't help but see the Iteeche who knelt before him. Except for chains, they wore nothing. No, a lot of them had a lot of black and blue marks on their skin.

They must have fallen down a lot while playing with their kids. I hope their kids weren't hurt that bad.

Then it hit me. These guys hadn't been playing around. The Iteeche did something that only bad Humans did. They beat up their prisoners. Suddenly, it dawned on me. These were the kidnappers I'd come to watch pay a most Painful, Sincere and Very Complete Apology to the Emperor.

There seemed to be an awful lot of them. I tried to count them but there were rows and rows of them and a lot in each row. What couldn't be missed were the three Humans in the back row closest to the clan lords.

I wondered why they were here, however, Gramma Trouble shushed me before I could ask the question.

I remembered something from talking with my Iteeche friends. One of these executions began with a snake bite and ended with the Iteeche's head being cut off. They'd seen the last execution; it was showed to all those in the Palace of Learning. The Iteeche wanted kids to learn about these things fast.

That was one of the reasons I was here. If the Iteeche kids could watch one of these things, I should be able to watch the Iteeche that almost killed me do their apology to my friend Tranna.

Gramma told me this one would be different, and I saw how it was when the Emperor waved his fan.

The lid stayed on the crystal bowl that held the snake. Instead, each Iteeche in red stepped forward and inserted the short needle from an ampule into the neck of the Iteeche.

Three Marine corporals did the honor for the three Humans.

All of them stepped back.

For a long moment, nothing happened. Then the chained Iteeche and Humans began to scream and collapse onto the floor.

I studied the Iteeche closest to me. The Iteeche have smooth, white skin. They can be quite lovely, in a fishy kind of way. These, of course, had black and blue marks, along with scratches. Now, however, the muscles under their skin began to knot.

I'd bumped my knee and arm enough times to know when it needed ice to take down the swelling. This wasn't that kind of knotting. I'd gotten a cramp once, and it hurt like the dickens. That was what this looked like . . . only a lot worse. There were more knots, then knots on top of those knots.

And the screaming! Oh, the screaming! One of my nannies had shown me pictures drawn by old masters of souls in the Christian hell. Those people were there for taking bribes and betraying those they were loyal to. She said they screamed in pain.

I'd wondered how bad a scream could be. After all, we kids screamed pretty loud on the playground.

Now I knew.

The Iteeche screamed as they rolled around the marble floor, writhing in pain.

A whimper escaped me. I didn't mean to whimper, it just got out of me. I reached out for Gramma's uniform pants. She reached over and rested a hand on my shoulder.

Somehow, without meaning to, I kind of slipped over closer to her. I didn't hide behind her. No. At least not yet. I still watched, but my stomach hurt like it had never hurt before.

Then the Smart Metal™ streamed up from my epaulettes to form tight earbuds that made the sound go away. More formed a shield in front of my face. I suspect people could see me, but I could only see one of my favorite stories. I was hearing it as well.

Now Gramma's hand on my shoulder urged me to return to my place in the line. I did, doing my best to look serious and attentive while ignoring what was actually going on while I watched something a whole lot better.

Still, the execution seemed to go on forever. Gramma offered me a pill. Usually Mom and Dad as well as Grampa and Gramma Trouble were in agreement. No medicine that you didn't absolutely have to take.

So, when Gramma offered me a pill, I took it.

It seemed to make my tummy feel less of what it was feeling. I could also breathe easier.

I found myself thinking more than watching my story.

Poor Tranna, he also had to watch this. If this rebellion went sour, Mom and Dad would make sure that Johnny and I were safe as she ran for home. Tranna *was* home. If he was unlucky, he might get his throat slit in the middle of the night.

If he wasn't, he was the one who might be down on the floor, apologizing to the guy who stole his throne.

Johnny loved to watch a cartoon made from an old classic. It had lots of dragons and knights. It called itself Game of Thrones. If you tried for the throne, you ended up dead more often than not.

These Iteeche had tried to play me and Johnny in their reach for some throne. If not Tranna, then some Clan Chieftain's seat. Now they were paying the price.

Still, Johnny or I could have been smashed like so many pawns in that story.

I loved it when Mom and Dad called me princess. I knew Mom was a real princess. I kind of wonder if I'm one too, or if I'm like so many other little girls whose folks call her that.

For the first time in my life, I realized that some people might take me being a princess seriously and that I could get killed for it. There was a reason why our nannies and teachers carried sidearms, and why there were always armed Marines close at hand.

I bet they got in trouble when we slipped out on them, I thought without realizing it.

I felt regret that I might have caused them trouble. Then there was the young Iteeche woman who went with us kids. She had been so nice to us. I never saw her afterwards. *Had something bad happened to her?*

Suddenly, I was overwhelmed by just how big the world was. How big was the ocean I was swimming in. Yeah, I know, Mom and Dad and a lot of people were doing their best to help us float, but still, the ocean was wide and it had a lot of big fish in it.

Daisy, could you kind of dim the shield in front of me a bit. Let me see just a ghost of what's happening.

ARE YOU SURE, RUTH?

YES, I'M PRETTY SURE. JUST BE READY TO TURN IT BACK TO DARK.

OKAY.

The screen went opaque. I could still see my story, but showing through was the scene in front of me. I couldn't hear anything, so it didn't seem real.

The chained prisoners on the floor were moving a lot less. Then, of course, their muscles were awfully knotted. How could they move? The guys in black were supposed to chop off their heads and end the pain, but none of them moved from where they stood behind them.

I tried to get a good look at where the three Humans had been. The Marine Corporals stood at attention; their swords were held high in front of them. There was blood on the blades. I guess the Humans had lost their heads a lot sooner than the Iteeche.

Of course, it's because Humans are smaller. It would take far less poison. Or maybe we made sure the Humans got more and died sooner. I wouldn't put that past Grampa and Gramma Trouble.

We Longknifes are a sneaky bunch. Mom says we got it from a whole lot of our grandparents. I think she's right.

I focused on Tranna where he sat on his throne. He was stuck playing this game. No wonder he'd asked Mom to come and help him. Mom was a great admiral and a good princess.

Could I be a good princess?

I had ten or twenty years to find out. I think Mom is a really good princess to learn the business from.

I needed to talk to Mom when she got back.

There was a lot more to being a Longknife and a princess than anyone had told me.

Yeah, we needed to talk.

I darkened the screen and went back to watching my story. I didn't need to see any more of this. It wasn't like I'd ever forget it.

ABOUT THE AUTHOR

Mike Shepherd is the National best-selling author of the Kris Longknife saga. Mike Moscoe is the award-nominated short story writer who has also written several novels, most of which were, until recently, out of print. Though the two have never been seen in the same room at the same time, they are reported to be good friends.

Mike Shepherd grew up Navy. It taught him early about change and the chain of command. He's worked as a bartender and cab driver, personnel advisor and labor negotiator. Now retired from building databases about the endangered critters of the Northwest, he looks forward to some fun reading and writing.

Mike lives in Vancouver, Washington, with his wife Ellen, and not too far from his daughter and grandkids. He enjoys reading, writing, dreaming, watching grandchildren for story ideas, and upgrading his computer – all are never ending.

For more information:
https://krislongknife.com
mikeshepherd@krislongknife.com

RELEASE INFORMATION

In 2016, I amicably ended my twenty-year publishing relationship with Ace, part of Penguin Random House.

In 2017, I began publishing through my own independent press, KL & MM Books. We produced six e-books and a short story collection. We also brought the books out in paperback and audio.

In 2018, we began the year with Kris Longknife's Successor, followed by Kris Longknife: Commanding, and Vicky Peterwald: Dominator.

In 2019, we published Kris Longknife: Indomitable, Vicky Peterwald: Implacable, and ended the year with Kris Longknife: Stalwart.

2020 will be an adventure! In April Longknifes Defend the Legations will be published. I'll also be writing two Kris novels, and a Vicky novel. In the fall, you'll also get the release of Boot Recruit, the short story that premiered last year in an anthology, that explains a bit about why Kris chose the Navy.

Stay in touch to follow developments by friending Kris Longknife and follow Mike Shepherd on Facebook or check in at my website https://krislongknife.com

MORE BOOKS BY MIKE SHEPHERD

～

This is what we include in all of Mike Shepherd's publications. If you enjoyed this book, here is a list of more books by Mike Shepherd, including some of his early works and short story collections. All have hyperlinks for the purchase of your choice. Enjoy!

～

Published by KL & MM Books

Kris Longknife: Emissary

Kris Longknife: Admiral

Kris Longknife: Commanding

Kris Longknife: Indomitable

Kris Longknife: Stalwart

Kris Longknife's Relief

Kris Longknife's Replacement

Kris Longknife's Successor

Longknifes Defend the Legation

Rita Longknife: Enemy Unknown

Rita Longknife: Enemy in Sight

Vicky Peterwald: Dominator

Vicky Peterwald: Implacable

～

Short Stories from KL & MM Books

Kris Longknife's Bloodhound & Assassin: A Duology

Kris Longknife's Maid Goes on Strike & Other Short Stories

Kris Longknife's Maid Goes On Strike

Kris Longknife's Bad Day

Ruth Longknife's First Christmas

Kris Longknife: Among the Kicking Birds

Kris Longknife's Bloodhound

Kris Longknife's Assassin

Ace Science Fiction Books by Mike Shepherd

Kris Longknife: Mutineer

Kris Longknife: Deserter

Kris Longknife: Defiant

Kris Longknife: Resolute

Kris Longknife: Audacious

Kris Longknife: Intrepid

Kris Longknife: Undaunted

Kris Longknife: Redoubtable

Kris Longknife: Daring

Kris Longknife: Furious

Kris Longknife: Defender

Kris Longknife: Tenacious

Kris Longknife: Unrelenting

Kris Longknife: Bold

Vicky Peterwald: Target

Vicky Peterwald: Survivor

Vicky Peterwald: Rebel

Mike Shepherd writing as Mike Moscoe in the Jump Point Universe

First Casualty

The Price of Peace

They Also Serve

Rita Longknife: To Do or Die

Ace Science Fiction Short Specials

Kris Longknife: Training Daze

Kris Longknife: Welcome Home, Go Away

The Lost Millennium Trilogy by Mike Shepherd, published by KL & MM Books

Lost Dawns: Prequel

First Dawn

Second Fire

Lost Days

The Lost Millennium Anthology

Award-Nominated Short Story Collections by Mike Shepherd, published by KL & MM Books

A Day's Work on the Moon

The Job Interview

The Strange Redemption of Sister MaryAnn